THE CALM
AND
THE STRIFE

THE CALM
AND
THE STRIFE

A Historical Novel
About Gettysburg

by
David J. Sloat
and
John W. Sloat

CCB Publishing
British Columbia, Canada

The Calm and the Strife:
A Historical Novel About Gettysburg

Copyright ©2012 by David J. Sloat and John W. Sloat
ISBN-13   978-1-77143-031-9
First Edition

Library and Archives Canada Cataloguing in Publication
Sloat, David J., 1968-
The calm and the strife : a historical novel about Gettysburg /
by David J. Sloat and John W. Sloat – 1st ed.
ISBN 978-1-77143-031-9
Also available in electronic format.
Additional cataloguing data available from Library and Archives Canada

Cover artwork: A cannon at the Gettysburg Battlefield at sunset.
Picture taken at the "High Water Mark." ©Dwight Nadig | iStockphoto.com

Disclaimer: This is a work of historical fiction. It is based on actual events and characters, but many of the motives and relationships in this novel are either products of the authors' imagination or are used fictitiously.

Extreme care has been taken by the authors to ensure that all information presented in this book is accurate and up to date at the time of publishing. Neither the authors nor the publisher can be held responsible for any errors or omissions. Additionally, neither is any liability assumed for damages resulting from the use of the information contained herein.

Publisher: CCB Publishing
                British Columbia, Canada
                www.ccbpublishing.com

This book is dedicated,
with love and appreciation,
to:

Amy Beth Fox Sloat

and

Helen Elizabeth Burdick Sloat

The Winds of Fate

by Ella Wheeler Wilcox
From *Poems of Optimism* (1919)

One ship drives east and another drives west,
With the self-same winds that blow,
’Tis the set of the sails
And not the gales
That tell them the way to go.

Like the winds of the sea are the winds of fate,
As we voyage along through life,
’Tis the set of the soul
That decides its goal
And not the calm or the strife.

Contents

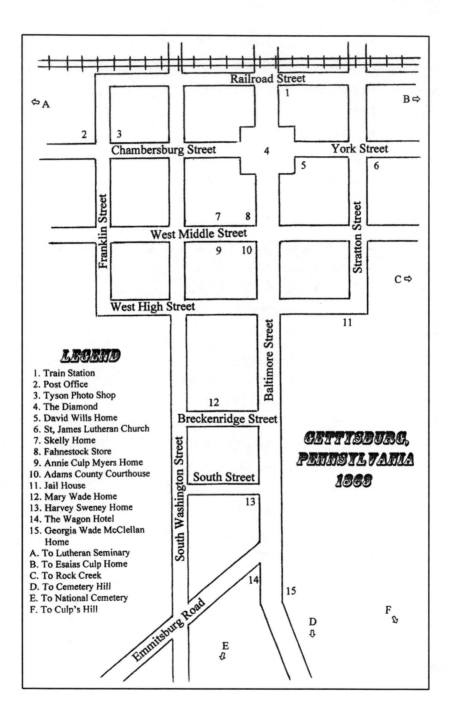

Railroad Street

1

⇦A

B⇨

2   3

Chambersburg Street   4   York Street

Franklin Street

5   6

7   8

West Middle Street

9   10

Stratton Street

C⇨

West High Street

11

Baltimore Street

LEGEND

1. Train Station
2. Post Office
3. Tyson Photo Shop
4. The Diamond
5. David Wills Home
6. St, James Lutheran Church
7. Skelly Home
8. Fahnestock Store
9. Annie Culp Myers Home
10. Adams County Courthouse
11. Jail House
12. Mary Wade Home
13. Harvey Sweney Home
14. The Wagon Hotel
15. Georgia Wade McClellan
    Home
A. To Lutheran Seminary
B. To Esaias Culp Home
C. To Rock Creek
D. To Cemetery Hill
E. To National Cemetery
F. To Culp's Hill

12

Breckenridge Street

South Washington Street

South Street

**GETTYSBURG,
PENNSYLVANIA
1863**

13

14   15

D
⇩

F
⇩

Emmitsburg Road

E
⇩

Prologue

HOMECOMING

Gettysburg, Pennsylvania
July 2, 1863

John Wesley Culp stood watching as Confederate troops swirled past him, moving in obedience to orders from distant commanders. He looked around Gettysburg, the newest prize of Robert E. Lee's army, and shook his head in disbelief. A wry grin twisted his mouth as he imagined the eyes that peered out behind shuttered windows. To them, he must appear to be just one more gray uniform in a vast sea of gray.

But Wes Culp knew he was different from all the others as he stood looking silently down Baltimore Street in the twilight. He had been gone for what seemed like a lifetime, but now the pilgrimage that had begun when he turned his back on Gettysburg seven years ago had brought him here again. To the other men in gray uniforms, this was an alien place, enemy country. To Wes, it still looked like home.

He peered down the road toward the small, two-story building half a mile away. In it was a woman who was unaware of his return, to say nothing of the message in his breast pocket, a message that would change their lives forever. Patting the pocket for the thousandth time, he set off toward the distant house.

Gettysburg had changed so little that it seemed to Wes as if he was waking from a dream. The buildings, the trees, even the rocks along the street were painfully familiar. The night could have been any night from his childhood – running along these streets, playing in these yards, hiding behind these trees. And yet tonight he saw the town with a startling clarity.

He had run so hard to get away from this place, from the memories and the people – his father, his family. He had run from the other children and their cruel taunts. And, he now saw clearly, he had also run from her.

But the running would stop tonight. The past had snared him so securely that he could no longer struggle against it. He smiled at the irony. Back in the very place he had been so desperate to leave, he no longer felt the need to escape; he had brought with him a whole new future. It was a boy who had run away from this place, too frightened to stand up to its challenges; but the man who stood here tonight was no longer afraid.

1

He had just come from visiting his sisters in a house half a mile back. Annie and Julia had greeted him as if he was still one of them, and the excitement of their meeting gave hope that they might recapture something of the old days. But it quickly became obvious that the naïve happiness of the past was gone forever. There had been too many changes.

His brow creased as he wondered what kind of reception awaited him at the house to which he was now headed. Ginnie Wade's reaction was much more important to him than that of his sisters'. He was certain that, regardless of all that had happened between them, their dreams were still within reach. No longer would they talk of places or houses or wealth, but only of being together. Now, each step down Baltimore Street brought him that much closer to their final goal.

The cries of the day's wounded echoed from several temporary hospitals, marked by red flags that now hung limply in the July dusk. The air was laden with smoke and the acrid smell of gunpowder. But Wes was oblivious to it all. Up on the crest of the rise to his left, Federal cannon boomed into the night, firing occasionally at targets that were becoming invisible. Wes smiled as he watched the cannons belch their fire, feeling not fear but an exuberant joy. The hill upon which the guns sat was as familiar to him as the streets he now walked. It was known as Culp's Hill, named after his family which had settled on the land generations ago. Tomorrow, his brigade would capture the hill and take those guns, winning the battle and probably ending the war.

He had reached the bottom of the hill, only a few hundred yards from the house where Ginnie was staying temporarily, when a guard sitting on a fence rail to his right hailed him.

"Where you headed there, boy?"

Wes stopped and turned to the man. In the dark, he could make out only a huge, featureless form in gray. The man moved forward, clearly suspicious, his rifle lying easily in the crook of his arm. As he approached, his gray hair and ruddy face suddenly flared in the phosphorescent glow of a match. He lit the pipe clenched in his teeth, then eyed Wes. "I say again, where you headed?"

Wes pointed to the house. "There. My girl is staying there."

The guard nodded thoughtfully, sucking on the carved pipe in his bandaged hand. "Northern girl, eh?"

Wes nodded, impatient to be on his way. He took a few steps but the guard's voice halted him again. "You might have a rough time of it if you go much farther, son. The Yankees hold that house. It's inside their lines." After a moment, he added thoughtfully, "Course, I suppose they'll be more'n happy to entertain a visitor who's dressed in gray." He grinned, then asked in a tone that left the next move up to Wes, "You reckon she's worth it?"

Wes stopped in the middle of the street, squinting hard to make out the house. He could see fires burning behind it up the hill, and could just make out a crude barricade adjacent to the house, thrown up to protect Federal sharpshooters. He stood silently for a long time, staring at the house. He had anticipated this meeting for so long; it was torture to get this close and then be barred from going the last few feet.

"Been a long time since you've seen her?" The guard's voice broke into Wes' frustration. The man smiled sadly, apparently entertaining memories of his own. Wes nodded.

"Yep. It's been a lifetime." He spoke quietly, not so much to the old man as to himself.

After a time, the man gave a single, resolute nod and turned to hitch himself back up onto the fence. "Then, you can wait one more day to see her, can't you, son?"

Wes sighed. He was right. One more day was nothing. But the thought did not calm his clawing disappointment. Finally, he turned grudgingly and started to walk back the way he had come.

The guard laughed, his cackle stinging Wes. "You'll just have to fight harder tomorrow, boy. She'll still be there. Unless the Yankees get to her first." His bitter laughter crackled through the night air.

Wes took a breath to respond angrily, then thought better of it. Like it or not, the old man was right. He was just going to have to wait one more day.

Chapter 1

DREAMS

Gettysburg, Pennsylvania
July 4, 1856

The normally quiet town of Gettysburg, Pennsylvania was awash in a sea of red, white and blue. Shouting figures waved at the parade of wagons moving slowly down Baltimore Street. Even from his vantage point on the hill, half a mile to the south, Wes Culp could sense the bonds that united the tiny forms into a single celebrating mass. He was alone by choice, preferring to watch the festivities from a distance, away from the crush of people, perched in his favorite tree.

It was expected to be the greatest day in Gettysburg's history: a dual celebration of the fiftieth anniversary of the town's incorporation and the eightieth anniversary of the country's founding. The students had worked for weeks to build floats for the parade, and now those floats, their sides draped with children happily waving to the crowd, made their way through town. They were coming slowly south from the Diamond, the town square, where the largest group of spectators had gathered to view the parade. Wes watched as each wagon arrived at the lower end of Baltimore Street, heading in the direction of his hill.

There had been no end of preparation in the past weeks, and it seemed that everyone was caught up in the excitement. Even Wes' father, Jesse, who was usually somewhat reserved, had been chattering about it. But when the day arrived and the crowds began to gather, Wes slipped away by himself. He knew that his mother would be searching for him, wondering why he wasn't with the family. It rankled that she still felt it necessary to look out for him. He was seventeen, well past the age that required a mother's supervision, and he no longer attended school since he started working with his brother, Will, at the Hoffman carriage factory. Even so, Margaret Culp still treated him like her baby although he was the third of four children.

A cruel prank of nature had made him much shorter than most other boys. This, compounded with an almost painful shyness, made it difficult for him to get along with others his age. Children, and even some adults, teased him relentlessly. His mother had counseled him not to worry about it, telling him

5

that he would eventually grow taller, like Will and their father. But, as time passed, it became apparent that he would never be like Will. And he had no desire at all to be like his father. As a result, he fell into the habit of keeping mostly to himself.

The frown on Wes' face grew deeper as his dark eyes watched the joy in the valley below. He flicked the brown hair back from his forehead and squinted at the float now coming into view down Baltimore Street. The wagon, filled with children, bore a banner proudly heralding the handiwork of the eighth grade class. Wes knew that his younger sister, Julia, was one of those aboard. She would be disappointed that he wasn't in the crowd watching her. Of course, she would forgive him as she always did, but he still felt a twinge of guilt. It was the only thing he regretted. Except...that Ginnie Wade would be there too. She and Julia would be sitting beside each other, their legs hanging over the wagon's decorated sides.

The July heat was beginning to build as the parade came to an end. Many of the young people escaped from the confines of their families and climbed the hill toward Wes, heading for the cool waters of Rock Creek. Wes' family had settled along this ridge generations ago, and people in Gettysburg referred to it simply as Culp's Hill. Wes felt somewhat proprietary about the land, even though his father had no claim to it. His father's cousin, Henry Culp, was the current owner. But Wes had played there since he could walk, and he knew the hill from top to bottom, every rock, every tree.

He watched silently as the line of teenage boys stormed up the hill toward him, finally veering off to his right toward the creek. Afraid of being seen by the invaders, Wes moved back among the branches to watch from his hiding place as the swimmers frolicked and splashed in the water. He resented the way they felt at ease with each other; he wanted to be able to jump into the creek along with them. But they all knew him and took delight in humiliating him, making fun of his size and his nervous stutter. He had earned a reputation for being yellow, because he had run away so many times from fights with bigger boys. He wore the pain of his continual rejection like a dead weight around his neck, allowing it to drag him further into his own isolated world. Eventually, his resentment built itself into a hatred of everything about Gettysburg.

He often imagined running away from home, leaving his family and his tormentors behind, searching for some place where no one knew him, where no one treated him like a child or made fun of his small stature. People would see him for what he was inside, and would not judge him for what he looked like on the outside. In this dream place, he would become rich and powerful, the town's most important citizen, and everyone would know him and like him and seek out his company. Then and only then would he come back to Gettysburg to let everyone discover how wrong they had been about him. He smiled as he imagined these boys, now playing in the creek, respectfully coming before him on some future day to apologize for the way they had treated him, then begging him for favors or money.

"Where were you?"

Wes, startled out of his reverie, looked down to see Julia climbing the hill toward him with a look of disappointment on her face. Her blue dress was dotted with red and white buttons, and a matching ribbon pulled back her dark brown hair. She stood with arms akimbo and stared for a moment at Wes.

"I l...l...left," he stuttered.

"It was a bore anyway," she said with a shrug. Wes knew she didn't mean it, but it was her way of forgiving him. She looked back toward the swimming hole, adding casually, "Ginnie was wondering where you were."

Wes slid closer toward her along the branch. "W...what did she say?" he asked with poorly disguised excitement.

"She just asked where you were."

"And what did you say?"

"I said you were probably up here. I told her you don't much like crowds." Wes could feel the heat rising up his neck, embarrassed at the thought of having his personal feelings exposed to Ginnie. She went on, "I also told her that you were madly in love with her."

Wes' head snapped up, but then he realized that she was teasing. "No, you didn't," he laughed.

"But you wish I had, don't you?" She giggled, looking wise beyond her thirteen years. She found her brother's infatuation with her best friend extremely entertaining and, while she would never deliberately hurt him, she frequently joked about the relationship when they were alone. "She's down at the swimming hole, waiting for me, if you want to tell her." When he failed to respond, she set off toward the creek. Glancing back to confirm that he wasn't coming down, she called, "All right, suit yourself. I'll see you at home."

Wes, cursing himself for his timidity, slid back among the branches where he could search the crowd of children by the creek. Finally, he spotted Ginnie, standing by herself on the bank, dressed in white, watching placidly as the boys splashed around in the icy water. From the cover of the branches, he had the opportunity to study her without self-consciousness. She was tall for thirteen, half a head taller than Julia and already as tall as he was. There was a poise about her, a personal dignity that showed itself as she stood by the water, just far enough back to avoid getting wet, yet close enough to enjoy the cool air off the creek. The light from the sun, streaming through the trees, came to rest on her dark hair like a halo.

Julia walked up to her, whispered something in her ear, and Wes saw Ginnie turn to look in his direction. Unconsciously, he pulled back into the shadows, but not before he thought he saw a look of disappointment on her face. He wished he had accepted his sister's invitation, but now there was no way to come down gracefully from his hiding place.

A moment later, a shout from down by the water attracted Wes' attention. He saw that several of the boys had come out of the water to seize a girl who had been watching them. They dragged her, fully clothed, into the water with them while she screamed in a mixture of pleasure and shock. Before she had even had a chance to surface, the boys set off in search of other prey. Suddenly realizing that they had focused on Julia and Ginnie, Wes found himself reacting before he had time to think.

Breaking through the branches, he jumped to the path below and reached them just as Julia landed in the water with a shriek. She surfaced immediately, sputtering, her mouth agape. Wes tried to get between the boys and Ginnie, but they brushed him aside and yanked her toward the water. He reached for the person closest to him, but the boy's slippery arm slid through his grasp and Wes succeeded only in clawing his flesh. Then Ginnie was in the air, screaming, and a second later she landed with a splash beside Julia.

The boy Wes had scratched now turned to look at his attacker. Wes saw that it was Jack Skelly, the son of a well-to-do shop owner. Of all the town's bullies, Wes despised Skelly the most. He was an arrogant kid, already taller than Wes even though he was two years younger. Skelly knew Wes hated being ribbed about his size and never missed an opportunity to make some snide comment.

"Well, look who showed up. The runt!" he shouted to his friends. The other boys laughed, forming a circle around Skelly and Wes. Skelly examined the long red welts on his arm where Wes' fingernails had raked him, then looked back with a sneer. "You scratch just like a girl, runt."

"Why c...couldn't you leave them alone?" Wes stuttered, glancing nervously around at the others.

"C...come on and make me," Skelly aped, to the great amusement of his friends. He walked up to Wes and started giving him short, vicious shoves in the chest with the heel of his hand, pushing him backward, challenging him. "Why don't you do something about it?"

Wes' anger suddenly bubbled over and he rushed forward, lowering his head to try to butt Skelly in the stomach. But Skelly saw him coming and sidestepped, grabbing his coat and spinning him around toward the water. Off balance, he teetered for a second until Skelly gave him a final shove. Wes toppled into the water with a huge splash alongside Julia and Ginnie who were struggling through the water toward the bank. He rose instantly, rage flaring through his entire body. Laughing boys lined the bank of the creek, pointing and jeering. Several of them slapped Skelly on the back in admiration.

Wes watched as Ginnie and Julia allowed two of the boys to help them out of the water. They both looked back at Wes and for a moment he thought they were going to join in the laughter. This was too much for him. He turned away and struggled toward the opposite bank, clawing his way out of the water with the help of a tree branch. Running south along the creek to get out of sight of the jeering faces, he crossed the stream again and ran back up the hill. His wet boots slipped on the rocks and he nearly fell several times, gasping from his frantic effort to escape the mocking laughter. He kept running long after he was out of sight, but the sounds of derision continued to float in the air, chasing him farther and farther away.

His anger and exhaustion congealed into tears which he wiped away savagely with the back of his hand. The branches and undergrowth tore at the skin on his hands and face as he shoved his way upward toward higher ground. He imagined the boys laughing and joking with Ginnie, helping her down the hill toward town as she blushed under their attention.

He finally reached his tree and leaned against its familiar bark to catch his breath. His muscles ached from the rapid climb and his jaw clenched as he thought of ways to get back at Skelly for today's humiliation. He looked up into the canopy of green overhead. Then, as he had so many times before, he climbed, using the toe-holds he had cut years before.

He had discovered this tree with Julia when they were both much younger. There were two trees, actually, side by side. Julia and he had been walking in the woods one day when she climbed a big maple and proclaimed it her "house." Wes, playing along with his little sister, had climbed the tree next to it, a majestic elm, and sat himself on a branch across from her. They pretended that they were grown up and living in houses next door to each other. It was an escape from childhood, from Gettysburg, from everything that made Wes feel badly about himself. The view through the dense branches was beautiful and he could see the farmlands for miles around. Later, he had frequented this place to think and dream. Now, settling himself on a large branch fifteen feet above the ground, he ran his fingers over his initials which he had carved high on the trunk that first day long ago.

He was shivering, partly from emotion and partly because the breeze was chilling his wet clothing. He struggled out of his coat, hanging it carelessly over the branch above him, and listened to the cicadas and the bird calls, willing them to drown out the laughter which still echoed in his head.

"Wesley, are you up there?"

Julia's voice, shockingly loud in the silence of the forest, caught Wes off guard a second time. He remained quiet, hoping she would give up her search and go home. He had no desire to talk to anyone, not even his sister.

"You're dripping, Wesley. I know you're up there."

Wes sighed, closing his eyes in frustration for a moment. "What do you want?" he grunted, not bothering to disguise his irritation.

"Come down here," she ordered. "I want to talk to you."

"No!"

After a moment, Julia said in a softer tone, "There's someone here who wants to see you."

Peering down through the branches, Wes caught a glimpse of white and froze for a moment. Then, summoning his courage, he grabbed his coat and started to work his way down through the branches. Dropping to the ground, he confronted them silently. But when he glanced at Ginnie, he was surprised to see a red swelling around her eyes that told him she too had been crying. It hadn't occurred to him that Ginnie might have been upset by what the boys had done. He thought she was enjoying the attention. He was irritated, however, by this intrusion into his private space, and he turned to Julia.

"Why'd you bring her here?"

Ginnie's face fell and she turned away to head back down the hill. Julia took hold of her arm, stopping her, then turned to glare at Wes. "Because both of us are soaked to the bone and we don't want to go home and get yelled at."

"Oh," was as much as Wes could manage.

Ginnie pulled away from Julia. "It's all right, I'll just go."

She took a few steps before Wes found his voice. "Wait! Please." He touched her arm lightly and, as she turned, Wes saw hurt and loneliness in her eyes and it brought a rush of compassion.

"Please come back," he said. "You can dry out before you go home."

She allowed him to lead her toward Julia's tree. Julia climbed up and seated herself on one of the lower branches where she could catch a bit of the afternoon sun. Wes laid his coat on the lowest branch and beckoned to Ginnie. She considered the coat, then looked at him, raising an eyebrow. "It's soaking wet."

"So are you," he responded lightly. She laughed at the comment and sat on the coat, dangling her feet. Her white dress stuck to her legs and dripped on the ground, and the disconsolate look gradually returned to her face. Several wisps of wet hair escaped from the hairpins that usually held them neatly in place. They hung before her eyes betraying an inner misery.

Wes knew little about her personally but, along with everyone in Gettysburg, he knew about her family. Her father, James Wade, was a drunkard who several years ago had stolen some money, gone to Richmond for a week and apparently spent it all on alcohol and women. The authorities arrested him when he returned to Gettysburg and he landed in jail. This left Mary Wade, Ginnie's mother, the sole support for Ginnie, her older sister, Georgia, and two younger brothers. Mr. Wade returned home when he had completed his sentence, but his outrageous behavior finally forced Ginnie's mother to have him committed to the town asylum.

The family's reputation, tarnished by this whole affair, was even more defamed when Mary conceived another child during this period. The scandalmongers, always eager for new material, debated as to whether the child was legitimate or not. But, regardless of its origin, there was now another mouth to feed. Ginnie's mother, assisted by Georgia, worked constantly as a dressmaker to keep food on the table for her family, while Ginnie helped around the house and looked after the boys.

The repeated scandals had made the Wade family outcasts of a sort. Wes saw them going about their business quietly, keeping to themselves most of the time. He knew that some of the local tailors employed Mrs. Wade during their busy season, but they did it furtively, without the knowledge of their customers. Wes' father however, also a tailor, had never offered her any work and derided those who did, preferring not to associate with her.

Something in her manner drew Wes outside his shy shell and he smiled at her, searching for something to say that might cheer her up. It made his own hurts seem less urgent. "I'm sorry, Ginnie. I'm sorry I couldn't stop them."

Ginnie looked at him and Wes saw in her eyes the beginning of a smile. "At least you tried. Thank you for that. You looked like Sir Galahad charging into the battle. I'm sorry that you got into a mess trying to help me."

Julia chimed in, "Wes, you sure made a big splash down there." The girls both started to laugh, and Wes felt his anger begin to melt away. He grinned, then joined in their laughter.

Ginnie giggled for a moment, then retreated into her somber mood. "I wish they'd just leave us be for once." Wes nodded, noting the subtle connection implied in her statement.

Julia looked off down the hill into the distance. "That Jack Skelly is such a brat."

The mention of Skelly broke Wes' quiet excitement and brought the anger surging forward again. "Someday he'll be sorry." He shot a black look down the hill.

Ginnie looked at Wes sternly. "You mustn't bear a grudge, Wes. It isn't Christian."

"Christian?" Wes scoffed. "You call throwing people in the creek Christian?"

"Well, we mustn't be like them," Ginnie said, as though speaking to her young brothers.

Wes held his tongue but he resented her pious remark. He believed in God to a certain extent, but when somebody hurt you, you had to get even. He imagined a dozen ways in which he would make Skelly pay for today's outrage.

Ginnie spoke again, but this time her voice was quiet and reflective. "My father came from Virginia. Someday I'm going to move there and get away from all of this. I'm going to marry someone with land and money and he's going to take me to his mansion in the South. Everyone there will treat me like a lady, like somebody special. Not like here. No one will make fun of me or my family. They'll respect me. And I won't have to work all day, doing the chores...and doing my sister's work, too. We can just spend the whole day sipping lemonade and discussing anything we want." She waved her hand lightly, as though dismissing all the unpleasantness of Gettysburg.

As her voice trailed off into the wind, Wes stared at Ginnie, unable to speak. He was deafened by the sound of her words, blinded by the images in her dreams. She had just described his own daydream. She had exactly the same hopes for the future that he did. In that instant, Wes knew that someday it would be *he* who would carry Ginnie Wade off to the great mansion, it would be he who would sip lemonade with her, talking the day away.

Julia jumped from her branch, shattering the mood. "Well, I'm going home. Might as well get the yelling over with. All this dreaming has made me hungry." She turned to Wes and Ginnie. "You coming?"

Ginnie hesitated for a moment, looking at Wes. He held her gaze, then broke into a shy smile. "Stay for a while."

Ginnie smiled back, calling to Julia who was already starting down the trail, "I'll see you later." Julia shook her head in amusement and set off for town alone.

Chapter 2

RESOLUTION

Gettysburg, Pennsylvania
August 1856

Ginnie ran the last three blocks to her house on Breckenridge Street, returning from her meeting with Wes. She had seen him as he left work almost every day during the past month, and their afternoon walks had become a habit which made the rest of her day bearable.

But today was different. The usual excitement she felt after such meetings was nothing compared to this afternoon. Her joy brimmed over as she raced to tell her sister and mother the news. Wes was moving to Virginia with his job and had asked her to wait for him. He planned to return to Gettysburg when he had earned enough to marry her and take her south with him. To Ginnie, it was too good to believe and she could barely contain herself. She rushed into the house out of breath, calling, "Georgia! Georgia! Mama!"

It was soon obvious that no one was home. Ginnie sat heavily on the divan, sighing in frustration. After a long, impatient wait she heard the door open, and ran to the front room as Mary Wade led her children into the house, the voices of Ginnie's younger brothers filling the place. Ten-year-old Jack was full of mischief, most of which was directed toward his five-year-old brother, Sam, who at present was yelling about some recent grievance and chasing Jack around the room. Ginnie's older sister, Georgia, came in behind the boys carrying the newest Wade, Harry, born only eighteen months ago. Georgia maneuvered her way through the rambunctious boys to put Harry in his crib.

Mary closed the door and gave Ginnie an angry look. "Where were you? You knew we had an appointment with Dr. Greene this afternoon."

Ginnie's excitement instantly drained away. The appointment had completely slipped her mind. Harry was ill with a fever, but her mother had told Ginnie to meet them in the doctor's office so he could examine her, too. Mary had made it clear that they could not afford repeated trips to the doctor. She scowled as she removed her hat, and Ginnie waited for the inevitable reprimand to begin. Georgia marched by her younger sister wearing a superior look.

Mary continued, "You were seeing that Culp boy again, weren't you."

"Yes," Ginnie responded defensively.

"Well, this will be the last of it. You are forbidden to see him anymore. You have too much work to do around here. I can't afford to have you go running off to see him every afternoon."

Ginnie was speechless for a moment, her mouth open in shock. Eventually she found her voice, speaking rapidly and with great force. "Well, it just so happens that Wesley is moving to the South and he has asked me to wait for him. He's going to return in a few years and we are going to be married." Immediately, she knew that this was the worst possible way to share her news.

Mary turned, her face reflecting astonishment. Georgia rushed from the other room when she heard the statement, shouting, "What did you say?" Ginnie had known that Georgia would be jealous of the news because she was older and didn't yet have any male callers. Mary put her hands up to quiet her daughters, trying to regain her own composure.

"You will do nothing of the sort, young lady," she shouted. "You will tell that boy tomorrow that you will do *nothing* of the sort."

Ginnie felt her resolve beginning to crumble but stuck out her chin, determined to make her mother agree. "I already told him yes."

"I don't care a fig for what you told him. You're too young to be making any such decisions. If you won't tell him, then I'll go see his father and that'll put an end to it. I have half a mind to have him arrested for immoral behavior toward a child. Now, you go to your room. There won't be any dinner for you tonight."

Ginnie's composure dissolved as the tears coursed down her face. She rushed past her brothers, who were enjoying the family fireworks, and into the room she shared with Georgia. She slammed the door dramatically before falling onto the bed and giving way to her frustration and rage.

Awaking early in the morning, she found Georgia in the bed beside her as usual. She stared at her sister in the gathering light. Georgia was only two years older than Ginnie, but those years seemed to make a great difference. Georgia, being the eldest, was responsible for helping Mary run the business. That left Ginnie to perform the chores that Georgia never got around to doing, claiming she was too busy helping her mother sew. Ginnie felt that her sister treated her like a slave and that Mary let her get away with it. As Ginnie looked at her in the morning light, she remembered the look of superiority on her face the previous night and could not bring herself to remain beside her for another second. She got up quietly and dressed, then slipped out the front door onto Breckenridge Street.

With a quick glance back at the house, she hurried away. Her mother would be rising soon. Ginnie held her breath as she headed toward Baltimore Street, expecting at any second to hear her mother's voice calling her back.

Finally she reached the corner, turned left and sighed in relief.

Baltimore Street was peaceful in these early morning hours. It was wider than the side streets, used by the larger carts and carriages. Ginnie could see several carts already moving through the mist up toward the town square, farmers with loads of hay and produce for the wealthier families residing in the center of town. As the morning light played over the mist, Ginnie could almost imagine she was in a dreamland in which everything was all right. Here there was no one to judge her or tell her what to do, no people to stare at her as she passed, whispering behind their hands when they thought she couldn't hear. She was alone in her own world.

But reality began to creep back as she noticed once again how the houses increased in size the farther north she walked. It was a reminder of the social distinctions that were important to so many residents. Everyone knew who was at the top of the social ladder and who was at the bottom. The judge who had taken her father away from her had cast a mark on her family, and people did not forget these things. Her friends were fewer now, and many people simply avoided her. She had done nothing wrong, and yet everywhere she went people whispered and stared.

She hurried through the village square where the main roads met to form a cross. Continuing north, she wondered whether her mother had discovered her absence yet. Mentally, she replayed the argument from the night before, rethinking her responses. In this version, she was the one who made all the forceful and convincing points, so that her mother eventually relented, begged forgiveness, and granted her permission to go south with Wes.

She knew it would have been different if her father had been there to stand up for her. In former days, the family lines had been drawn more fairly, with Mary and Georgia on one side and Ginnie and her father on the other. But her father had been gone for six years now, first in prison for a "misunderstanding" as he called it, then in the Poor House north of the city. The boys, as they grew, had naturally sided with their mother so that Ginnie always felt that she had no support.

She missed her father's company and backing desperately. Mary and Georgia sometimes referred to him with contempt, as though they were embarrassed to be related to him. Ginnie found it hard to believe all the things they attributed to him. She had seen him drunk, of course, and had watched, terrified, as he smashed things in his rage and threatened the family with harm. But this was not the real James Wade. Ginnie remembered the man who got up in the middle of the night to kiss her gently on her forehead when she had bad dreams. She recalled how he had carried her on his shoulders during their long walks in the woods while he talked endlessly about his life in the beautiful hills of Virginia. He had teased her with special secrets, whispering that she was his only real daughter, that he loved her more than anyone. He said that he had named her Virginia for his beloved birthplace, and that someday she should go there and marry a rich plantation owner.

But that James Wade was gone. What remained was only a hollow remnant, his mind ruined by alcohol. Four years ago, Mary had him committed as "incorrigible and insane." A year later, repenting her action, she applied to have his status changed to voluntary commitment so he would be free to visit home during his rational periods. He made several such visits and was always eager, it seemed to Ginnie, to make amends. Ginnie was glad for these visits, but after one final violent episode the judge had him committed permanently. His last visit home had been more than two years ago, the main legacy of which was a new child, her brother Harry. Another mouth to feed for a family already stretched to its financial limits.

From time to time, when the house became too crowded or the fights with her mother or sister grew too intense, Ginnie would head north, as she was doing this morning, to the Poor House to see her father. She knew her mother would punish her with extra chores, but it no longer mattered. Behind her mother's angry eyes she sometimes glimpsed a silent sympathy. Mary never spoke of it, but Ginnie believed that her mother still loved her father and understood her need to go see him once in a while.

The sun was above the eastern horizon by the time Ginnie arrived at her destination. It had been months since she had seen her father and she felt a bit of trepidation. Over the past year he had become more haggard, his face drawn and hopeless. He was only forty-two years old, but his hair had grown a shocking white which made him appear ancient. On each visit, he seemed to have deteriorated a bit more. There were times when he was too ill to leave his bed and the men at the door would turn her away.

She stood for a time looking at the low, dirty building set back from the road in an ill-tended field. Trees blocked much of the view, planted discretely to hide these men the county seemed determined to forget. The Adams County Alms House, or the "Poor House" as people called it, housed all the county derelicts, emotional as well as financial. Most had gambled or drunk away their savings and then, having lost everything including their self-respect, had been ordered into the Poor House by unsympathetic courts and angry creditors. Some, like Ginnie's father, had been declared dangerous to the community and placed there for lack of a more appropriate facility. It was an odd assortment of men with a variety of backgrounds, but all shared a reputation as failures.

Each morning the men were escorted to the outhouses prior to an early breakfast. Ginnie tried to time her visits to coincide with these walks since the attendants would not permit her inside the building itself. Soon after she arrived, the door opened and a line of men spilled forth. They walked casually in twos and threes, talking quietly. For the most part, nothing appeared unusual about the group; they might have been laborers leaving for their jobs in the morning. She strained to find her father among the crowd. For a moment, she was afraid he might not appear; perhaps he was ill again. Then she saw him, his white hair standing out boldly in the sun's low morning rays. He walked by himself, quietly smiling at some inner dialogue.

Ginnie moved forward, walking down the path that led to the building. Off to one side stood a large man with his arms crossed, watching the procession. He was the attendant charged with supervising the more disturbed of the House's inhabitants. Ginnie approached him cautiously, trying to make her presence known so as not to startle him. The man turned, caught sight of her and a scowl darkened his face.

"Excuse me," she began as respectfully as possible. The man managed a grunt, allowing his eyes to slide down the length of Ginnie's body. His leer made her shiver and she lowered her eyes. "I'm here to see my father."

The man continued to stare at her with suspicion, even though he recognized her from previous visits. "And who might that be, young miss?" His voice was low, sounding more animal than human.

"It's all right, Samuel. She's here for me."

Ginnie turned to see her father walking slowly toward her. She ran to him, throwing her arms around his neck. "Papa!" He embraced her for a moment, then stood back to admire her. "I'm so glad to see you," Ginnie sputtered. But she stopped when she saw his face. It was badly bruised on one side where a nasty-looking welt ran down along his left cheek. She reached for it but he pulled away from her hand. "What happened to you?" she asked in a tiny voice.

He looked away, but could not hide the discomfort in his eyes. "Nothing. I was someplace I shouldn't have been."

Ginnie turned to glare at the attendant who hovered nearby. He returned her stare impassively. Despite her father's white hair and haggard face, Ginnie felt a kind of maternal pity for him. He seemed so innocent and naïve, more like a brother than a parent. His eyes darted around the groups of men huddled in the yard, some of whom stared back at Ginnie with interest. Feeling protective, he took her by the arm and led her back toward the building, away from the others.

"You've been fighting with your mother," he said knowingly. His eyes, despite their hollow look, maintained something of their old sparkle.

Ginnie couldn't help but smile. "Yes."

He nodded. "You'll have to stop that. Your mother needs you now that I'm not there, and she can't be worried that you'll run off every time you have a disagreement." He sighed sadly. "Was it about me? I've caused your mother a lot of pain. I'm better off here where I can't embarrass her. You should forget me. I'm not worth the effort."

17

"Don't say that," she scolded gently. "I think you are. That's why I came. To get your opinion."

He smiled thinly. "Why would you want a crazy old man's opinion?"

"You're not crazy," Ginnie said emphatically. On days like today it was almost possible to believe that he was normal.

He nodded vacantly and stopped to pick a wild flower for Ginnie which he slipped into her hair. "Now, what did you come all this way to ask me?"

"It's about a boy," she began hesitantly.

Her father's face showed surprise. "A boy? God a'mighty, you're too young to be thinking about such things." He looked at her piercingly, then shook his head with some dismay. "Well, maybe not. No, I suppose you're starting to grow up."

Ginnie couldn't help blushing. She had turned this moment over and over in her mind, thinking how she would approach the problem. But now that the moment had come, she was afraid that her question might sound ridiculous.

"So, what is it?" He dropped his voice. "You're not in trouble …that way, are you?"

"No!" she cried, her face flushing with indignation. "No. He just wants me to wait for him. He's going south to work and wants me to wait until I'm old enough to go with him."

"I take it your mother wasn't thrilled with that idea," he said, trying to look solemn. She couldn't tell if he was laughing at her or not.

"No. She doesn't like him. She doesn't like the South. She wants me to stay here." Wringing her hands nervously, she was afraid she might start to cry. Her father rubbed at his cheek and shook his head.

"I suppose I had something to do with her not liking the South. And how do you feel about it?"

"I think I'm in love with him," she laughed, unable to believe what she was saying.

"Then wait for him," he said decisively. After a moment he shook his head again, leaning toward her. "Just don't tell your mother," he whispered.

A thrill of joy ran through her. She had been certain that he would be on her side. But then she covered her mouth in surprise when she thought of the implications of what he had suggested. "But that means I'd have to lie to her."

Her father pondered this idea for a moment. "You can be forgiven if you go to the church and confess it to God. Anyway, she'll find out in due time. And you can apologize on your wedding day."

Ginnie laughed again, feeling the excitement of the night before returning. She hugged her father warmly, gratefully, tears of gratitude washing away her previous frustration. Then with a quick peck on the cheek she bade him farewell. If she hurried, she would have time to slip into the church for a quick prayer and still get back in time for her morning chores.

Chapter 3

FREEDOM

Gettysburg, Pennsylvania
August 1856

There was a palpable silence in the room when Wes' brother, Will, finished speaking. It seemed for a moment as if time had stopped and rendered those around the table incapable of movement. The carefully prepared Sunday ham sat untouched at the head of the table. Wes, afraid to break the stillness with the smallest gesture, scanned the faces across from him without turning his head. Julia and his older sister, Annie, sat with their hands in their laps, their eyes fixed on their father. He sat stoically at the head of the table, his weathered skin and sunken eyes inscrutable in the light of the flickering gas lamps. Wes watched him out of the corner of his eye, dreading his father's response to the idea of his sons leaving Gettysburg.

The rumors had been whispered around the carriage shop for over a month. Mr. Hoffman had for some time been making arrangements to move his company south, and it was only a matter of time before word began to trickle out to the community. The majority of Mr. Hoffman's customers lived in the south, and thus the move was logical. When Hoffman finally made the news public, there was turmoil in Gettysburg since almost fifty wage earners were faced with the loss of their jobs. Hoffman, however, gave his workers the option of moving to Virginia if they wanted to retain their positions. While some refused to move away from family and friends, for Wes it was just the chance he had longed for. Virginia was the very place he most wanted to be in order to build a new future for himself…and Ginnie. He had waited patiently while his older brother made up his mind. Will had a wife and child to consider and the thought of not being able to support them had finally forced him to agree to the move.

The elder Culp had assumed that his sons would quit their jobs to work for him, and Will's announcement that he had decided to join the migration south had caught Jesse off guard. Now, as their father pursed his lips and glowered at the ham, they watched in silence, waiting for his tirade to begin. The quiet was shattered by a hacking cough from Wes' mother, which served to heighten the tension at the table. For the past few weeks, they had listened as she struggled to catch her breath between the wracking fits of coughing that came more and more frequently.

Jesse, raising his eyes for the first time, took a deep breath. Wes tried to keep from wincing as he anticipated the angry words that were certain to follow. But his father simply looked at Will for a long moment and then nodded his head, a motion so slight that it was almost lost in the gray shadows of the flickering lamps. But Will and Wes both saw the sign of assent and stiffened in surprise. When their father finally spoke, his voice was breathy and hoarse, sounding infinitely tired.

"Of course, I knew that this day would come sooner or later. You're grown now and you have a family to look after, a wife and a three-year-old son. I don't like the thought of you being far away. Your mother will miss you. But you have a good job, and you must do what you think is right."

Never once did Wes' father take his eyes from Will's face. He had made a point of not including Wes in any of his words, and Wes' anxiety continued to rise. When his father paused, Wes could resist no longer.

"Father, can I go, too?" Immediately, he chided himself for interrupting his father, and for the childish sound of his request. He did his best to maintain a positive expression on his face, but the look faltered when the old man turned his gaze toward Wes.

"Of course not." His father's lips barely moved when he spoke, and the words came out sounding sarcastic and condescending. Anger poured into Wes' body, building into rage at being treated like a child. But all of his carefully thought out arguments failed him when he looked into his father's scornful eyes. He stuttered for a moment in one final attempt to argue his case, but all that came out was a whimpering "W…why not?"

There was a moment's pause before his father spoke again. The old man's voice was steady and even, but what Wes heard was pure contempt.

"Because you still act like a little boy. Because you're too young to go off by yourself. Because your mother needs you here, and God knows you need a mother to look after you. And because I wouldn't burden Will with the responsibility of looking after you. He's got enough to worry about with his wife and child to care for in a town full of strangers. You can just start looking for work right here in Gettysburg. And in the meantime, I'll see to it that you're not idle."

Wes had prepared a hundred things to say in support of his case. But as he opened his mouth to say them, the words ran out of his head before they could reach his lips. He could think of nothing that would soften the granite face at the end of the table. And so he deliberately pushed his chair back from the table, stood without looking at anyone and walked toward the door.

"Come back here!" his father's voice boomed after him. Wes could

20

imagine the old man's face flushing red. "I didn't excuse you from this table!" But Wes willed his feet to keep moving and stepped though the door into the kitchen, then opened the back door and escaped into the warm afternoon. Before he pulled the door closed, he heard his father mumble, "See? It just proves my point. The boy is just a stubborn child." Wes heard the sound of his mother weeping and slammed the door before he could give way to his own tears.

As the time for the move approached at the end of September, life dissolved into a flurry of preparations. It became harder and harder for Wes to drag himself out of bed each day to get to work, which now involved crating up all the various materials and machines used in manufacturing the Hoffman carriages.

The more vacant the once-crowded shop became, the more Wes' co-workers were filled with excitement. With few friends in the shop, he hung around his brother and his brother's friends, Ed Skelly and Billy Holtzworth, who chattered non-stop about the big move and all the novel sights that would await them in Virginia. Nearly half of the employees were going, and it was all they seemed able to talk about. Wes could do nothing but stand back and listen to the enthusiasm of the others, each day hoping that his father would change his mind, and each day being more certain that he would not.

Even Will was caught up in the excitement. "I've never been out of Gettysburg," he mused one evening as they walked back toward the house. "I wonder if it'll be much different. It'll be so nice not living with Ma and Papa. Do you think the people will be much different?" It was an endless stream of random thoughts, each biting deeper into Wes' resentment. He could not remember seeing his brother so worked up about anything before. But Wes held his tongue, preferring to keep Ginnie's and his dreams to himself. And his jealousy was tempered to some extent by happiness for his brother because, as Wes listened to him talk, he understood Will's excitement better than anyone knew.

To Wes, Will had always been the lucky one. He was tall and ruggedly handsome, but there was a gentleness to him which made him easy to like. He had a talent for making difficult things look simple. As a child he could throw a rock further than anyone else; as an adult he could shoe a horse or fix a machine without effort. His easy nature had won him many admirers, and the young ladies in town had fought fiercely over him. That contest had been won by Salome Sheads, who was not only beautiful but talented and gracious as well. The couple – everyone agreed they were a perfect match – were soon married, producing a son and a daughter in quick succession. Will's luck had failed him only briefly when a fever had struck the year before and carried their daughter away. Her death pulled the small family more tightly together and made their son, Willbertus – "Bertie" – even more precious to them.

Wes, studying Will out of the corner of his eye, admitted to himself that it was hard not to like him. But Wes had good reason to resent his brother. Will was everything that Wes could never be and everyone knew it, especially their father. To the elder Culp, Wes was a poor imitation tagging along in the wake of a perfect original. And so Wes listened in silence as Will talked about the future, a future which for Wes was becoming more distant and unreachable.

At the end of September, just before Hoffman's shop was to move, the foreman told Wes that he no longer had a job. That same week his mother took a serious turn for the worse, and since he was no longer working, Wes spent much of his time with her. The doctor had ordered her to bed, and while Annie and Julia took care of her needs and ran the house, Wes stayed by her side.

At night he would sit for hours holding her hand and listening to her labored breathing. Sometimes he would read to her in the late hours when she couldn't sleep, struggling to make out the words in her battered copies of Elia's essays and Donne's poetry, two of her favorites. Most of the time they sat in silence, Wes watching her struggle with pain and with the knowledge that she was dying. The sorrow he experienced at the thought of losing his mother merged with the loneliness of being left behind. It created a dull, black hopelessness that constantly tugged at him, sucking his spirit down into a deepening depression.

He blamed his misery on the hostile relationship he had with his father. Only death could end the fierce despair into which he was falling. Perhaps when he died of a broken spirit, his father would finally feel some remorse for his attitude.

It grew worse in the following weeks. Will and his family left with the others for Virginia. The summer heat was gone, replaced by the relative cool of fall. All around, the green foliage ignited in a blaze of red, yellow and orange as the leaves burned their lives away. But Wes saw none of it. Without a job to go to in the morning, he spent more time in his room or beside his mother. He could see her condition deteriorating, and regardless of how many visits the doctor made, she slipped a little farther away from him each day. Wes felt himself slipping away with her, cut off from any kind of meaningful life. Ginnie came with Julia after school one day to visit, but Wes would not see her. His plans for them had been defeated and he was too ashamed to face her and confess his impotence.

As the weeks wore on, his father repeatedly demanded that he go out to look for work. But he continued his vigil at his mother's bedside since she was now in a coma from which the doctor said she would not recover. Wes felt as if he was peering at life down a long, empty hallway filled with distant echoing sounds. There were only scattered moments of clarity in his days. He remembered once seeing Julia standing on the other side of the bed, caressing their mother's head lovingly and then looking with a strange and worried expression at him. He remembered looking through the window and seeing people proceed in a kind of slow motion to destinations that had nothing to do with him. He remembered studying the big oak tree visible from his mother's bed, watching the leaves fall one at a time, certain that when the last one finally let go both he and his mother would depart with it.

Then one morning he woke to find his mother looking at him, her eyes focused and clear, a smile on her face once again. After a week of senseless babbling while racked with fever, her sudden clarity startled Wes. He got up, knelt by her bed and took her hand.

Her voice sounded high and frail, but it was clear. "Wesley. Why are you here?"

He was surprised by the question, wondering whether she was looking for someone else. "Do you want me to get Annie or Julia?"

She shook her head. "No. I'm glad you're here. I've been lying here looking at you." She paused, trying to catch her breath. When she spoke, the words came out in short gasps.

"When you were young, I remember how different you were from your brother. Will and your father were so practical. But you were a dreamer. Like me." She smiled softly, sadly. "Promise me something." Wes nodded, carried away by her intimate words. "Don't let them stop your dreams. I've had my life and it's been a good life. I wanted lots of things that never happened. But my dreams held me up and kept me going. You fight for your dreams because without them you'll be lost."

She slid off into silence and closed her eyes. Wes thought she had fallen back to sleep. But a moment later she looked at him again. "I always knew that, of all my children, you were special. There is so much promise in you. I have a feeling that you'll do great things. I only wish I could be here to see them." After another silence she fell asleep again, a peaceful smile on her face. Eventually, Wes moved back to his chair. He stared out the window for a long time.

She died the next morning, never having wakened again. There was a flurry of activity in the house as friends and neighbors stopped to offer condolences, bringing food and wreaths. The casket maker came to take the measurements and returned later with the casket. Julia and Annie were constantly busy cooking, cleaning and entertaining visitors who thought it proper to make sympathy calls. The family dressed in mourning and there was an oppressive silence in the house, a cloud of sadness that obscured their perceptions and muffled their words. Wes' father seemed to carry on as usual, rejecting any show of emotion.

Wes felt distanced from everyone, as if he was watching them all act out their parts in some strange play for which he was the only audience. Aunts and uncles, cousins and children of all ages constantly filled the sitting room, talking, moving about, creating a quiet commotion. He tried to stay to himself, to avoid having to deal with any of them.

But when Will came home, everything changed. With a few words, he rekindled the hope which Wes had thought was lost forever.

Wes suddenly became eager to see Ginnie, but the funeral and other family duties prevented him from going to her. On the third day after his mother's death, Ginnie appeared nervously at the door to pay her respects. Overjoyed to see her and grateful for the opportunity to escape his gloomy family, he quickly accompanied her outside.

Ginnie's face mirrored an inner uncertainty and after a few steps she turned to him. Hesitantly she said, "I was afraid you didn't want to see me anymore." Wes realized how he had neglected Ginnie in the past weeks and how differently he felt from the last time he had talked to her.

"It's been very difficult," he said. "I'm sorry I wouldn't see you that day. It was just t-t-too hard. But I'm glad you came today. I've missed seeing you. I was going to come to your house as soon as the family left so I could t-t-tell you the news."

"News?"

"I'm leaving Gettysburg. I'm going south to work with Mr. Hoffman, like I wanted to in the first place."

Ginnie's face fell for a second before she recovered, feigning excitement. "Oh, that's wonderful. But I thought your father said you couldn't go."

He smiled confidently. "I'm old enough to make my own decisions now. I've been t-t-talking a lot to Will since he came home for the funeral. He's given me the money for a ticket and told me that Mr. Hoffman will hire me if I go down. My father doesn't have any say in the matter anymore."

Ginnie accepted this pronouncement in silence as they continued their walk out past the family farm to the foot of Culp's Hill. Finally, when the silence had become awkward, Wes turned to Ginnie.

"This doesn't change anything between us. I still want to come back for you, Ginnie."

The hopelessness which had been his constant companion for the past weeks had magically departed, replaced by a new confidence in their dreams. His mother's words sounded inside his head, leaving him nearly dizzy with elation. Her death had not signaled the end of his life, but had brought into being a whole new future. His sorrow was mitigated by an overwhelming sense of freedom. He no longer felt tied to his father, and Will's simple words, asking him to come south with him, had released the final bond and freed him to pursue his goals.

He took Ginnie's hand and led her up the slope to the familiar grove of trees that stood as sentinels toward the top. The trees were naked, but the

24

breeze still held a bit of the autumn softness. Below, the town began to twinkle as the street lamps came on one at a time.

He turned to her at length and asked, "Do you ever wonder if you're meant for greatness?" Her blank look revealed her confusion at the question. "I mean, we're all here for some reason, right? But some of us are here to be a part of something bigger. The people in this town are so shortsighted. They only see who you are now, they only know where you came from. Tomorrow I could be a great man. But they wouldn't understand how it happened because they knew me when I was a boy, when I was nothing, and they thought I would always be nothing. That's why I have to leave here. Do you see that?" She paused in contemplation, then nodded with bright eyes. Wes sighed, looking down at the town again. "Don't you ever think that when you get older you'll be a great person?"

Ginnie looked out on the town and said softly, "I never really thought about it much. But I guess I'd rather have a family and happiness and health than fame. I mean, when you're great you don't have time for your family, and everyone is jealous of you. They resent you and say mean things about you."

"They say mean things about me *now*," Wes responded. "But if I was someone important, they would look up to me. When I get to the South, I'll save up all my money and buy lots of land. Then I'll be making enough money to build a big mansion on a hill somewhere, a hill just like this one, where we can look down on the town. And then I'll come back to Gettysburg in one of the fine big carriages that Mr. Hoffman makes, and I'll pick you up in it and take you away with me."

"It sounds like a fairytale," she said.

"But it'll come true. I just know it will. Everything will be better when I get away from here." He grasped her hands again and pulled her closer. "You *will* wait for me, won't you?"

Startled to be so near to him, she looked into his face, her eyes wide. He could smell her hair and see her face coloring with excitement. "Yes, of course I'll wait for you. And I do believe you'll be a great man someday, Mr. Culp."

He laughed, then suddenly leaned closer and kissed her lightly on the lips. She tensed at first, then relaxed and kissed him back. When he drew away to gaze at her, he saw that tears of joy sparkled in her eyes.

"And you will be the wife of a famous man, Miss Wade, or should I say 'Mrs. Culp'?"

They laughed at the thought, then melted together in a gentle embrace, holding each other close. The touch of her hair on his face, of his breath on her cheek, joined with the caress of the wind to complete the enchantment. Then, reluctantly, they began their descent back down into the real world, to the place of relatives and noise, of death and rejection. But their hands were joined and their hearts united in a vision of the future that the others could not see.

Chapter 4

DEPARTURE

Gettysburg, Pennsylvania/Shepherdstown, Virginia
November 17, 1856

The rhythmic clatter of the train's progress blurred the world outside into a gray streak. Wes sat uncomfortably in his best suit, his face pressed to the window watching hopefully for any changes. They had been traveling for an hour already and would soon be approaching Shepherdstown, but the landscape looked the same to him.

Will and his family slept across the aisle, oblivious to the excitement. Wes envied their easy familiarity with something that was so completely new to him. He wished for the day when he could take such a trip with the same utter disregard. He had never been on a train before. Although it seemed to move with breathtaking speed, each new hill only revealed more hills beyond. The landscape was endless, the people they passed numberless and each new second carried him further into the unknown.

For most of the past week, Wes had waited for the formalities to end following his mother's burial. He knew he should mask his eagerness to leave, but every now and then his sorrowful facade slipped and the impatient excitement shone through like a ray of sunlight. Julia had noticed, and Ginnie, and perhaps even his father because on occasion he found them staring at him with a look of mild reproof. Wes' father had aged in the past week. He took his wife's death stoically, its full impact hidden even from himself, but at times Wes could see the pain steal through the opaque barrier of his eyes. Wes, anticipating his own future, realized that his father could look forward only to sorrow and this sudden emptiness.

That morning, Wes had walked past his father's door and caught a glimpse of him standing by a dresser. The old man tenderly held a silk scarf in one hand, rubbing the material between his fingers. He was staring out the window, and if he heard Wes' approach he gave no indication of it. Wes moved on, leaving him to his reveries.

Jesse Culp had argued when Wes once again announced that he was moving south, but not so vigorously as before, and Wes knew that he had won. For just a moment before his father relented and gave his consent, Wes detected remorse in the man's eyes, a subtle sorrow. It was a little thing, but in that sad moment Wes nearly regretted leaving. His father had always seemed so large and commanding, and Wes realized now that he was neither. With new eyes, Wes saw him not as a bellicose adversary but as a lonely, tired old man. Perhaps the pity showed, for his father's granite stare was quickly back in effect, never again to be broken in Wes' presence.

Talking to Ginnie had helped a great deal. She was a willing ear for his tumultuous thoughts, refining his dreams with glimpses into her own small world. Together they laid out the landscape of their future. They walked long hours along the crest of the hill above Henry Culp's farm, holding hands and rehearsing over and over again the hopes they had already expressed many times.

This morning had dawned like all others; people went about their business oblivious of the importance it held for Wes. Sleep had been impossible the night before and he was wide awake long before the rest of the house. Will and Salome calmly ate their breakfast before leaving for the new train station, while Wes nibbled distractedly at a chunk of bread. He had said his farewell to Ginnie the day before since her classes would force her to miss his departure. With all the loose ends neatly tied, Wes' single focus was getting onto the train.

When they arrived at the station, Mr. Emery, the station master, announced that the train would be late. Wes nearly screamed in frustration, pacing nervously along the track while his father, sisters, Will and his family sat on the benches. Finally, the distant chug of the engine broke on the crisp November air. Wes' heart raced, as if trying to adjust to the thundering pulse of the locomotive.

As he turned back to the others, he saw Ginnie on the platform, her hands self consciously smoothing her blue dress. She looked more like a little girl than Wes had remembered. Her presence disturbed him; now he would have to find some way to say another goodbye. But as he approached her, he saw the tears in her eyes.

"What is it?" he asked, taking one of her hands.

"I just came to say goodbye." She was struggling to keep from crying, but a single drop broke free from the corner of her eye. He glanced at his family down the platform, watching them rise as the train steamed into the station. She followed his look, pushing back the hair from her eyes. "I shouldn't have come," she mumbled. "Miss Jenkins will miss me and I'll be in for it."

Her pain was nearly tangible and Wes was overcome by a tender concern. The train whistle deafened them and for a moment they could only look into each other's eyes. When the whistle stopped, Wes took both her hands. "No. I'm so glad you did."

Now that the impatient hours of waiting for the train were over, Wes felt pressured by its arrival. He would have given anything for another five minutes to spend with Ginnie. He realized, however, that more time would only prolong the pain.

He pressed her hands tightly, gazing into her eyes. The train's whistle sounded again, warning the passengers to be aboard. "I'll come back for you, Ginnie. I promise. It will be just as we planned it." She attempted to smile, but was overcome by emotion. Wes could think of nothing to say. "D...d...d...don't cry, Ginnie," he stammered, overwhelmed by his feelings.

Will called from down the platform and Wes looked up. "I've got to go." She nodded. He ran down to where his family was standing, shook hands with his father and gave Annie and Julia a hug. Julia hung on to him and he couldn't miss the tears glistening in her eyes. He smiled at her, kissed her on the forehead, then ran to help his brother load the cases up the narrow steps into the car. When the conductor yelled a final warning for passengers to board, hoping to regain the lost time with a short stop, Wes found a seat and pressed his face to the window. His family had gathered below and his eyes touched each of them briefly before passing on to look for Ginnie. For a frantic moment he thought that she had left, going back to school before the train departed. But then he found her, backed into the shadowed overhang of the station's eaves. He waved to her and she stepped forward to wave back.

The shrill steam whistle startled him again, and he looked down to see Julia smiling up at him, the proud look on her face replacing the tears. As the train lurched forward, Ginnie's wave became more animated and she stepped out into the sunlight. Now he could see that she was smiling and he knew that everything was all right. He waved until she was out of sight, grinning wryly at the irony. For years he had been desperate to leave Gettysburg; now, when the moment had finally come, he found himself crying.

All that was a hundred miles ago and the Maryland countryside had given way quickly to Virginia. The conductor walked briskly past, his hand glancing off the seats for balance. "Next stop, Shepherdstown!" he bellowed in an odd nasal tone which drew out his vowels and elongated the words.

Will and Salome stirred from their rest, and Bertie began to cry, rubbing his sleepy eyes. Wes turned back to the window as the trees thinned out and the buildings began to crowd in. He noticed with disappointment that the whitewashed fronts and dirt lanes looked much like a rearranged version of Gettysburg. But here and there he caught sight of majestic elms and willows hiding pillared buildings. On the road he glimpsed a lady in billowing pink stepping from a jet black carriage, her parasol in hand. But what affected him most was the strangeness of the faces on the platform. He scanned the crowd of thirty or more who stood staring up at him; not one of them was familiar. A new beginning!

After dropping Salome and Bertie at the house where they were letting several rooms, Wes and Will made their way to the boarding house to inquire about space for Wes. As they walked through the town, Wes eyed the surroundings curiously. It was not what he expected. While there were traces of grandeur in several of the buildings, there were no lofty mansions set along tree-lined ways. He didn't see any rich men and women in their finery waited on by attentive slaves. The people were strangers, but in many ways they were identical to those he had left behind in Gettysburg.

The woman at the boarding house sized Wes up, her wrinkled lips tightly pinched before she agreed to board him for $2 a week. After an awkward pause, Wes realized that he was to pay the first week in advance and hurriedly looked at Will who, with a sigh, handed over the money.

They went next to the new shop to see Mr. Hoffman. The building which housed the carriage works sat back from the main road to the south of town. It was easily twice the size of the building in Gettysburg and Wes gazed at it in amazement as they headed around back toward the office. Will rapped on the door, then stepped through without waiting for a reply. Wes followed, hat in hand. Despite the larger building, the office was a cramped room with papers and books strewn on every surface. There was a musty smell about the place, a mixture of damp parchment, fresh ink and the unwashed smell of Mr. Craflion, the office manager. Craflion, half hidden behind an enormous roll top desk, brusquely rose to greet them, informing them that Mr. Hoffman was away on business. Wes studied the man carefully, deciding that his primary trait was the ability to look annoyed no matter what the circumstance. Craflion stared over his pince-nez with a raised eyebrow, apparently wondering why Will and Wes had not fled upon hearing of Hoffman's absence.

Will said, "My brother has come from Gettysburg for the upholsterer's job." Craflion's face descended into an even deeper level of annoyance as he let his gaze shift to Wes. Wes was certain that the position had been filled, that he would be left without a job in a strange town, worse off than he had been in Gettysburg.

Finally, Craflion dropped his eyes and returned to his books. "See that he's here first thing in the morning. Mr. Hoffman will make a decision when he returns."

Will nodded slightly and turned, heading out the door without a further word. Wes, flustered by the abruptness of his brother's departure, nodded nervously at the office manager who took no notice of him.

Outside, he caught up with his brother. "Hey! Wait a second. What did all that mean?"

"You just got your job back," Will said without breaking stride.

"But doesn't Mr. Hoffman have to...."

Will cut him off. "Hoffman'll take you back. That old walrus in the office likes to give everybody a hard time. But the position is still open which means he'll take you in a second. He won't have to train you."

Wes followed as Will ducked into a dark hallway, then stepped out onto the factory floor. The shop was huge in comparison to the one in Gettysburg. The old equipment was laid out differently but it was a comfort to see familiar machines. Ed Skelly and Billy Holtzworth saw the two of them enter and called a greeting.

"Hey, look who's back," Ed shouted cheerfully.

Holtzworth jumped off the carriage on which he was working and wiped his hands on his pants. "And look who he brung with him."

Until that moment, Wes had enjoyed the obscurity of the new town, but seeing familiar faces brought a sudden sense of warmth. He shook hands eagerly with men who would have ignored him back in Gettysburg. A couple of months ago he could not have called them friends, but now they felt like lost comrades. The others asked about news from Gettysburg, offering condolences for the loss of their mother. Wes looked around the factory and caught the eye of several of the other workers. Some appeared friendly but others were suspicious, as if he was intruding.

Ed slapped him on the shoulder. "Let me show you around." The tour took no longer than five minutes and Wes met most of the new workers, forgetting their names as soon as he heard them. One man, however, did not bother to come greet him. He sat in the backseat of one of the carriages reading a newspaper. Ed stood below him for a moment. "Frank. Hey, Parsons! Come meet a friend of mine." The man ignored Ed and continued to read.

A sandy-haired man with a boyish face appeared from behind one of the company wagons and walked up to Ed and Wes. Smiling, he said, "Just ignore old Frank. He likes people to think he can read, but he's just looking at the pictures. My name's Ben Pendleton." He stretched out his hand and shook Wes' firmly. "Welcome to the party."

From his perch in the carriage, Parsons looked over his paper at Ben with a frown. Wes caught the man's eye for a second and the look of animosity. He waved uneasily, then turned back to Ben.

Glancing at Parsons out of the corner of his eye, Ben said with a grin, "Don't worry, I'll introduce you to the better element in town. I've been after your brother ever since he came down here to join us at the Guards. You need to meet some people, and maybe now that you're here, he'll come along too. We're meeting over to Bridger's Tavern tonight. After you get settled, come over and have a beer with us."

There was a warmth about Ben that made Wes like him instantly. Looking across the shop, Ben indicated some of the others. "Hell, you can drag all the rest of your Pennsylvania buddies with you. I've been trying to get them to join us, but I guess they're afraid us Virginians'll drink them under the table."

Ed chuckled. "You never out and out challenged us like that before. Now I can't turn you down."

"What are the Guards?" Wes asked, trying not to look in the direction of Parsons who had laid his paper aside and was openly glaring at the group below.

"Hamtramck's Guards. Colonel Hamtramck was in the war in Mexico. He thought the local boys could use something to keep 'em out of trouble, and I guess he was just plum bored with farming. So he organized the group, and now a bunch of us dress up and march around and keep fit and defend the honor of Virginia and Virginia's women. But most of the time we hang out at Bridger's and drink and tell lies about battles we never fought."

Ed turned to Wes with a grin. "You should see 'em out there in that field marching around like a flock of sheep. And Ben here won't be satisfied until he turns all of us into sheep. Ha!" Ben ignored the remark and turned back to Wes.

"So, what do you say?"

"Sure," Wes said, eager for the acceptance that seemed to be offered so easily.

"Good," said Ben. "I'll come over with Ed here after work and pick you up."

Wes nodded and started to walk away. He glanced up at Parsons who suddenly opened the carriage door and jumped down in front of him. Startled, Wes had to look up to meet his eyes. He noticed the crooked, yellow teeth and the faint smell of whisky on his breath. There was a ring of sweat on his collar, and three days growth of stubble on his tanned face. Wes recognized in him every bully he had ever faced, and he felt the old familiar weakness creep into his knees.

Then Ben was between them, moving Wes off toward the door with Ed and Will following. "Just forget him, Wes. He tries to scare everybody like that."

"I wasn't scared," Wes mumbled, trying to keep his voice from quaking.

Ben, Ed and Billy arrived after Wes had eaten dinner and the foursome headed off to the other side of town. A moment after they emerged from the boarding house, they heard derisive laughter from the porch of a saloon across the way. Wes recognized Parsons, standing with three other toughs, puffing a cigar.

"Hey, Ben," Parsons called sarcastically. "You takin' up shepherding?" The others laughed and began bleating, louder and louder, trying to outdo each other.

"The shepherd of Shepherdstown," someone said mockingly, and the whole flock in front of the tavern roared in amusement.

Ben merely smiled and said loud enough so that all the locals could hear, "Looks like the garbage collector missed some this evening." The bleating and the laughter stopped abruptly. There was an icy silence as the tavern toughs eased onto their feet.

Parsons stepped off the porch and came face to face with Ben. Ben didn't back away, didn't flinch, and the smile never left his face, even though Parsons towered over him. To Wes, he looked like a giant, but Ben kept smiling. "Don't you want to take that back, Pendleton?"

Ben's smile widened. "Now, why would I want to take back the truth, you buck-toothed, pea-brained piece of dung?"

Parsons' face went into contortions as his mind struggled to cope with the sheer magnitude of the insult. Finally, his rage congealed into a bellow and he raised his fists to swing them down on Ben's head and shoulders. Ben stood his ground while Wes and the others unconsciously took a step backward. Parsons brought his hands crashing down, but at the last second, Ben stepped aside and Parsons lost his balance as his hands swished through empty air. Ben's fists flew faster than Wes could see. Falling to his knees in pain, Parsons clutched his stomach.

An odd silence settled over the observers as they stared at each other, uncertain what to do next. Then, as though someone had given a signal, they all jumped at the same instant and came together with a crash, swinging, cursing, yelling.

Up against a slightly larger boy who swung wildly, Wes did not have to duck, realizing that in a fight his shortness was an advantage. He had been in his share of brawls, with his brother and with schoolmates, but he had always known the person he was punching. Now, he was fighting a total stranger in a strange town. He had usually been beaten, pinned by Will or knocked senseless by one of the others. Because he was small, he assumed he would always get beaten, and so he usually pleaded for the fight to end.

But not today. Some inner force, fired by rage, broke loose at that instant. As his opponent swung again, missing him a second time, Wes rocked back and timed his punch so that the boy stepped into it, with the weight of both their bodies behind the blow. He had aimed for the kid's jaw but missed and hit him in the nose. The boy backed off, unsteady, stunned. A warm gush of bright red blood exploded down his face, covering his shirt. He grabbed frantically at his wounded nose, hopping around and yelling as though he'd been shot.

Wes grinned, feeling the surge of adrenaline in his blood. A moment later, he received a heavy blow to his back and stumbled forward onto his hands and knees. He got to his feet, turning to face his new attacker, when he saw that Parsons had his arms wrapped around Ben's head. They had bumped him in their struggle and now Parsons' back was directly in front of Wes. Without

33

conscious thought, Wes launched himself into the air, feet first and connected squarely with Parsons' lower back. Ben fell free as Parsons again dropped to his knees. Wes rolled to his feet quickly, catching Ben's eye as he did. Ben's face was red and his sandy hair disheveled, but the smile was still firmly in place.

Ben focused again on Parsons and was about to finish him with a blow to the face when a gunshot made them all jump. They looked toward the sound and there in the center of the street was an older man holding a huge pistol skyward.

"All right now," he said in a quiet voice. "What seems to be the problem? What's got you boys so riled up?"

Ben turned to the man. "Well, Sheriff, Frank and his thugs saw fit to offer my new friend here their kind of welcome, and things got a little too friendly."

"I guess they did, at that." The sheriff walked through the group and helped Parsons to his feet. "Frank, my boy, you look even worse than the last time. You don't learn very fast, do you? Run along home, now. The next time you start a scuffle like this, I'll let you think it over in the cooler."

Parsons and his friends moved off down the street. Wes glanced at the boy whose nose he had broken. He was just a kid, looking scared and foolish, and Wes felt bad for hurting him. Then he caught Parsons' eye again, and saw a look of black hatred. But Wes was no longer intimidated. He had stood up to him and won. Elation was just beginning to hit him when the sheriff put a hand on Wes' shoulder.

"Now, you boys are new here. I know you didn't start this, but it takes two to make a fight. I hope this isn't going to become a habit because I don't like fighting in my town." Then he turned to Ben.

"Ben, you should know better. I'm disappointed in you, and your father will be hearing about this. But the rest of you – well, consider this your one and only warning." With that, he released Wes and was off down the street.

Wes and the others crowded together, watching him go. As he passed out of sight around the corner, they burst into excited chatter and headed the other way. They compared stories and sized up each other's bruises. Ed had caught a punch under the eye from one of the bigger fellows, but had knocked him down in return. Ed and Billy jabbered on, talking over each other. But Wes was quiet, filled with an inner joy that he was not ready to put into words. Ben noticed this and fell in alongside him.

"You're one hell of a fighter, Wes," Ben exclaimed. "When I saw you come flying through the air like that, I thought the cavalry had arrived." Wes smiled happily at the compliment.

Bridger's was a tavern at the east side of town. When the group arrived, they found the large room packed with men in odd, dark gray uniforms. Ben loudly announced their arrival and a path opened through which Wes and the

34

others moved. Grabbing a beer and climbing onto one of the tables, Ben yelled for the group's attention, then proceeded to introduce the newcomers and retell the story of their battle in detail. The group was appreciative and jovial, and Wes found himself slapped on the back by numerous strangers and toasted with raised beer mugs when Ben finished the story.

Ben elbowed his way to Wes' side. "Well," he said, "these are the boys. What do you think?"

"I think you tell a good tale," Wes yelled over the roar of laughing voices.

Ben took a swig, then looked at Wes. "You should join us. It's a hoot. And the women love it. You know, if you're in a uniform, they'll do anything for you." He gave him a laugh and a wink, emptying his mug in one long swig.

Wes looked at his newfound friend in wonder. It was hard to believe that only a few hours earlier he had been in Gettysburg saying goodbye to Ginnie. He wished she could see him now, surrounded by a whole group of new friends. Things were starting off just as he had hoped they would. His grand plan was in operation. And the first step had been getting away from Gettysburg.

Ben peered back at him. "What do you say, Wes? Are you with us? Do you want to join the Guards?"

"You bet," said Wes without hesitation. "Count me in."

Chapter 5

A GATHERING STORM

Shepherdstown, Virginia
October 4, 1860

Wes could see the smoke hanging in a lazy black column long before the train was in sight. His heart pounded with anticipation as he nervously smoothed his hair. The October sun, unusually warm for this time of year, made his woolen Guard's uniform even more uncomfortable, and he wiped a bead of sweat from his brow as the train chugged into sight.

His nephew, Bertie, now seven years old, stood next to him holding Will's hand. Looking first at his father and then his uncle, he jumped up and down whining, "I want to see the engine. Lift me up."

As Will raised his son to viewing height, Wes pushed forward impatiently through the throng. For three years he had waited for Ginnie to visit him in Shepherdstown. In his letters and during his trips home he had begged and cajoled her, but to no avail. She seemed willing enough, but her mother consistently refused the request: Ginnie was too young, she was needed at home, the South was too dangerous for a lone woman traveler, and so on. No time was right and Wes had begun to fear that she would never make the trip.

Then one day last August a letter arrived reporting that Ginnie's mother had agreed to let her come in October. Ginnie had asked for the trip as a special gift for her eighteenth birthday, still seven months away, and her mother had agreed since Julia would be coming for a visit and could serve as a traveling companion. Wes had been in agony, impatiently waiting for fall to arrive. With only his work and the Guards to occupy him, the time had dragged.

As the train hissed and clanked to a stop at the station, Wes tried to look at all six cars at once as they began to disgorge their passengers. He leapt onto a bench from which he could view the entire train. At that moment a young woman disembarked from the next to last car, assisted by the conductor. She moved gracefully forward, nodding her thanks to the man before looking into the waiting crowd. Wes' gaze passed over her, then returned with a start when he realized that it was Julia. She wore an attractive floral dress and bonnet and looked older and more mature than when he had last seen her. He called her name and waved at her, all the while searching the faces behind her for Ginnie. But there were only strangers. When Julia waved and came toward him without a backward glance, he was certain that she was alone.

Leaping off the bench, worried about what she was about to say, he greeted her with a hug. She gave him a radiant smile and kissed both Will and Bertie warmly. Wes was afraid to ask the question, but Will looked around the platform.

"Where's Ginnie?" he asked.

Wes watched her sister's face closely for a reaction. She looked for a moment at Will before turning to Wes. "I'm sorry, Wes. She's not coming."

He nodded stoically but the burst of disappointment hit him like a physical pain. For months he had imagined how he would feel when she arrived, the pleasure it would be to show her his home and his new life. Yet he had always fretted that she might not come, that something would happen at the last moment to ruin everything. His secret fear was that she might not *want* to come, that in the four years since he had left Gettysburg she had changed her mind about their plans.

After retrieving Julia's bag, Bertie and Will took her hands and led her off the platform, Wes following a few paces behind. They walked the short distance to Will's home while Julia related all the latest news from Gettysburg. Wes, trying to deal with Ginnie's absence, longed to corner Julia for a moment to learn the reason.

Salome greeted them warmly at the door, giving Julia a big hug. Then she stepped back, looked around in puzzlement, and asked, "Where's Ginnie?" She searched Wes' face, but he could only avert his eyes.

"She had a problem at the last moment," Julia said, trying to cover the awkward moment. "She felt really badly that she couldn't come. She'd been so looking forward to the trip." She glanced at Wes sympathetically. Then, trying to divert the conversation, Julia looked at Salome with a smile. "Bertie is just beautiful. He's so grown up I hardly recognized him."

Salome leaned close to Julia and said in a whisper, "I'm going to have another baby in March." Julia squealed her excitement and the two women walked into the house together. It was not until after supper that Wes and Julia finally had some time alone as they walked together to visit his rooming house.

Julia sighed. "I'm so sorry it turned out this way."

"What happened?" he asked impatiently.

"It's her mother. She told Ginnie at the last minute that she couldn't come. Something about the presidential election and the South being too dangerous to visit now."

"What?" Wes exclaimed angrily. "Too dangerous? Danger from who?" He shook his head in exasperation. The country was full of agitation about the election. Many southerners were violently opposed to the idea of Abraham Lincoln, an abolitionist, becoming President. With the vote only a few weeks away, several southern states implied that his election would result in their secession from the Union. However, none of this, in Wes' mind, had anything to do with Ginnie's trip.

His anger flared. "I can't believe this. That old woman doesn't know what's going on down here. Anyway, the election isn't 'til next month. Maybe some people in the *far* South will be upset, those who own the slaves. But do you see any slaves around here?" He swept his hand out toward the town. Julia shook her head meekly. "No!" he said, answering his own question sarcastically. "That's because there *aren't* any. People around here are too poor, and lots of them even oppose slavery. Hell, there are more blacks in Gettysburg than there are here."

"But they're free blacks, Wes," she said quietly.

"I don't care what they are," he yelled. "Nobody knows what's going to happen. It's all guesswork. And it has nothing to do with Ginnie and me." He shook his head, then sighed again. "That woman hates me, Jules. No doubt about it."

"Surely not, Wes."

"Yes, she does. She has it in for me. She doesn't think I'm good enough for her daughter."

"Oh, Wes, that's not true." Julia looked at him with a sisterly compassion in her eyes. "But it doesn't matter whether she likes you or not, so long as Ginnie still does. She'll be eighteen next year, and then she can make up her own mind."

Wes looked at her urgently. "*Does* she still like me?"

Her eyes softened with affection. "Of course she does! When she came down to the station to see me off, she was in tears. She was that disappointed." This assurance pacified Wes somewhat but it did nothing to dim his anger toward Mary Wade.

As they rounded the corner near the boarding house, Wes saw Ben sitting on the porch waiting for them. Wes noticed him eyeing Julia.

As they walked up on the porch, Ben rose and came toward them with a broad smile. Wiping his hand on his pant leg he offered it to Julia and, before Wes could make the introduction said, "You must be the lovely Ginnie."

Blushing in amusement, Julia responded gamely, "No, I must not be," but shook his hand regardless. Ben frowned at Wes in a silent question.

"Ben, this is my sister Julia. Julia, my friend Ben Pendleton. He works with me at the factory."

"And I play soldier with him in the Guards," he said, the self-assured smile back in place. He turned to Wes. "So, where's this mysterious Ginnie of yours hiding?"

39

Wes smiled ruefully, his embarrassment at Ginnie's absence replaced by the knowledge that it had been beyond her control. "She won't be joining us, unfortunately. The climate here is not to her mother's liking – the political climate, that is. Perhaps she's afraid her daughter might catch the southern bug and never go home."

Ben looked confused again, but Julia smiled at Wes and said, "Well, at any rate, I'm happy *I'm* here."

Wes put an arm around her shoulders and hugged her. "I'm glad you're here too, Jules. I've missed you."

"Well, Miss Julia," Ben said, "I'll make it unanimous then and say that I am also very happy that you're here. If you were Ginnie, Wes would have kept you to himself. But since you are his sister, perhaps I can intrude and help Wes show you around our fair city." He was looking at Julia with obvious interest.

"It would certainly be no intrusion, Mr. Pendleton," Julia responded coyly.

Ben switched his attention to Wes. "Have you told her about the dance?"

"Dance?" Julia exclaimed, turning to Wes with an inquiring look.

Ben hurried to explain. "The Guards are throwing their annual ball at Rodger's Barn this Friday. I was afraid for a moment that, if you were the fair Ginnie, this hound would already have filled your dance card. Perhaps, now that I know your true identity, you would be so kind as to reserve the first dance for me?"

Julia blushed, but could not help smiling broadly. "I should be happy to keep that space available for you, Mr. Pendleton. Providing, of course," she added, turning to Wes, "my brother assures me that I will be safe in your hands."

Wes scratched his chin thoughtfully, examining Ben out of the corner of his eye. "I don't know," he said. "He could be one of them secessionists. We'll have to keep an eye on him."

Ben laughed, said his goodbyes, jumped off the porch and, with a final wave, disappeared around the corner. Wes watched him go. "I believe Ben has taken a fancy to you, 'Miss Julia.'" She slapped him on the shoulder in rebuke, and they went inside to examine his room.

The next days flashed by for Wes who kept busy during the day at work and at night escorting Julia through town, usually in Ben's company. Wes found it amusing to watch his friend rushing to open every door for Julia or offering her an arm up and down even the smallest steps. For her part, Julia was properly cordial to Ben, not wishing to seem unladylike in front of strangers. But Wes, who knew her well, noted the bounce in her step whenever Ben was near.

The day of the ball finally arrived. Wes stopped by to see Julia on his way to work and found her already up and barraging Salome with questions: how she should do her hair, what color her bouquet should be. Julia barely nodded at Wes, completely occupied with a myriad of details that he found trivial. When Wes came back for dinner eight hours later, the conversation was still in progress. Wes went home after dinner to change into his Guard's uniform, then returned to wait for Julia. Standing in front of the parlor looking-glass, he admired the Guard looking back at him: steel gray uniform trimmed in yellow lace, white epaulettes, blue cap with its white plume. He smoothed his hair into place and patted his whiskers to even out his scraggly beard.

Will came in and caught him preening. "Look at the soldier boy," he said sarcastically. Wes eyed him in the mirror hoping that his brother would not start another argument about the Guards. Will had considered joining the group when they first arrived but, along with the others from Gettysburg, had been disenchanted by what he saw. The Guards had a reputation for wild escapades when they were in uniform. Also, their extremist politics were the cause of much discussion, and they were generally thought to have been responsible for an incident a month ago in which the crops of a local abolitionist had been burned. A number of other charges, none of them proven, had been privately laid at the Guards' door across the years. But the locals, many of whom agreed with the actions, never made any formal complaints.

"Do you think Julia will be safe among all those uniforms this evening?" Will asked innocently. Wes knew his brother was trying to bait him, but he refused to give him the satisfaction.

"I'll do my best to protect her."

Walking up to him at the looking-glass, Will pretended to straighten the braid on Wes' shoulder. "Don't you feel a little funny…" he asked.

"Don't start!" Wes growled. He walked out onto the porch to wait for Julia.

After an hour, he grew so impatient that he climbed the stairs to look into the master bedroom where she was dressing. His knock was answered by Salome who assured him it would be only a few more minutes. With a sigh he sat down again in the parlor. Will threw him a rueful smile. "You can't hurry them, Wes."

There was a knock on the door and Ben stuck his head in. "Are you still here, Wes?"

"What's it look like?" Wes answered in a frustrated tone. "Come on in and join the party."

"I couldn't find you at the barn so I thought you might still be here."

"Good guess," said Wes, shaking his head. "She's only had since morning to get ready. Maybe you ought to come back next Wednesday."

Ben wore a uniform identical to Wes' and, as he walked into the parlor,

Will stood and saluted him. Ben, immune to this sort of ridicule, grinned and returned the salute before flopping down in the chair across from Wes.

"Well, do you think she might have escaped out a back window?" Ben asked at length, looking at the grandfather clock when it chimed the quarter hour. "Did you give her a bad report on me or something?"

Wes shrugged. "She said she'd be ready in a few minutes."

"How long ago was that?"

"Half an hour," Wes answered with a straight face, prompting a laugh from the others.

Eventually Salome appeared, hurrying down the stairs with an air of suppressed excitement. The three men stood quickly as Salome stopped at the bottom of the stairs and turned to look back up. Julia appeared and began her descent with the poise and charm of a princess. Wes glanced at Ben who stood like stone, spellbound by Julia's radiance.

Her gown was gorgeous, white with hints of yellow under the lace that covered her arms. The bottom of the dress flared outward with the help of hoops, giving the impression that she floated as she moved into the room. Her bonnet was of matching fabric, topped with a yellow rose similar to the flowers in the corsage on her wrist. She curtsied fetchingly as all three chorused their praise.

Will, who kept one of the Hoffman wagons at home to run errands for the shop, had hitched it to his horse. Ben helped Julia up onto the seat alongside Will, then clambered up and sat with Wes on the floor boards behind the seat. Will snapped the reins and they were off.

They arrived after a few minutes' ride and, climbing down, bid farewell to Will. The threesome set off toward the lighted barn with Julia in the middle. Several of the Guards were milling around the doorway chatting with each other. All conversation stopped, however, as their eyes settled on Julia. She did her best to ignore their stares by talking with great animation to her escorts.

The interior of the barn had been carefully cleaned and was decorated with streamers and bunting. Chairs sat along the sides and a large table at one end bore an enormous punch bowl. There were at least thirty of the Guards already in attendance and an equal number of ladies.

"I've never seen so many pretty gowns," Julia exclaimed. Her eyes flew around the room taking in the excitement.

Ben smiled. "But none to match yours, Miss Julia."

"How gallant you are, Mr. Pendleton." The brief flush on his sister's cheeks did not escape Wes' notice.

A reel began, the music floating down from a hay loft overlooking the dance floor. A number of couples formed lines facing each other and began the dance. Ben offered his hand to Julia. "May I have the pleasure?" he inquired, dipping his head in a slight bow from which he peered at her beseechingly from the corner of his eye. Julia laughed and took his hand.

Wes, left to himself, poured a glass of punch and carried it to a corner of the barn to view the dancing. There was something formal about the night, as if the Guards were playing their part in some traditional drama. He had seen them drunk and into mischief, he had seen them ankle deep in mud out in the fields. But tonight they looked like proper gentlemen and Wes felt tremendous pride that he was one of them. His pride was tempered with sadness, however, that Ginnie was not there to see him among his friends.

After several more dances Julia and Ben rejoined Wes, laughing about some private joke. "Oh, Wes," she cried, "are all your friends such good dancers?" Wes couldn't recall seeing her quite so happy.

Ben indicated a corner of the barn to Julia. "Did you see the picture of Colonel Hamtramck? He always came to these events since he organized the Guards. But he died two years ago, and we really miss him."

Wes walked Julia over to examine the photograph. Splendid in his dress uniform, the colonel's chest was laden with medals and ribbons from his military service in Mexico. His white whiskers gave him an air of regal authority which Wes greatly admired.

Julia grabbed Wes' hand, stirring him out of his reflections. "Come on, big brother. We have to get you onto the dance floor at least once tonight. If you don't do it now, my card will be filled."

On the floor they moved to the sounds of a slow waltz, swirling around with the other couples, enraptured by the setting and the night. "Oh, Wes," exclaimed Julia, "there's nothing like this back in Gettysburg." Wes had never danced with his sister before, and was amazed at how accomplished she was. She smiled up at him. "I like your friends, Wes. I'm sorry Ginnie couldn't come. Her mother was wrong, you know. These people are marvelous." Wes nodded.

They danced for a time in silence until Wes put a troubling thought into words. "Do you think I'm a fool, Jules?"

"What do you mean?" she asked, frowning.

"I mean, do you think I'm good enough for Ginnie?"

"John Wesley," she scolded. "You are certainly good enough for any woman. Ginnie would be crazy not to wait for you."

As the evening progressed, Julia grew tired from dancing and the threesome found a quiet corner in which to sit and talk. "This has certainly been an education for me," she admitted.

"What do you mean?" Ben asked attentively.

"Well," she said slowly, "you know all the rumors that are flying around. People think that you're all hot-heads down here. Some people don't like the fact that Wes has joined the militia. They think it's not patriotic."

43

Wes snorted. "Let me see if I can guess who. Mrs. Wade."

But Julia was suddenly serious. "No, Wes. Lots of people. They're scared of what may happen."

Ben asked pointedly, "And what do *you* think about us?"

"I'll have to go home and tell them that you're as nice a group of gentlemen as I've ever met." She nodded her head emphatically. "But this talk of war frightens me."

Ben pulled his chair closer. "Miss Julia, may I try to explain that to you?" he asked earnestly. "I don't think there'll be a war. Not unless the people in Washington start it. We don't want a war. We just want to be left alone. And if there is a war, it will only last a day. All of us'll stand at the line between the Federal states and the southern states, and when the army sees us they'll go away and let us live in peace. At least, that's my hope."

Julia thought for a moment. "May I ask you a question, Mr. Pendleton?"

"Ben, please. Of course."

"Ben. What about the Guards? Isn't the reason you have the Guards so you can fight against the army if there *is* a war?"

Ben pondered how to answer that loaded question. At length, he asked Julia, "If you were traveling and someone asked you where you were from, what would you say?"

Julia was confused by the question, unable to see its relevance. "Why, Pennsylvania, I suppose."

"Exactly," he went on, "and I would say Virginia, not the United States of America. Virginia and Pennsylvania existed long before the United States did. When the government was formed, it was with the idea of equal representation among the states, that no *one* state would have more power than any other. Now there are people in the North who want to change that, who want to tell the South what's right and wrong. I wouldn't presume to tell some New York banker what to do with his money, so why should he decide what's right and wrong about my business?"

"But do you think it's right to own another man or woman?" Julia asked.

"Slavery?" Ben scoffed. "Slavery has nothing to do with this. A few powerful leaders in the North are using slavery to get their people all worked up. Most of those men once owned slaves of their own, so how can they be so hypocritical as to tell the South to get rid of theirs?"

Wes had never seen his friend so worked up. Ben was pleading for Julia to understand. But she frowned, troubled by a new thought. "So the Guards would fight if it came to a war?"

Wes spoke now, his voice low and firm. "Yes."

"Wes is right," said Ben. "We would fight. I hope it doesn't come to that but, if it does, we'll be ready."

"That sounds like revolution, Ben," she said in a hushed tone.

"Right," he said forcefully, startling her. He smiled broadly, as though she had finally understood. "This country was started by a revolution against tyrants who wanted to tell us what to do. We may just have to have another one to make people remember what we stand for."

Julia shook her head. "That's very frightening."

"It is. That's why I don't think it'll go that far," Ben said. "Now, enough of this talk, we should be rested enough." He held out his hand to her. She took it slowly, distress still apparent in her eyes. She looked at Wes for a moment before disappearing into the mass of dancers.

After midnight the ball began to break up. Ben offered to walk with Julia and Wes even though he lived on the opposite side of town. Wes followed behind to give them some privacy. Alone with his thoughts, he wondered if Ginnie was thinking about him, and that made him resolve to write her that night. Watching his sister and his best friend walking together, he felt isolated and lonely.

Chapter 6

SKELLY

Gettysburg, Pennsylvania
December 21, 1860

The postmaster shook his head when Ginnie walked through the door of the post office. She waved her thanks and turned back to the street, a ritual repeated time and again over the past four years. There had been little mail from Shepherdstown, but the few letters that did come made the long wait bearable. Wes hadn't been much of a correspondent to begin with and, as the months became years, he seemed even less inclined to write regularly.

That was why the flurry of mail in the past weeks had been so unusual. Since she had canceled her visit to Shepherdstown, Wes had written almost weekly, telling her how much he had missed her company and assuring her that he knew she had been forbidden to come. The warmth in his letters gave her new hope that the relationship was still solid and full of promise.

She was glad for this reassurance because that special summer with Wes four years ago seemed to be part of a different lifetime. He had been home only three times, riding the train up for a day or two. Each reunion was increasingly awkward, a meeting between strangers who never had quite enough time to get reacquainted. Every effort to recapture the intimate relationship of that long ago time seemed frustrated, and before she could be certain of their connection, he was gone again, off to pursue what he considered their common dream. She had hoped that her trip to Shepherdstown would allow her to become part of Wes' new world. But her mother's refusal to let her go had dashed those thoughts.

She pulled her wrap closer around her head to combat the bitter chill of this first day of winter. Another year was slowing down into frozen immobility, in the same way that her dreams were stagnating and she was becoming like everyone else in town, resigned to the ordinary.

She had saved nearly enough for a train ticket to Shepherdstown and by spring, with luck, she would be able to make the trip. Julia was planning a second visit and was anxious to have Ginnie accompany her. Since Julia's return, Ginnie had questioned her endlessly for information about the trip, but Julia could only talk about a certain gentleman she had met. Ginnie, thrilled to hear about Julia's new friend, was grateful that she felt compelled to return so soon.

There remained only the matter of convincing Ginnie's mother to let her go this time. Ginnie hoped that her faithfulness in the relationship would convince her mother that she was serious about a future with Wes in the South. In any event, she would be eighteen in May and was hoping that her mother would agree that she was old enough to make her own decisions.

But she was still filled with unspoken doubts: It wasn't that she didn't want to be away from Gettysburg or that she didn't love Wes anymore. It was just that the whole idea seemed to have faded, like the bright red paint on a barn that peels and flakes off as the storms relentlessly wear it out. The innocent plans of a thirteen-year-old seemed more and more childish to the seventeen-year-old she had become.

She walked slowly down Baltimore Street to the Skelly house to begin her day's work. During the past summer, she had begun to help the seamstress in Mr. Skelly's shop with odd jobs. Pushing through the door, Ginnie closed it quickly to keep out the bitter wind. Madeline, the seamstress, looked up from behind the dressmaker's dummy on which she was fitting a gown.

"I'm glad you're here," Madeline called. "Henrietta, here, is rather dull company."

Ginnie smiled. They had privately named the dummy after one of their more bothersome customers. Ginnie took off her coat and knelt to assist Madeline. She often wondered about the woman's age, which could have been anywhere between thirty-five and fifty. She wore her hair pulled tightly up into a knot which had the disagreeable effect of making her unpleasant features more noticeable. She was unmarried and said quite frankly that she had no desire to be otherwise; her negative attitude toward men was no secret. But she had a sweet nature and she was kind to Ginnie. They talked often about Wes and, while Madeline envied Ginnie her great plans, she made it clear that Wes was not nearly good enough for her.

"Any mail from the South?" she asked in her habitual greeting, having already read the answer in Ginnie's face.

Ginnie shook her head, tied on her smock and sighed. "I wonder sometimes if I'll always be stuck in this town."

Madeline looked up, her eyes squinting. "There are worse places."

"I know," Ginnie said apologetically. "I have some good friends here. It's not just for the sake of leaving that I want to go."

"Oh, dear heart, you don't have to explain to me. The people here can be atrocious sometimes. But I've lived lots more places than you, and they can be atrocious just about everywhere."

Ginnie shook her head. "But it seems so much more…romantic in the South."

Madeline laughed scornfully. "Romantic is all in your head, Ginnie. Men are men wherever you find them. But hot! It's miserable there in the summer. And the flies! God o'mercy! That just about finishes any romantic ideas for me, thank you very much."

Ginnie frowned. "But you've never been there."

"No. But my sister moved to Atlanta a few years back and she writes me all the time. I do know about it. I don't even want to go down there to visit, especially now with all this talk of secession." Ginnie slumped onto the sofa in the corner, staring numbly at Madeline's fingers as they flew up and down the dummy with quick, precise movements. A moment later, Madeline stopped and looked at Ginnie. "It's not the place but the man you should be thinking about. You're almost of age. When is this great successful man of yours going to come home in his big carriage and carry you off?"

Ginnie blushed, feeling a little foolish. She hadn't told many people about that dream, but when she had first shared it with Madeline it had seemed so special. Now it just sounded silly. She shook off her embarrassment by venting her frustration. "It's been so long, I feel as if I don't even know him anymore."

"You could catch the eye of a good many boys anywhere you went, Ginnie. There's always a better fish in the next pond. If Wes won't even write you for months at a time, I wouldn't expect him to come riding up on no white horse, no time soon. No, ma'am!"

"I got four letters since Julia went down," she said somewhat defensively.

Madeline snorted and shook her head. "He wants something," she said. "Men never do anything for you unless they think they'll get something out of it."

Ginnie wondered whether Madeline might be right. Mentally, she drifted off, listening to the inner debate all over again. Madeline interrupted her. "At any rate, it's not a good time for a girl to be going south."

Ginnie was suddenly furious. Her mother had been using the same argument for months and she was tired of it. She didn't care what a bunch of politicians had to say about slavery or war or secession. But after Mr. Lincoln's election last month, it seemed to be the only thing anyone could talk about. "That has nothing to do with Wes and me," Ginnie said with some heat.

Madeline looked up with raised eyebrows. "Oh, no? You know so much? What if there's a war? What if you get stuck down there when the shootin' begins?"

The question disturbed Ginnie. She covered her annoyance by scoffing, "War? It'll never come to that."

"Haven't you read the newspapers? This new president, Mr. Lincoln, has made a lot of people in the South very unhappy. So unhappy that they might very well do just that."

The door opened quickly and a bundled mass shuffled through, slamming it quickly behind her. As the client turned toward them, Ginnie stood. "Hello, Mrs. Comfort. Nasty day, isn't it?"

Maria Comfort unwrapped her heavy cloak, set down the package she carried, and rubbed her cheeks to warm them. Ginnie had known the woman all her life, having lived across the street from her until a few years ago. Mrs. Comfort was a warm, motherly woman who had frequently cared for Ginnie and her sister while their mother was at work. Georgia was still very close friends with her and they visited often.

"I didn't realize how bitter it was out," she muttered, rubbing her hands. "I need my Christmas dress refitted again. I don't know why it keeps getting smaller every year." All three of them chuckled as Mrs. Comfort patted her round figure.

Madeline rose from her work and unwrapped Mrs. Comfort's package containing the taffeta dress. Leading her into the back room, she helped her put it on. The ladies reappeared a few minutes later and Madeline helped her up onto the fitting stand. Ginnie knelt beside Madeline, handing her pins with which she expertly marked where the dress needed to be let out. Still upset with Madeline, Ginnie held her tongue, listening to Mrs. Comfort talk about the townspeople. The conversation eventually drifted to the subject everyone seemed unable to avoid: politics.

Mrs. Comfort's voice drifted down from above. "My husband has been a Democrat all his life. But he says that President Buchanan, even if he is a Pennsylvanian, has not helped this country. So Henry switched parties and voted for Mr. Lincoln."

Ginnie could not contain herself. "Do you think there will be a war, Mrs. Comfort?"

"Mercy, child. I pray not. No, there are too many people trying to stop that from happening. These southern states just want to have their say. They'll make a little noise and force everyone to listen to their complaints, and then the people in Washington will make some changes and it'll all be settled. It happens every time." She continued in a hushed voice, as though she was sharing gossip. "Henry was just reading me the paper this morning – there's a senator in Washington right now, Critterden or something like that. From Kentucky. He has a plan that'll settle the whole business. Compromise, that's the word. We need cool minds to settle this hubbub down. Why, the whole idea's foolishness. These states that are talking about leaving the union, they know they can't make it on their own. You mark my words. It'll be settled before the new year."

Madeline glanced meaningfully around the edge of the dress at Ginnie. "But if there is a war, Ginnie dear, Wes would have to come home. Maybe that's the only thing that'll get him back here!"

50

"Oh, what a horrible thought," Ginnie exclaimed. Startled by her own vehemence, she explained, "I mean, I'd be glad to have him home, but not if it meant there had to be a war. I mean, it would spoil all our plans." She shook her head again. "I think Mrs. Comfort is right. I think it'll all be settled soon."

At that moment the door to the house flew open and Mr. Skelly's son, Jack, came thumping in, holding his arm tenderly. Ginnie looked up and saw that he was covered with granite dust, the gray powder on his face contrasting with his chilled red ears. His left arm was wrapped in a filthy rag soaked dark red with clotted blood. He passed through the hallway, noticed the women, retraced his steps and grinned at them boyishly.

"Close the door!" Madeline yelled and Jack rewarded her by slamming it loudly. His head was bare, his hair tousled and there was a boyish excitement in his eye.

"Did you hear? South Carolina has seceded. They voted themselves out of the Union yesterday." The women paused in their work to look at him, their faces shadowed by a sudden anxiety. Jack pushed them for a response. "Well, what do you think?"

Ginnie asked, "Is that true?"

"Yup. It just came over the wire a few minutes ago. I was cutting stone over by the telegraph office when it came through, and old Mr. Holland was hollering so loud you could hear him all over town. So, there's sure to be a war now."

Ginnie frowned and went back to work, wanting to ignore what sounded like terrible news. Maybe Jack was making the whole thing up just to scare them. She knew he liked to play pranks on people.

"You're joking," Ginnie said, trying to ignore him and concentrate on her work.

"It's true!" he insisted.

"Just go about your business, young Jack," said Madeline in an authoritative tone, "and let us go about ours, if you please." But he sauntered casually into the room, trying to decide how to irritate them further. Madeline turned her sharp voice in his direction. "Get out of here, Jack! You're filthy. If your Pa catches you in here, he'll give you what-for. You'll get that dust all over everything."

Jack suddenly tottered, his eyes rolling back in his head. "I'm bleeding," he said, feigning dizziness. "They sent me home because I got hurt. I've lost a lot of blood. I feel faint. In fact..." and he proceeded to collapse on the floor in front of the startled women.

Ginnie shouted, "Jack!" and ran to his side. Picking up his injured arm, she touched the large spot of blood on the bandage and found it wet. When she unwrapped the wound she discovered a large, ugly gash that was bleeding freely. "He's really hurt," she said, looking up at Madeline who was trying to ignore the whole affair. "There's a big hole in his arm. He's bleeding. You go on with the fitting. I'll take care of him."

Jack opened one eye to peer at her secretly, then closed it again when she turned back to him. Slipping a hand under his neck, she leaned down and said, "Jack, do you think you can get up?"

Letting out a sarcastic laugh, Madeline said, "There's nothing wrong with that one that a good scrubbing won't fix."

Jack let out a pitiful moan, grabbed his left arm and mumbled, "Oh, the pain. The drill almost went clear through my arm!"

"Get him out of here, Gin," Madeline commanded, tired of the game. "The only thing ailing him is this female audience."

Ginnie stood up. Jack opened both eyes and stared at her from the floor. "Aren't you going to patch me up? I'm sure my Pa would be grateful," he said, his face twisted in theatrical torment.

"Not while you're lying on the floor, I'm not," Ginnie said, smiling in spite of herself.

Slowly, he picked himself up and headed for the kitchen. "I don't know how much blood I've lost, but you better get this bleeding stopped or I may not make it through the night." Ginnie laughed, led him to a chair at the kitchen table and sat by him to unwind the soaked bandage.

"How'd you do this?" she asked.

"One of the guys has rotten eyesight," he said, peering at her face from a foot away. "He thought my arm was a block of granite." He looked sympathetically at his arm which, unwrapped, had begun to bleed again. "I should have taken his chisel and wrapped it around his neck," he said in disgust, adding, "but that's kinda hard to do with one hand."

Ginnie started to laugh. "I can't tell if you're really hurt or if you're just crazy."

He looked at her in surprise. "You think this blood is make-believe? Take a close look at that hole in my arm!" Ginnie glanced at it again, then looked back at him. With an edge to his voice, he said, "That hurts, if you want to know."

"I'm sorry," Ginnie said. "But you're so funny. You make me laugh." She got water and washed the wound, fitting a dressing that neatly stopped the bleeding.

He inspected his arm. "You're pretty good," he said, flashing her a smile. "Where'd you learn to do that?"

"I know how to do lots of things," she said coyly.

"I'll bet you do." He looked at her intently.

"Is what you said about South Carolina true?"

He nodded, his face suddenly serious. "Yeah. And you watch. The other states'll do the same thing. Do you think Wes'll come back if there's a fight?"

The sudden switch caught her off guard. She busied herself wrapping his arm to cover the dressing. "I suppose so. What else could he do?" she asked, feigning indifference.

"That's too bad." He smiled slyly.

Ginnie continued to work on the wrapping but glanced into Jack's dark eyes. She realized suddenly that he was very attractive, despite the dust that made his black hair look gray. His chin was solid and his face strong. But it was his eyes that caught her attention. They penetrated into her, warm and intimate, and the wry smile at the corner of his mouth was worldly and teasing.

"What's too bad?" She tried to sound casual, but working on his arm put her only inches from his mischievous eyes and she could feel the blush starting to work its way up her face.

"It's too bad that you're with him. There are lots of men in town who wouldn't mind courting you."

She snickered, doubtful. "Oh, sure. Name one."

"Me."

She looked up too quickly, truly startled. Caught again by his stare, she looked away in embarrassment and quickly finished her work. "There," she said, standing up and heading for the door, hoping to get away before he said anything else.

He reached out, caught her arm and stopped her. Reluctantly, she looked at him again. He smiled warmly and, holding up his bandaged arm said, "Thank you." She nodded and fled back into the safety of the fitting room.

In the afternoon, as she was leaving the house to walk back to Breckenridge Street, Jack was in the yard waiting for her. He fell in alongside her as she started down the walk.

"Where are you going?" she asked, slightly ill at ease.

"Oh, I thought I'd walk you home," he said.

"I can walk myself home, thank you."

"Oh, no. There's lots of bad people out there waiting for young girls who walk home alone. I'm going to protect you."

"It's broad daylight. I don't need protecting."

"Good, then you can protect me. Remember? I'm injured."

She looked at him, smiling in spite of herself. "I think that chisel really hit you in the head."

He immediately started to totter as though overcome by dizziness. "Oh, I think you're right. Maybe we should go back so you could bandage my head, too."

She kept walking and in a moment he caught up with her again. "If there's a war I'm going to sign up," he said abruptly.

"What?" she asked, not understanding his meaning.

"The army. I'm going to enlist if we have a war."

She stopped short, facing him in surprise. "You are! Why?"

"If there's a fight," he said, more subdued, "I want to be in on it."

Shaking her head in disbelief she asked, "Why would you want to fight? Why would anyone want to fight?" Pointing to his bandaged arm she added, "You could get hurt a lot worse than that."

"These southern hotheads are getting too big for their britches. I never did believe that slavery is right, but now they want to bust up the country so they can do whatever they please."

Ginnie shook her head. "It seems so silly to me. Who cares what they do down south?"

He looked at her intently. "Do you think we ought to let people break up the country any time they want to?" Without giving her time to answer he said, "They're only doing it because there's so much opposition to slavery in the North. England freed the slaves twenty-five years ago. We have to do it sooner or later, too, and we'll have to fight the slave owners before it happens. I'd rather it happens now, while I'm young, instead of later."

His intensity surprised her; it was the first time she could remember hearing him talk seriously about anything. Then his smile was back and he said, "If the fight takes too long to start, I won't be able to get in on the fun."

"Fun!" she said sarcastically, starting to walk away. "Shooting people is not my idea of fun."

"Depends on who you're shooting at," he said with a grin, amused at how easily he could upset her.

They walked in silence for a while, each of them trying to guess what was going on in the mind of the other. After a minute or so Jack said, "I got a letter from my brother, Ed, the other day." Ginnie mumbled an acknowledgment, curious about why he had mentioned this fact. Jack went on, "He sees a lot of Wes, since they both work for Hoffman." She glanced at him in spite of herself, wishing that he would stop mentioning Wes' name. "Seems Wes has joined an army militia group down there."

"I know. He told me all about it," she said, sounding defensive.

Jack gave his head a skeptical shake. "Don't you think that's a bit odd?"

"Why?"

"He's a northerner. Or at least he's supposed to be. What's he doing with those southern radicals, running around playing soldier?"

Ginnie felt herself getting tense. "He said it's a social club, not really like the army."

"The hell it is," Jack said in disgust. Ginnie recoiled slightly at his profanity. "How many social clubs do you know that march around with guns and shoot at things? It's the closest thing they have to an army down there, and if war comes it's going to put him on the wrong side."

"Please stop talking about Wes," she said in a voice full of emotion. "There's nothing wrong with what he's doing." Jack was about to retort when she had a sudden inspiration. "And anyway, Wes told me that your brother joined the group, too."

Jack suddenly stopped and grabbed her arm. His voice lost its angry tone and became urgent. "That's just it, Ginnie. Ed fooled around with the group when he first went down there, just to find out what it was all about. But he quit years ago. He quit because they hate the North and they hate northerners. Everybody from Gettysburg got out...everybody except Wes."

Ginnie tried to pull away from him but he would not let her go. In a softer tone he said, almost beseeching her, "Don't you see? That's what I meant when I asked you earlier if you think Wes'll come back if there's a war." She looked away, offended, intensely aware of what he was implying. "How could he stay in the group," he asked, "if they hate northerners?" He paused a moment, then spelled it out. "He could only do it if he's one of them, if they convinced him to move over to the southern side."

"That's ridiculous," Ginnie almost shouted as she turned away, wanting to be home, to be away from Jack. He caught up to her and kept pace as she hurried south. When they arrived at the corner of Breckenridge Street, she turned right toward her house, without a word, hoping that he would leave.

"Ginnie," he called in a quiet but firm voice. She stopped and waited while he took the few steps to her side. When she refused to look at him, he gently turned her so he could look into her face. "Ginnie, I'm sorry if I upset you. I didn't know if you knew what people were saying about Wes, and about you for being his...friend. I don't want you to be hurt by what he does." Ginnie tried to turn away, but he kept his hold on her arm. As softly as he could he said, "I respect your feelings for him. I would never interfere with that. But I want you to remember that, if he doesn't come home, I'm here."

She wrenched her arm loose and, in a flurry of conflicting emotions, ran down the walk toward her house.

Chapter 7

DISSOLUTION

Shepherdstown, Virginia
April 11, 1861

Wes watched from the doorway of Bridger's Tavern as the burning effigy of President Lincoln was dragged down the street. In the darkness, flames trailed behind it, emitting a wake of burning sparks like the tail of a comet. The scene had an infernal appearance to it, a tumbling mass of moving fire wreathed in smoke and punctuated by the laughter of spectral figures silhouetted by the flickering light.

The inauguration of President Abraham Lincoln the previous month had been the signal for extremist groups in the state to demand that Virginia separate itself from the Union. Events like the effigy burning were commonplace as many Virginians felt the need to voice their opposition to the result of the election. Following South Carolina's secession on December 20, 1860, six other states had also left in as many weeks. Jefferson Davis had been inaugurated almost two months ago on February 18, at Montgomery, Alabama as the first president of the Confederate States of America. Since there was no chance that Virginia would remain as part of the North when the rest of the southern states were withdrawing, many wondered why its officials were hesitating; if the thing were to be done, let it be done now.

On the porch of the tavern several members of the Guards had gathered to watch the spectacle, gulping their ale and shouting obscene encouragement to the hangmen. Wes, however, did not feel like laughing. He glanced at the others, examining their faces in the amber light that spilled from the tavern. There was only one topic of conversation: secession. For half a year, the tension had been escalating rapidly; what had formerly been only a theoretical discussion was now a passionate cause.

There was an enormous rift in the town, and each person was labeled by whether he stood on the north or the south rim of the political chasm. Geographically, Shepherdstown was south of the invisible line that separated North from South, but barely so. Because of this, there were many in town whose sympathies lay with the Union against secession. The Guards, on the other hand, were firmly for disunion.

Wes was not sure which label fit him, since he had no firm conviction about either one thing or the other. He had come south for personal, not political, reasons. Will, concerned about both the mounting hostility generated by Lincoln's election and the expected birth of their second child, had sent Salome home with Bertie two months ago. Their baby girl was already two weeks old.

Then, when it became clear that the problems would not be resolved peacefully, Will and several of the others from Gettysburg decided that the time had come to return home. They were packing, planning to leave on the morning train. Wes didn't really blame them. There was a silent accusation in the eyes of many of those in town, as if having grown up in the North automatically made a man the enemy.

Ben came out of the smoky tavern to lean against one of the columns near Wes. He watched the dying flames in the distance and, speaking to no one in particular said, "I don't envy that man his job."

"Who?" Wes asked, keeping his eyes on the flames.

"Lincoln. Poor man has barely had his job for a whole month and he's sitting on a powder keg with a lit fuse."

Wes nodded thoughtfully, then asked, "Do you think we're going to war?"

Ben turned to look at him, taking a long pull on the cheap cigar he was smoking. The ash glowed, then darkened. "I think it'll be sad for the country if somebody doesn't stop what's going on in Washington."

Wes nodded and turned his attention back to his own thoughts. The blaze in the distance divided itself into several smaller fires as the effigy broke apart.

Ben shuffled hesitantly, then asked, "Are you leaving with Will and the others."

Wes looked up, trying to read Ben's face. The words seemed passively curious, but somewhere hidden in the question was a challenge. Wes figured that most of his friends expected him to run back north with the others. It would be the natural thing to do, and perhaps it was the smart thing as well. But Wes knew that leaving now would mean giving up his dreams with Ginnie, returning to a place he despised and to people who despised him. Going back would be admitting failure, and Ginnie would see that at once.

"I was thinking of going up just long enough to bring Ginnie back down here with me." There was a long silence from Ben, with only a nod to show that he had heard. "I just wonder what she'll say," Wes whispered to himself. The fires died and blackness enveloped the town once again.

At noon the next day, Wes arrived at the railroad station a few minutes before the train was due and bought his ticket. On the platform, Will looked up from the crowd and saw him. "Well," he called with a tinge of sarcasm, "I'm glad you decided to join us. I thought maybe you were going to stay!"

Wes clenched his jaw and nodded, not ready to start an argument by revealing his plans.

The train ride was a quiet affair. Northerners filled the car, rushing home to avoid the coming unpleasantness. To a person, Wes noticed, they each had a pensive look about them that masked a common fear. They wondered what lay in their future, in the country's future. There was laughter and conversation from time to time, but it repeatedly fell off into a silence broken only by the clack of the train wheels.

As they neared the station in Gettysburg, Wes looked out on well-known scenes and even saw familiar faces in the street. The town seemed so small and constraining to him, as if the place had the power to recapture him and tear him from his new life. The paint on the buildings along the Diamond seemed to have gone drab, and the center of town had a used look that depressed him. He tried to pinpoint why everything had changed so drastically in such a short time and decided that it was not the town that had changed; it was he who was different. After months of inner doubt, it took only one look at the place for Wes to be absolutely sure: Gettysburg was no longer home.

They disembarked late in the afternoon and Will paid a wagon driver twenty cents to haul them and their cases to their father's house. As they settled uncomfortably in the back, Will raised his hand in farewell to Ed Skelly and Billy Holtzworth. Wes saw him sigh with resignation as he glanced around at the familiar Gettysburg landmarks to which they had been forced to return. Will caught his brother looking at him, smiled and said, "I'm glad you decided to come back with us. I wasn't so sure there for a while."

"I'm not staying." Wes held his brother's gaze for a second to underscore his determination. Will's face lost its smile as he tried to understand what Wes was saying.

"Then why'd you come?"

Wes looked down Baltimore Street as it dipped into the valley before rising up sharply again into Cemetery Hill. He thought for a moment before answering. "Ginnie. I want her to come back with me."

For some reason, he had assumed that Will would not care what he did, and was surprised by the black look that suddenly burned in his brother's eyes. "How could you?" Will growled.

Wes shrugged innocently. "How could I what?"

This served only to further anger Will. "Are you blind? There's going to be a war, Wes. It's only a matter of time before Virginia joins the rebellion. If you go back, you'll be fighting against us, against your own family."

Wes sighed as he looked at Will, realizing how much he resembled their father when he was angry. He took a breath to respond, then realized that it was useless to try to explain himself to either one of them. After a moment's

59

silence, Wes jumped from the wagon onto Baltimore Street just before the driver turned east. Telling his brother, "I'll be back later. I'm going to see Ginnie," he turned and began walking south, trying to ignore the angry glare burning into his back.

Ginnie's house on Breckenridge Street was quiet. Wes stood for a moment looking at it, waiting for the memories to come. But the house failed to inspire him; it was just a dull boxy two-story building. He was fearful for a moment that the sight of Ginnie would also fail to excite him, that the reality might not live up to the idealized image in his mind. Swallowing his anxiety, he knocked on the door. Ginnie's brother, Jack, answered and told Wes that she was working at the Skelly shop. Wes thanked him and set off back toward Baltimore Street.

As he rounded the corner, he saw her immediately, walking slowly home. She did not notice him at first, since her attention was focused on the young man walking with her. They were talking about something and her smile revealed her pleasure with his company. For a moment, Wes thought he was mistaken about her identity, but Ginnie had changed little since his last visit, looking perhaps a bit more adult and self-possessed. She wore a dark blue dress and had her braided hair pulled up attractively on her head. Wes shifted his eyes to the man with her. He was tall and rugged, his sandy hair carefully combed. His work clothes were neat and pressed as if he had taken pains to prepare himself for this meeting. Then it struck him – it was Jack Skelly.

For a moment, he was back at the swimming hole with Skelly standing over him, that infuriating smirk on his face. Anger was pulsing through his body when Ginnie happened to look up. She saw him standing motionless in the middle of the street. Her face first registered shock, then joy as she broke into an enormous smile of recognition.

Leaving Skelly alone, she ran the last few steps to him. "Where did you come from?" she cried in amazement, grasping both his hands.

Wes' rage subsided somewhat in the face of her excited welcome, but he glanced sullenly at Skelly who was sidling up to them. Wes demanded in a low growl, "What's he doing here?"

"He's just walking with me." She said it casually and Wes noticed that she did not turn to look at Skelly but continued to gaze intently into his eyes.

Skelly said with forced joviality, "Wes! Welcome home." Wes nodded without a smile. An awkward silence hung around them for a moment until Skelly cleared his throat. "Well, I guess I'll be on my way. Ginnie, I'll see you later." He locked eyes with Wes again and, for a moment, Wes thought he caught the beginning of a smirk. Then he was gone and they were alone.

"Why didn't you tell me when you were coming home?" Ginnie said, feigning irritation.

"I meant to surprise you," he responded, casting a meaningful glance down the road toward Skelly's retreating back.

Sensing his jealousy, she touched his arm lightly and smiled up into his face. With that one intimate move, Wes felt his anger begin to drain away.

"I'm glad you're home," she whispered.

It was not his home, but he decided not to make an issue of it. Then he realized that she, like everyone else, expected him to stay in Gettysburg. Before he could explain, however, she began chatting happily about everything that had happened to her since they last talked. They walked west, arm in arm, finally settling on a rail fence near the Seminary. Ginnie grew quiet and Wes began to sense a question working its way up from somewhere inside her.

"Wes? I need to know something."

He braced himself, his jaw clenching visibly. "What is it?" he asked.

She debated with herself for some time before curiosity won the battle. "Why did you join that militia group? I mean, don't they hate all northerners?"

After preparing himself for something troublesome, Wes couldn't help being amused by the absurdity of the question. "Who have you been talking to?" he asked as innocently as possible.

"No one. I've just heard other people talking." She looked guilty and his mind raced to connect the pieces.

"What people? Who would be talking about the Guards up here?" Then the answer snapped into place. He looked at her. "Ed wrote to Jack, didn't he? And Jack told you." Her silence confirmed the truth.

Julia had been right, people had been talking about him. But he hadn't believed that Ginnie would be a party to it. He had been nervous about asking her to come south with him, for fear of her mother's reaction. But it had never occurred to him that she herself might argue with him about it. Skelly was poisoning her mind before his plans could be fully worked out.

She continued to stare at him, waiting for an answer. "The Guards are my friends," he said. "The first true friends I've ever had. They don't hate northerners. How could I be one of them if they did?"

Ginnie looked at him in genuine confusion, then shook her head as if to clear it. "Well, you're back now for good. That's all in the past. It doesn't matter any longer."

"I'm not back for good, Ginnie," he said firmly. "I still want to make our dream come true."

She looked at him in shock. "What? Wes, our dream was the dream of children. Everything is…different now."

His anger finally spilled over. "No!" he shouted, the word striking Ginnie with almost physical force. "No. It's not different just because Jack Skelly says it is. It's still our dream. What's happening now won't last."

"But what if it does last?" Then, somewhat less forcefully, "What if there *is* a war?"

Wes smiled, trying to reason with her, to get back to a point on which they could agree. "There isn't going to be a war, Ginnie. My brother and the others are just a bunch of worried old women. There wasn't any reason to leave the South. They just got scared."

"Does that mean you're going back?" she asked in disbelief, shaking her head as though trying to influence his answer.

He grimaced in frustration. "You don't understand, Ginnie. That's my home now. That's where all my friends are."

"And if you go back, will you stay in the militia down there?" she asked in a voice tinged with accusation. He knew where she was leading him, but he was powerless to avoid the truth.

"Yes."

With growing bitterness she asked, "And if there's a war, will the militia be part of it?"

He sighed deeply. "Ginnie, all of this is just a temporary interruption. If we give up now, we'll never make our dream come true. I don't know what the Guards are going to do. All I know is, they're my friends."

"Then why did you come back?"

He looked into her eyes and spoke with great intensity. "I came back to get you, Ginnie." He watched carefully as his words registered.

Her eyes widened. "You want to take me down there, *now*? You want to take me down where they hate northerners?" There was astonishment in her voice. She slid off the fence rail and stood uncertainly in front of him, not quite able to face him. In a quiet, controlled voice she said, "Well, your friends may be in Virginia, but mine are here in Gettysburg." She turned to him slowly and said, as though she were having trouble believing her own words, "Jack thinks you've become one of them, that you want to be a rebel." She spoke quickly, as if her courage might fail her. "I didn't believe him. But now you say that you're going back to the Guards, even though there may be a war, even though that means you'd end up fighting against your own people." She almost shouted the last words, then wavered for a moment as if she were faint.

Wes was stunned. He looked at her for a long moment without emotion, watching the tears flow down her face. Shaking his head in bewilderment he asked, "*Jack* thinks? Ginnie, how could you listen to him?"

She turned toward him, her frustration boiling over, her arms held stiffly at her side, fists clenched. "Don't you understand, Wes? Everything has changed. There's going to be a war. I *can't* go with you!" A moment later, bursting into tears, she turned and ran for home.

Wes, too shaken to follow, could only stare at her retreating form. He sat frozen on the fence, feeling shock settle over him like a suffocating blanket. He had waited so long for this moment when they would finally be together for always. But now everything was crumbling. He waited for her to turn back, but she finally slipped out of sight around a distant corner.

The sun had set behind him before he moved. The numbness had dissipated and only his rage remained. His feet knew where he had to go and carried him there mechanically as his mind focused on the damage Jack Skelly had done. No one seemed able to understand his faith in the future because they were all blinded by uncertainty about the present. He was looking beyond the trouble to what was certain to happen when everything returned to normal. Will, Ed, Jack and all the rest could only see the threat, could see him as nothing more than a traitor to their beliefs. But their beliefs never had been his. And Ginnie had always shared his hopes. Until now. She had been unfairly influenced, turned against him by his worst enemy. The rage built into a roar that drove him toward town.

Jack and his friends were on the porch of a ramshackle tavern behind the train station. Wes had known he would be there, with Ed and Billy and the rest of the demons from his past. But there was no longer any fear in him. In the darkness he could hear their self-satisfied laughter, knowing that in all likelihood they were laughing about him. He marched up to the porch where a half-dozen men sat surrounding Jack, drinking, illuminated by the eerie light of a couple of swinging lanterns. Wes faced him, ignoring the others.

"Well, if it isn't the runt," Jack sneered. The group laughed.

Wes paused, realizing that the taunt, far from infuriating him, gave him energy. Breathing deeply to keep from stuttering, he spoke firmly, never taking his eyes off Jack. "After all these years, is that the best insult you can think of? I may be short in height, Skelly, but you're short of brains."

There was a sudden silence, and then someone hooted sarcastically at the insult. Jack stood and swaggered to the edge of the porch. The others clustered behind him, ready to watch the two square off. But Ed came and put his hand on Jack's shoulder, trying to make him reconsider.

Wes shifted his glare to Ed. "I thought we were friends, Ed."

Ed turned to Wes. "What?"

"You've been writing to your brother, feeding him lies so he can steal my girl."

Ed stared at Wes for a second, then glanced at Jack with a shrug. He took his hand from his brother's shoulder and stepped away.

Wes looked back to Jack. "So? Are you trying to steal my girl?"

"I don't steal nothin', Culp. Nobody thought you were coming back. Ginnie and I are friends. If she doesn't want you anymore, it's not my fault. Maybe you should've thought of that before you turned into a southern boy."

"A southern boy?" Wes smirked.

Jack's anger was beginning to surface. "That's right. Marching around with your little boy soldiers."

"Those boy soldiers are better men than you or anyone else in this town."

There was fire in Jack's eyes and Wes waited for him to throw the first punch. But instead he said, "Culp, you're a traitor and a coward."

Wes swung quickly, catching Jack flatfooted, striking him hard on the cheekbone. Jack almost fell backward, the look on his face more shock than pain. Then he charged, tackling Wes before he could dodge him. The two fell to the ground wrestling, churning over and over on the road. Wes clawed and punched, his toes desperately digging the ground for support. For a moment he gained the upper hand, but Jack was too strong and flipped him on his back, pinning him. With one hand holding Wes' hands, Jack punched him in the face, then grabbed his hair to knock his head against the ground. The burst of pain ignited a wild surge of energy in Wes and he broke free long enough to slam his head viciously into Jack's face, hearing him grunt in pain. The two stood, hunched and bloody, facing each other. Dust-covered, their hair disheveled, Wes thought that Jack had the look of a wild animal.

Jack wiped the blood from this mouth, spit some onto the ground and leered at Wes. "Your brother tells me that you're going back south. Good riddance is what I say. I always knew you were a rotten rebel, a traitor. I can hardly wait 'til the war starts. I'm going to join up just so I can have the pleasure of killing you. But I wonder who's going to look after Ginnie while you're gone." He smiled, his white teeth reddened with his own gore.

This time Wes charged, trying to tackle Jack, to bring the bigger man down hard. But Jack sidestepped, tripping him. Wes fell heavily, rolling over painfully in an attempt to regain his feet. Before he could do so, Jack kicked him squarely in the ribs and Wes felt a savage pain as the air rushed from his lungs. Jack kicked him again and again before a host of hands pulled him back. Wes lay curled in the dust, his arms covering his head. He heard voices above him, whispering, like bees buzzing.

One voice, closer than the rest, said, "Wes! Wes, are you all right." Then it seemed to fade away. "We've got to get him home." Several hands lifted him, and he groaned as a searing pain cut into his chest like a knife.

When he woke, he was lying on the porch of his father's house. He looked around in the dark, listening, but heard only silence. A while later he woke again when someone shook him. "Wes. Oh, my God! Wes!"

He opened his eyes and was surprised to see the darkness disappearing with the coming of dawn. His eyes took a moment to focus before he saw that it was Julia leaning over him. He managed a smile. "Jules. How are you?" His throat was dry and his voice crackled.

"What happened?"

He stood with great effort, Julia assisting him, and leaned heavily on the porch column. As his dizziness gradually cleared, he realized that his chest ached badly, as did his right eye; he probed it with a finger. When he was able, he sat on a bench near the door, looking up at Julia through a half-closed eye.

"What happened, Wes? Who did this to you?"

"Just the Gettysburg welcoming committee," he tried to joke, but Julia didn't smile. He did not want to argue anymore. All he wanted was to get as far away as possible. He stood again, ignoring the pain that raced through his body. Walking into the house, he went to the kitchen and allowed Julia to clean up his face as well as she could. Then, without a word, he found his bag in the front hall, picked it up and headed outside. As Julia followed him, he turned for a moment to touch her face gently.

"Goodbye, Jules." Then he set off, trying to ignore her voice as she ran inside yelling for Will and their father. He turned for a moment as he rounded the corner onto Baltimore Street and caught a glimpse of his family watching him. They were all there, Will and his father, Julia and Annie. Will held Julia as she struggled to give chase. He waved as he passed from their sight, grateful that no one was pursuing him.

At the station he bought a ticket, boarding the morning train when it finally chugged in. He had little trouble finding a window seat on the vacant train. No one was going south these days. Looking through a streaked window at the empty platform, he hoped that Ginnie would somehow miraculously appear. But she did not, and the train pulled out a few minutes later.

Chapter 8

INTO THE FIRE

Shepherdstown, Virginia
April 13, 1861

The tower bells in the Episcopal Church rang continuously, denying Wes any hope of sleep. He rose with a groan, his chest and head aching from the beating he had received two nights ago. He steadied himself against the bedpost until the room stopped spinning, then staggered the few steps to the window, his curiosity about the bells greater even than his physical suffering. The streets were crowded for the early hour, with people hurrying to and fro. Teenage boys ran about shouting incomprehensible things to their friends, while men grouped in clusters to discuss something of obvious importance.

What were the bells doing ringing on Saturday morning, Wes wondered. Something momentous had occurred but, even though he opened the window to listen, he could not make out what was being said. He had decided to get dressed and investigate when the door burst open and Ben rushed in.

"Wes! You're back!" There was a tone of wild excitement in Ben's voice that was unusual for him. He started to say something else, but stopped short when he caught sight of Wes' bruised face. "What the hell happened to you?" His whole manner changed to concern.

Wes sat heavily on the bed, wincing in pain. "Nothing." He waved the question off with his hand. "What's all the noise about?"

Excitement returned to Ben's face. "It's war! South Carolina fired on a federal fort in the harbor at Charleston yesterday!" Wes stared at Ben in shock while he tried to digest the announcement. Standing in front of him, gesturing wildly, Ben was almost shouting. "Virginia has to secede now. I don't see how we can wait any longer. The rest of the southern states are supporting the attack. This is what we've been waiting for."

Wes was too dizzy and sore to share his friend's enthusiasm, and gingerly rubbed his aching head. This time Ben would not be put off. "What happened to you? Who the hell did this? How come you're back so soon? And where's Ginnie?"

But Wes was overwhelmed by a swirling confusion of thoughts. He rubbed his forehead trying to sort everything out. The war had begun, and he was here when it started. That meant that he would be part of whatever happened over the next days. If he had not left Gettysburg when he did, he would most likely have been trapped in the North. He almost smiled at the thought of Skelly doing him that favor, but his jaw hurt too much. He had chosen to be here with his friends. His brother and the rest of them had chosen to run back north. And Ginnie, too, had made her choice. There was no turning back now.

"Wes!" Ben's voice broke through his fog. "Where's Ginnie?"

"She's not coming," he answered quietly.

Ben appeared taken aback. "Why not? If she doesn't come now, she won't be able to." The insistence in Ben's voice grated on Wes' nerves.

"She's not coming!" he bellowed with a furious glare. "She made up her mind to stay with her mother." He paused, then said in a softer, almost puzzled tone, "She thinks I'm a traitor, Ben. So does the rest of the town." He pointed at his bruised face. "This is what they did to me because they think I'm a traitor." He pulled up his shirt to reveal the even uglier red welts and purple bruises that covered his chest and back.

"My God," Ben whispered, stunned out of his exuberant mood.

"They stole her away from me, Ben." Suddenly, he was afraid he might cry. "They poisoned her mind with lies about me. They think I'm a traitor because I'm in the Guards. Now that the war's started and I'm down here, they'll be sure of it." The words were forced out through his clenched teeth, firing a rage which he hoped would avert his tears. He looked at Ben and saw the pain and compassion in his friend's wide eyes. "I didn't believe you, Ben, when you said there'd be a war. Well, I was wrong. I've seen what they think of southerners. There's going to be a hell of a fight, all right, and I want to be right here in the front ranks."

Ben nodded, his eyes locked on Wes'. "I'll be right here with you, my friend."

Wes dressed as quickly as his injured ribs would allow, then headed over to Bridger's with Ben. The tavern was crowded with members of the Guard and the place rang with the jubilant excitement of a spontaneous holiday. Wes' entry caused something of a stir as men rushed forward to examine his bruised face.

Ben proudly explained that Wes' wounds were the result of his defending the southern cause back in the North. He became an instant celebrity, even among some who had previously avoided him, suspicious of his northern upbringing. Now his injuries were marks of honor, branding him as one of them. Ben added details in retelling the story which inflamed the group even further, saying that the attack was specifically directed against the Hamtramck Guards.

As Wes listened with quiet pleasure to Ben talking about him, he let his mind try to grasp the tumult that had overtaken the nation, puzzling as to where he fit into it. So much had changed in recent days. Everything he had worked for and dreamed about in the past four years had been ripped away from him. But instead of causing him to feel desolate, that fact brought him a revelation: he saw clearly where his future lay. It was not in a feeble attempt to gain power and prestige through money and land; it lay instead in the coming battle. For five years he had marched and trained with the Guards for just such a moment. It had never seriously occurred to him that his membership in the group had any meaning other than friendship. But, without realizing it, he had been preparing himself for his personal destiny, that of a soldier.

New reports arrived hourly during the next day. Rumors overran the town and a thousand willing voices were ready to pass them along. Each bit of information was discussed, debated and argued about until the wind blew in another rumor for them to chew on. There were reports that President Lincoln was amassing an army in Washington, getting ready to attack Richmond and burn it to the ground. Even more ominous reports told of bands of escaped slaves from the Carolinas which were heading north toward freedom, liberating blacks along the way and indiscriminately slaughtering whites, including women and children.

The Guards continued to cluster near their headquarters, waiting for some official word about how they were to respond to the crisis. Runners from the telegraph office arrived at regular intervals with the latest news from Fort Sumter, the previously unknown Federal installation on a tiny island in the North Carolina harbor. The eyes of the nation were focused on Charleston and the besieged fort, with those south of the Mason-Dixon Line seeing the assault as the first blow in their struggle for freedom.

On April 13th, Fort Sumter fell to the forces of South Carolina, and was abandoned by the Federal troops that had vainly attempted to hold it. When the news reached Shepherdstown, the place erupted into jubilant celebration. Any who still opposed the war decided to keep off the streets and away from the joyful crowds. Wes and the Guards led the celebration, marching through the streets in hysterical self-congratulation until late into the night.

On the next day, sobering news came that President Lincoln, in response to the attack, was calling for seventy-five thousand volunteers to put down the rebellion. He had asked loyal governors to immediately send as many men as they could muster. Virginia, not yet having seceded from the Union, was included in this request. Many in the Guard were enraged by the President's action, and by the fear that Virginia's Governor Letcher might bow to the President's wishes. Wes heard whisperings among the Guard members about riding further south to join the armies in seceding states that were massing to combat Lincoln's Federals.

By Wednesday, the 17th, Wes, tired of the unresolved tension, was ready to join those going south to join the Confederate Army. He, Ben and several of the others were sprawled on the grass near Bridger's, discussing that option when a stranger walked up to them and stood looking down at Ben. After squinting up at the stranger for a second, Ben's face lit up with pleasure. He jumped to his feet and the two men exchanged a noisy bear hug.

"Wes, meet one of my oldest friends. This here is Henry Kyd Douglas." Douglas shook Wes' hand, while Wes sized up the newcomer. He looked to be in his early twenties and was dressed in a gray uniform similar to that of the Guards. He was tall and bore himself with an easy grace, his intelligent blue eyes partially hidden by a mop of light brown hair.

Ben slapped Douglas on the back. "Where'd you come from?"

"St. Louis, of all places. I was there when they started shooting at Fort Sumter. So I boarded the first train that would get me back here."

Ben turned to Wes. "Kyd here is one of the original Guards. Can't you tell from the look of this tattered old uniform he's got on?"

Kyd looked offended. "My mother was up all night mending this thing so I wouldn't miss the fight."

"Fight?" Ben snorted. "What fight? We've been lying around for days waiting for a fight. We're about ready to leave and go further south to get some action. What do you say?"

Kyd frowned for a moment, his eyes focused on the distance. "That might be premature," he muttered. Ben and Wes turned to see a horseman galloping down the street at full speed. The rider dismounted, not waiting for the horse to come to a halt. He landed gracefully a few feet from the Guard's commander, Captain Butler, who stood at the door to the saloon. The entire Guard quieted expectantly.

The messenger saluted. "Captain Butler, I bring a message from Governor Letcher. You are to proceed with all haste to Harper's Ferry and gain control of the armory there. Other militia groups are headed there now, and together you are to compel the Yankees to leave."

Wes was close enough to hear all of this clearly and, with a surge of excitement, he and the others looked at each other and cheered. The captain straightened himself, pulled his hat firmly onto his head, cleared his throat and bellowed, "Form up!"

It was just as they had practiced it hundreds of times, but this time they jumped to it with a tingling sense of anticipation. The lines straightened and the men stood stiffly, awaiting orders while the captain mounted his horse and rode to the front of the line.

"Boys," he said, "the governor is calling upon us to fight for our rights. We have grown up free and independent citizens of a free country. Now, the politicians in Washington have decided that they know more than the founding fathers did. Well, let's find out how they change their tune when they see the Guards coming. Now, *follow me!"*

With one voice, the Guards cheered, holding their caps high in the air. Wes was carried away by the moment, waving his cap with abandon and yelling until his throat hurt. The captain turned his horse and moved slowly down the road as the sergeant screamed orders, barely audible over the cheers. The front ranks lurched ahead and the rest followed, the files becoming ragged as the later ranks hurried to catch up.

Wes saw that Kyd had an old pistol tucked in his belt and Ben was wielding what looked like the handle of an old axe. Looking around, he noticed that most of the others had brought assorted weapons with them, everything from hunting rifles to rusty sabers. Feeling conspicuously naked with his hands empty, Wes broke ranks and dashed to the side of the road to grab a good-sized branch. He fell back into line and, as he walked, started to convert his prize into a weapon by trimming it with his knife and smoothing it to fit his hands. Along the road, people gathered to witness the impromptu parade, waving kerchiefs and hats and shouting good wishes.

Kyd, talking to one of the telegraph operators in town, had learned that Governor Letcher had finally responded to Lincoln's call for troops with a cable that said simply, "You have chosen to inaugurate civil war." Having broken its ties with the Union, the Virginia legislature began debating whether to join its sister states in the new Confederacy. But the governor's order for the state's militias to attack and capture Harper's Ferry seemed to make that decision inevitable.

Wes had been to Harper's Ferry two or three times over the years and knew a little bit about the place. It had been the scene of an infamous uprising a few years earlier during which John Brown and a group of radical abolitionists had tried to seize the armory and raise an army of former slaves. The plot had failed and Brown and his followers had been hanged. Wes, aware of the irony of the moment, wondered whether things would be different this time; he and other bands of rebels were now on their way to capture that same armory.

As if reading his mind, Kyd, marching beside him, spoke up. "I was there when they dragged John Brown out of the engine house. It feels strange to be going back there. I never thought it would come to this."

"I know what you mean," Wes said thoughtfully.

Kyd squinted at Wes. "Ben says you're from Pennsylvania." It wasn't an accusation, but it wasn't a question either. Wes stared back at Kyd, trying to decide what he meant by the statement.

Kyd understood Wes' reaction. "I only ask because I've spent a lot of time in the North myself." Then, looking up the road ahead of them he said quietly, "I don't believe any man should be the slave of any other man." He glanced at

Wes, who was clearly surprised by this statement. "And yet I can't stand by and watch the government push Virginia around. Is that why you're here?"

Wes thought about all the reasons that had brought him back, but realized that the answer was too complicated to put into a few words. Looking at Kyd, he nodded his head. "Yeah, I suppose that's why I'm here, too." Kyd smiled approvingly and Wes felt as if he had just passed another test. He wondered how many more tests awaited him.

They completed the ten mile trip before dark, every foot of which was torture for Wes, still bleeding from his beating at the hands of Jack and the others. Atop the hills overlooking the little village of Harper's Ferry, they met another militia group from Charlestown. The two companies eyed each other suspiciously as their captains talked the situation over. After a few minutes, the group from Charlestown led the way down the hill, with the Guards following close behind. By the time they reached the outskirts of town, darkness had fallen.

Wes was quiet, like most in the group, nervously listening to the sounds from up ahead. Off to their left, the Potomac flowed noisily away into the darkness. Approaching the outskirts of the town, they noticed a glow in the sky and were assaulted by an acrid smell. Word spread through the ranks: *"Fire!"* The Yankees were burning the armory. They had seen the militia coming and were trying to destroy the place to keep the munitions out of rebel hands. The men surged forward. Wes, Ben and Kyd lost sight of each other as the formation broke and men ran in confusion toward the fire. When they reached the center of town, they discovered at least three buildings ablaze.

The first men on the scene were yelling for buckets and trying to organize the troops into a fire line. In the distance, riding up the hill to the southeast, Wes could see a few dark shapes with torches galloping away from the fire. Some of the Guards on horseback took off in pursuit. Buckets appeared and the men formed lines from the river up to the burning buildings. Wes found himself on the front end of one bucket brigade, throwing water directly on the flames. Shouts rang though the night as men ran chaotically in every direction, silhouetted by the leaping flames. The heat was like a wall and the fire licked out at him as he ran forward, repeatedly hurling buckets-full into the thirsty flames. His arms grew heavy, his face stung viciously from the heat, and his bruised body protested every effort, but he ignored the pain.

The work continued for an hour, until Wes, faint with exhaustion, was scarcely able to lift another bucket. The heat was becoming almost unbearable and, despite their best efforts, new fingers of flame kept leaping out of the building, reaching for him. Eventually the fire began to subside, and as the heat lessened, men came forward to pull away the charred wood and smash the burning embers with the flat of their shovels.

When the fire was under control, a relative quiet returned to the town. The shouting subsided and darkness returned as the last flickering flames died away. Men patted each other on the back, exhausted but pleased with their efforts. Wes and some others found a stable nearby and lay down on the soft straw to rest. He was instantly asleep.

When he awoke, the sun had just risen and around him men moved slowly. Some wandered out to examine the fire's damage. Wes stood and stretched his aching muscles. He had marched ten miles and then fought the fire long into the night, still suffering from the effects of his beating.

He walked over to the building which he had tried to save. It had apparently been a storage facility for military equipment. A large hole had burned through the roof leaving fragments of wood hanging down at odd angles against which the low morning sun cast eerie shadows. The wreckage still smoked and crackled, giving off an overpowering stench. At the far end of the ruin were what was left of several horse stalls. Wes assumed that army mounts had been stabled there.

A voice from behind startled him. "They pulled out, all of them."

He turned to see Captain Butler examining the damage, talking to an officer from one of the last militia groups to arrive. "Most of them were gone before we got here. The rest set the fires when we got close. But we did good. Most of these buildings can be saved."

"How about the weapons? Did they burn the arsenal?"

"Some were destroyed. But we saved about half the rifles. Thousands of them."

The other officer nodded and the two moved off down the street. Wes explored the rubble for awhile, then, when he saw some of the others rising, set off in search of breakfast. He begged a loaf of bread from one of the shops, whose baker was happy to trade it for details about the action of the previous night.

Wes made his way up a steep hill. At the summit he found a church which looked down on the spot where the Potomac and the Shenandoah Rivers meet to embrace the town. The sign indicated that it was a Protestant Episcopal Church. Wandering hesitantly inside, he found the sanctuary empty and sat in the back pew, resting for a moment and listening to the quiet.

He was not a praying man, but he had been raised in a religious home. His parents had taken him to church every Sunday and, although he had the feeling that they did it for the sake of appearances, deep in his heart he knew that it all had a serious meaning. He peered through the gloom of the dimly lit church. A single light hanging in the chancel caught his eye, and for a moment the world around him lost its focus.

He found his thoughts wandering back to Ginnie and the memory of her running away from him. He could feel again the heavy weight which pressed on him, keeping him from pursuing her. If only he had tried harder to convince her, she might have come with him. But then the old doubts crept back into his thinking, the certainty that she had never loved him, that he had been a fool all along. Instead of loving him, she despised him, thought he was a traitor.

Traitor. That word made little sense to him anymore. Each day made him more certain that he was a true patriot. The northerners were the real enemies of freedom; they were ignorant of the significance of what Washington was doing, and too indifferent to take action to stop it. Everything that mattered to him, everything that he cared about, was now in the South.

He wondered if his mother was watching over him. In this place, he could almost imagine her there beside him. Knowing that she would be able to answer his questions and soothe his inner turmoil, he closed his eyes tightly and pictured her face.

"Can I help you, son?"

Wes turned quickly to see a priest standing beside him.

"No, sir. I just stopped in for a moment." He stood abruptly, anxious to leave.

"It's all right. You're always welcome here. No matter what side you're fighting for." The priest gave him a wry smile. "God doesn't take sides, you know. We're all his children." He moved off toward the chancel humming to himself and Wes slipped out the door back into the sunlight.

About noon, the sergeants gathered the Guards together. The group chattered excitedly, pleased with their success in foiling the army's attempt to destroy the town. Wes found Ben and Kyd, sat down alongside them and listened to their stories about last night. They had helped fight the fire at the arsenal itself, and related in comic detail how the fire was just about to reach the gunpowder when they had finally doused it. They all felt as triumphant as if they had already won the war.

Captain Butler gathered the men around him. "I have a message from the governor congratulating you on your success in driving off the Federals last evening. He is calling for troops to join in the fight against the North. The day before yesterday, our legislators voted on a resolution to sever Virginia's ties with the United States. The resolution was passed." The Guards cheered wildly.

The captain continued, "We are no longer a part of the United States, but a free and independent state. As the militia, we are called upon to defend our state against the attacks of all outside forces. Therefore, we will be calling you forward singly to fill out the proper papers. From that moment on, you will no longer be Guards. You will be members of the Virginia Volunteers." There were more cheers. "And," he concluded, "you will be paid eleven dollars a month for your services."

The men cheered even more enthusiastically at this announcement, then lined up to sign their names in the regimental book. When it came Wes' turn, the sergeant handed him a pen which he dipped solemnly in the ink. Carefully, he spelled out his name and date of birth, then hesitated when he saw the line marked "Birthplace." After a moment's reflection, he scrawled "Gettysburg" as illegibly as he could, purposely omitting the state name. He looked at the sergeant to see if he would object, but the man, bored and tired, was oblivious.

Wes looked again at his name, tucked under many others, in drying black ink. With a sudden thrill, he realized that now he was really a soldier. There would be no more play-acting at war, as the Guards had been doing for years. This was for real, and he was going to be a part of it. Here was the opportunity to prove himself, at long last, a success.

Chapter 9

A NEW ALLIANCE

Gettysburg, Pennsylvania
April 17, 1861

It was a declaration of war on the South and it signaled that there would be no turning back. Ginnie struggled to maintain her balance among the jostling people as she read the shocking words. Henry Stahle, editor of *The Compiler,* Gettysburg's Democrat newspaper, had just displayed in his window the front page of his latest edition. The street in front of the little clapboard building, only a block north of Ginnie's home, was filled with people shouting the news to one another. Ginnie read the proclamation quickly, feeling her anxiety increase with each word.

Whereas the laws of the United States have been for some time past and now are opposed...in the States of South Carolina, Georgia, Alabama, Florida, Mississippi, Louisiana and Texas by combinations too powerful to be suppressed by the ordinary course of judicial proceedings or by the powers vested in the marshals by law:

Now, therefore, I, Abraham Lincoln, President of the United States, in virtue of the power in me vested by the Constitution and the laws, have thought fit to call forth the militia of the several States of the Union to the aggregate number of 75,000, in order to suppress said combinations and to cause the laws to be duly executed....

I appeal to all loyal citizens to favor, facilitate, and aid this effort to maintain the honor, the integrity, and the existence of our National Union and the perpetuity of popular government and to redress wrongs already long enough endured.

I deem it proper to say that the first service assigned to the forces hereby called forth will probably be to repossess the forts, places, and property which have been seized from the Union....

Done at the city of Washington, this 15th day of April, A.D. 1861, and of the Independence of the United States the eighty-fifth.

ABRAHAM LINCOLN

Ginnie looked at the faces around her, seeing in them a mixture of fear and determination. The Capital was in desperate peril due to its proximity to Virginia, which was expected to secede at any time. Lincoln, determined to protect Washington, had initiated historic actions which were moving faster than people's ability to keep pace.

Pennsylvania's governor, Andrew G. Curtin, an old friend and close political ally of Lincoln's, had been the first to respond to the proclamation. He had announced that, by the end of the week, he would be sending five militia companies from Harrisburg to the defense of Washington. Army officers had already arrived in Gettysburg and were at that moment setting up stands on the Diamond to begin recruiting a company of local men. This news was the only topic of conversation in Gettysburg. The governor's call had created in the residents of Gettysburg tremendous alarm, and they were determined to be among the first to come to the defense of the nation.

But, while every man under the age of thirty seemed anxious to go to war, Ginnie was appalled by the whole idea. She could not understand why the entire country seemed to have erupted into hatred, or why any of the southern states should want to secede, or why the North should want to stop them if they did. None of it made any sense to her.

She kept thinking of Wes and the way they had parted. The day after their argument, she had gone to his house only to find that he had already left town to go back south. Over and over she pondered their argument, trying to figure out how she might have responded differently. If she had been more moderate in her reaction, could she have persuaded him to stay, at least until the war was over? He was no traitor, she was certain of that. She knew he loved the South and was trying to make a future for them, but why couldn't he understand that the war had temporarily interfered with their plans? His hatred for Gettysburg and its people had originally driven him away, and she wondered if, because of her refusal to leave with him, he had decided that she was just one more person who rejected him.

Distracted by her thoughts, she walked slowly north with the crowd toward the sound of military music which was playing somewhere near the village center. When she reached the Diamond, she discovered that the soldiers had built a crude platform on its south side filled with tables and chairs so that men could sign the company rosters. Behind the tables, the band stood in formation playing loudly, while privates ran around tacking up posters which promised all sorts of rewards, monetary and moral, to those who had the manliness and national spirit to sign up. Word spread quickly that the recruitment would begin at noon, and by that time a crowd of six hundred or more had gathered, a quarter of the entire population..

Ginnie saw Georgia standing on tiptoe under a tree scanning the crowd for her boyfriend, Lou. Georgia waved to her, then turned back to the gathering crowd. "Have you seen Louis?" she shouted in an anxious voice.

"Not today," Ginnie said, joining her. "Do you think he's here?"

"Of course he's here someplace. Everyone in town is here by the looks of it."

Before Ginnie could respond, a shouted order was heard followed by a volley of rifle fire. Ginnie and Georgia both jumped at the noise, then laughed nervously at each other. In the distance they could see Mr. David Kendlehart, president of the Gettysburg borough council, mount the platform. He paused for a dramatic moment, surveying the faces before him, then lifted his large voice so he could be heard by those on the fringes of the crowd.

"On behalf of the citizens of Gettysburg, Pennsylvania, I want to welcome to our town these officers and men of the army of the United States of America." Enthusiastic applause greeted the statement.

"They have come to be with us in these perilous times, to help protect our fair city. But more than that, they have come to accept into their honorable ranks those young men whose love of freedom, whose devotion to their mother country, and whose hatred of tyranny will leave them no choice but to volunteer their services to help protect our state in this hour of her greatest peril." Cheers drowned out his last words, and he smiled indulgently at the effect he was having on the crowd.

"In a moment," he continued, "I will introduce to you the officers of this company, and they will tell you how they will accept young men, qualified young men, into this glorious and righteous force of arms which will remove from our great nation this threat to all that we hold so dear. But first, we must seek the blessing of Almighty God on our proceedings."

He introduced the Rev. George Bergstresser, the elderly pastor of the Methodist Church on East Middle Street, who was helped to his place on the tiny platform. He shouted, "Let us pray." The men removed their hats, and the agitated throng settled into a reverent silence. The Rev. Mr. Bergstresser prayed, at length, for the nation, the president, the town, and for those who would soon be risking their lives on this national crusade. When he was finished, Mr. Kendlehart stepped onto the platform again, accompanied by two officers in full uniform, and made the introductions.

"I have the great honor and the distinct pleasure of introducing to you the commander of the regiment which we are helping to raise this day, Colonel Frederick S. Stumbaugh, commanding officer of the Second Pennsylvania Volunteer Infantry Regiment." It seemed to Ginnie that Stumbaugh had been born in a uniform. He saluted smartly and then stood at attention as the civilians cheered in welcome, admiring his blue uniform and military bearing. Ginnie, swept up in the crowd's emotion, clapped until her hands smarted.

Kendlehart then turned to the other officer and continued, "We also have with us Captain Charles H. Buehler who is here to raise a company of soldiers which will be made up entirely of Gettysburg boys. Captain Buehler will command this Gettysburg company, which will be part of the Second Pennsylvania Volunteer Infantry Regiment, commanded by Colonel Stumbaugh." Again the crowd cheered, as Kendlehart turned to the colonel and invited him to speak.

Col. Stumbaugh, whose nasal military voice commanded immediate attention, spoke of the requirements and the benefits of volunteering now: the period of enlistment was only three months, probably more than enough to settle this business with the traitorous rebels; the pay was $13 a month, twice as much as many men were making, especially in those parts of the North where unemployment was widespread; food and uniforms would be provided, as well as travel and shelter, all at no cost; the training in military discipline, physical conditioning and the use of firearms would benefit the men for the rest of their lives; and those who waited until later to sign up might entirely miss the greatest experience of their life.

Then, as he began to speak of the rebellion of the southern states, his voice took on a higher pitch and the movements of his arms became more pronounced. He looked angry as he referred to "the southern traitors," and Ginnie could almost hear the glee in his voice as he spoke of the retribution which the army would visit upon these rebels for their attack on Fort Sumter.

Ginnie glanced at Georgia and saw the excitement in her eyes, the breathless attention with which she followed every word. Looking around, Ginnie noticed on many other faces the identical expression, as if the colonel were inviting them to share in some great religious crusade. But, in Ginnie's mind, the colonel was not speaking of the hoards of southern militia gathering for battle, he was speaking of Wesley Culp. As she pictured Wes facing the seventy-five thousand soldiers that would soon be sent south, she recoiled with guilt at what she had driven him to do.

The colonel was still speaking. "You men of Gettysburg must stand firm against the tyranny being displayed by the southern states. We must defend our borders, our cities, our families from harm. What man among you would not rush to arms for such a cause?" He went on in the same vein for a while, needlessly, because the last part of his discourse was almost entirely drowned out by the roar of the crowd. Men surged forward while he spoke, struggling to be among the first to reach the tables bearing the books in which they would record their names as members of the Gettysburg company. The soldiers, having received orders not to begin the enrollment until the colonel had completed his motivating speech, had all they could do to protect and defend the safety of the company rosters.

The colonel finished speaking and immediately the tables were thronged with eager young men competing for the lowest enrollment numbers on the roster. The recruitment troops snapped into position, forming the mob into somewhat orderly lines, shouting commands, answering questions about serving in the military, running errands for the officers, and generally keeping order.

Ginnie stood on her tiptoes to get a look at the men who were signing up. Alongside her, Georgia started to wave, calling, "Lou! *Louis!*" Ginnie saw Georgia's boyfriend, John Louis McClellan, fighting his way toward them through the crowd. Lou was tall and slightly awkward, the son of the proprietors of the local McClellan Hotel. He had just turned twenty-three and was trying to complete his degree at Pennsylvania College in town. They were not officially engaged yet, but everyone assumed that it was only a matter of time. The crowd parted to let him though and he smiled down on the girls.

"I'm so glad I found you," Georgia said, grabbing his arm possessively, her eyes shining in excitement. "You're still going to join up, aren't you?"

Lou looked at the long lines in front of the enlistment tables, shook his head and looked back at her, his serious face a dramatic contrast with her enthusiasm. "I'm not sure."

She turned on an encouraging smile and pulled him closer. "You'll look so handsome in a uniform. It would make me so proud. Why don't you go up before all the places are gone?"

Ginnie frowned at her sister's enthusiasm, aware of Lou's hesitation. Ginnie had always liked Lou despite his apparent poor taste in befriending her sister. There was an intelligence in him that was rare among the boys she knew in town. She noted the serious doubt in his eyes as he watched the others in line, but Georgia continued to goad him. "It'll all be over soon, Lou. I don't want to be the only girl in town whose beau isn't in uniform."

Lou frowned down at her again, shaking his head in silent frustration. When he spoke, his voice was quiet and intense. "This is going to be a messy business. It won't be as easy as that man thinks. And I don't relish the thought of shooting anyone."

Ginnie nodded, but Georgia, oblivious to all but her own feelings, continued to push. "You don't want them to think you're a coward, do you? How could you stand that?"

"I'm not a coward...." he said firmly.

"Of course you're not."

Lou sighed, nodding slowly as if reluctant to accept the inevitable. He turned and made his way through the packed bodies to the rear of one of the lines.

Ginnie tried to keep track of those who had signed the roster books by watching as they ran by on their way to the Courthouse, two blocks south of the Diamond on the corner of West Middle Street. Individually or in groups of two or three, some accompanied by parents or girlfriends, they streamed south down the sidewalk: Nick Codori, Will Weikert, the three Sheads boys, Willie

Pierce, John Arendt, Sr. and his son, John, Jr., Henry Critzman, as well as many others whom she knew by face but could not name. She watched in wonder as the line of excited faces flowed down the west side of Baltimore Street, each group or individual flushing with pride as bystanders applauded them, hailing them as though they had just accomplished some momentous task.

Then, out of the crowd, Jack appeared, running up to her with a broad smile on his flushed face. "Well, I did it. I'm in."

Ginnie could not mask her surprise. She was not surprised that Jack had joined up – he had already told her he was going to do so. Rather, she was surprised that he would choose to tell her out of all the people in the crowd. Still unable to determine what his feelings toward her might be, she was always on the defensive around him, as though he might be playing some game with her feelings. He stood so close to her that she unconsciously backed away, flustered, but he grasped both of her hands. Wondering how to respond, she managed to sputter, "Congratulations."

"I'm headed over to the Courthouse with the others to get my uniform. Can I stop by to see you later?" He looked into her eyes, his face beaming with satisfaction. Ginnie blushed, sensing her sister's eyes on her, and wished she could politely refuse the request.

"I guess I can't stop you."

"Good. I'll be over this afternoon." Then he was off, running down the street after several of his friends. Ginnie, perplexed, watched him go, feeling the weight of Georgia's curious eyes pressing on her.

"What was *that* all about?" Georgia asked with a suggestive look that annoyed Ginnie.

"I have no idea. We're just friends," Ginnie responded, refusing to look at her.

The men continued to file past, heading to the Courthouse with that same look of pride on their faces. Ginnie saw Billy Holtzworth with Jack's brother, Ed, and Wes' brother, Will, in one group. She wondered again if Wes would really end up fighting against these people he had known all his life. Lou rejoined them, reporting that he had to go to the Courthouse with the rest of the recruits, so Georgia and Ginnie went home to wait.

A little after one o'clock, there was a knock on the door of the Wade house. Georgia ran from the back of the house calling, "I'll get it!" Pausing to compose herself, she opened the door with a flourish. Ginnie waited for Georgia's voice to greet Lou, but when she heard her sister say with surprise, "Jack!" an electric shock surged through her body. She was surprised to realize that she was happy to see him, that she had been hoping he meant it when he said he would visit her.

She hurried to the door to greet him and saw that his clothes had been replaced by an outfit which looked as if it had been cut out of old rags. Hanging baggy in some places and pulled tight in others, the trousers were at least four inches too long and dragged on the ground. The uniform, if it even could be called that, consisted of a blue flannel shirt with the tails hanging outside of dark gray trousers, the whole of which had no military markings at all. In addition, he wore his own shoes, and the forage cap he had been issued was several shades lighter in color than his shirt. Ginnie found herself stifling a laugh, despite herself.

"Do I look that bad?" he asked with a wry face.

"Worse," she moaned, covering her mouth, and they both laughed.

From inside, Mary's voice boomed, "Ginnie, don't be rude. Invite him in."

Sincerely pleased to see him, she opened the door wide. "Won't you come in?"

Jack greeted her mother politely as Sam and Harry rushed up to him, stroking his uniform in awe. Sam grabbed the kepi and put it on his head at a rakish angle, and immediately a fight broke out about whose turn it was to wear it. At that moment, there was a second knock and Georgia ran to the door again. Lou walked in with a disgusted look on his face, spreading his arms in dismay to show off his so-called uniform which was just as disreputable looking as Jack's. The boys, whooping in delight now that they each had a kepi to wear, donned them and ran around the house shooting each other with loaded fingers and playing war at the top of their lungs.

Settling themselves in the sitting room, the new soldiers related what they had learned at the Courthouse. The company was to pull out in two days, Friday, the 19th, for Harrisburg where it would be joined by other companies to form the Second Pennsylvania Regiment. They would find out at that time what their company identity would be, a letter of the alphabet between A and J. There would probably be ten companies of about a hundred men each, forming a regiment of approximately a thousand. Already the Gettysburg company had enrolled fifty-nine men, and the day was only half over.

They went on to explain that the army was democratically run. When they got to Harrisburg, they would elect their own officers. Of course, they knew that Capt. Buehler would be company commander, but they would need corporals and sergeants and a lieutenant. Jack was so excited about the prospects that the women let him talk without interruption for half an hour or so. Georgia noticed that Lou seemed to be catching something of Jack's enthusiasm, and was overcoming his initial reluctance to be part of the military.

Finally, Jack looked down at his uniform again. "I didn't think we'd look like this," he said, making a wry face. "It doesn't look like the uniforms I've seen."

"This isn't our permanent uniform," Lou broke in. "They said this was an 'enlistment' uniform, to get us from here to Camp Curtin in Harrisburg where they would fix us up with permanent uniforms."

"I know," said Jack, "but it doesn't even look like a uniform." Then, glancing at Ginnie with a raised eyebrow he said, "They said we could alter them, if we wanted to."

Ginnie and Georgia looked quickly at each other, then at their mother with a single thought. "Oh, of course," Ginnie said sarcastically. "We wouldn't want you looking unfashionable while you shoot each other."

"We'll alter them for you," Georgia assured them, ignoring her sister. "Bring them back here and we'll remake them to look more like regular army uniforms." Jack and Lou, pleased with the suggestion, left for home immediately to change clothes.

As soon as the front door closed, Georgia and Mary turned to Ginnie.

"Well...Jack Skelly?" Georgia exclaimed in a tone of voice that made Ginnie grind her teeth. "When did all this happen?"

"When did what happen?" Ginnie asked, pretending ignorance.

Mary said, "Ginnie, Jack's father is our employer. I'm not sure it's wise to...." She couldn't find the diplomatic way to say what was on her mind.

"It's not wise to do what?" Ginnie shouted, her frustration boiling over. "See him? That's what you said about Wesley. Is that what you're going to say about everyone? I don't know that anything has happened. He's talked to me once or twice, and he wanted to show me his uniform. What's wrong with that?"

Mary and Georgia were silent for a moment, taken aback by Ginnie's outburst. But Georgia couldn't restrain herself. "Tell me," she murmured, "do you think he's interested? He certainly seemed interested." She turned to her mother. "He was holding her hands. Right out there in the middle of the street. In front of everyone."

Ginnie glared at her. "He's excited. It's part of the fun." She hated having to defend herself like this.

"So, this is just for fun?" her mother asked mildly.

"We're just friends. Why does everyone want to make something out of it?"

"Because," said Georgia in a low, meaningful tone, "he's a great catch. He's one of the more desirable young men in Gettysburg. Why, maybe some day you could even take over his father's tailoring business."

"Heavens," her mother shouted, throwing up her hands. "Don't talk nonsense. He's been here once to pay a casual visit, and you have Ginnie taking over his father's business. Such rubbish."

Turning to Ginnie, Georgia whispered, "Maybe at least we could have a double wedding. Wouldn't that be fun?"

"George!" Ginnie squealed in frustration. "I don't even know if I like him yet." But Ginnie's anger was beginning to flag and she couldn't help laughing, secretly enjoying the thought.

When Mary left for her afternoon work at one of the other tailor shops in town, Georgia immediately cornered Ginnie. "You've got to come with me," she demanded.

"Where?" Ginnie asked, bristling at the order.

"My friend, Maria Comfort, is coming by in a while. We're going over to Mr. Tyson's Photographic Shop. You have to come."

"Why are you going there?" Ginnie asked, puzzled.

"To get our picture taken, of course. Everybody's doing it. For the soldiers. I'm getting one made for Lou to take with him."

"And you want me to go with you? Who's paying for all this?"

"Maria, of course."

Ginnie looked at her, totally confused. "Why would she pay for us to have our pictures taken?"

Georgia sighed impatiently. "I couldn't ask Mama for the money, and I didn't have enough to pay for it myself. Maria said she would pay for half of it if we had our pictures taken together. Then she could have a picture of me, too. This way, it would only cost me half as much."

"And who's paying for the other half?"

"Maria," Georgia said, laughing at Ginnie's expression. "Well, she's lending me the money. I can pay it back a little at a time and Mama will never know." Then, brightening, she added, as if finally getting to the point, "But, if we all get our pictures taken together, we each have to pay only a third of the cost."

"What am I going to do with a picture?" Ginnie asked indifferently, shaking her head.

Georgia stopped her. "Give it to Jack, of course!"

This thought, though she realized it should have been obvious, had not occurred to her. She pondered it for a moment. "I don't know. That seems a little...."

Georgia sighed heavily. "You don't *have* to give it to him if you don't want. Do it for me then. I want you to be there. We've never had our pictures taken together. Please."

Ginnie closed her eyes, resigned to the fact that her sister would badger her until she got what she wanted. "All right, I'll get ready," Ginnie said without emotion.

Maria arrived shortly afterward and helped each girl braid her hair and arrange it in a crown on top of her head. With a final look in the mirror and an admonition to their brother Jack to watch Sam and Henry, they set off. The three women walked up to Chambersburg Street to where Charles Tyson maintained a photography studio in his home, west of the Diamond. They sat for several poses, most of which showed Maria in the middle with Georgia on her right and Ginnie on her left, their hands and arms linked in friendship and affection. Mr. Tyson assured the girls that he could have the pictures ready the next morning, in spite of the fact that many other women in town had the same idea.

They returned home and set to work on the two uniforms. By bedtime, some striking alterations had been made. They added dark stripes down the sides of the trousers, substituted brass buttons for the black bone ones that came with the blouses, and stitched piping around the cuffs, collar and front. Also, they reworked the shirts so that they fit properly. Lou stopped by early the next morning and sat impatiently while Georgia hurried to finish her sewing. Ginnie, having been flustered by Jack's attention, made a point of running an errand so as not to be home when he stopped by.

When she returned, the men had collected their uniforms and reported for more indoctrination. The house was empty. Ginnie sat for a while staring out the window. Her inner chaos matching the chaos in the streets, she realized that she was more confused than ever. Her feelings for Wes had not changed, but in the past few days she found her thoughts wandering more frequently to Jack. She didn't have the same kind of feeling for Jack that she had always had for Wes, but she could not deny the strange elation she felt when his name was mentioned or when he looked at her. Her mind was filled with questions that she had no way to resolve and, worse, she had no one to talk to about her problem. She wanted to be true to Wes, but she had no idea if he was ever coming home. Should she wait for him? Everyone said that he was a traitor and that she was suspect for harboring feelings for him. Jack was attractive she had to admit, and his style was far more polished than Wes'. It was a compliment to have him show an interest in her. But what about Wes?

She slipped back out of the house before her mother was due and headed north, determined to talk to her father about her inner turmoil. She made the familiar trip quickly, pausing only to catch her breath before knocking on the door of the Poor House. The large attendant with the dead eyes opened the door a crack, leering at her from the darkness.

"I need to see my father."

Another voice came from inside, "I'll take care of this, Samuel." The attendant stood to one side and a tall, thin man whom Ginnie had never seen before appeared. "May I help you? I'm Mr. Kemp, the superintendent."

Ginnie was relieved to have someone more pleasant than the brutish attendant to deal with. As Kemp squinted at her through his pince-nez, she stuttered, "I'm...I need to see James Wade...my father."

"Do you, now?" he asked contemptuously. "This is not a boarding house, you know. We don't have visitors here." His curt manner made it apparent that argument would be useless. But Ginnie was determined.

"Please, sir, just for a moment. I have to see him. It's important." She smiled hopefully, trying to hide her shaking hands.

"Mr. Wade is not himself today. I'm afraid he would not recognize you, even if you might be his daughter." Before she could express her resentment at his comment, Mr. Kemp nodded a farewell and shut the door in her face. Loneliness and confusion overwhelmed her as she made her way back to the road, where she found herself weeping. She paused for a final glance at the front window, hoping to see the face of her father. But there was no one.

On Friday morning, most of the town gathered again, this time at the railroad station, two blocks north of the Diamond. Everyone wanted to bid the new soldiers goodbye as they left for war. Railroad Street was thronged with clusters of people – parents bidding sons farewell, wives and lovers making the most of their sweet sorrow.

Ginnie walked to the station with Georgia and Lou, who were oblivious of her presence. Wondering whether she would see Jack, she looked around the crowd, impressed by the number of young men in uniform. There seemed to be so many, but she knew there were fewer than a hundred in all. She tried to imagine the seventy-five thousand soldiers that Lincoln had called for, all gathered in one place, but found that her imagination was not up to the challenge.

A tap on her shoulder brought her out of her reverie. She turned to see Jack dressed in his newly tailored uniform. "Come to see me off?" he asked with a grin.

A flush of pleasure warmed her cheeks. She smiled and said, "I thought I'd come see if you'd messed up my handiwork yet."

He snapped to attention, turning around so she could examine him. "It looks wonderful," he said with a smile. "Thank you so much." Grabbing her hand, he pulled her away from Georgia and Lou. She was too surprised to object.

"I wanted to see you yesterday to ask you something, but you weren't home when I came for the uniform." Ginnie felt a flush of guilt. He looked down at her intently. "You know that Wes isn't coming back."

She frowned at the mention of his name. "I don't know what he's going to do...."

Jack cut her off. "He's not coming back, Ginnie. He's made up his mind to quit this town for his new friends, and that means giving you up as well. I think he's wrong and I don't want to see you get hurt."

She felt herself begin to tingle with resentment. "You never liked Wes," she said heatedly. "You're glad that they're calling him a traitor." The indignation in her voice caused him to pause.

"Ginnie," he said, pleading for her understanding, "this has nothing to do

87

with Wes. It has to do with you and me. I'm going away and I have to say this before I go. I like you, Ginnie. I think you know that. I didn't want to come between you and Wes, but now he's gone and I don't want to miss my chance."

Ginnie opened her mouth to speak, but no words would come. Jack looked at his feet nervously, and Ginnie realized that he was embarrassed. She had never before seen him at a loss for words and it amused her. He cleared his throat a few times before speaking. "I...I mean, I was wondering if you would consider...being my girl."

Although she knew what he was going to say, she still felt both shock and thrill when she heard the words. She stared at him for a moment until he finally found the courage to look at her. She had often wondered how she would answer such a question, but now that the moment was here it seemed hard to say anything but yes.

She nodded her head slowly. The look of embarrassment on Jack's face was instantly replaced with a huge smile. He grabbed her hands and shook them awkwardly, babbling, "Oh, I'm so happy."

The train whistled and Captain Buehler shouted for the men to get aboard. There was a flurry of activity as people said their last goodbyes. Jack looked at her, his lip quivering.

"May I kiss you, Ginnie?" he asked in a hurry.

Ginnie felt herself begin to tremble as he stooped and touched her lips lightly with his, then kissed her again, harder. She grasped him tightly around the neck feeling his strong arms support her and hold her close, and they embraced for a long moment. When he pulled away, she was surprised to see his eyes glittering with tears. "I wish I had something of yours to take with me," he whispered.

It was only then that Ginnie remembered the picture in the pocket of her dress. She pulled it out and handed it to him, captivated by the light in his eyes as he studied her likeness. Then he was off, lost in the crush of poorly uniformed figures all trying to board the train at the last minute.

Jack found a window and she caught sight of him again just as the train began to chug slowly north toward the state capital. Around her, hundreds of others waved and called out names, but she was oblivious to the clamor. Her brimming eyes were filled not with the sadness of loss but with the joy of discovery.

Chapter 10

JACKSON

Harper's Ferry, Virginia
April 23, 1861

Wes paced the dark street trying to keep his mind from wandering. Down the slope, the town was silent. It was, after all, the middle of the night when only spirits were abroad. The rivers gurgled in the distance, the wind whispered through the trees, and Wes shivered, feeling small and alone.

It had been a week since they had come to Harper's Ferry. He and the other Guards had been among the first to arrive but, with the governor's call to arms, the Ferry had become the focal point for troops because of the armory which was located there. At last count, there were well over four thousand men from cities all over the western part of Virginia. The streets were filled with carts, horses and various other articles of war. Daily, new militia units marched down the long hill to join the crowd, filling to double and triple capacity the already overcrowded buildings serving as makeshift barracks.

Wes had never seen so many people in one place at one time. There were men in wildly colorful uniforms with baggy pantaloons and strange, flat hats with tassels. There were men who had come right from the farm and who carried axes and pitchforks instead of rifles. There were men in coonskin hats and bearskin coats who looked as if they had never before been in a town. Morale was high and almost everyone enjoyed "playing soldier." The various units engaged in daily marches up and down the streets in the center of town as officers struggled to learn how to move masses of men in the same direction at the same time. The Guards, because of their previous experience, performed better than most and, as a result, were required to drill for only an hour or two a day. The rest of the time was reserved for enjoyment, and they worked hard at it.

Whisky and ale were plentiful, appearing in huge quantities each night as if by magic. Wes had never been with people who drank so much, and he had spent most of the past week either drunk or hung over. During one of his stupors, he had apparently said something to an officer which was not appreciated. He didn't recall the incident, but it had resulted in his pulling

89

extra guard duty outside the town.

So he walked, trying to keep warm and awake because, even though there was little possibility of the Federals attacking tonight, he knew that if he were caught asleep at his post he would be thrown into the stockade – or worse. Several men in his company had already been caught asleep on duty. There had been talk of firing squads, but so far the offenders had merely been locked up for a while.

After a few hours, boredom set in and Wes began to fantasize in an attempt to stay alert. Various noises became approaching Federal scouts whom he surprised and captured. He imagined pointing his gun at the frightened enemy soldiers and herding them off toward town where he would sound the alarm. Then all the others would come storming out and see what he had done, congratulating him and praising his courage.

With a start, Wes came out of his reverie. What a moment ago had been nothing more than wind in the trees now formed itself into real hoof beats coming down the road, straight toward him. Instantly, all his boldness vanished. He fought off a painful fear that paralyzed his arms as he struggled to raise his gun in the direction of the approaching horsemen. Peering down the dark road in dread, he knew it was unlikely that another militia unit would be arriving this late.

The horsemen broke around the bend in the road with a suddenness that terrified Wes. His guard post was lit solely by two lanterns, one on either side of the road. He planted himself squarely between them and waited, aware that the lights made him a better target.

"Halt, or I shoot!" He had tried to yell it convincingly, but it came out more like a strangled soprano. The group, seeing him standing in their path, slowed and reined in ten yards away, their uniforms still obscured by the darkness. Wes pointed his gun unsteadily at them, knowing he should say something. With as much fierceness as he could regain he shouted, "Who goes there?"

The lead horsemen edged forward a few steps and the tall figure in the center spoke in a calm voice. "I'm here to take command, son. If you'll relax for a few seconds, I'll show you my orders." The man waited a moment, then said, "Please put that gun down, soldier. It'd be a poor start to get shot by one of my own men." The horsemen behind him laughed quietly in the darkness.

When Wes lowered his musket slightly, the man reached into his knapsack, pulled out a sheet of paper, leaned over and offered it to Wes. In the feeble light, Wes could see that the man was wearing the blue coat of the United States Army. This sent a confused shockwave through Wes. What if he was an enemy pretending to be a friend? Rather than taking the piece of paper, he raised his gun again, stepped back and said, "That uniform says you're a Yankee."

He could hear the officer sigh. "You're doing your job well, soldier. But we don't have any Confederate uniforms yet, now do we?" Wes shook his head as he began to understand the problem. "So rather than ride into camp in my long johns," he continued, "I thought I'd wear the uniform I was wearing before the war started." He paused, waiting for Wes to react.

Wes lowered his musket again and mumbled, "You may pass."

"Oh," said the horseman. "Now you don't want to see my orders?" Wes glanced at the sheet of paper the man held out to him a second time, but in the dark he couldn't make it out and, in any event, he was too rattled to read it. He handed it back and the man asked, "Who's your commanding officer?"

Wes came to attention. "Um, Colonel Allen, I think."

"You think?"

"Well, th-that is..." Wes stuttered, "he's my commander. I-I'm not sure who his commander is."

Looking down on Wes from high atop his horse, the new commander said, "Well, why don't you take me to Colonel Allen, Private, and we can get this all sorted out."

Wes, still trembling, knew he should lead the group to company headquarters. But he hesitated because there was an irrational feeling tingling up his spine that, if he turned around, they would shoot him in the back. The man on the horse said with impatience, "Son, I don't think the Federals are going to attack tonight. And if we were the enemy, one of us would probably be dead by now. So, why don't you just take us to your officers."

"Yes sir," Wes responded, his anxiety somewhat allayed. He turned and trotted off down the hill into town, glancing back every so often to make certain that the horsemen were not just illusions in the dark. They remained a few paces behind him, the large horses bobbing their heads nervously, bidding their riders to turn them loose.

Arriving at the house Colonel Allen was using as his headquarters, Wes marched up the front steps and knocked on the door. After a long, tense wait, during which he kept glancing nervously at the newcomers, the door was opened by a bleary-eyed young man wearing a disheveled lieutenant's uniform.

"What?" the officer demanded unpleasantly.

Wes, standing as straight as he could, said, "I need to see Colonel Allen."

The officer scoffed indignantly. "Who the hell are you?"

"Private Culp of the Hamtramck Guards." Before the lieutenant could respond again, Wes felt a hand on his shoulder. He turned, realizing that the lead horseman had dismounted and come up behind him.

"It's all right," the new commander said to Wes. "I'll handle it from here. You did a fine job." Then he turned his attention to the man in the doorway. "I'm here to see Colonel Allen. I'm the new commander, Colonel Jackson. Be

91

so good as to wake him for me." His tone was quiet but authoritative, and Wes felt suddenly secure beside this man whose face he still had not seen clearly. The lieutenant responded instantly to his commanding tone. He opened the door wide for him, then climbed the stairs to get the colonel, while the other horsemen followed their leader through the door. Wes, not knowing what was expected of him, stood quietly outside the open door.

Colonel Allen came down the stairs holding a lamp in one hand and trying to button his shirt with his other. The young lieutenant scurried behind him, holding another lamp aloft. As Allen reached the landing, his visitor stepped forward. "Good evening, Colonel. I am Colonel Thomas Jackson. I'm carrying orders from General Robert E. Lee authorizing me to take command here. I apologize for waking you, but I thought it best to begin straight away." He handed Allen the sheet of paper he had shown Wes earlier.

For the first time, Wes could see Jackson's face. It was thin and stern, with a drawn look which seemed to mask some inner pain. His reddish brown hair was receding, but was complemented by a healthy beard. He carried himself with a regal air made more pronounced by his perfectly erect posture. A tall man by any standard, more than six feet in height, he towered over Allen. But it was the Colonel's eyes that Wes found most striking. They were pale blue, stern, yet kind. Wes found himself staring at him, momentarily forgetting that he should return to his guard post.

Allen cleared his throat as he finished studying the orders. "Yes, well...allow me to offer you my welcome, Colonel Jackson. I'm sorry I didn't know you were coming. We would have turned out the men to greet you. But tomorrow I shall personally conduct you on an inspection tour of the encampment."

"That will be appreciated. Now, if you would be so kind as to show my staff where they can sleep."

Wes wondered if he should stay or silently vanish. As the lieutenant rushed out the door to seek shelter for the new commander and his men, Wes decided to make his escape. He turned to go, but Jackson's voice halted him. "Private."

He turned to face the dimly lit doorway. "Thank you for your help," Jackson said quietly. "Now, don't you think you should return to your post? I trust you will continue to guard the road with the same diligence you showed when we arrived."

Wes felt a fierce pride rise though his body. He snapped to attention and saluted with a smart, "Yes, sir!" Then he was back out into the night.

For the remaining hours of the watch, Wes had little trouble staying awake. He was relieved by a bleary-eyed young private, who looked more asleep than awake. Wes fell into bed just in time to be routed out again by the morning cannon. He frowned, wondering why the call had sounded so much earlier than usual, several hours before first light. The rest of the Guard stirred, moaning and swearing softly. Several got up but the majority stayed in their bedrolls and soon fell back to sleep. Wes, tired but not sleepy, turned out along with Kyd and several of the others to see what was happening. Putting their heads outside the barracks' door, they saw horsemen at the far end of the main street, two of whom held torches over their heads to drive away the darkness.

"Who the hell is that?" asked the man beside Wes.

After several others offered their uninformed opinions, Wes spoke up. "That's the new commander. Name's Jackson. Came in last night while I was on guard duty."

His pride in being the only one to know the situation was quickly dashed when his companion said, "Well, he must be one crazy son of a bitch to rout us out this early." Wes started to defend Jackson but held his tongue when several of the others indicated their agreement. The Guards' officers began yelling at the men to fall in, unceremoniously dumping several of the more reluctant members out of their beds. Still dressed from duty, Wes was the first man in formation. It took several more minutes for the entire Guards' complement to muster. He glanced around and saw the shadows of several other companies forming on either side of them. The darkness came alive with the sound of shuffling feet and coughing men.

All the while, Jackson sat quietly on his horse watching the men form up. His face was impassive in the flickering torch light, but he seemed filled with a kind of patient energy as he waited. Wes saw Colonel Allen ride up to Jackson, salute and say something. The former commander was apparently unhappy with this change in routine. Jackson never took his eyes from the men assembling in front of him, but raised a hand high above his head as if waiting to be called upon by a teacher. This curious gesture apparently confused Allen and he ceased his complaints.

Finally, everyone was in place and waiting expectantly for Jackson to give his orders. Instead of speaking to the silent troops, he turned his head toward one of his subordinates, who listened respectfully, then galloped up to the nearest company and shouted loudly, "Right face!" This order was repeated by other non-coms down the line, and the regiment turned clumsily to face down the road. "Forward...*March!*" echoed across the way and the men stumbled forward, grumbling, to a clearing north of town.

As the sun rose, they began practicing a number of different maneuvers, each executed more awkwardly than the last. This continued into the morning until several companies became so entangled that their officers nearly came to blows trying to separate them. Jackson, meanwhile, remained on his horse, watching the proceedings with fatherly patience, occasionally raising his hand above his head in the same curious gesture.

After breakfast was eaten at a makeshift mess line, the maneuvers continued. By the noon meal, Wes was so weary from having missed an entire night's sleep that he could barely stand. All afternoon, the drilling continued and the grumbling became louder. Several of the more churlish soldiers from other companies started yelling obscenities at their officers, much to the delight of their comrades. At this, Jackson, who had sat impassively until now, spurred his horse toward the profanity. With the help of several officers, the culprits were weeded out and hauled off under guard. This startling action served to stifle further verbal comments, at least those which could be heard beyond the individual rank. They marched until dark, practicing the same simple maneuvers over and over again until they could move through them half asleep, as Wes had been doing for the last several hours.

Supper was a quiet affair, after which the weary troops collapsed into informal groups. The primary topic of discussion was their new commander. Wes and Ben moved through the mess line and, as they carried their food back to join the rest of the Guards, overheard several young lieutenants talking among themselves.

"I knew Jackson at the Institute. He was one of my teachers. Worst one there. Couldn't speak worth a damn. We called him 'Tom Fool' because he was crazy as a loon."

Wes moved on, but had heard enough to make him reconsider his initial impression of Jackson. It was difficult to see what good all this drilling would do. Everyone knew that the war would be over in a few weeks. Soldiering was mostly an excuse to get away from the homestead, to drink and enjoy a good time with other men. Drilling the whole day was no one's idea of a good time. He shared his thoughts with Ben and Kyd who also expressed their doubts about the new commander.

Suddenly, a voice in the shadows behind them spoke up. "Well, I'll tell you something. This pitiful bunch has to have a leader if it's ever going to be an army. I think Jackson is just what we need." They turned and saw Patty McGuire sitting nearby, his back to a tree, quietly poking at his meal. McGuire was one of the few veterans in the Guards, having served during the war in Mexico. He was a sergeant now and most of the men, as well as the younger officers, looked to him for lessons in the ways of warfare.

"You see, lads, an army isn't just a bunch of men marching around in circles. It has to be a unit. Individuals don't count. You've got to learn to think and act as a group. That takes a long time and a lot of marching. It may seem pointless now, but when you get into battle you'll thank heaven you learned it." He chewed for a moment. "And I'll tell you another thing, lads. It's no party we're getting ready for. The Federals aren't going to turn and run if we just yell 'boo!' This fight is going to last a while, and a lot of people are gonna get hurt."

An hour after dark, several carts rumbled across the field and men began to unload canvas tents, the army's shelter for the night. Wes realized that there would be no more sleeping in the comforts of town. Although others griped as they pitched their tents, this new element finally made Wes feel like a real soldier. He helped set up his tent with something close to excitement after which he, Ben, Kyd and another man crawled in and promptly fell asleep.

The next days brought more drilling. Many of the groups were reorganized and broken up. Their officers were sent home or back to the lines and replaced with Jackson's own choices. The many diverse units were merged under the official sounding name "Army of the Shenandoah." Between the hours of marching came more hours of digging, as they began work on what would eventually become twelve miles of defenses surrounding Harper's Ferry. Guard duty, which until now had been somewhat careless, became serious business at all hours of the day and night.

Gradually, the men lost their own identities as they blended into the larger formations, moving mechanically in relation to all the others, performing maneuvers so often that they became second nature. The drills were more complex, with several simple maneuvers being combined into more demanding field exercises. Each time a new maneuver was mastered, an additional evolution was added. Jackson watched it all from his horse, moving quietly around the perimeter of the sweating troops. Every once in a while, the men would see his hand rise into the air, to be held there for several minutes. Wes and the others discovered that this was the Colonel's own prescription for keeping the blood flowing evenly through his body. But regardless of his strange habits, Jackson appeared to be a good, if somewhat eccentric, officer. He paid particular attention to how his officers commanded their units, and frequently spoke privately with one or another of them. Wes watched as he offered advice, and observed how the junior officer was then able to help his unit maneuver more smoothly. Through it all, Jackson was a silent, dominating presence.

When the men were not marching, they practiced loading their weapons and firing at targets. Wes had a problem managing his gun. The barrel was so long that it was difficult for him, with his short arms, to use the ramrod properly. When he tried to shoot, he consistently missed the target altogether. The men began to take notice, heckling him, making fun of this Yankee who couldn't hit the broad side of a southern barn.

"I hope all Yankees shoot as good as you do, Culp," one of them called one day, amid the laughter of his comrades. "'Cause if they do, we got this war won already." The taunts made it harder to concentrate, and his performance continued to plummet. Wes fumed with resentment and, despite his best efforts, failed to improve.

One day, Sgt. McGuire pulled Wes aside and told him to fetch his gun.

95

Wes carried it to McGuire's tent and found the sergeant sitting on a small stool holding a saw in his hand. Grabbing the musket, McGuire looked it over, mumbling, "Let's see now." After a moment, he rose, placed the musket on the stool, planted a foot on it and began sawing on the end of the stock. At first, Wes was too shocked to object, but when McGuire's saw was halfway through the stock, four inches in from the end, Wes asked in bewilderment, "What are you doing, Sarge?"

The sergeant ignored him, whistling contentedly. When he finished, he brushed off the splinters, inspected his work with satisfaction and handed the musket back to Wes. "There, now try that." Wes took the gun, making a face as he examined its mutilated stock. "Aim it," prompted McGuire. Wes raised the musket, sighting down the barrel, and felt it fit more snugly under his chin, the sights noticeably closer than before.

He was amazed at what a difference those four inches made. Not only could he load the musket more efficiently, but the next day he found he could hit the target three times out of four. The jeering of his fellow soldiers turned into grudging compliments, and even their initial jokes over the amputated stock soon died away. A night later, after Wes hit the bullseye five times in a row, he went back to his tent and carefully carved on the shortened stock the letters, "W. CULP."

When they began to hear rumors that the Federal army was moving toward them, the drilling took on a new urgency. Rain or shine, reveille sounded at five a.m. Discipline increased, and the men began to act like professionals. Shirkers, who tried to escape the drudgery of army life by applying for sick leave, were examined first by Colonel Jackson, so that many simply gave up and returned to the ranks before ever seeing a doctor.

The men were reorganized into new units. The Hamtramck Guards from Shepherdstown became Company B of the Second Virginia Volunteer Regiment. There were nine other companies in the regiment made up of men from all over the state: Winchester, Martinsburg, Charlestown, Clark County, Floyd County. All told, the army at Harper's Ferry consisted of eight other regiments like the Second, each approximately the same size, plus four regiments of artillery.

On May 23rd, General Joseph Johnston arrived with orders from General Lee to take command of The Army of the Shenandoah. Colonel Jackson, during his four weeks in charge, had succeeded in preparing the raw troops for battle and was satisfied to turn command over to the senior officer. By this point Wes, along with many others, had to confess a grudging admiration for Jackson. They acknowledged that he had transformed them from farmers into fighting men, from civilians into soldiers. Many of the men, who only weeks before had talked of their hatred for the man, were now reluctant to see him replaced by Johnston. They were pleased, therefore, when General Johnston divided the Army of the Shenandoah into two brigades, giving command of the first of these to Jackson. This resulted, appropriately, in Jackson being promoted to Brigadier General. Wes' 2nd Regiment was one of four which composed Jackson's 1st Brigade.

This change of command brought about a corresponding change of attitude on the part of the men. Jackson became increasingly popular with his troops, who had learned to trust him. Now, when he rode by, he was greeted with loud cheers instead of whispered oaths. He was proud and fierce, and this pride communicated itself to his men, who stopped calling him "Tom Fool" and adopted the more respectful "Old Jack," or "Old Blue Light" in reference to the fierce sparkle that lit his eyes when he was angry or excited.

Days and weeks passed, the endless drills made more urgent by renewed rumors of Federal advances. Suddenly, in the middle of June, without prior warning, Wes' regiment was told to pack for a long march. By nightfall they were a dozen miles back toward Shepherdstown, leaving the rest of the army behind. Everyone talked excitedly about the possibility of a battle, thinking that they had been chosen over the rest of the brigade to start the fighting.

When they arrived in Shepherdstown, the day had begun to fade. It was quiet and there were no signs of Federal troops anywhere. Colonel Allen, now the regimental commander, ordered them north of town to a bridge that spanned the Potomac River. He dismounted and surveyed the location while the troops stood by.

Kyd nudged Wes gently. "We're going to burn that bridge, I'll bet."

Wes nodded in agreement. Then he saw Kyd looking up the hill at a large house that sat on the opposite side of the river. The home looked beautiful in the fading light. Wes was surprised to see a great sadness in Kyd's eyes. Moved by his friend's apparent distress he asked, "What's wrong?"

"That's my home over there," he said quietly, indicating the house on the hill. Then he pointed to the wooden span which Colonel Allen was inspecting so carefully. "My father is one of the owners of that bridge." He shook his head. "This is how it begins. We burn our own property and cut ourselves off from our own families. I pray to God that he watches over us because after tonight there'll be no turning back." The two of them stood staring across the once friendly river which the war had now transformed into a barricade against the enemy.

Soon orders were given, torches were lit, and Company B was sent forward to set the fires. They moved over the bridge, crossing the dark waters which separated friend from foe. The weathered wood was set ablaze and the men came rushing back to the southern end to watch the bridge die. The flames grew higher and higher, lighting the buildings with an eerie glow. For a long time, the thousand men of the regiment were completely silent, realizing the symbolism of what they were doing: they had now physically cut themselves off from their former countrymen in the North. Finally, after a quarter hour, the bridge began to sag, moaning like a dying animal. There were scattered cheers from various members of the Guard. Wes and Kyd did not feel like cheering.

Before noon the next day, they arrived south of Martinsburg, rejoining the rest of the army which had marched up from Harper's Ferry. They made camp, setting up their tents and shelters, and were given the luxury of relaxing for the rest of the day. They bivouacked near a line of railroad tracks and several trains passed them before nightfall. After dark, the regiment began ripping up the tracks which ran through a stretch of land north of the town.

The following day, they were posted along the gap in the tracks, waiting for the first train to steam into sight. It arrived several hours later. The engineer, seeing the break in the tracks, brought his engine to a stop opposite Wes and his companions. With shouts of delight, they rushed into the cab, blowing the whistle and ringing the bell in celebration of their capture.

Other companies went through the passenger and freight cars where they found luggage and supplies destined for the North. In addition, they discovered half a dozen Northern sympathizers trying to make their escape before the traffic north was halted and trains were no longer allowed to cross the Mason-Dixon line. A spontaneous party broke out after the capture, lubricated by bottles of whiskey liberated from the train, with entertainment provided by the disconcerted passengers-turned-prisoners whose flight north had been so rudely interrupted. Over the next week, the brigade captured all of the trains coming north along the track until the engines were stacked for a mile back along the Virginia countryside.

One day, Kyd received a message from a college friend by the name of DeWitt Clinton Rench. Kyd's friend lived in Williamsport, Maryland, twenty miles upriver and on the opposite side from Shepherdstown. Rench had visited Kyd in camp and had met Wes and Ben and some of the others. The visit had so excited him that he had made up his mind to cross the Potomac permanently and join them, enlisting as a private in Company B. He was due to arrive three days later.

Kyd was obviously excited by the news and was up before dawn on the day of Rench's scheduled arrival. By noon, the new recruit had still not arrived, but Kyd kept his vigil, constantly watching the road from the north. The next morning, another letter addressed to Kyd arrived. He opened it with some apprehension. As his friends watched him read the letter, they saw his face turn ashen. He dropped the note and walked away from them, obviously wanting to be alone.

Ben picked up the letter and read it to Wes. It was from Rench's father, reporting that several people in Williamsport had learned that Rench was going south to join the rebels. He said that the anti-Confederate feeling was so strong in town that a mob had pulled him from his horse, brutally beaten and then shot him. They had left his body lying in the street as a warning to others who might want to turn rebel.

Ben went off to find Kyd while Wes reread the account of the boy's death. A cold fear swept over him as he realized that the same fate might be in store for him if he ever returned to Gettysburg. He sat in thought for a long time, staring north into the darkness.

A few days later, the brigade received word of another Federal advance. When they arrived in the area of the sighting, the brigade was divided in half, the Second remaining in place with the Fourth while the other two regiments continued on toward the enemy. This time there was a tension among the officers that Wes had never felt before. Everyone seemed to sense that this was the real thing, at last.

The quiet was suddenly broken when hundreds of guns began firing up ahead. A deathly silence fell over the two reserve regiments as the troops watched the horizon intently and listened to the sounds of battle. Several minutes later, a horseman galloped over the hill at full speed. It was one of the younger officers on Jackson's staff. He proceeded to Colonel Allen who was waiting impatiently on his horse several hundred paces in front of his men. The two consulted for a moment, after which Colonel Allen spurred his horse back to the waiting troops. Wes watched him breathlessly, excited but almost dreading his words.

"By rank, forward...march!" The men moved ahead mechanically, heading directly toward the clamor of battle. Wes, feeling as though he was walking in a dream, knew that his first real test as a soldier had arrived. All the preparations had been leading him to this place, equipping him for this moment.

As they came up over the rise, they were met by the other regiments retreating toward them. No one was running, but the two forward units were marching slowly back in Wes' direction. As they came, they fired into the distance behind them, the smoke from their guns obscuring their targets. The smell of gunpowder stung his nose and an electric energy hung in the air, creating a sense of both excitement and dread.

Then, a shifting breeze lifted the smoke and, for one heart-stopping moment, Wes could see another group of men, this one in blue, firing in his direction. His heart pounded as he realized that he had just caught sight of his first Federal soldiers. They were moving directly toward him.

The Second was ordered to halt, to stand in place while the other regiments passed through them and formed in the rear. Wes was now standing in the front line of Confederate troops, looking down the road at the approaching enemy. There was no one between him and these men whose only purpose was to kill him and his friends. Wes ducked instinctively as a bullet whizzed by. It was a familiar sound to him but altogether unnerving when he realized that he was the target. He waited to be hit, every muscle in his body tensed with fear. The bullets continued to fly past but he and the others managed to remain in place, waiting until the enemy got a little closer before they fired their first volley.

Then Wes realized that the bluecoats were no longer moving. They had stopped and were holding their position just beyond range of the first rebel volley. After a few minutes of incredible tension, during which the two sides sized each other up, the Federals began to move away. It took Wes a moment to realize what was happening. Then everyone understood, and a wild cheer went up from the men in gray.

It was unbelievable, too much to comprehend. Wes' mind whirled as he cheered at the top of his lungs along with the rest. They had met the enemy. And they had beaten them.

Chapter 11

MANASSAS

Winchester, Virginia
July 17, 1861

For a week after they met the Federals, Wes and the rest of the company could talk of little else. The other regiments had fought a majority of the battle, but it was the arrival of the fresh Second Regiment on the field that had put the Yankees to flight.

Now, back in camp at Winchester, the military drills no longer seemed quite so harsh. Talk of going home had almost ceased, and the men yearned to have another shot at the Yankees. Wes could not forget the thrill of facing the enemy across a field, standing firm, and seeing him turn and run away. He thought back to that moment again and again, obsessed by their success.

It was the seventeenth of July and the heat had risen to an oppressive level. Wes, Kyd and Ben shed their woolen coats and sat down to dinner with the rest of the company after a hot morning of drilling, chatting like veterans about the ways of war.

"I think those northern politicians are having second thoughts about this whole thing," one of the privates was saying. "I bet they're pulling their armies back to Washington and we won't even see them again."

Sgt. McGuire snorted and scooped up a mouthful of broth with his hardtack, shoving it into his mouth and wiping his mustache. "Well, you boys are quite something, God's truth."

The others quieted, turning to look at McGuire. "What do you mean, Sarge?" one of the men asked.

"I mean, you're all sitting here, talking tough, thinking tough. And ain't a one o' you been in a battle yet." He chuckled sarcastically to himself.

The men protested, talking at once, backing up each other's claims about the regiment's accomplishment. Wes watched McGuire quietly continue his meal. Tommy Green, one of the boys whom Wes knew fairly well, spoke up. "What do you call what we did last week, Sarge?"

McGuire shook his head, a condescending smile on his face. "I call it an afternoon's outing. 'Twere barely a scuffle. You boys don't know what a real fight is. But you will. Them Yankees ain't gone. They're just testing us. They

101

want to see if we're really serious."

Tommy struck a manful pose, thumping his chest. "Well, just bring 'em on, is what I say. We can whomp any damn Yankee any damn day."

The others laughed and chorused agreement. McGuire looked at them, shaking his head, then retreated into silence, preferring to let the boys' ignorance play itself out. Wes wasn't laughing, however. He suddenly sensed that McGuire was right. He had stood there, staring at the northern soldiers, feeling that dreadful, exquisite fear crawl up his body, and he had known that, the next time, the Federals would not just walk away.

Tommy sat again, then leaned close to Wes. He had misread the serious expression on his face and said apologetically, "I didn't mean you, Wes, when I was talking about the Yankees, you know."

Wes nodded absently. He was watching a horseman gallop toward the captain's tent. It was apparent that something was about to happen. A moment later, Captain Butler called McGuire over. The old Irishman jumped up and jogged the short distance. Ben was laughing at Tommy along with the rest of the group when Wes nudged him. "We're moving out."

Ben continued to laugh for a moment, then turned to his friend with a puzzled look. "What did you say?"

"I said, we're moving out. Just wait. Here comes the Sarge."

McGuire hustled back, a stern look on his face. He yelled over the boisterous laughter, "Form up!" The men froze for a second, slow to realize what was happening. Anticipating the order, Wes had grabbed his gun and was first in place. The others formed around him quickly, searching anxiously for some clue as to what was happening.

McGuire stood in front of the group, waiting for them to settle down. Then he snapped out the order in a tight, serious tone. "You've got five minutes to break camp and get ready to march. We're going for a walk, boys. Now, *MOVE!*"

This last word was a roar, and the men shouted their approval. Chaos exploded within the camp as men tore down their tents and gathered their belongings. It took only seven minutes. By the time the men were back in line, Captain Butler had appeared, sitting high astride his horse. He examined the men carefully, then shouted the order to fall in line behind Company A. They began moving out even before some of the other companies had formed. Obviously, something important was going on. Wes noticed Jackson, already mounted, consulting with General Johnston. Junior officers hurried about them like worker bees, carrying messages to all parts of the army.

They were was marching southeast; the Federals were north. Even a child could figure out what was going on. Winchester, a little town too far north for its own good, was being deserted by the only people who could save it. A sense of betrayal was written on the faces that Wes saw. People lined the road, silent, resentful. Wes imagined their thoughts. They had worked all their lives to be free; they didn't care about slavery because most of them were poor; it was the rare man in these parts who owned even one slave. This was the rich man's fight, and now the army was being pulled back to protect the rich people further south, and the poor were being abandoned. In a fight that really didn't concern them, they would be the first victims.

Wes' company was in the van of the army, Wes himself only a few ranks behind the front line. Company A, being used as skirmishers, had been sent on ahead. Thus, it fell upon Company B to set the pace for the entire army. The men were proud of this honor, determined to make their unit look good.

Captain Butler flashed up on his red roan, which screamed in protest as he yanked on her reins. The sun shone down on the captain's face as he halted the men for a moment. When he spoke, his deep voice carried easily to the hundred or so troops gathered before him.

"I've just had a word with General Johnston. He wished me to convey to you the urgency of this operation and the vital part we will play in it. The Confederate Army is drawing together near the towns of Centreville and Manassas, just south and west of Washington. General Beauregard is there with a good sized army, but he is presently threatened with attack by a much larger northern force. We are to make our way to Piedmont as fast as possible, where we will board trains which will take us to the aid of General Beauregard's men."

He paused to let his words sink in, taking his hat off and rubbing his forehead thoughtfully. "Men, if we do not reach our destination in time, General Beauregard may be defeated. His defeat may mean that we cannot rid ourselves of northern rule." Wes was entranced by the rising passion in the captain's voice. "We must not lose this battle. It's time to fight for our beliefs. We must show that we are tougher and stronger than any northern unit ever formed." He paused for effect, looking at his company with an expression of paternal pride. "Now, let's *move out!*"

As one, the company broke into cheers, with Wes yelling as loudly as the rest. By now he had stopped thinking of himself as a northerner. A mere accident of birth could not outweigh the sense that he had become as southern as any man alive. He belonged here more than he had ever belonged up north. He was not fighting for the politicians or the rich and the powerful; he was certainly not fighting for the slave owners. He was fighting for his friends, fighting to defend his home, the only place where he belonged.

He began to run with the others, shouting, ecstatic. Their yells raised a stir which spread through the regiment, to the brigade, to the entire army. They ran to join Beauregard, the hero of Fort Sumter, to take their place by his side in history.

It was well after noon when they reached the Shenandoah River. Much of their earlier elation had evaporated, replaced by a grim determination. The intense heat made it difficult to maintain the pace. When, after a few hours, General Jackson called a halt, the men searched for shade and collapsed. Ten minutes later, the commander urged them forward again, setting a cycle which repeated itself for the remainder of the march: fifty minutes of marching, ten minutes of rest.

The men watched Company A, across the river, frolicking in the sun. Apparently, crossing the water had not been much of a problem. McGuire stripped off his uniform, rolled it into a bundle which he placed on his bayonet, and marched knee deep into the river. Turning to look back at his astonished men, he taunted, "Well, come on, lads. Are you a pack of old ladies, or what?"

As he turned to plow through the water, the men, hooting and laughing, stripped naked and followed him. The water felt so refreshing that Wes wished he could remain there all day. It reminded him of the water hole in Rock Creek back home. He knew it would be filled on a hot day like this. But then, he reasoned, most of the boys had joined up to fight with the North. He wondered where his brother was, whether he might be marching at this moment to confront him in the oncoming battle.

The water seemed to revitalize the company spirits and they set off again at a brisk pace. On they marched, as mile after mile fell behind them. Wes' feet had grown numb as he stumbled on, past the point of pain, a human machine moving without conscious thought. The rest periods felt shorter each time and there was little talking in the ranks, only the lonely sound of thousands of shuffling feet. When the halt was finally called, it was well past midnight and Wes was asleep in an instant.

He woke with the bugle, so tired it felt as though he had not slept at all. His legs were badly cramped from the previous day's effort. He and Ben stood quietly, sipping hot coffee and trying to ease their stiffness. Kyd rushed up from somewhere, looking fresh and ready for another day. "Did you hear about Old Jack?" he asked with a glow in his eye. Wes and Ben shook their heads as Kyd grabbed some coffee and took a gulp. "Well, after we called it quits last night, no one turned out for guard duty. The officers were going to kick some of the boys awake but Old Jack, he just told them to let us sleep. He stayed up all night and guarded us himself."

Wes and Ben shook their heads in wonder and looked over to where Jackson sat on a fence rail, sipping coffee and reading from his Bible. He was by himself, absorbed in his reading, but just then he happened to look in Wes' direction. For a mystical moment, Wes fancied that his commander was looking him straight in the eye. Then the general dropped his head and went back to his reading. Wes felt strangely invigorated, as though some of Jackson's strength had flowed into him.

Kyd talked on and on about what a great leader Jackson was. He told them that he was writing some friends to see about getting an appointment as an officer, so he could become an aide for Jackson.

They set out as the sun rose, and in a few hours reached the town of Piedmont. It consisted of a few buildings around a new stop on the railroad. As they came over the rise into town, Wes saw three locomotives standing by the platform, a string of boxcars behind each one.

They halted near the trains and fell out of formation, using the time to relax, eat, and talk about the upcoming fight. Many of the men still didn't believe there would be a battle. Wes did not share that opinion. On the contrary, his mind was troubled by what might lie ahead. He wondered what it would be like if he had to face a former acquaintance in battle. Then he remembered all the accumulated insults and humiliations he had endured across the years, the people in Gettysburg who had made fun of him, his brother who had always belittled him. Somehow, in that moment, all the frantic fist fights and painful defeats he had suffered throughout his life blended into one long battle which he had never been able to win. Now even Ginnie was lost to him, another casualty in his private war. The thought generated a rage that burned away considerations of friendship and home, even of compassion. He sat listening to the others, but in his mind he was fighting a new battle, one for which he had waited all his life. This time he would be victorious.

When the rest of the brigade arrived, they all filed onto the train, several cars for each company. Wes was pulled up into a dark and musty freight car that smelled of manure. There was barely enough room to sit, and many of the men found it more comfortable to stand. After a long wait, the train finally jerked into motion, slowly picking up speed. The clacking of the wheels produced a soothing rhythm and a cool breeze flowed in through the open door. Wes was soon asleep, knowing that he would have little time to rest in the days to come.

They off-loaded late in the afternoon, uncertain where they were. They could not hear any gunfire, but the acrid smell of gunpowder in the air made Wes wonder if they had missed the battle. Ordered to form up, they set off again, passing a row of fresh graves. No words were spoken as the men walked by, but all eyes were focused on the mounds of dirt.

They made camp in a row of pines, and taps was beat early. Wes lay awake for a long time, thinking about the next day. He heard others nearby tossing restlessly in their bedrolls, and knew that they too were wondering about their fate.

He awoke with a start as a distant explosion shook the earth. The sun had barely risen. Wes sat up, listening as the booming continued. McGuire announced, "Cannon off to the north." He was already up, making a pot of coffee. Wes struggled out of his bedding and sat on the log beside the sarge. The cannon fire was not close, but Wes couldn't help feeling frightened. He tried to mask his fear from McGuire who was stoking the fire. "God-awful sound, ain't it?" McGuire commented.

Wes glanced down at the sergeant and was surprised to see a flicker of fear in his eyes. He blurted out the question before he could stop himself. "Are you scared, Sarge?"

McGuire stopped his work, looked up at Wes and smiled. "Of course I'm scared, son. I'd be stupid not to be." He struggled to his feet. "Trouble with you young tikes is that you're afraid of your own fear. Fear ain't bad unless it takes control of you. I've seen it happen to many a brave man. They hold it all bunched up inside themselves, pretending they ain't scared. Then they see the enemy and their legs are running before their brains can stop 'em." He poured himself more coffee, then stared at Wes. "Don't be afraid to admit that you're frightened, son. It'll keep you humble. And it may just keep you alive."

Wes mulled this over as he sipped McGuire's coffee. After a few minutes, there was a flurry of activity and shouted orders. The stiff and sleepy men grabbed their things and formed up, marching off to cover a distant bridge threatened by the Federals.

They had been standing for nearly three hours, waiting for the Federals to attack their bridge when, just before noon, a courier galloped up to Capt. Butler and delivered a message. A moment later, Sgt. McGuire ordered an about face and Wes found himself running back the way he had come. They jogged more than a mile, moving along a slight rise which bordered some woods. To their right sat a little farmhouse overlooking a valley in which, from the sound of it, the fight was happening. The brigade formed, the 2nd Regiment toward the left, next to the 33rd. Wes was sweating freely by this time, anxiously trying to see what was happening. They formed two double rows. Wes was in the second rank of the front row, so that he was looking over the head of the man who was kneeling in front of him.

The pounding from the big guns was getting louder and each new explosion etched deeper anxiety on the men's faces. They faced the white farmhouse, a hundred yards to the north. Beyond, in the valley, a cloud of smoke hung, blue and ominous in the afternoon sun. Capt. Butler walked across the front of the line and yelled at them to lie down. They fell on their bellies, gratefully hugging the cool grass. The explosions marched toward them until the shells were roaring overhead. The noise was overwhelming, intermingled with moans, and Wes began to feel real terror for the first time. From the valley in front of them, they could hear the sounds of men screaming, but the battle itself was still invisible.

Then, over the rise, came a group of bloody men, running as fast as their wounds would allow them. They were in gray, although it was difficult to tell because of the grime and gunpowder and blood that covered them.

"We're *beaten*," one particularly bloody soldier yelled. "Go back. Save yourselves while there's still time." The men shot frightened looks at each other. Ben's eyes were enormous and bright with fear, and Wes felt his terror intensify, realizing that he was surrounded by people who were as frightened as he was. McGuire stood and began to walk among the prostrate men, talking all the while in a soothing voice. "Steady boys. Steady. They'll have to do better than that to scare us."

The retreating soldiers passed through the Second and disappeared over the hill behind them. Another wave of soldiers came after them, a little more military in their bearing, loading their guns and turning to fire as they retreated. They moved through the Second and the 33rd, then paused just behind them in front of the woods.

Wes' heart was beating so violently that he could feel it in his throat. He knew that no one was left between him and the Federals. The thunder of the guns in front of them seemed to redouble as the bluecoats found the range to the top of the hill. Suddenly, several deafening explosions sounded to the right. Wes quickly realized that these were their own cannon returning the fire. Although the waiting was difficult, it felt good to know that someone was shooting back at the Federals coming up the hill toward them. Wes could still see nothing of what was going on in the valley below him; billowing tempests of smoke obscured nearly everything.

McGuire yelled to the men over the incredible noise of the battlefield, but Wes could only hear a few words. He saw others beginning to load their guns and he did the same. It was a difficult job because his hands were shaking badly, but Wes put the stock on the ground, the barrel pointed upward. Reaching into the pack at his waist with one hand, he grabbed a charge, tore off the edge with his teeth, the familiar taste of gunpowder burning his tongue. Carefully he poured it down the barrel, pressing the wadding and minie ball into the barrel after the gunpowder. He pulled the rammer from its place under the barrel and flipped it around, hammering the minie ball down tight. After he replaced the ramrod, he carefully opened the tiny tin that carried the caps. Picking one up with trembling fingers, he replaced the cover, put the tin away in his waist pack, cocked the musket's hammer and tried to press the round cap onto the firing pin. It took him three attempts before he succeeded.

With his musket loaded, Wes felt a little more secure. The cannon fire was getting louder, and suddenly there were explosions to the left and a howling noise that ripped close over their heads. Several shells hit at once near the cannon to the right. Wes could see the troops off to his left begin to move back toward him as they retreated from Federals who were firing obliquely into their flank. Two Federal cannon were only a few hundred feet away and

Wes could see their crews working feverishly to reload them. Since each was serviced by only a few men, Wes wondered why the 33rd was running away from them.

Those retreating men spilled over them in a wave, forcing Wes and the others in his regiment to fall back in confusion. But others, on the far left of the 33rd, sensing perhaps what Wes had seen, began yelling for their comrades to return. The tide shifted again, reversing its course, and the 33rd flowed back to its former position. The confusion made it difficult to understand what was happening: horsemen rode in all directions, cannon fire on Wes' right was answered by Union artillery from the bottom of the hill, geysers of earth erupted all around him, blasting screaming men into the air.

Suddenly, another great cheer rose from the men of the 33rd. They were running down the rise away from Wes toward the two cannon. The whole regiment charged at the battery as the undermanned Federals tried to reload their pieces. To this point, Wes had seen nothing of the bluecoats except the tiny battery that the 33rd was attacking. The firing intensified dramatically as Wes tried to make out what was happening with the large mass of men struggling off to his left. The smoke covered their frantic contest, obscuring all but muzzle blasts and an occasional glimpse of flailing barrels and bayonets. Drawn into this desperate struggle, the entire regiment seemed to disappear before Wes' eyes, devoured by the smoke.

Then, looking toward the rise, he saw the 33rd returning in disarray, many of the men being dragged back by comrades. The straight lines and crisp formations had been shattered, and all that remained was chaos. As they approached, Wes turned to look for Jackson. He sat calmly on his horse, tall and straight, looking through his binoculars at the valley below. Wes could see the intense expression on his face. He gave orders to several mounted men who galloped off.

Captain Butler paced the lines with McGuire, calming and helping where he could. As the men from the 33rd fell back through their lines, many of the troops from the 2nd tried to follow, jumping up and heading for the rear. But Butler and the junior officers worked them back into place, trimming up the lines once again. An officer raced up to Butler, who listened intently to the message from the colonel. He saluted and turned to the men. They all watched him expectantly. "Bayonets!" he roared. As one, the men pulled their knives free and shoved them home over the barrels of their muskets.

"Now, men," Butler cried, "wait until they are fifty yards away. Then fire and fire well. Aim low. After the volley, we will charge, and when we charge we will scream like the furies of hell and frighten them back to Washington."

They stood, nervously watching the confusion ahead. Gradually, like evil apparitions, rows of men emerged from the smoke, marching toward them, their guns lowered, the sun glinting from their bayonets. Wes felt his throat tighten. Jackson rode by yelling, "Steady, men! Steady! Don't forget to yell when you charge." Wes watched the blue-coated men grow larger as they surged up the hill. The Federals opened fire and a few men near Wes were hit and fell out of line, cursing loudly, but most of the shots missed completely. The Federals kept coming, and Wes ached to fire at them, impatient for the signal.

Time slowed, each moment seeming an eternity, waiting, waiting. Then McGuire yelled, "Fire!" Wes fired, not really aiming. He pulled the trigger, then started to run down the hill, following the men in front of him. All around him the air was filled with a high-pitched wail which rose over the din of battle. Wes added his voice to the hellish sound. They could see the Union soldiers stop, shaken by this unexpected charge. The blue line faltered, then began to turn back, but those in front ran into the secondary lines. The perfect order which had existed a moment before dissolved into frantic disorder, and Wes and the others rushed forward, plowing madly into the enemy on a full run, abandoning every thought in their insane passion to kill.

Instantly, they found themselves in a horrifying nightmare, all order gone, man battling man, hatred smashing into rage as elemental instincts broke loose. The roiling mass of men turned into maddened animals filled with a consuming blood lust.

Wes faced a terrified young boy who pointed his gun tentatively at him. Wes deflected the gun with the barrel of his musket, then rammed his bayonet into the boy's chest with such force that the blade pierced his back. The boy shuddered and fell, pinning Wes' gun to the ground. Wes, momentarily disarmed, was panicked by the realization that three or four men were charging directly at him. Desperate, he stood on the corpse's belly and tore his bayonet loose, ripping the boy's small chest apart in the effort.

Wes charged on, following the front wave as it continued forward. All around him, a maniacal scene was acting itself out. Muskets exploded at close range, the wounded shrieked in agony, metal clanged on metal as bayonets dueled, the air filled with the grunts of men straining to kill other men, curses and yells rose louder than the gunshots.

The ground beneath him became slick with blood and he lost his footing, falling face down into a mangled mass that had been a Union soldier. Rolling off, he looked down at himself, smeared with blood and, for one mad instant, thought he had been killed. But, realizing it was the blood of other men, he jumped up and moved on. Ahead of him, one of the men he knew fell to the ground holding his eye, blood trickling between his fingers.

McGuire ran to and fro, yelling at his troops, warning them of imminent attacks, punching, tearing, stabbing, shooting at everyone in front of him. He turned toward a cannon guarded by three Federals, running the nearest one through with his bayonet. The others turned to run, but were pushed back into position by a blue-coated officer. Wes and several others arrived at the same moment to help McGuire. Tommy Green was beside Wes and, using his musket like a club, he smashed the head of one of the remaining bluecoats. As the man fell away, another Union soldier tried to stab Tommy but ran into Wes' bayonet as he charged by. He hung there for a moment, turning to Wes with a stupid look on his face, before crumpling to the ground.

With the cannon's crew down, only the officer was left standing behind the piece. He was armed with a large revolver which he pointed coolly at McGuire. Just as Wes yelled a warning, the officer fired. McGuire staggered, paused, then reached down to his chest which had a huge black hole in its center. A moment later, the black turned red and McGuire slid to the ground. Wes, screaming in rage, turned to see the officer reloading his revolver. Racing toward him around the cannon wheel, Wes held his musket out for a bayonet strike. But in his blind fury, he missed his thrust and crashed into the man, knocking him flat and dropping his gun. The officer, lying on his back, frantically tried to reload his weapon. When Wes leaned over to retrieve his musket, the Yankee grabbed Wes' collar. Trapped, whimpering with terror and exertion as he stumbled on top of him, Wes butted his head viciously into the man's nose, then rolled off and scrambled to his feet. With a howl of animal rage, he smashed his musket butt like a pile driver into the man's face.

Spotting McGuire on the ground, he ran and knelt by him and stared into the old man's pale face and glazed eyes. The sergeant tried to speak but no sound came. Wes bent low, trying to hear his words, but the Irishman only choked, spitting blood all over the side of Wes' face. Then he was silent, his eyes staring up at the sky. Wes wiped the blood off his own face with revulsion, as if the death it had brought to McGuire might be contagious.

Standing again, he looked around self-consciously, realizing that for a whole minute he had been vulnerable, oblivious to everything except McGuire's body. Anyone might have come up and killed him. But the tide of battle had moved on, its roar having subsided into a constant low moaning from the wounded, sprawled everywhere among the dead,

The remainder of the fight was a blur. He was numb, unthinking, unfeeling. The hand-to-hand combat continued for some time as Jackson's men chased the Federals back into the valley and beyond. Wes, able to find only the fringes of the fight, was too dazed to understand any longer what was happening. At one point, it seemed to him that the overwhelming horror and excruciating effort of this battle blotted out all memory of the rest of his life, that it distorted his consciousness to where he believed that he had always been in the midst of this ghastly nightmare, knowing that at any second he might die screaming.

The two sides fought to an exhausted standstill, until fresh Confederates arrived and drove the remaining Federals into a flat-out retreat. By then, Wes had been reduced to a mindless machine, running, pausing to reload, firing, running again, until there were no targets left to shoot.

Darkness finally made it difficult to see more than a few yards ahead. When the fighting finally wound down and the halt was called, Wes realized that he didn't recognize any of the Confederate soldiers around him. He turned back and began searching for the rest of his company.

Chapter 12

PROMISES

Gettysburg, Pennsylvania
July 28, 1861

Ginnie was restless with anticipation. She had risen early, trying to keep herself busy with housework, but her mind kept wandering. Georgia, looking drained, came out of her room and slumped in a chair beside her. "I can't stand it any longer," she moaned to Ginnie. "Time is just crawling by. They said they'd be home days ago." Georgia's frustration and anxiety were so pathetic that for once Ginnie could truly sympathize with her sister.

News of the first big battle of the war had swept the town a few weeks earlier. Near a small creek called Bull Run south of Washington, the Federal army had been thrown back in chaos. Ginnie tried to imagine Jack in the battle, wondering how he had fared. Since the battle, she had not heard a word from him, and she had no idea if he was all right. Lou, on the other hand, had sent Georgia a wire saying that he and the rest of the company were coming home because their three-month enlistment had expired.

But after the wire there had been no word at all, and the town was gripped by a silent tension. People in the northern part of town would stop and gaze up the tracks toward Harrisburg where the regiment was supposed to be stationed. Anxiety hovered like a gray cloud over the town since most of the people knew someone involved in the fighting. A few weeks ago it had all seemed unreal, as if the military maneuvers were a staged political drama designed to frighten the South into settling the dispute peacefully. But Bull Run had changed all that. Some were saying that three thousand Federal soldiers had been killed, wounded or captured, three whole regiments. The hopes of peace had been swept away, leaving only fear and determination.

A train whistle broke the town's quiet at 11:00 am. Ginnie and Georgia, working blocks away in their home, heard it. They looked at each other in excitement, then raced for the door. By the time they arrived at the station north of the Diamond, the train had arrived. The ex-soldiers had not even had a chance to detrain before the station was flooded with ecstatic wives, lovers and parents. The returnees were preceded from the train by functionaries whose duty it was to escort the soldiers home, make certain that the

113

paperwork was done properly and then, if possible, to re-enlist the men for an even longer term.

President Lincoln, suddenly realizing that the war would not be easily or quickly won, and faced with the expiration of short-term enlistments, called for 300,000 more recruits.

The accompanying military staff chased the civilians back from the train, established barriers to keep the public at bay, and only then allowed the company personnel to get off the hot, crowded train. Although the men were officially civilians, most of them wore their uniforms for lack of other attire. Non-commissioned officers yelled orders at them and they formed into ranks from sheer force of habit.

As they lined up, they scanned the crowd for familiar faces, a few here and there waving and smiling as they caught sight of loved ones. Only about fifty of the original seventy-five men were on the train, the rest having left the company for various reasons. Some had been discharged earlier because of illness or when it was discovered that they were unsuited for military life, others had already re-enlisted and chose to remain in Harrisburg. Still others had simply decided to go elsewhere, and a few families were distressed to find their men missing from the train with no notion of where they might be.

As the company formed, the spectators marveled at the splendid sight they presented, far different from the stumbling recruits in baggy temporary uniforms they had seen fourteen short weeks ago. They looked like soldiers. The men were tanned and toughened, their uniforms were official and fairly neat, they wore them like veterans, and they stood to attention in even rows, their eyes straight ahead of them.

When the company had formed, Capt. Buehler stepped down from the train. Ignoring the crowd, he stood before his command and spoke a few words. He was pleased by the way they had adapted to military life, proud of the opportunity to serve with them, and anxious that they re-enlist, now that they were experienced veterans. Pointing to the recruitment officers who would take care of the paperwork, he explained the benefits of signing up once again, in money, rank and glory. Finally, he said his farewell and climbed back onto the train. The men did not move until the sergeant screamed, "Dismissed!"

Then there was pandemonium.

Georgia and Ginnie were standing in the middle of the crowd, halfway down Carlisle Street, which was as close to the station as they could get. From there they could see little more than the smoke from the train's engine. The crowd jostled them as people shoved forward to get a better view of the troops. When the word "Dismissed!" was heard, a roar erupted from the station platform as the men broke ranks and ran madly in every direction, looking for family, embracing loved ones, shouting, laughing, crying. The hubbub continued for almost half an hour, and turned a quiet Monday into an instant celebration.

The two girls waited in the crowd, craning for a view, while those around them jumped up and down, calling to their men. As they worked their way closer to the station, Georgia finally spotted Lou and yelled his name. In an instant, they were in each other's arms. Ginnie, only half noticing their embrace, searched the mass of faces in blue forage caps. Suddenly, Jack was behind her, his voice in her ear, "Hi, Ginnie." The look of excitement on his face erased any doubt about proper conduct, and she gave herself to him as he swept her in his arms and hugged her close, rocking back and forth in pleasure at being home, at being with her.

Both men went to their homes to change, and in the afternoon met again at the Wade house. After a polite half hour in which they shared their stories with Mary Wade, they escaped with Ginnie and Georgia, each one to spend the afternoon seeking some corner of town where they might find a little privacy. The problem was that two or three dozen other men had the same idea. As a result, the next several hours were spent walking around town with their girls, greeting members of the company who were doing the same thing and joking about how odd their civilian clothing looked.

That evening, Jack returned to take Ginnie for a walk, telling her that he had something important to discuss. They walked south on Baltimore Street, eventually finding themselves on a ridge just east of the cemetery from which they could see in every direction. It was a warm July evening, but on the hill a light breeze brushed their cheeks. As they reached the crest of the hill, Jack turned to Ginnie, reaching for her hands.

"I thought about you all the time I was gone," he said suddenly. She flushed at this bold confession. "I was glad I had your picture," he went on. "You don't know how lonely it got in camp, doing nothing but drilling all day, marching somewhere and then marching back again, setting up camp, tearing down camp. All I could think of was getting home." He grinned nervously, then added, "and seeing you."

Ginnie could not think of anything to say. Her face felt hot and she was aware of his hands holding hers. She tried to look into his eyes, but was disconcerted by their boldness and looked quickly away, nervous but flattered.

"Well?" he said after a moment's pause, waiting for her to say something. "Did you think of me all the time, too?"

Retreating into coyness, she teased, "What? With two boys to take care of, a house to run and all that sewing to do? I had lots of things to think of."

Taken aback, he scowled. "Come on, admit it," he demanded. "You thought about me a lot."

"I thought about you every time I got a letter," she said, throwing him a playful smile. "Exactly twice in three months."

115

"We were busy all the time," he said defensively. "We...."

"If you were so bored and lonely," she countered, "and were thinking about me all the time, like you say, you might have written me more than twice."

He turned away, irritated, and started to walk farther out the Baltimore Pike. She followed a step behind, delighted to have gained the offensive. Trying to sound indignant he said, "I only got three letters from you. So you didn't do much better."

Catching up with him she said deliberately, "I wrote you first, and I answered both of your letters. I was waiting for another letter. If I'd gotten a third one, I would've answered that one, too."

Feeling that he was losing this verbal battle, he stopped and turned to her. "You don't know what soldiering is like," he snapped. "It's hard and tiring. I was so exhausted when the day was done, I just fell on my bedroll and I was gone."

Ginnie nodded her head sympathetically. "I know how you feel," she responded, then added innocently, "I'm tired when my work is done, too."

He was no match for her repartee, and he knew it. He said harshly, "Women are supposed to keep up the morale of their soldiers. They have to write their men, whether they write back or not. It's part of their job."

Ginnie gritted her teeth. "I didn't ask for the job, Jack. You drafted me. Remember?" She turned her back to him and began walking away. He stopped her after a few steps.

"Wait...wait. I'm sorry. It's just that I thought...." His words trailed off.

She glared at him again. "Well, you should stop thinking so much. I gave you a picture. That's all, Jack."

He was silent for a while, but she could see that he was hurt and that his hurt was making him angry. "Most of the men had pictures of their girls," he retorted. "If you didn't have a picture, they thought you weren't a real man, that you couldn't get a woman back home. And if you did have a girl's picture, she was supposed to write regularly."

She looked at him questioningly. "So that's why you wanted my picture?"

The statement stung him. "No," he said, "of course not. I like you." He fumbled for words. "I showed the picture to lots of the men," he said more quietly, his tone indicating that she should feel honored. "I even told some of them that you were my... fiancée."

"You what?" she said in astonishment. "You told them what?" He was surprised at how perturbed she sounded. She asked sarcastically, "Don't you think I should have something to say about that?"

Trying to soothe her, he shrugged. "You know, it's something you say around the men. They didn't know the difference."

Her eyes opened wide as her indignation bubbled over. "Oh, so this is all

116

just another one of your jokes. To make you look good in front of the men."

Realizing that he was making a fool of himself, he stopped and looked at her, completely lost for words. His mouth worked silently as his face reddened. Finally, recovering lamely, he said, "I didn't mean that. It's coming out all wrong."

She looked at him for a moment, trying to decide what she felt toward him, anger or pity. When she couldn't make up her mind, she changed the subject. "What did you bring me out here to talk about?"

He didn't say anything at first. Finally, he asked, "Can we walk together?" He took her hand and pulled it through his arm. They walked silently for a while, and she was surprised to feel the tension in his arm. His discomfort softened her.

He stopped, looked at her, took a deep breath, and said, "Maybe we can get married." He sighed in relief now that the words were out, echoing in the silence between them. He was too embarrassed to press for an answer, afraid it might be negative; she was too entranced by the moment to spoil it with words. Regardless of what she felt for him, a man had just proposed marriage to her – a very eligible young man.

When the silence was no longer tolerable for either of them, she said quietly, "I feel very honored that you asked me." They relapsed into silence, continuing to walk as an excuse not to look at each other. "When do you think we might do it?"

He looked at her out of the corner of his eye. "Gin, there's something else I have to tell you." She was surprised at the sudden apologetic note in his voice. "I'm going to join up again. Most of the boys are. They need us now more than ever and, anyway, it won't last much longer."

"You're going to re-enlist?" She said it quietly, but the shock hit her like a physical force. "For how long?" she managed.

He grimaced, knowing she would not like the answer. "Three years."

"Three years!" She broke away from him, too upset to speak or cry. What was he trying to do to her? Asking her to marry him, then casually announcing that he would be gone for the next three years. She turned for home, desperately wanting to be away from him.

"Please, Ginnie," he begged, starting to follow her. "There's no way it will last that long. It will probably be over before the end of this year. And then we can settle down here and be happy. Anyway, all of the fellows are joining up again. Even my father is talking about joining."

Although she was still too hurt and confused to speak, she stopped trying to escape. Jack kept trying to say the right things. "We could even be married when I come home on leave," he said eagerly.

"Jack...stop." When she finally spoke, her voice was firm. He took a step backward, startled by the change in her voice. Struggling to make him understand, she said, "I just don't know. It's not what I wanted. When I get married, I want to be *with* the person. I don't want them running off all over the place. It seems that everyone is always doing the same thing to me. Running away."

His eyes were angry now. "How can you be so selfish? This country is tearing itself apart and all you're thinking about is what you want. I don't want to be in the army, but I know that it's my duty." Ginnie listened to his self-righteous lecture as though he were speaking to someone else. She thought about her father who had run off to Virginia with stolen money when she was just a child. She thought about Wes who had gone away to Virginia, too, and who had gotten so involved in his own dream that he forgot about hers. And now here was another man who claimed to love her but who was preparing to leave her alone again.

She stopped and he caught up with her. "I want to marry you," he said earnestly, "and I don't want to wait three years."

"Why do you have to go back into the army?" she asked, her voice full of disappointment.

"You heard about Bull Run last month. We lost about three thousand men. Three *thousand*. They have to pay for that, Ginnie. I knew some of those men. I have to fight, for them."

"And what about me?" she asked quietly, staring out at the lowering sun through the gates of Greenwood Cemetery.

"I'll be back, Ginnie."

"What happens if you get added to that list of three thousand?" He was quiet for a long time. She didn't move, but continued to stare at the sun until her eyes burned.

"There are never any guarantees. I could come back here after the war and fall off some building I was working on. You have to take your chances with life."

Ginnie turned around to look at the woods and streets and open places where she had played as a child. It had all been so simple back then. She looked out toward Culp's Hill. "Do you remember," she asked, pointing to the hill, "how we used to swim in Rock Creek in the summer, and then run through the woods looking for berries?"

He followed her eyes and his jaw clenched as he saw her looking at the hill, as he imagined her thinking of the man whose name it bore. "Yeah," he said, "and I remember that time we threw Wes into the creek with all his clothes on. You tried to start a fight with me over that."

"So I did, Jack. You always were a bit of a bully." She nodded slowly, wondering how things could change so quickly. That day seemed like yesterday and like a thousand years ago.

Jack made a disgusted face. "He made people want to beat on him. He was just a little coward."

"Wes was a dreamer. And I liked him." She stared at him defiantly. "He wanted to make a new life for himself. You boys drove him away. He wanted to find some place where he could make a new beginning."

Jack laughed scornfully. "Oh, so it's my fault he turned traitor." Ginnie shook her head in frustration. He pushed on thoughtlessly. "I'm trying to save you from him. If he came back for you, even after the war, you'd be disgraced. You'd never be able to live in this town again." She looked away, aware that it was useless to try to make him understand. Jack peered into her face. "I'm trying to save your reputation," he said, his voice full of concern. "Too many people already think you have rebel sympathies. If we get married, it will stop all that talk."

"Oh," she said, as if a new light had dawned. "You're doing me a favor by marrying me?"

He raised his hands in helplessness. "Why are you so damned difficult to reason with? You know that's not what I mean. We both belong in Gettysburg. We can make a nice life here, together. This is our home."

She nodded. "It's Wes' home too."

"Not any more it's not," he said emphatically. "Wes is a traitor. He probably killed some of our own boys at Bull Run."

Ginnie closed her eyes, shocked by that thought. She had visualized Wes in the South, in uniform, with the Confederate army, even fighting in battles. But the others in the picture had always been faceless. She could not bring herself to believe that he would shoot people he knew. Being a rebel was one thing, but killing friends was something else. What if Wes and Jack should one day face each other over the barrels of their rifles? She shook her head as if to erase the thought. It was too terrible to consider.

Jack was going on. "You have to get Wes out of your mind. There are people in town who think you'd be happy if the South won the war."

"Who says that?" she demanded indignantly.

"Oh, people. I've heard them say that your father was a crazy Virginian, and that you have the South in your blood, and that's why you still like that rebel; you want to live in the South after the war." He turned on her in exasperation. "How can you go on liking him when everyone else in town is ready to shoot him if he ever comes back?"

"People are terrible sometimes," she said, choking up. "Wes grew up in this town. He's only been down there a few years, and he's only been in the army a couple of months. Why is everybody so quick to condemn him?"

"Because if he was a real man, he'd have come home and fought with us against those rebels. He's still a coward," Jack said with a sneer, "just like that time I threw him in the creek."

"He's not a coward. It took courage to stay there when everyone here condemned him for doing it."

Jack looked at her, speaking deliberately. "Now, think, Ginnie. When the war's over, all those rebels are going to hang. So he'll either get shot in battle or he'll hang after the war. Either way, he's done for. I don't see how it was so smart for him to stay in the South. I think he was crazy to do it. There's no way he can get out of the mess he's gotten himself into."

Ginnie's eyes filled with tears of pity for Wes, with regret for how things had turned out, with pain over lost friendships, and with resentment at Jack's blind prejudice. He noticed her tears, and said with some lack of feeling, "You still love him, don't you?

She shook her head. "It's not that. It's just all so sad."

Jack had lost the mood with which he had begun the evening. He had been full of enthusiasm to make Ginnie his fiancée; now he felt outwitted by her conversation, frustrated in his desire for an exclusive relationship, rejected. He turned to her and said, "I guess I'd better take you home."

"Don't be mad at me," she said, taking hold of his arm. "It's all so confusing. I didn't know this was what you were going to say to me. I'm honored that you think that much of me. But I have to get my mind straightened out before I can give you an answer."

"What's to straighten out?" he asked, close to sarcasm. "You have no future with...him. We could have a nice life here together. It's a simple decision."

They walked back toward Breckenridge Street, both deep in thought. After a time she said timidly, "Why me, Jack? We haven't had anything to do with each other since school, and we hardly knew each other then."

He grabbed her hand suddenly and led her off to the right of Baltimore Street, down the hill to where the trees started, searching for a little privacy. When they arrived at the edge of the woods, he sat in the grass and patted the ground beside him.

He looked off toward the east where the lacy clouds were flushed pink from the sunset. He studied them for a moment, then turned to her and said, "I know you, Virginia Wade. I've always known you." He looked at the clouds again, as though in hopes that their beauty might somehow inspire beautiful words. "When we were in school, I used to look at you when you couldn't see me. You were always the smartest girl in your class, the prettiest girl in school. I knew you were a hard worker because your father didn't live at home. When the others made fun of you, I felt bad. You were more grown up than the rest of the girls."

He looked at the grass, poking a stick aimlessly into the ground as if trying to pry something loose. Ginnie felt herself begin to tremble at this dramatic change in his attitude.

"I never could understand," he went on, "why you took up with Wes Culp instead of me. I came from a better family, I had better prospects, I was better looking, the others at school liked me better." He paused, as if contemplating the mystery of what he had just said. "He was four years older than you, and yet when I saw you together, you seemed older than him. You were as tall as he was, even though you were younger. And you were a lot smarter than he was. I always thought you could find someone better than him." He looked straight at her for the first time. "Ginnie, I'm here and he isn't. I can give you things he can't. And," he hesitated, "I love you. I've loved you for a long time."

Ginnie was dizzy with emotion. A minute ago, Jack was inarticulate and almost hostile, and she was upset enough to want to go home. Now this. "I didn't know you felt that way," she said, almost whispering. She looked straight into his eyes, which no longer threatened her. She was drawn by their honesty, by their bare emotion. Something within her melted, something which less than five minutes before had been resisting his insensitive pronouncements. She saw a side of him which she never knew existed, a tender side.

Seated facing one another on the grass, they gazed into each other's eyes, bathed by the rosy light of the setting sun. His smile embraced her, open, vulnerable, and it filled her with a glow that made her giddy. Slowly he rose, helped her to her feet and embraced her, holding her tightly in his arms as though he had dreamed of this moment for his whole life. Then he looked at her mouth, touching her lips with his. The kiss was infinitely light, lasting only the briefest moment, yet it sent an electric shock through both of them which changed everything, opening new doors, locking others forever.

When they drew apart, still holding hands, and climbed back down to the road, something had been settled. They walked toward her home in silence although their heads were filled with the sound and celebration of love. They kept glancing at each other, unable to keep from smiling when their eyes met.

Halfway up Baltimore Street, Jack finally spoke. "Now that we've got all this settled, I think you had better write Wes and tell him of our decision." The echo of his words, like acrid smoke, trailed after them as they walked. "Maybe when you write the letter, it'll finally straighten everything out," he added, unable to disguise the subtle note of triumph in his voice.

She said nothing, bitterly resenting the fact that he had picked this time to say it. As he dropped her in front of her home on Breckenridge Street he said goodnight, then added, "I want to see the letter before you send it." She looked at him for a long moment, then turned without speaking and walked quickly into the house.

Chapter 13

IN THE ENEMY'S LAND

Winchester, Virginia
March 1862

The sun had melted the last of the snow, leaving the camp a quagmire of mud stirred up by the movements of Jackson's four thousand men. But the sun had also lifted the heavy spirits of men who had been trapped in inactivity for several months by mother nature. The monotony had been plagued by questions concerning Jackson's fitness to command, as officers and soldiers alike argued about his New Year's Day march.

Rather than allowing them to hibernate in their winter quarters, as armies had always done from late November until the spring thaw, Jackson had undertaken a campaign in January to attack the Federals, hoping to catch them unaware in their winter camps. But it had been a failure and was called off after repeated protests from the senior officers. Its only accomplishment was the deterioration of morale among nearly everyone in camp.

The onset of spring, however, was bringing an end to the grumbling, and each day the army, hardened now into seasoned soldiers, expected the fighting to begin again.

Wes carried his tin through the mess line and found a dry branch to sit on, while waiting for Ben and his other tent mates, Old Pete and Charlie Sims, to join him. The faces around him were familiar, the conversation easy, and the spring sun brought a feeling of new hope. He smiled to himself as Ben perched on a rock and began to eat his gruel, dipping the hardtack in hopes of softening it a bit. Wes flicked a weevil out of his stew.

Old Pete, always first to know what the rumor mills were grinding out, shared what he had just heard – the Federal army was marching south toward them, due to arrive at any time. The estimated size was given as something between 25,000 and 100,000 men.

Rather than being frightened by the thought of facing the enemy again, the morale of the regiment was high. Since the victory at Manassas the summer before, Jackson and his army had become legends. The papers had frequently quoted the remark of General Bernard Bee about Jackson and his men. Bee had seen Jackson's unit standing, unmoving, at the top of Henry

House Hill. Thinking they were unwilling to engage, he pointed them out and shouted to his own officers in disgust, "Look! There stands Jackson like a stone wall." Bee had died soon afterward, but Jackson's later success had made the words memorable, not as criticism but as apparent praise of his strength and courage. Now it seemed that everyone referred to the general as "Stonewall" Jackson and to his unit as "The Stonewall Brigade."

The nearness of the Federals brought increased activity in the brigade and, as Ben and Wes ate in silence, they watched the officers ride to and fro, expertly maneuvering their horses through the milling men. Near the captain's tent Wes could see Kyd, spotless despite the abundant mud, standing proudly in his new lieutenant's uniform. His promotion had come through, aided, everyone knew, by pressure from friends and family. They had seen little of him since his promotion, and Wes felt a tinge of jealousy as he watched him. Wes saw Ben staring in Kyd's direction too, his chewing arrested for a moment, and Wes knew he was not alone in his jealousy. Together they slogged on as foot soldiers, hoping to achieve the ignominious rank of corporal before the summer began.

After lunch, Wes followed Ben and the others over to the mail wagon which was crowded with anxiously waiting men. As the sergeant bellowed the names, Wes let his mind drift. Mail call was always slightly depressing since he never got any mail. He knew no one in the South, and northern mail was unable to get through. For that reason, it took him a second to hear his name called.

"Patterson, Nelson, Culp," the sergeant yelled.

Ben nudged him. "Culp," he repeated. Wes shook off the surprise and pushed his way through the group.

"Culp!" he said, reaching for the crumpled envelope. His hand closed around it and he moved back through the crowd, unable to do anything but stare at the handwriting. The familiar curve of the letters that spelled his name filled him with a thrill of recognition, but he was unable to believe it was true. It was from Ginnie. Ignoring a flurry of questions from Ben and the others, he ran to his tent, unfolded the letter and read it in the gathering dark, his heart pounding wildly.

Tue evening

Dear Wesley,

I hope this letter finds you well. You have been much on my mind since the awful fight that separated us. When I heard that you had returned south to Shepherdstown I was afraid that I had caused you to leave. I realize now that it was only your true nature, that you were standing up for your beliefs. I'm sorry I can't agree with your decision. The war has changed everything.

While I know that this letter will come as a surprise to you, we thought it best that you know as soon as possible. Johnston Skelly and I have decided to be married. He has joined up and so the marriage will have to wait until he is home again. He wanted me to send this letter to you, so you would know what we plan. He says he can have it taken through the lines by an exchanged prisoner.

I'm sorry if this news makes you unhappy in any way. But I am sure you have plenty of southern belles to call on and have forgotten all about me. But I will never forget you, Wes. Perhaps if the war had not changed things so much our dreams could have come true. But I must go ahead with my life and make the best of the chances that I have. May God bless you and protect you.

Virginia

Below this was a postscript, scribbled in a different hand. Wes had to squint to make out. It said:

If you come back to G-burg I'll see you hang from the nearest tree! Stay away, traitor! J. Skelly

There was a roaring in Wes' ears, a crushing weight shoving him down, down, until he could barely breathe. Coming after almost a year of silence, her news was devastating. Wes sat down on his bedroll, unable to move or think. A ray from the setting sun stole though the flap of his tent. Absently, he let his eyes follow the patch of light which it drew on the ground, not looking away until it faded into darkness.

Eventually he lay on his bedroll, unable to keep from turning the words over and over in his mind. His dreams always had one of two endings. In the first, the South won the war and he returned home as a conquering hero with all sins forgiven. He swept Ginnie off her feet, took her south to live on the plantation as they had planned, and all their dreams came true. In the other scenario, Ginnie forgot him and turned her attention to someone else, someone wealthier and more handsome. Someone taller. Someone from the North.

It seemed that the nightmare was now coming true. But the more he reread the letter, the more he felt that between the lines Ginnie was trying to say that she still cared for him. Looking at the postscript again, Wes felt rage building inside him. It was almost as though Skelly had forced her to write the note so that he could gloat that he had taken Wes' girl.

What rankled him most about Skelly's note, however, was not that Skelly had read this supposedly private message between Ginnie and himself; it was not even that he had threatened him with death and called him a traitor. What rankled was that it was true. He probably would be hanged if he ever went home. He thought again of what had happened to Kyd's friend in Maryland and was certain that many people in Gettysburg might be tempted to do the same thing to him.

And that fact gave Skelly a free field on which to make his move toward Ginnie. Wes imagined him filling her mind with all manner of foul thoughts – how Wes had been changed by his years in the South, how badly southern men treated their women, how Wes had abandoned Ginnie for some criminal cause. He saw how Ginnie's feelings toward him might slowly have been manipulated by Skelly's lies. If he could just get to her, somehow, if he could only talk to her for a few minutes, he could make her see that he still cared for her, that he had not left because of her but because of Skelly and the rest of them.

Up until this minute, he thought that he had gotten her out of his system, that he hated her. But it was a lie, and a few words on a crumbled piece of paper brought back all of his feelings. Suddenly he knew: he had to see her! Others had gotten permission to visit loved ones. Surely he could find some means of getting away.

Ben, Charlie and Old Pete filed in silently a while later. They were quiet and respectful, sensing the cloud that hovered over the tent because of the letter's arrival. Sleep was long in coming, and Wes stared at the few stars that shone through the flap. Outside a guard paced, the sole of his boot flapping with each step.

It was still dark when reveille blew, greeted with a chorus of moans as Wes and the others fell into line automatically. After roll call came the command to pack up and prepare to move out. This brought an instant change, transforming the group of sleepy individuals into a well-organized fighting force.

Wes could sense the eyes of his tent mates on him as they packed their gear away. Charlie, unable to check his curiosity any longer, blurted out, "Well, ain't you gonna tell us who it's from?"

"No," Wes answered evenly, pausing to look into Charlie's eyes for emphasis. A chill settled over the tent as they silently hurried about their duties.

When Old Pete and Charlie took the canteens to the stream to fill them, Ben said simply, "It was from her, wasn't it?"

Wes merely nodded. A wave of sorrow passed over him briefly and Ben sensed his pain. "What did she have to say after all this time? She's sorry you got beaten."

"She's getting married, Ben." Wes' voice was fierce. "She's marrying that bastard who beat me."

Ben could think of no way to respond except, "Oh, that's shitty, Wes."

Wes mumbled, not so much to Ben as to himself, "I've got to get away.

I've got to see her and tell her that she's making a mistake. If I only had a few minutes with her, that's all I'd need."

Ben put his hand on Wes' shoulder. "You should go to the Captain. Maybe he'll give you leave."

Wes looked at him scornfully. "So I can go north? He knows where I'm from. Everybody does. Besides, there's going to be a battle. If Old Pete's right, the odds are ten to one against us. Do you think he'll let anyone go now?"

Ben sighed. "All right. But what are you going to do?"

There was a fire in Wes' eyes when he looked at Ben. "Whatever I have to, Ben."

"If you go absent, they'll shoot you. Hell, even if you get away from us, you'll have to outmaneuver the whole damn Federal army. They'll catch you and hang you as a traitor. Or a spy. You're being stupid, Wes. She's not worth it."

Wes pulled away savagely and shouted, "I'll decide if she's worth it or not."

Old Pete and Charlie returned, looking quizzically at Wes and Ben. They could sense the tension and reluctantly held their tongues. The sergeant yelled for the company to fall in, and the men sprinted to gather the last of their belongings and toss their tent bundles into the carts. They marched out of the muddy field that had been their home for two months and started north. Black hatred smoldered inside Wes, making him eager for the next battle. Every face across the lines would be Skelly's.

They halted at the top of a rise that overlooked a long valley. On the far side Wes could see the smoke from hundreds of campfires. The Federals seemed to reach as far as the horizon. Wes amused himself by imagining those thousands of troops milling around, terrified that they might have to fight the great Stonewall Jackson. The officers conferred, looking through field glasses at the Feds. Orders were sent to each company captain. The 2nd Regiment was marched down the hill a half mile and placed at the far right of the army's flank. Wes and Ben in B Company were placed at the far right of the regiment.

They dug in and waited, watching across the lines for any movement. There was none. After noon, the company officers suddenly busied themselves. The sergeant ran over to the line shouting for volunteers. Wes stood immediately, anxious to do anything at all. Ben stood too, giving Wes a suspicious look. They were pulled out of line with ten other volunteers and brought as a group to the captain who was busy consulting a map with Kyd. He looked up when the group had quieted. "I'm sending you men down the hill with Lt. Douglas here. There's a road about a half a mile away that I want to secure. Any questions?" There were none and the captain smiled. "Good.

Move out, then."

As they trotted down the hill, Wes looked at Ben. "You didn't have to come, you know."

There was a question in Ben's eyes and Wes realized that his friend knew what was in his mind. "I couldn't let you go without at least trying to talk you out of it one more time."

Wes sighed. They moved through the dense trees quietly, passing a small creek. After a mile, the group paused and Kyd studied the map again. The road had not appeared as anticipated and it was apparent that they had missed their mark.

Finally, Kyd threw the map down in frustration. "All right. We'll split up in pairs. If you find anything that looks like a road, give a yell." Ben and Wes set off together toward the left.

Once they were out of sight, Ben stopped Wes with a hand on his arm. "Wes, listen to me. I know what you're thinking and I'm not going to let you go. I can't."

Wes frowned at him in frustration. "Ben, you can't stop me. If I don't go now, it'll be too late. She'll be married."

"But she doesn't love you any more, Wes. Face the facts!" Ben's voice was loud and angry.

Wes put his hand up to quiet him. Forcing himself to be calm he said, "Ben. I'll be back. You have my word. I'm not giving up on my duty to the regiment. But I can't give up on Ginnie either. She means too much to me. I know she still cares for me. She wouldn't have written if she didn't. Don't you see, Ben? I have to go. The letter was begging me to do something."

Ben was quiet for a long time. Wes took the silence for agreement. "I'll need your help. If they think I deserted, they'll look for me. If you tell them I was captured, then I can come back after I get this settled." Ben shook his head slowly, and Wes could see that his resistance had weakened. "You're my best friend, Ben. If I can't count on you, who can I count on?"

"You'll be captured."

"Maybe," Wes nodded. "But maybe I won't. I have to take the chance."

"All right. But you have to promise me that you'll come back."

"You have my word," Wes assured him.

Ben stuck out his hand and Wes could see the anguish in his friend's eyes. He grabbed Ben in a rough bear hug. "I'm sure I'm doing the right thing."

Ben released his grip and stepped back. "You have to come back."

Wes laughed. "I will, Ben. You're my best friend."

Ben turned back up the hill and began to walk away. Before he reached the top he turned again for a last look. Then he raised his rifle into the trees, fired off a shot and began yelling. With a last wave he ran over the rise and disappeared. Wes quickly turned in the opposite direction and fled.

He ran for what seemed an hour, passing the road that Kyd had been trying in vain to find. He stopped from time to time, listening for any evidence of pursuit. But all was quiet. He decided that it would be best to head due east for the rest of the day and try to circle around the Federals after dark. Pressing on until night began to fall, he was suddenly worried that he had not come far enough to avoid the Federal pickets.

Stumbling though the darkness, he found a road which ran north and followed it for a mile or so before fear of discovery pushed him into the woods. Invisible branches whipped his face and tore at his clothing, and he tripped repeatedly, stumbling over underbrush. At one point, he swore out loud but was immediately terrified by the sound of hooves. A troop of cavalry pounded by without stopping, torches held high. Their boldness was a good sign since it meant that he had cleared the pickets and was firmly in Federal territory.

He moved off again and for the next four hours paused little in his trek. He guessed it was about three in the morning when he thought it safe to try the road again. He made better time this way, and stayed on the road until the black sky began to turn deep blue. Then he returned to the woods and melted into a dense grove where it was nearly impossible to see him. Here he spent the day, quietly listening to the sounds of wagons and men moving further south along the road. Most of the wagons that he could see were filled with supplies, which meant that he had made it to the Federal rear. As the afternoon shadows grew longer, the road quieted completely, until there was nothing at all moving on it. The Federals were following Jackson south, away from Wes.

As evening fell, Wes sorted through his pack, making a pile of the things he would no longer need. Without his ammunition, his pack was several pounds lighter. He looked at his rifle for a long time before deciding that it was useless to him now. Tracing the carved initials in the stock with his finger one last time, he covered it and the ammunition with a pile of branches. For an instant, he had the irrational thought that he would reclaim it on his way home. Slipping out of his hiding place and heading north again, he realized that there were still at least thirty miles to go before he reached the Pennsylvania border. With a sinking heart, he knew that the trip would take much longer than he had anticipated.

He began to wonder if perhaps Ben was right, that he was acting foolishly. If he were caught now, who would mourn him? How could he get into Gettysburg in uniform, and how risky would it be to use civilian clothes as a disguise? He had left his only friends to go to a place where everyone was the enemy. Except for Ginnie. He needed to get to Ginnie. That single thought kept him pressing forward. If he could only see Ginnie, it would be worth the risk.

The darker it got, the more his courage returned and he moved back onto the road. In the starlight, he began to make good progress, his military conditioning serving him well. He walked well into the night, only seeking cover three or four times. By three a.m., however, his strength was waning and he decided not to risk his safety by getting so tired as to become careless. Pleased by the distance he had come since dark, he found a grove of trees, plunged into them until he was far from the road, and fell asleep surrounded by dense brush.

A persistent scratching on his nose awoke Wes a few hours later. He rubbed it and heard a gasp in response. In an instant, he was fully awake. It was broad daylight. Staring at him, only a few paces away, were two young boys. The older one held a long twig with which he had been touching Wes' face. He turned to his friend and said with satisfaction, "See, I told you he wasn't dead."

The smaller boy stared at him, mouth agape, as Wes struggled to his feet. The first boy looked at Wes without the slightest hint of fear. "Mister, are you a Johnny Reb?" he asked boldly. Wes could not think how to respond and held his tongue. The boy nodded as if confirming the fact. "Well, you don't look like no monster. My Pa says all Rebs are monsters."

Wes was considering whether to capture the boys and tie them up when the younger one walked up and pointed at Wes' belt. "Is that a canteen?" Wes nodded. "What's in it?" he asked. Wes took the canteen from his belt and offered it to the boy, who took it, removed the cap and smelled the contents with grave interest. Handing it to his friend to examine, he asked, "Can I keep it?"

"No," Wes said, smiling to soften the refusal. "Maybe I'll give you a button off my blouse. See, it says 'C.S.A' on it. But you have to promise me something." The boys nodded with great earnestness. "You can't tell anyone that you talked to me. Understand?"

The boys nodded again and, before Wes could say anything else, the taller one snatched the cap from Wes' head and bolted away, bounding happily through the trees, whooping about his captured treasure. Wes started after them, then thought better of it and watched them go. He wanted to put as much distance as possible between himself and this place now that he had been discovered. But since the sun was up, it would be safer to find a good hiding place. He chided himself for sleeping so late and, even worse, for avoiding the entire Federal army and then allowing himself to be found by a couple of small boys. Within a mile, he found a shallow cave and crawled inside.

For several hours he listened to every sound outside, sure that the army would come for him at any moment. But there was only silence and he convinced himself that the boys had not turned him in. He dozed a while. When he woke, he was instantly filled with terror. Hounds were baying nearby, hot on the trail of some prey, which Wes could only assume was himself. The sun was high in the sky and there was no way he could run without being spotted by the search party. He moved as far into the cave as possible, hiding behind a small outcropping of stone. The baying got louder by the minute and Wes felt himself washed by waves of panic. Helpless, he saw the long silhouette of a man suddenly block the entrance to the cave. Wes could see by his shadow that he carried a shotgun in his hand.

"Hey, Matt, come over here a second."

Another shadow joined the first. This one had a pack of dogs attached to it and their baying echoed in the cave. Wes, trapped like an animal, waited to be torn to pieces by the dogs. There was nothing to do, nowhere to run. The two shadows tried to decide what to do. They hadn't seen him yet, but the dogs had certainly scented him and were tugging at the ropes, yelping to be let at him.

The man with the dogs pulled them away from the cave, and Wes thought for a moment that he had escaped detection. But then the first man spoke directly to him. "Boy, I know you're in there. I'm not going to mess around with you. You either come out now or I'll let the dogs loose and there won't be anything left of you to bring out." He paused, waiting for a response. Wes didn't move. "I'm gonna count to three. One...." Wes could imagine the dogs ripping at his legs and arms. "Two...." The dogs would slaver all over him, reaching for his throat as he tried futilely to push them away. "Three!"

"All right!" He crawled out toward the light, too frightened to think. The man raised his gun and pointed it at Wes' head. For a moment, half expecting the man to pull the trigger, Wes braced himself for the impact. But when he looked up, he saw the man's grinning face. "Boy, did you get lost or are you just plain stupid?" Wes didn't answer. He stood, trembling in fear, furious at his carelessness.

The man tied Wes' hands behind him, then led him back toward the road. He was joined by the man with the dogs. The animals, catching Wes' scent again, strained to get at him, barking viciously and snapping at his heels. By the time they reached the road, a small group had gathered to stare at the captured rebel as he was marched past them to the man's cart. A woman stepped from the crowd and stood blocking Wes' path. He looked up into her face and was chilled to see a look of shimmering hatred. She spat on him and the warm spittle slid down his cheek as he was shoved roughly up into the cart.

Turning, he caught sight of a familiar face, the taller of the two boys he had seen earlier. The child, wearing a gray Confederate cap, smiled innocently and waved at Wes.

Chapter 14

A LOST CAUSE

Harrisburg, Pennsylvania
March 1862

Wes wrapped a weary arm around his aching ribs and shifted his body in a vain attempt to get comfortable on the rough wooden floor. Pain rippled through him, causing him to gasp involuntarily. It had been nearly a week since his capture and the white hot dagger in his chest had not subsided. He decided that he had a broken rib or two. It was not surprising, considering the vicious beating to which his captors had subjected him.

He had almost been glad to be handed over to the Federals. They, at least, were professionals; they had treated him roughly, but they hadn't beaten him. He wondered if they would have been more vicious had they discovered that he was a northerner. The civilians who caught him hadn't cared where he came from. All they knew was that the uniform he wore was gray. They did care about their brothers and neighbors who had gone off to fight him and the rest of his friends, and so they figured they were helping in their own way by beating up one lonely rebel. Wes would have laughed, but the pain in his ribs prevented him. The irony was too great. They thought they were protecting their neighbors; in fact, it was one of their neighbors they were abusing.

Once he had been turned over to the Federal army, he had been moved from place to place, joining larger and larger groups of captured rebels. At first, there were only three or four of them. The men were strangers to Wes, but in every sense they were more his brothers than the northerners swarming about them in blue. After a few days, there were enough of them, about two dozen, to move to more permanent quarters. They were marched up the road to a train stop, loaded aboard a freight car like so many cattle, and moved north. Wes, knowing roughly where the rail lines ran, wondered whether the journey would take him near Gettysburg.

As the train crawled north, stopping at every little station to pick up civilians and occasionally another prisoner-of-war, he peered anxiously between the slats of the car waiting for familiar landmarks to roll into view. Just as he feared, he began to recognize the hills from his youth. The train was in fact nearing Gettysburg. He closed his eyes and listened, praying that they would keep rolling, that they would stop anywhere but there, someplace where no one knew him. But the train pulled into the north end of town and stopped at the station. Perhaps they were just picking up passengers, Wes thought. But soon, the doors slid open and the group was told to get out. Wes descended, afraid to look about, fearing that someone he knew might be nearby. He saw a group gathered at a distance down the platform. Wes couldn't make out the faces in the dim light, and was relieved to realize they couldn't recognize him either. He turned to face the train so it would be harder for anyone to catch sight of him.

Suddenly, he heard voices approaching, young voices, high and happy. He noticed a group of boys just as they discovered the twenty-five disheveled prisoners. They stopped in the middle of the street and stared. Wes was turning back toward the train when something crashed against the door of their freight car. Startled, he turned and saw that the boys were throwing things at them. Several impacted the ground in front of them, spraying their shoes with bits of rotten apple. As the prisoners raised their arms to protect themselves from the barrage, one of the Federal guards shouted, "You boys get out of here!" The boys jeered at him.

A crowd gathered to watch the spectacle and Wes' apprehension grew. Fortunately, the guards were even more concerned. The sergeant of the detail ordered them back into the car, and Wes scrambled up quickly, relieved to be out of sight of the townspeople. He stared through the slats at the boys who were calling the prisoners every unpleasant name they could think of. One particularly loud participant threw another apple toward the train. It banged against the side, echoing through the wooden car. Wes saw a woman step from the crowd, move toward the culprit, and call in a voice that was high and piercing, "Harry Wade, you come home right now."

Wes felt a moment of dizziness. He stared at Mary Wade as she dragged her boy away from the group. Holding him by the ear, she marched him to the far end of the platform where another figure waited. Wes could not see the other person clearly, but he pressed his face against the slats, desperate to discover who it might be. The figure turned and walked away. Was it Ginnie? As the three moved beyond his range of vision, Wes sank to the floor, overcome.

That scene replayed itself again and again in Wes' mind as the train rolled on toward Harrisburg. When they arrived, their guards could not find room for them in the temporary stockades so, as a result, the rebels ended up in the city jail. Wes shared his cramped ten by ten foot cell with twelve other soldiers. Given no beds or blankets, they had to make do with what they had, pillowing their heads against each other, crowding together for warmth during the drafty nights. After a few days of repeated pleas, Wes finally had his ribs tended to by an aged doctor who reeked of liquor and resentment. He wrapped the bandages too tightly and made the pain even worse. Wes rewrapped the bindings as soon as he returned to the cell, and the pain in his chest subsided somewhat.

Life as the prisoner was life in hell. He had lost everything, literally everything. None of his dreams remained. Ginnie was lost to him; there was no doubt about that. His friends in the South were now lost too. He had risked one for the other and had lost both.

There was only one person who would still accept him, only one who would be willing to look beyond his mistakes to his dreams: Julia. Wes knew that Ginnie would never understand him now, especially since he was a prisoner. He would be a reminder to her of the sins of her own father. But Julia would understand. The idea kindled a faint light in his soul.

From one of the other prisoners he got a scrap of paper and then begged a pencil from a guard. In his desperate need to reach out to someone who still cared for him, he wrote Julia, asking for help, for supplies with which to bribe the guards for his basic needs. He asked her to consider coming to visit him, feeling that merely seeing her face again would bring a ray of light into his darkness. And he asked that she keep the truth about him quiet.

Getting the letter sent was easier than he had imagined. He promised the guard that sending it would bring a relative who would pay him for his services. The guards, who cared little for politics but a great deal about lining their own pockets, were willing to listen to anything that promised them money. Wes picked one of the guards whom others in the cell had found willing to help. At first, the man was hesitant about taking the letter, until he found out that the recipient was a young woman.

A week passed and they began to hear that they might be moved north to a prison camp near Lake Erie. This rekindled Wes' anxiety; he imagined Julia arriving in Harrisburg the day after he left. But the only move that materialized was to a barbed wire enclosure, a holding pen for Confederate soldiers on the edge of Camp Curtin in Harrisburg. It was somewhat larger but even less comfortable because it consisted of a roof supported on posts but without walls. There was practically no protection from the weather.

The days settled back into an endless and mind-numbing routine. The others played cards with a makeshift deck and chatted idly, sharing rumors about the fighting further south. One of the more literate Yankee guards spent his afternoons reading newspaper articles to the prisoners, stressing how the South was losing every engagement. But the effort proved to be therapeutic because it kept Wes and the others in touch with the world that existed outside of their miserable environment.

Many of the articles were about The Stonewall Brigade which earned Wes some small notoriety among the others. Jackson was running around the Shenandoah Valley, totally confusing a Federal army twice his size. He continued to surprise the enemy forces, constantly outguessing and out-maneuvering them. Wes listened with pride but also with a bit of trepidation, wondering how Ben and the others in his company were faring. Eventually, his worry turned to jealousy as he realized that, since he was no longer with the 2nd, he could not share in the victories which were making his friends immortal.

At night, after the lamps were extinguished and the others tried to sleep, Wes lay thinking about all that had happened. In the quiet, he cursed God for taking away everything that he loved. There was a strange consistency to his life: each time he loved something, it was ripped out of his hands. He had chosen to leave the North and that had cost him Ginnie and his family. Now, he had chosen to leave the South and that had cost him his friends and his chance at fame. And perhaps his life.

A foot in his back woke him in the morning a week later. The sun was high and the others were already playing cards. Wes looked up to see one of the guards.

"Culp?"

"Yes." Wes tried to stand but his legs had cramped in the night and threatened to give out. He braced himself against one of the roof posts and stood upright to look the man in the eye. The others had stopped their cards and were watching the interchange with interest since the guards rarely took such personal interest in them.

"You've got visitors."

Wes stood still for a moment, letting the information sink in. Visitors. Who would have come with Julia? Maybe Annie, or perhaps she had been unable to keep it from Will and he had gotten off and come with Julia. Then again, perhaps someone had learned that the captive they held was a northerner, a traitor, and they had come to take him away. His mind swam with that frightening possibility.

The guard opened the gate, which creaked noisily on its rusted hinges, allowing Wes into the outer pen, the exercise yard. "Who's out there, Culp?" one of his fellow prisoners asked with a hint of jealousy.

Another man answered, "Maybe old Stonewall's come to escort him back personally." The others laughed.

The guard shut the pen door and locked it, motioning for Wes to follow him around the corner of the main prison building. Despite the pen's openness, it was gloomy, bathed in shadow. So the light outside tore at his eyes and Wes tried to shield them with his hand.

The guard led him toward a side gate, hidden from the main entrance. He said gruffly, "You have ten minutes," then stood in place, obviously planning to monitor the visit. As Wes' eyes adjusted, he could make out the gate twenty yards away in the corner of their muddy exercise yard. On the other side of the fence stood two shadows whose faces he could not make out. Both seemed to be female. So, it was Annie who had come with Julia. That made sense. She might be unpleasant to him, but at least it wasn't Will.

Wes stumbled forward, trying to keep his footing on the uneven ground. Between his sleepy leg and the bright light, he imagined that he looked like a madman. But it didn't really matter. Julia was here and she would forgive the way he looked.

"Julia?" he asked as he got close enough to identify her features. She was even more elegant than when he had last seen her, in a dark dress and bonnet. Then he looked at the other figure and felt his heart miss a beat. "Ginnie?" It was a whisper, a choked cry of joy. He felt that he was hallucinating and that at any moment he would awaken back in the pen.

But the moment passed and she was still standing there, more beautiful than he remembered. He forgot everything for an instant. Nothing existed but the two of them. He grasped the wire mesh between them frantically, searching her face. She smiled a sad smile that communicated pain and pity. It was warm but it was also distant; she seemed to be horrified by what she was seeing.

"I can't believe you're here," he said in amazement, his eyes immediately welling up uncontrollably. He was astonished at his own weeping, but was powerless to stop it. He reached through the fence to touch them. Julia, who had been able to master her emotions to this point, lost all control and began to sob. She grasped at his hand protruding through the wire, and touched it lightly to her face. Wes tried his best to quiet her and looked to Ginnie for help. She moved closer to Julia and put her arm around her friend's shoulder.

Julia gained some control, wiped her eyes and looked up at Wes. "I'm so sorry this all had to happen."

Wes, barely able to speak, finally managed to choke out, "Thank you so much for coming. It's so good to see you." He studied their faces, as though their presence could somehow nourish his starving soul. He turned to Ginnie. "I can't believe you're here. I didn't think I'd ever see you again. I thought I saw you when we went through Gettysburg on the train." Fresh tears choked him and he couldn't go on.

Ginnie said quietly, "Julia asked me to keep her company. I didn't think she should make this trip alone."

He looked at her in wonder, as a person catches a glimpse of paradise at the moment of death. "It's so good to see you. I've missed you so much." At this, Ginnie began to lose her own composure. Wes, only half aware of what he was saying, mumbled, "Things were so much simpler before I went away. If I could only do it over...." But he could not continue. Julia nodded in agreement.

"How are Will and Annie?" he asked.

"They're both well. Will's safe. He hasn't been in any big battles, so far as I've heard."

"And Papa?"

Julia's face fell. "Wes, he passed on."

Wes felt as if he were watching himself from outside his body. His face grew rigid and his breath was expelled in a long silent sigh. But the emotion had left him. Somehow, he had known what she would answer. He watched himself nod to Julia, with no emotion on his face. Who was this person who could cry at seeing the girls but shed not a tear at news of his father's death?

"When?" was all he said.

"A year ago. Last June. He wasn't sick very long." She wiped her nose with a small handkerchief. "He never got over Mama's passing, you know."

He nodded, then looked at Ginnie who was still standing with her arm around Julia's shoulder. "It was good of you to come with her." Ginnie squinted her eyes in a brief smile that Wes remembered well. It still stirred his heart. "I got your letter. I didn't think I'd see you again, after what you wrote. After what...Jack wrote."

"I'm sorry about that," she said, revealing her discomfort. "The war...well, the war changed everything."

"It doesn't have to," he heard himself saying.

"Wes," she said, moving close to the wire, her voice tense. "It's too late. It's over. Everything has changed. I just wanted to come see if you're all right. I wanted to say thank you for...for thinking about me all these years. You're a good man, in spite of all this." She glanced around the prison enclosure. "I'll always remember you."

They were beautiful words, but they were terribly final. His trip north to change her mind had been doomed from the start. He had been the captive of a hopeless cause, and now his pursuit of that elusive dream had made him an actual prisoner. A final desperation flowed through him.

"But Skelly? Ginnie, please. Think about it. He's a bully. You weren't meant to be with him."

Ginnie's face fell, her eyes beseeching him. "Wes, he's changed."

He studied her face. "Do you love him?" he asked quietly.

She looked at him for a long time before answering. "Yes. I suppose I do."

"Then I'm happy for you," he said. He thought about the fight that had forced him from town. His ribs began to ache again as if to underscore the memory. But there was no point in causing her any more pain. The best thing he could do for her was to let her go.

"We brought some things," Julia told him. "The things you asked for."

Ginnie reached back and pulled a sack up to eye level. The guard behind Wes came forward quickly. "I'll take that, ma'am. No gifts for prisoners, that's the rule." The women looked upset but Wes held up a hand, quieting them. "It's all right. They're for the guards anyway. It will help me get along better here." They nodded slowly as his meaning registered.

The guard unlocked the gate to retrieve the bag and said to them, "You ladies will have to go soon, before the captain gets back."

They looked at each other and then at Wes. He reached out to Julia through the wire mesh. Her eyes were puffy and full of pain as he grasped both her hands. "I love you, Jules," he whispered.

She walked a few paces away from the fence and out of reach, unable to look into his face any longer. Wes watched her, then turned to Ginnie. He could think of nothing more to say.

"I'm sorry things worked out this way, Wes," she said. "I truly am." She looked down at the ground in front of her. "There are so many things I wish could have been different. But we have to make the best of what is." Her eyes searched his. "Don't we?"

"Yes." His voice was a whisper. She was so close, inches away, but she was as unreachable as if she had been on the moon. She put her hand through the gate, her eyes glistening. He took it in both of his.

"I hope you'll be happy," he said. "We might have had a chance, if the war hadn't come. But now, you'll be better off with...him." He couldn't bring himself to speak Skelly's name. He held her hand for a long moment. At length, unable to stop himself, he tried to say, "I'll always love you." But no sound came from his lips and he was uncertain whether she heard him. He knew at that moment that this was the last view he would ever have of her.

"Thank you," she said. "I'll always pray for you." He nodded, then turned to go, unable to endure any more. Even prison would be better than the agony he felt standing here.

She turned away and walked to Julia. Wes, watching them in spite of himself, saw them wave one final time before they moved off toward the town. He felt numb, as though his muscles had turned to stone. The guard had to nudge him three or four times before he roused himself enough to stumble back to the pen.

He sat apart that night, quietly staring into nothingness. The others stopped trying to pry information out of him. Initially, they had been jealous of his having visitors but, when they saw the effect it had had on him, they decided to leave him alone. The numbness continued for days. It was a blessing, perhaps, since the pain it masked would surely have destroyed him.

A week later, the group was rounded up and moved under guard to the train station. Most of the men speculated about whether they were being exchanged. There had always been talk of prisoner exchanges, second- or third-hand stories of cousins or friends who had come back from captivity. Wes paid no attention to the rumors, and life itself was mostly a blur to which he paid little heed. He remembered only snatches, like wisps of smoke floating through his half-conscious mind. There was the cold drizzle of spring, the endless sitting, and then the jolt of the train's first movement accompanied by groans as the men realized that they were headed north. The ride seemed to take forever, but he spent most of it asleep, or perhaps unconscious – he no longer could tell which. The slow pace of the train matched the dragging rate at which his life moved, and the deadly lack of activity made even time itself slow to a crawl.

He didn't remember arriving at their destination, and could not say how many days they had been on the train. He was aware of marching through the mud, his feet cold and wet, of flopping down on a wooden floor which seemed to be rocking. He vaguely remembered being moved to another place one night well after darkness had fallen. He did not know where he was, nor did he care. Most of the others were talking and laughing, exploring their surroundings. Their voices were muffled in Wes' mind, but he covered his ears with his arm to block out the world.

When he awoke the next day, he looked about his new room trying to force his mind to make sense of what his eyes saw. One of the other men saw him. "Hey, look. It's alive," he called. Men chuckled.

"Where am I?" a voice asked. It took a moment for Wes to realize that it was his own.

"Why, you're on Johnson's Island, son. Don't you remember?" Wes looked at the speaker, an older man with whitish hair. Wes had heard the man's words, but they didn't convey any meaning. There was the sound of laughing.

"But since you don't look like no officer, they stuck you in this cage. So's you could have the pleasure of our company!" More laughter. "What's the matter, boy. Yankees got your tongue?"

"Just let him lay," someone said quietly. "Looks like he's had a rough time of it."

Quiet returned and Wes was left alone with his thoughts. He tried to remember the details, but they hung out there just beyond his grasp. He felt hot. He lay back on the floor, waves of heat flooding over him, his muscles twitching out of control, drowning him alternately in seas of vicious fire and icy water. Voices floated above him somewhere.

"He's burning up." "We'd better get someone." There were other voices, but he couldn't tell if they were real or not. Then all was quiet. Blackness.

When he opened his eyes, it was as if he had been asleep for a century, as though he had just been born. He heard a quiet flutter and felt a cool breeze. Someone hummed lightly, a pretty female voice, a tune he did not recognize. It felt as though he were swimming upward through ocean depths. He could hear the sound of water trickling and sense a blessed coolness on his forehead.

Wes forced his eyes open, blinking quickly to adjust to the bright sunlight.

It took a moment to focus on the shadow that moved above him. The humming was coming from the silhouette and Wes watched transfixed as the figure's hands dipped into unseen water, then moved to replace the coolness on his brow. The person paused for a moment and Wes saw a smile.

"You're awake."

Ginnie. His mind produced a name that meant something to him. He tried to remember what it was. He squinted at the shadow, finally distinguishing brown hair and a pleasant face. He cleared his throat lightly, testing his voice. His mouth was drier than fall leaves. The woman pressed a glass to Wes' lips and cool water ran over his tongue and down to his throat. It was the taste of heaven.

"Thank you, Ginnie," he managed in a rasping voice.

A peal of laughter emanated from the form. The sound was delightful, like music. "You're welcome. But, I'm Rebecca." Wes pondered the name as the washcloths came and went on his forehead. "We didn't think you were going to make it for a while," Rebecca said conversationally. Wes was content simply to listen to her beautiful voice. "You've been asleep for a long time, nearly a week. Dr. Starr was ready to give you up." She paused, then added with a giggle, "But *I* wouldn't let you go." Another pause. "Who's Ginnie?" she asked softly. "Your girl?"

Wes tried to think of the answer to this question, but nothing came to mind, so he merely nodded. "I'll bet she's a very nice girl. She's lucky to have someone as faithful as you. You've been talking about her all week. And you know what?" she went on, chattering happily. "You'll be seeing her soon. The army is preparing a big prisoner swap, maybe next month." Wes nodded again.

Another week passed during which Wes gradually regained his painful memories, almost making him wish he could forget again. He was amazed to discover that he was in the infirmary of a new prisoner of war camp on Johnston's Island, two miles out into Lake Erie, near Sandusky, Ohio. He had no recollection of being aboard the boat which had brought him here.

The talk of a prisoner exchange increased every day, but nothing happened. News from the South told of a pitched battle in which a general named McClellan was trying to take Richmond. Most of the guards seemed to think McClellan would succeed and that the war would soon be over. Wes had his doubts, but somehow none of it seemed to matter anymore.

In another week, he had regained enough strength to stand and walk short distances and eat solid food. Rebecca spent as much time with him as she could, walking him, her arm lightly supporting his efforts. She chatted easily, keeping Wes' mind from plunging back into the depths. In time, he was returned to the prisoners' barracks, weak but certain that he would recover.

141

However, his release from the infirmary meant losing the sound of Rebecca's voice. To Wes, stripped of everything else, that final loss was the most devastating of all. But he grew stronger and, as the weeks passed, he focused on the one hope he had left: a prisoner exchange.

One morning, early in August, the captain arrived after breakfast to announce that those who were well enough to walk would be leaving that day. They were to be exchanged immediately. Wes dressed and joined the line heading for the infirmary. After the doctor checked them, indicating who could go and who would have to remain, Rebecca came to say goodbye to some of the men.

When she reached Wes, she took his hand warmly. "Goodbye, Wes," she said with her usual bright smile. "Say hello to Ginnie for me. Tell her she's found herself a true gem." Wes could only nod. He wanted to thank her, but by the time he had recovered his voice, she had moved on to the next man.

The trip back south was a succession of rides on different trains and long hours of waiting. When they finally reached Richmond, they were processed by a bored major and a young private who carefully copied each name into a large ledger. When each man identified his regiment, the bored major checked a long list, noting the current location of that regiment, and wrote a note which he handed to the man before dismissing him. Wes unfolded his note and read "Gordonsville." He had no idea where Gordonsville was or how he was supposed to get there.

He turned back to the major, who was busy searching the list for the next man. "Excuse me, sir."

The major looked at him with an angry expression. Almost shouting, he asked, "Do you want to stay here?" Wes shook his head in alarm. "Then, get moving," the major ordered.

After asking a dozen people, Wes was directed to a dirty sergeant who was tying down a load of lumber on an overly full cart. "I'm trying to get to Gordonsville."

"Well, ain't we all, sonny."

"Can you give me a ride, if you're headed that way?"

"If you don't talk too much or smell too bad. Because my Nelly," he said, thumbing toward his white nag who looked as though she had about three miles left in her, "she don't like it when things smell bad."

Wes doubted this assertion since the sergeant himself smelled like something between week-old garbage and dead skunk. But he nodded and climbed up into the seat. As it turned out, Wes didn't need to work at being quiet since the sergeant talked enough for both of them.

After a few miles, he no longer heard the man's chatter; his mind had turned to thoughts of being reunited with his company. When they reached the camp outside of Gordonsville, a few inquiries led him in the right direction and soon he was standing outside the captain's tent. The new captain questioned him for several minutes before sending him on his way. Wes walked as fast as he could, feeling the excitement building inside him. There was so much to tell, so many things to catch up on.

Then he saw them, Company B, his friends, his family. Some faces were missing and the rest looked tired and drained. But the men jumped up as soon as they laid eyes on him. Wes found himself looking around, soaking in the sights and sounds that he had missed for so long – the happy shouts of the men, the smell of food cooking, the sight of thousands of gray uniforms. Old Pete welcomed him warmly with a pat on the back. Wes looked around for Charlie and Ben.

Old Pete shook his head sadly and said, "Charlie's gone home. Caught a bullet in the knee at Kernstown."

Then before he could press Old Pete about Ben, he felt a rough shove against his shoulder. He turned and saw the stern face of his friend. Ben looked older and different, an extra stripe decorating his shoulder.

"Salute your superior, soldier," Ben barked.

Wes snorted, "Well, look who's got all high and mighty."

Ben's face cracked into a warm grin and he grabbed Wes in a rough bear hug. They embraced warmly, and Ben, his voice choked with emotion, whispered, "Welcome home, Wes. I wasn't sure I'd ever see your ugly northern face again."

Chapter 15

A SOLDIER'S RETURN

Gettysburg, Pennsylvania
April 6, 1863

Monday's mail brought a special treat for Ginnie which she had not fully expected. There was a letter in the mail postmarked Winchester, Virginia. Under her name the address, in Jack's familiar handwriting, said simply, "Gettysburg, Adams County, Pennsylvania." She ran her fingers over the envelope, feeling a lump which indicated that it contained something else along with the letter. Smiling to herself, she knew instantly what it was.

She tore the letter open and out fell what she had hoped for, a *carte de visite*, a photograph on a small card of Jack in uniform. She picked it up with a surge of joy, studying it intently. He was seated in a chair, his uniform blouse buttoned carefully to the throat, his kepi fixed squarely on his head, his rifle lying easily in his lap, the barrel pointing out past his right arm. She stared at it as closely as she could, drinking in all the details. He had grown a mustache since she had seen him last. In one of his letters, he had told her about it, and she wasn't certain that she would like it. Now she stared at it, trying to adjust to his new appearance. It made him look older, more handsome, and she decided she liked it. It appeared that he might also be growing a small goatee, but it was partly hidden by his collar and she couldn't be certain. He looked as though he had lost weight, but seemed to be tan and fit.

His corporal's stripes showed clearly on the left arm of his blouse, showing the rank which she knew made him proud, and which he had earned by signing on for a tour of three years. He pointed out in his letters that, out of the more than one hundred men in Company F, 87th Pennsylvania, only ten now outranked him, and four of those were commissioned officers.

She tried to recall what the real Jack looked like in person. But there was only the dimmest memory of the sound of his laugh, or the curl of his smile. Suddenly self-conscious at the thought of being caught looking at the picture, she slid it into the pocket of her apron.

She read the accompanying letter slowly, hoping that it would mention something about his next leave or perhaps even about their marriage. In the past year and a half Jack had never again made mention of his desire to marry her, and she was growing impatient for some definite information. It seemed once again that she was being forced to postpone her happiness. Each new battle brought increasingly bad news as the end of the war stretched farther and farther into the future.

The letter contained only a few short lines about what he had been doing, but somehow it warmed her heart, giving her some small peace of mind to know that he was alive and well. It was dated March 22, two weeks previously. She checked the postmark: Winchester, Virginia, March 24. It was taking mail two weeks to get back home from Winchester, less than a hundred miles away.

Mary walked through the room and Ginnie quickly hid the letter in her pocket. It wasn't that her mother didn't know about Jack; she did, of course, and Ginnie believed that Mary even liked him a little. But the letter and picture were private, not something she wanted to share. She couldn't even talk to Georgia about Jack. Every time she began, Georgia shifted the conversation to Lou and the impending birth of their baby. They had been married a year ago, the month after Ginnie and Julia had visited Wes in the prison-of-war camp.

Early that afternoon, Ginnie went to the Skelly's house to help the seamstress, Madeline, with a fitting. As soon as she arrived, Madeline pulled her into the back room and closed the door secretively. She listened for a moment, then turned to Ginnie.

"I wanted to make sure Mrs. Skelly doesn't hear us."

Ginnie looked perplexed as Madeline pulled a chair close and spoke in a conspiratorial tone. "I overheard something Mrs. Skelly said about you."

Ginnie felt the blood draining from her face. Mrs. Skelly didn't like her, and liked even less the fact that her son was developing a relationship with her. Ginnie had sensed this from Mrs. Skelly's behavior; the woman treated her like a common servant, ordering her around and refusing to address her by name. But Ginnie had never heard anything firsthand about her future mother-in-law's true sentiments. "What was it?" she asked with trepidation.

"Well, I overheard Mrs. Skelly talking to one of the old biddies in town about you. She was telling her about how you went to Harrisburg with Julia to see Wes. Well, she said that you've always been a rebel sympathizer and that you were sending General Lee messages about what Jack's company was doing." Madeline laughed lightly. "Isn't that the silliest thing you ever heard?"

Ginnie felt a flush of anger rise in her throat. "I can't believe she could say that."

"Oh, it's true," she said emphatically, nodding her head. Ginnie squinted at Madeline, knowing that she had a reputation for being a gossip. But in this

146

case their shared dislike for Mrs. Skelly made it unlikely that she was lying. Madeline smiled again. "Virginia Wade, She-Rebel." She giggled, and Ginnie couldn't help laughing with her, realizing how absurd it all was.

Madeline went on, her tongue loosened by the laughter. "Did you hear about Jack's father?" Ginnie shook her head. "Well, Mrs. Skelly was telling the parson that he got ill down south in the army, and then, when they were shipping him up north to a hospital, he got lost."

"What do you mean, he got lost?"

"That's what she told the parson. She said he disappeared and no one seems to know where he is. Personally, I think the idea of coming home to Mrs. Skelly was too much for him, and he took off somewhere to escape her." They both broke into laughter. A noise from upstairs cut the humor short, however, and they hurried back to their work with mock seriousness. But every time Ginnie met Madeline's eyes, they broke out in laughter again.

Later that afternoon, when they had almost completed a fitting, the front door opened, then banged shut. Ginnie went to the fitting room door to greet the newcomer. Instead of the next client, however, she saw a soldier standing in the foyer, holding his kepi in his hands and looking up the stairs. When he turned, a sudden electric shock surged through Ginnie. It was Jack. She hadn't recognized him at first because of his new moustache.

They looked at each other for a moment, then Jack's mouth curled up into the familiar smirk. "Surprise!" he said lightly before sweeping her off her feet. She squeezed him tightly as though to convince herself that he was not a mirage.

Then his grip loosened and as she looked up at him, Ginnie found his attention focused up the stairs. Turning, she saw Mrs. Skelly frowning down over the banister. But her angry look dissolved when she realized that the soldier was Jack. He rushed up the stairs and embraced her. "Hello, Mother."

"Jack! Oh, thank God. Did you get my message about Father?"

"Yes. And I came as soon as I could."

"Oh, thank God." She looked greatly relieved. Ginnie felt a brief prickle of guilt about her unkind thoughts toward the woman. "But how are you supposed to find him?" Mrs. Skelly asked.

"I haven't a notion. I'm going to Harrisburg and I'll try to ask some questions while I'm there."

Ginnie asked, glancing briefly at Mrs. Skelly, "But how did you ever get to come home? Lots of soldiers must be missing. Do they send someone to look for each one of them?"

"Well," said Jack, enjoying the moment, "come on into the parlor and I'll tell you all about it." He led his mother down the stairs. As they moved through the archway into the parlor, Mrs. Skelly said, "Virginia, you need to go back and help with Mrs. Brecker's fitting."

147

"No," interjected Jack. "I want Ginnie here."

There was a tense pause as Ginnie waited to see what the next move would be. Jack walked into the parlor, pulling her by the hand. Mrs. Skelly glowered at him for a moment, then followed.

When they were seated Jack said, "Well, it's all in who you know. I found out that you don't get into the parlor by knocking on the cellar door." He saw that they were waiting for an explanation, so he lifted his arm and pointed to his corporal's stripes. "Rank counts. I told the captain what I needed to do and I offered to stand extra duty. I just happened to know," he said with a wry grin, "that the colonel had a prisoner and paperwork that needed an escort to Harrisburg, so I volunteered. I have to be back on the twentieth." He gestured with both hands to indicate that he had explained his point. "So, here I am."

"How long can you be in town?" Mrs. Skelly asked.

"I got on the train in Winchester this morning at six o'clock, got here about an hour ago, took my prisoner to the county jail so he wouldn't run away, went over to see Ginnie," he said, glancing at her with a smile, "but I guessed she was here." Ginnie tried to hide her grin as Mrs. Skelly glared at her, upset at the thought that Ginnie claimed his first attention, even before his own mother.

Jack continued, "There's a five-thirty train to Harrisburg. We'll be there by dark, I'll hand my man over to the provost marshal at the stockade at Camp Curtin. Tomorrow, I'll deliver my paperwork and then I'll be free to find where they've got Father. I can be back here by Tuesday, if I get lucky. And I don't have to be back in Winchester until the following Monday. Pretty good, eh?"

"Well, you'll be hungry, I suppose." Mrs. Skelly led them into the kitchen and started to get him some food. Ginnie sat with him at the table. They chatted for a while as Jack regaled them with stories of army life which tumbled out one after another.

Madeline stuck her head into the kitchen. "Hello, Jack," she said without enthusiasm. Turning to Mrs. Skelly she said, "I could really use some help."

Mrs. Skelly fixed her eye on Ginnie. "Virginia, please go help Madeline."

Ginnie started to rise, but Jack caught her arm. "Not so fast, young lady. I want you with me."

Ginnie glanced at Mrs. Skelly who was looking at Jack with obvious irritation. "Really, Jack," his mother said, "business must go on, in spite of your unexpected arrival. Madeline needs Virginia's help."

"So do I," he said with a disarming smile, making it clear that he would not budge.

The older woman sighed and, after a moment, relented. She turned to Madeline impatiently and said sharply, "You'll just have to do your best. I'll be in shortly."

Jack rose and started for the door. "I'd better be getting to the station."

Mrs. Skelly hugged him briefly. "Do your best to find your father, Jack. I'm so worried about him." She turned to go assist Madeline. Ginnie walked him to the door, but he pulled her outside. "Come with me, so we can talk for a few minutes."

"I can't, Jack. I have to help your mother."

He stuck his head back into the house. "Mother, I'm taking Ginnie with me. She'll be back in a little while." The loud clearing of a female throat indicated that his message had been received. They ran down the walk in a flurry of laughter.

Ginnie shook her head. "She'll kill me. She doesn't like us seeing each other, and she doesn't like me to miss work. She'll take it out of my hide."

"Don't you worry," Jack assured her. "I'll tend to Mother." As they walked up the street, Jack took her hand. She felt slightly self conscious and glanced around to see if anyone was watching. But people passed by without a second glance, having become accustomed to seeing soldiers on leave escorting their young ladies around town.

He stopped before the jail house and turned to her. "You should probably head back. I don't want you around the prisoner, giving him any ideas."

She frowned but complied, turning to walk back up the street. After a few steps, she ran back and hugged him tightly. "I've missed you," she said quietly. He smiled and then leaned over and kissed her with an intensity that both startled and dazed her. He promised to be back on Tuesday and then disappeared into the jail.

Ginnie spent the next two days waiting for him to return, rushing to the door every time she heard a sound in the street. But he did not arrive until Wednesday night. He banged on the door while Ginnie was mending in the back of the house. By the time she rushed to the door, her brother Jack had already answered the knock and was talking with Jack. Ginnie pushed by her brother knowing that he would question Jack all night if she allowed it. Little Jack's greatest dream was to join the army, and he greeted every soldier he met with a sense of awe. Ginnie stepped outside and pulled the door shut behind her since it was clear that the boy planned to listen to their conversation.

"Did you find him?" she asked. Jack nodded, then took her hand and led her down the street away from the house. He told her the story as they walked toward the center of town.

His father, it seems, had come down with the ague, or swamp miasma disease, which is prevalent in that area of North Carolina. The regiment was camped in the middle of marshy ground filled with stagnant water and biting insects, and many of the troops had gotten sick. Finally, when some of the sick began to die, the authorities decided to evacuate them. They put a number

149

of them on a transport early in March and shipped them up the coast toward Washington.

"But," he explained, "when they got up into Chesapeake Bay heading for the Potomac, they were spotted and shelled. The ship caught fire, and many of the men drowned when they jumped overboard. Lots of those who made it safely to land didn't know the difference between Virginia and Maryland. Those who got to Virginia were captured for the most part, I guess. Others swam east toward Maryland and made it to safety. But, apparently, they were stranded there for a week before anyone found out about it and went to help them. Some of the troops were placed in a hospital in St. Mary's City, but no one reported the whole mess. That's why we hadn't heard anything."

"Well," she asked impatiently, "was your father one of those who drowned?"

Jack shook his head. "Oh, no," he assured her. "He's listed as one of those in the hospital. I don't know where he is now, or when he'll get to Washington. But apparently he's all right. It was the best I could do," he said, a note of frustration in his voice. "I had a hell of a time trying to get telegraph messages through, and a worse time trying to get the answers. At least we know he's all right."

Jack took Ginnie home and they spent the rest of the evening talking. In fact, they spent the better part of the next four days together. They were together so much that both of their mothers began to complain. Mrs. Skelly claimed that she needed Ginnie to finish certain tailoring jobs, and Mary Wade demanded that she help around the house, saying that, though it was nice to have Jack home, the work still went on.

On Saturday night, Ginnie made a picnic supper as a means of escaping family, and the two of them walked out the Baltimore Pike, each carrying a basket. They spotted the place where they had sat a year and a half ago, when they had agreed that it was serious between them. They glanced at each other with a grin, as though they both had gone there with the same thought. In a moment, they had spread the cloth on the ground just inside the tree line, and arranged the food between them as they sat facing each other.

It was a quiet April evening, cool but pleasant, and the sky was clear and blue. The breeze that had followed them up the hill stopped at the entrance to the woods, as though to respect their privacy. They ate and laughed. He told more stories, and she told him how much he seemed to have matured in the months he had been in the army.

They talked about everything, about how to stay together while he was away, about what would happen if he got wounded. "Ma wouldn't even go to Washington to see my father," he said moodily. "What do you think of that?"

She pondered a moment. "I think she was afraid," Ginnie said gently. "That's a long way, and it's a big scary city for a woman alone."

"If she loved him, she'd go. He's afraid, too, and alone – and sick." He paused. "I wouldn't want to be down there alone."

It was a moment before she caught his thinking. "You mean, if you were hurt and in a hospital somewhere, you'd want me to come."

He looked at her intently, then nodded. "Would you be willing to?"

"Of course," she said quickly, with more enthusiasm than she felt. Where? How long? What would she do while she was there? She didn't even want to *think* about him being wounded.

He was thinking, too. Without looking at her he said, "You went to see Wes when he was in that prison camp."

A cold flush washed over her. She had hoped they weren't going to get into another confrontation about Wes. Controlling her voice, she said as calmly as possible, "I went because Julia wanted me to go. She couldn't go alone." Another silence. "If I had to come see you, I'd probably ask Julia to come with me."

"It's not the same thing," he said, shaking his head.

She frowned slightly. "What do you mean?"

"He's the enemy. And you went to see him."

Ginnie closed her eyes and sighed deeply. "Please. I can't think of him as the enemy. Anyway, that's history. That's over. You and I are going to be married some day."

He thought about her statement for a minute. Then he looked at her directly and asked, "Do you mean that?"

She held his gaze for a moment before she answered. "Yes, of course," she said. "You're the only man in my life. I want to live with you and raise a family."

He started to pack up the picnic things, arranging them carefully in the baskets. When the baskets were filled and closed, he had put everything away except the blanket upon which they were sitting. He stood, carried the baskets into the woods where they were out of sight, returned to the blanket on which she was still sitting, picked up a corner of it and waited for her to move. She stood slowly, watching him intently. He folded the blanket over his arm, smiled at her, took her hand and led her into the woods where the undergrowth, speckled sunlight and shadows masked them from the view of passers-by.

"Where are we going?" she asked, suddenly uncomfortable.

"Where we can talk alone," he said evenly, as though it were nothing. He found a grassy spot on the south side of Culp's Hill, surrounded by scrub growth. Snapping the blanket open, he laid it smoothly on the grass and then lay on it, looking at her encouragingly.

Everything she knew warned her against this moment, yet deeper voices called to her, creating an emotional static that drowned out the voices of caution. He patted the blanket by his side and she sat down next to him.

He rolled onto his back alongside her, putting his hands under his head. Looking up through the trees, he said, in a voice so soft she had to strain to hear it, "When I was in Winchester, I went out on picket duty one evening before dark. There were six of us, and we were waiting for a reb company to come along. I was lying on my back like this, looking up through the trees, while we waited. As I was lying there, a breeze came up and it brushed across my face, and it felt...it felt like you were there beside me, and your hair was down and it was touching my face."

He was silent for a while, then went on as though there were no difference between this place and the woods in Virginia. "I knew there would be a moment like this some day. That's why I could hardly wait to get home. I wanted to see you so bad." Turning to look at her, he paused for a moment, then whispered, "I've never seen you with your hair down."

She gazed at him without blinking, surprised that she felt no embarrassment. After a moment, she reached up, unpinned her braids and began to unravel them. Combing her hair with her fingers, she pulled it down over her shoulders so that it framed her face.

He looked at her, breathless. "You are so beautiful," he said, shaking his head in wonder. "You should wear your hair like that all the time."

"I'm too old for that," she said, giggling.

"Yes, you are," he agreed. "Anyone who saw you that way couldn't help wanting you."

She had never before heard words like these. She was drawn farther into a vortex of pure emotions, elemental passions which she had never known existed and against which she had no defense. He reached up and drew her down to him. As her dark hair brushed across his face, he began to weep.

She leaned farther down, her face alongside his, embracing him, comforting him, asking, "What? What is it?" He struggled to control his quivering lips as the tears streamed down the sides of his face. "What?" she asked again.

"Down there," he said hoarsely, "down there nobody talks about love. Down there, there are only men who are trying to be tough. It's funny. We love each other, but we never talk about it. We fight and we kill people. We're terrified our friends are going to get killed, and we don't dare make new friends because that's just somebody else to lose. We'd die for each other, but we'd never say we love each other. It's a hard, man's kind of love." He wiped his eyes and looked at her as though he were in some terrible distress. His voice pleaded with her. "This is so different. You love me, I know that. You're so soft. I need you so much."

She leaned down, her hair bathing his face, and kissed him, kissed him repeatedly, devouring his mouth in a kind of absolute abandon that made her forget who she was, where she was, forget everything except that they were there together. He embraced her, holding her so tightly that she had to struggle for breath, and they wept together, the taste of salt tears running into their joined mouths.

Turning on his side, he reached over her to the edge of the blanket and pulled it up so that they were wrapped in a warm cocoon. She murmured, "No," as he began to caress her shoulder but he silenced her protest with a kiss. She struggled, more against her conscience than against him.

"I can't, Jack. I can't."

"Ginnie, please. I've been so patient. All the others in camp go with those...women, you know, who follow the soldiers around. I've never gone with them. I've had the chance. But I wanted to wait for you because I knew you would wait for me. When they laughed at me, I showed them your picture and said that I was waiting for you, and they stopped laughing."

She felt fire racing through her body, felt herself consumed by a frantic trembling that made her think she was going to faint. "We shouldn't...."

He kissed her neck, nuzzling her ear with his lips. "We're going to be married. I'm so afraid I'll get wounded and won't be able to...or I'll get killed and we'll never have time to be man and wife." His voice broke. "I don't want to die without having had a chance to make love with you, Ginnie. I love you so much."

His weight pressed her against the ground. His lips covered her protests and she found herself unable to stop him. She struggled for a moment, gasping at the pain. Then it was over and Jack lay beside her with a sigh, nuzzling her neck. The buzz of cicadas filled the night air. Ginnie listened to their sound, a quiet contrast to the noisy confusion inside her brain.

Chapter 16

NORTH AND SOUTH

North of Chancellorsville, Virginia
May 11, 1863

There was a deathly silence in the camp. Wes exchanged somber glances with those who passed by. Thousands of soldiers had been numbed into silence by one shocking death. A mere week after the greatest victory in the short Confederate history, the entire army had been plunged into gloom. General "Stonewall" Jackson was the reason for that victory at the small town called Chancellorsville, and for his success he had been given an ironic reward. In the darkness one night, his own men had mistaken him for the enemy and shot him. His wound had cost him his left arm, but pneumonia had eventually cost him his life. The news of his passing had arrived this morning and an agony of disbelief spread through the ranks.

Wes sat with men he barely knew. It seemed that, in one way or another, everyone had gone on without him. Some were promoted, like Kyd, and now Ben had finally gotten his stripes and was serving as an aide on General Walker's staff. Some had been wounded, like Charlie Sims, and were back home tending their farms. Many had met the ultimate fate in the fierce fighting a week before. Old Pete was one of them, caught in the throat by a bullet that tore the wind and the life from his old bones. And now Stonewall. They were all gone. Only he remained.

Things had been changing rapidly in the past few days. Officers were promoted, units were merged and reorganized to compensate for the losses at Chancellorsville. With Jackson gone, the command of 2nd Corps had devolved upon Richard Ewell. The men knew him as a division commander, but no one could guess how he would function in command of an entire corps. He was a strange man, profane and full of fire. At first, he had not liked Jackson, but later had fallen under his spell, becoming the best of his division commanders. But the men, who referred to him as "Old Baldy" for obvious reasons, doubted that he was capable of filling the large shoes he had inherited.

It was the new commander of the Stonewall Brigade, however, who evoked the most controversy. When the former commander, Frank Paxton, had been killed in action at Chancellorsville, Wes and the others felt that his replacement should come from the brigade itself. But James Walker had been appointed, having previously commanded one of Early's brigades. No one in Wes' company knew much about their new general except for one widely circulated story. Walker, while a student at the Virginia Military Institute, had been kicked out of Jackson's class one day for causing a disturbance. Later, he went to see his professor to argue for reinstatement. But Jackson, refusing to listen, had shouted him down. Angered, humiliated, Walker had foolishly challenged him to a duel. Jackson declined and had young Walker court-marshaled and expelled from the school for insubordination. Now Walker was to command Stonewall's old brigade.

But Wes no longer cared who was in charge. The battles still took place. Men still fought and died. He moved when he was ordered, fired when the enemy was in sight, ate when there was food available and slept where he fell from exhaustion. No longer proud of the cause that had pulled him away from Gettysburg, there was within him an almost complete indifference to both life and death.

The following weeks were interminable. In an endless hell of loneliness, misery and monotony, Wes felt trapped in a place where he no longer belonged. He was forced to scrape for information about the regiment's battle plans, since Old Pete's rumor mill had been permanently shut down. But no one would talk to him about where they were headed. Even Ben, when Wes saw him around camp, had become tight-lipped.

Wes' instinct told him that Lee would move the army north into Pennsylvania, and each day he became more and more anxious to know the truth. He began to have dreams about Gettysburg, of his sisters and brother in the house they shared in their childhood. But everything was somehow different. The figures he saw were his siblings, no doubt, but their features were different, and even the house was different. Outside, the landscape was barren, the trees shorn of leaves and bark, the grass withered and brown. Even so, he could not deny a deep yearning that began to beckon him home.

One morning, word came down to prepare for a march. A shiver of excitement ran down Wes' back as he stood at attention among the ranks waiting for the order to move. When it finally came, they began to march north, just as he had envisioned it, toward Pennsylvania. He waited at the end of the day for an order to countermarch, to return south again. But the order never came.

*   *   *   *   *   *   *   *

Southwest of Winchester, Virginia, June 13, 1863

Jack Skelly nibbled at his hardtack without much enthusiasm. Darkness was beginning to fall and he and three of the other company corporals were sitting on crates around a fire in front of their barracks, away from the troops. John Zeigler and Peter Warren, as usual, were deeply involved in their card game.

Billy Holtzworth handed Jack a pot of coffee and he poured some into his metal cup, then dipped his hardtack into the coffee in an attempt to soften it up so he could eat it without breaking his teeth. The men called them "sheet-iron crackers" because they were practically unchewable. Hardtack was delivered in crates marked "BC" for Brigade Commissary, but the soldiers joked that the stuff had been made Before Christ. Jack examined his piece. At least there were no weevils in this batch.

Peter threw his cards down in disgust, losing yet another round to John, who smiled and collected the small pile of rocks they were using as ante. They were playing with one of the "patriotic" decks that the army provided. In place of the symbols found in a normal deck – clubs, hearts, etc. – these contained shields, stars, flags and eagles, with the face cards portraying Federal officers, Miss Liberty, and other personages designed to appeal to the men's patriotism.

"Four Miss Liberties! How are you dealing that deck?" Peter roared. "That bitch'll be the death of me yet."

John smiled and dealt another hand. Peter paused as if he were going to stop playing but, with nothing else to do, he picked up the hand with a sigh. Shaking his head, he complained, "I'm tired of this shit. All I want to do is get this damn war over with, go back home to Gettysburg and farm that place 'til I drop. I'm never going to leave home again."

Jack nodded as he gnawed at the corner of his biscuit. "I hear ya, Peter. Sleeping in a real bed and eating real meals." His eyes glazed as he dreamed of his recent trip home. It was only a few weeks ago but it felt like ages. "I tell you, it's sure hard to come back to this," he said, waving his hardtack, "when you've had some good hot meals."

"I'll bet that's not all you were sorry to leave," Peter said with a leer. "Let me see that picture you always carry with you." The only one in the group who didn't know Ginnie, Peter studied the photograph, then grinned. "I can see it in her face. She could hardly wait for you to get home. Did she give you any?"

Jack caught John and Billy exchanging an amused look.

"Any what?" Jack asked, playing dumb.

Peter laughed. "You know, any...soldierly comfort, any horizontal refreshment?"

Jack made a sarcastic face. "Why should I tell you?"

"Well, I just wondered. You seem to like to go out of camp to see Blanche. I just wondered what you did when you were home."

Billy said, "Peter, you don't know Ginnie or you wouldn't ask that question. She's the most proper girl in Gettysburg."

John sputtered with poorly suppressed laughter, adding, "Peter, not even Jack, good-looking as he is, could get that girl into bed."

Jack couldn't stand it any longer. "Well," he said, with great drama, "it just goes to show that you've always underestimated me!"

There was a momentary silence during which all the men stared at Jack in disbelief. "You mean," asked Billy in astonishment, "that you *did* get her into bed?"

"Sort of," Jack said, relishing the attention.

"What does that mean?" Billy shouted sarcastically.

"It means I got her into the woods!" The three men roared in delight. Jack, carried along by the merriment of the moment, went on, "She wants to get married. So I told her this was our last chance, because I didn't know if I'd ever get home again, what with the war and everything."

"Oh, that's a good one," Peter laughed. "I'll have to use that one on my next leave."

"I told her we can't make it public yet, because both of our mothers are against it. So, she thought this was like an engagement pledge. You know what I mean?"

Peter nodded vigorously. "Something to remember you by, huh?"

"Yeah, like a promise that we belong together, that we won't do it with anybody else."

"You mean," Peter corrected, "that *she* won't do it with anybody else." They all laughed.

The laughing stopped as Will Culp, the company's first sergeant, edged over to the circle. Culp locked eyes with Jack for a second. "Keep your voice down, Skelly. I can hear everything you're saying." He turned back toward his own barracks, leaving the others momentarily silent.

"What's with him?" Peter asked, perplexed.

Billy looked at Jack, then explained, "Ginnie used to be his brother's girl."

"You mean his *reb* brother?" Looking at Jack, Peter exclaimed, "You mean, that reb used to go around with your girl?" He whistled dramatically as the light gradually dawned. "So you sort of got her to...declare her loyalty to the Union, so to speak."

Jack nodded, and with a parting glare toward Will Culp leaned closer to them. "And best of all, guess where we did it." He waited for the curiosity to build before he whispered, "Culp's Hill."

After a moment, Billy hooted in admiration. "Holy shit, Jack. You screwed both of them at the same time." Gales of laughter.

Jack smiled in satisfaction. "That ought to show Wesley Culp who's in charge back home."

After breakfast the next day, the mail cart rolled into the Federal camp, kicking up a plume of dust behind it. The soldiers raced for a place around the cart's perimeter and Jack made sure that he was near the front. The sergeant opened the white canvas bag and began calling names.

"Skelly!" was the third name called. Jack grabbed the letter with a grin and shoved his way back through the crowd, waving the envelope aloft for everyone to see. He sauntered over to his cabin where Billy and Peter were sitting, waiting to hear the latest from home.

He tore the letter open casually and scanned the lines. Expecting the usual mundane details of life in Gettysburg, the words struck him instead like a blast of ice water, and the blood drained from his face before he could turn away. They couldn't miss the look of horror on his face before he dove into the cabin to avoid their curious eyes. Sitting on the bedroll he read the lines again, slower this time, focusing on each word.

Gettysburg, May 28, 1863

Dear Jack,

I wish I could tell you this in person. I know you have enough problems just being in the army without my worrying you about things like this. But I have to tell you, and I knew you would want to know.

This is very hard to say, and you must keep it a secret between us. I think I am expecting a child. I know this is impossible to believe, but my sister is expecting one, as you know, and so I recognize all the signs. I have not told her, or anyone, but I have talked to her enough to know that I am probably not mistaken.

I know this all came about because we were planning to be married. If I could not depend on your faithfulness and your promise of marriage, I could not live with this situation. I will be disgraced if this comes out before we are married.

Is it possible that you could get home again so that we could have a quiet marriage ceremony as soon as possible? We can no longer afford to wait until your anniversary leave in September. If it was private, we could let people think that the wedding had taken place earlier. I need you to help me find a way out of this terrible situation.

I love you, and I know you will not leave me alone to face this problem. Please write me an answer as soon as you can. I will wait for your letter hopefully.

With my love, Virginia.

Jack stared at the words, too stunned to feel anything. Then the anger began to build inside him. She was doing this deliberately, he was certain. She was saying these things to punish him for forcing himself on her, hoping to hurry him into a marriage he was not certain he really wanted. His fists curled around the letter until the nails dug into his palm. At that moment, Peter popped his head through the door.

"Jack?"

Jack whirled toward the entrance. "Get out!" he screamed. Peter withdrew as if he had been shoved.

Jack sat alone in the cabin, his thoughts racing. During his last visit home, he had realized how much the war had changed him. Ginnie must have sensed this too, must have noticed some subtle difference in him. Perhaps she feared losing him, and this talk of pregnancy was a ruse to get him to marry her. But he had known then, and was even more certain now, that they had little in common. His life was filled with things that she would never understand. There was an unbelievable horror in the bloody battles he had endured which had burned itself into his mind. But there was also something intoxicating about army life. There was a kind of belonging, an excitement, a purpose here that he had never known and which was indescribable to outsiders. He had never realized what possibilities the world held until he had escaped from home. When he was with Ginnie that last time, he finally understood just how small and cloistered her world was. He could no longer imagine returning there for good. But she knew no other world, and now she wanted to pull him back into it with her.

He stood suddenly, moving quickly through the door and back into the circle around the fire. The others paused to look at him curiously, but they collectively held their tongues.

"Who wants to go with me to ride a couple of the gals?"

John and Peter shook their heads but Billy jumped up. "I'll go." Jack headed up the path without looking back. The camp was laid out in a grid pattern, prescribed by army regulations. Each company was billeted in a row of crude buildings, the front of each cabin facing the rear of the one ahead. To either side were other rows inhabited by other companies. At the head of each row of cabins were the buildings that the non-commissioned officers and the company commanders lived in. Beyond these, and facing the rest of the cabins, stood the houses of the regimental staff, considerably larger and more comfortable than those of the foot soldiers.

Outside of this temporary city lay the huts of the various hangers-on who followed the army wherever it went. There were traders and merchants, as well as undertakers and embalming surgeons, who sold their wares and services out of the backs of their wagons, retreating only when the fighting became too fierce. Separate from these wagons were several shacks which housed the army whores. Sometimes the women were allowed within the camp itself, but Major General Milroy, the army commander, was more prudish than some of his predecessors. He had banished the women to the outskirts of town, causing much grumbling among the men who were now forced to hike half a mile to seek the women's services.

Jack was used to the walk and it didn't bother him anymore since it got him away from the monotony of camp life. Captain Adair understood this need on the part of the men, having been a foot soldier himself. Some of the officers believed that discipline was the only way to keep the men in line. But Adair knew differently. Keep them happy, well fed and well sexed, and they would fight. So when they weren't drilling, which wasn't very often anymore, Jack and the rest frequented the whores.

Any guilt Jack felt over the visits soon faded in the face of hard reality: at any moment he might be killed. He had left mountains of corpses behind him on the long road to Winchester. Ginnie and the others could never understand what it felt like to live this way. So he went to the whores, trying to enjoy the moment while he could.

Billy tagged along with him, at first keeping his mouth shut. Finally, his curiosity got the better of him. "Did she throw you over, Jack?" Jack glared ahead, refusing to look at him. When he said nothing, Billy took his silence as an affirmative and Jack was too angry to tell him otherwise.

When they got to the shacks, Billy disappeared and Jack walked to the end of the row where the raven-haired Blanche worked. It was early enough so that there was no line outside. He didn't even bother to knock but yanked on the wooden door, pulling it nearly off its ancient hinges. Blanche protested the interruption but Jack waved his money in her face and she quieted down. He took his time getting undressed, pulling his boots off while sitting on the end of the bed. Blanche stretched out on the dirty sheets, her dark hair contrasting with the vivid red of her lips and cheeks.

She might have been twenty five, but she had a used look that could have meant she was as much as forty. She rarely stepped into the light, and her rouged cheeks and the darkness of the hut hid any lines that might suggest her age. She paused to spray some cheap perfume into the air from an atomizer. Rather than covering the hut's dank smells, the perfume merged with it to create a new fragrance that turned Jack's stomach.

In her best seductive voice, she cooed, "Come to Blanche, sonny."

Jack lay back, pulling her roughly to him. He kissed her hard, forcing his tongue into her mouth. Rather than resisting, she kissed him back with equal force. He thought of Ginnie and her prudish innocence, knowing how she would have reacted to such treatment. Pulling Blanche on top of him, he began to fumble with his pants. He had them only partly open when he heard the bugle.

161

"Shit," he swore savagely under his breath, quickly redoing the catches.

"Where are you going, sweetie? You just got here." Blanche looked genuinely disappointed, more from the loss of her fee than anything else. Jack flicked her a dime as he dashed out the door.

Billy was already outside in the mud pulling on his boots. Running the whole way back to the camp, they found the company at attention when they arrived and slipped into their allotted spaces. Will Culp gave them each an angry glare, but the verbal chewing out would have to wait until later.

Captain Adair came jogging down the street trying to strap his sword into place as he ran. His blue uniform was rumpled, the trousers splattered with mud. A corporal ran beside him trying to hand him orders. He stopped before the company, snatching the orders out of the courier's hand.

As he scanned the lines, all eyes focused on him, trying to guess what he was about to tell them. A colonel rode by at the end of the row of barracks, reining in and calling for him. Adair went to his side and the two men conferred quietly. The captain saluted and came back to the men.

"We're moving out," he said in a voice that carried to the farthest man. "There's a reb army on the move about five miles south of here. They'll be here before sunset and we're going to stop them." Adair took a deep breath. "The report says that it's an entire corps."

Even the slightest movement in the ranks stopped at this announcement. Jack felt his stomach double up. An entire corps, twenty-thousand men. There were only five thousand Federals in the whole camp. And Hooker was hundreds of miles away with the main Federal body. There was nothing between the rebels and Pennsylvania. Except them.

"So get your gear and form up as fast as you can. Fall out."

The men ran for their barracks. Jack pulled his knapsack from the corner and his rifle out from under his bed. Then, as a last thought before he dove back through the door, he grabbed Ginnie's letter, balled up at the foot of the bed, and shoved it into his pocket.

Marching out of camp onto the road a few minutes later, they merged with the other companies of the regiment, moving southward, toward the oncoming rebels.

Chapter 17

MAKING PEACE

South of Winchester, Virginia
June 14, 1863

The roads were familiar to Wes. How many times had they marched along them before? Fifteen? Twenty? As they neared the town, all was quiet. The farms were empty, the crops unplanted. A ghost town with ghostly fields. Such a waste. Such a dismal way to live.

Wes heard the men discussing the Federal troops who were awaiting them in Winchester. Three young boys nearby, as ignorant as they were innocent, talked excitedly about getting into their first battle. Where they had come from Wes could not imagine. He thought the Confederacy had exhausted its resource of men, that all those not presently in uniform were either too old or too crippled to be of service. But here were three young boys, untouched as yet by the hell of war. They still believed in what they were fighting for.

As they marched, the three boys kept looking at Wes, their expressions carrying a wide-eyed look that Wes finally recognized as awe. These boys, walking next to him, saw Wes as a wise and experienced veteran. He nearly laughed out loud at the thought. Being a veteran meant knowing something these boys had yet to learn, if they lived long enough. As a veteran, he knew that each battle you survived, each bullet that missed your head by a hair, was one battle closer to the one that would take you away forever. Wes no longer seemed to care; he had lost his fear of death, and that, more than anything, made him a veteran.

Winchester came into sight as the army moved over a hill, appearing as it had after so many other marches. They had captured it time after time, but it never seemed to stay captured. Someone told him that the town had changed hands over sixty times, that on one memorable day alone it had switched sides thirteen times. All he knew was that he had lost count. Now, they had been ordered to take it again. Looking around, Wes saw no sign of the Yankees. He strolled on, pretending to ignore his admirers.

Suddenly, they heard a deep thud in the distance followed by a high whine that grew rapidly louder. Wes instinctively jumped into a ditch by the side of the road, landing hard in the mud. The explosion ripped the air around him, slamming him further down into the ground. His back was singed by blazing heat that flared for a moment, then subsided. Waiting until the rocks and dirt quit raining down, he crawled back up onto the road. Without emotion, he glanced momentarily at the bloody remains of three boys who had never before heard a shell coming toward them, and who would never hear one again. The area was strewn with torn flesh that bore no resemblance to the naïve faces he had seen a few seconds ago. His only thought was: that's one more shell that missed me; now I'm one shell closer to the big one.

The battle did not last long. Wes and the others reformed and attacked. They fired at the lead group of Yankees and watched as they turned and ran. Running in pursuit down the same streets in which they had fought so many times before, Wes dove behind a rail fence for protection. Waiting out a volley from up front, he rose quickly to fire, then ducked again to reload. His arms worked rapidly and without conscious thought, his body becoming an extension of his weapon, efficient, cold, impersonal, firing every thirty seconds or so. Others lying near him were firing rapidly at any target that presented itself. Wes could hear the Yankee bullets whizzing past him, smacking the brick building a few feet away. Wood splinters from the rail in front of him peppered his face as the enemy fire increased.

Suddenly, Wes realized that their line was being flanked, that he was in danger of being trapped. He looked around, searching for the best route by which to escape. Waiting for the right moment to retreat, he fired steadily over the fence rail at the blue-coated men approaching down the road. He reloaded again and laid the barrel of his gun back on the fence rail. Raising his head, he could just make out a thin line of blue clad Federals directly to his front. Behind this row and to the right, Wes saw a man yelling orders, his chevrons marking him as the company sergeant. Wes carefully drew a bead on the man, waiting for the smoke to lift enough to give him a clear shot. Bullets slammed into the fence with new intensity as his head attracted the attention of enemy sharpshooters.

He looked at the Federal sergeant, caught in his sights, realizing that the slow movement of his trigger finger was measuring the final seconds of this man's life. He waited, waited, for the right moment. But his finger would not move that last fraction of an inch. The hairs slowly rose on Wes' neck. He stared at the man, pulling his eye away from the gunsight to study him more carefully. In a split second of clarity, amid the utter chaos of the battle, he realized that it was his brother, Will.

He started to stand, forgetting where he was, when a bullet smashed the post in front of him, shooting jagged pieces of wood into his face. He fell to the ground, wiping frantically at the wounds. When he looked at his hand, it was covered with blood, his blood. He waited for the intense pain to hit. But it did not come.

A yell went up from beyond the fence and Wes stood to see a large group of rebels crashing into the flank of the Yankees who had, until that moment, been firing at him. Now they were running, fleeing so fast that they were stumbling over one another. Wes looked for Will, but could see only a few Yankees running for the woods beyond the road.

Then they were gone. Wes wiped at his face again. This time there was less blood and only a little pain. His fingertips felt for the splinters of wood embedded in his cheek and, gingerly, he pulled them free.

Moving down the street which was now filled with Confederates, Wes thought about the man who resembled Will. There had been several times in the past when Wes was certain he had seen his older brother, but the chance of actually running across him in battle was very slim. It made him chuckle, now, to think how he had been fooled again, and how his momentary confusion had bought some northern sergeant a few more days of life.

Wes walked over to look at a group of captured Federals being led back through the town. There seemed to be hundreds of them and they badly outnumbered their guards.

A frantic Confederate officer rode up to Wes. "Well, boy, don't just stand there. Help with the escort here. We need every man." He galloped off to search for more men. Wes despised guard duty which was usually assigned to the dregs of the regiment, those too frightened to do anything else. But today he was tired of fighting. He had survived again. With a grimace, he fell into line beside the beaten bluecoats.

Most of the men marched with their heads slumped, exhausted, frightened. The rebel guards marched beside them every ten paces or so. Ahead of Wes, a wounded Yankee stumbled over a rock and landed heavily on the road. The guard nearest the fallen soldier kicked the man in the ribs, yelling, "Get up!" Too exhausted to move, the Federal simply curled into a ball, driving the guard to kick him again and again.

Images flashed through Wes' mind, memories of the way he had been treated as a prisoner. Suddenly, he could not bear to see this man abused, Yankee or no. He shoved the guard away, using the barrel of his musket as a lever against the man's chest. The rebel lost his balance and fell, his face a mask of rage. Wes stood over the Yankee, his musket at the ready, prepared to fend off another attack by the irate guard. At that moment, however, the mounted officer returned and quieted the outburst. The Confederate guard glowered at Wes, then moved to catch up with the prisoners.

Wes knelt to help the Yankee. The man uncoiled painfully, allowing Wes to assist him to his feet. Looking at Wes for a moment, his filthy face softened into a smile. "Thanks," he said. Then, gasping, he peered at him more closely. "Culp?"

Wes squinted at the man, trying to place him. The stranger's face

165

gradually transformed itself into one from his childhood. "Billy Holtzworth? Is it you?" The man nodded. He bore only the slightest resemblance to the boy Wes had known in Gettysburg. The two stood grinning at each other in amazement. Back in Gettysburg, Wes had despised Billy. Now, all of that seemed distant and childish. The surprise of seeing someone from his other life made him wonder who else might be here. What about the officer who looked like Will?

"The others?" Wes asked, searching Billy's face.

"Warren got away. And I saw your brother running off just before the line caved in." Wes drew a sudden breath, realizing how near he had come to killing his own brother. Billy continued, unaware of Wes' inner turmoil. "Jack Skelly and I tried to run, but they got him in the shoulder and I stayed by him until they dragged me off."

"Skelly? Where is he?" Wes said carefully.

"I left him with some other wounded men back up the road, under a clump of trees off to the right. Wes, do me one favor, will ya?"

Wes' mind was in a whirl, thinking about his brother and Skelly both being here. But Billy grabbed his arm. "Look after Jack, will you? I think he's hurt pretty bad. Maybe you can find a doctor for him."

Wes stared at Billy for a moment, frowning in an effort to comprehend all of this. He had suddenly been pulled back among people he thought were out of his life forever. Billy, Jack, Will had been mere shadowy memories until a moment ago, until this quirk of fate had thrown them together again.

Billy thought he understood Wes' hesitation. "Listen, I don't care much for this war and I'll wager you don't either. What matters now is getting home. Jack needs help. Please."

"Yeah, o' course I'll look after him," Wes mumbled. Billy nodded his thanks, then put out his hand. Wes took it and, for a long moment, held it warmly. Billy was pushed back into line by a guard and, with a final look over his shoulder, disappeared into the distance.

Wes left the guard detail and set off in search of Jack, feeling oddly light-headed. He had expected hatred and rejection from his former friends but, instead, Billy had seemed glad to see him. He wondered whether the present course of the war would change the feelings of some of the others, too. The South seemed to be winning. The rebels had shown such persistence that it was only a matter of time before the politicians put a stop to all the killing.

At the top of the hill, he saw a clump of trees with a group of wounded soldiers lying beneath it, just as Billy had said. Wes walked closer, looking at each face. Then a voice broke the quiet. "Culp!"

Away from the others, Jack Skelly lay against a tree, a bloody bandage wrapped around his right shoulder. Wes steeled himself for a hostile confrontation, expecting to feel a rush of anger against this man who had taken so much from him. But Wes saw only another sorry bluecoat, wounded and hurting. It could well have been his brother.

He walked slowly toward him, kneeling so that their faces were on the same level. "Hey, Jack."

"I sure never expected to see you again." Jack's pained voice was filled with amazement.

Wes tried to think of something to say. "It's been a long time."

"Yeah. You've changed. You look older. I hardly recognized you. But you're still short, aren't you?"

Wes laughed in spite of himself. In that other life, he might have lost his temper and punched someone for saying as much. But here, surrounded on all sides by the enormous issues which drove the war, the matter of his stature seemed laughable. Rather, it was more like a joke that now linked them. "How's that arm?" he asked Jack.

"It hurts pretty bad, but I think I got most of the bleeding stopped."

"We've got to get you to a doctor."

Jack nodded, the movement making him wince in pain. Wes stood, looking back toward the town, and searched for the red banner which would signify a hospital. He saw one on the far side of the road three or four hundred yards distant. Turning back to Skelly he asked, "Can you walk?"

"I don't know."

Wes bent, lifted under Jack's good arm, and helped him to his feet. Jack, obviously in great pain, sagged against Wes' body, his usable arm around Wes' shoulder. Wes led him off toward the hospital.

It seemed to take forever. Several Union prisoners stared at this unlikely duo, a man in gray assisting one in blue. Several times they had to stop when Jack fainted, and Wes ended by practically carrying him. Still, it was the better part of twenty minutes before they arrived at the hospital. The sound and the stench inside were nearly overpowering, and Jack, suddenly terrified, pulled back and tried to get away.

"Don't take me in there," he begged, his eyes wild, pleading. "I've seen what they do to you. I don't want to go in there."

Wes tried to soothe him. "They can help you. You have to see them. You'll die if they don't take care of you." In the end, it was only faintness and loss of blood that kept Jack from fleeing. He sagged limply against Wes as his legs gave out.

Sitting him against the wall outside the front door, Wes hurried inside to find a doctor. Two men were hunched over a table on which lay a young officer, writhing in pain. They were examining his left leg. It was obvious, even in the dimly lit room, that the man had caught a minie ball in the knee. The pulpy red flesh was peeled back to reveal white bone and ligament. Wes was used to seeing all manner of ghastly wounds on the battlefield, but his skin crawled as he looked at the man's knee. The doctor straightened, nodding to his companion. As the assistant took the officer's shoulders to hold him down, the man began to panic, yelling for heavenly intervention. He screamed at the doctors to leave him alone, to let him die rather than put him through this torture. But the doctor grabbed a bloody rag and, after soaking it with the solution from a brown bottle, placed the rag over the man's mouth. He quieted almost immediately.

The doctor turned and took a knife from a nearby table. Lifting the officer's leg, he sliced quickly through the flesh, circling the leg above the knee as Wes watched, horrified. Leaving a flap of skin to cover the stump, he picked up a large silver saw. Quickly – he had obviously done the same thing many times before – he lined up the teeth of the saw in the cut he had just made and yanked back firmly. Wes winced at the sound of metal against bone, turning away as his stomach started to rebel at the sight.

When the sawing stopped, he watched the assistant take the man's lower leg and toss it deftly over several occupied cots onto a pile of severed limbs in a corner of the room. The doctor was busy probing into the bloody stump with a needle and thread. When he was finished, the doctor straightened up, massaging his cramped back with bloody hands. Two men stepped up to the table and carried the officer away.

Catching sight of Wes he asked, "Well, what is it, boy? You've been standing there for too long to be hurt very badly. Come over and let me look at you."

"I'm not here for me," Wes informed him quickly. "I have a friend who needs help. He's hit in the shoulder. Can you take care of him?"

The doctor approached, and Wes got a good look at his face. He was tall with sandy brown hair and a huge mustache that hung boldly on either side of his lip. He peered down impatiently at Wes through wire rim spectacles. Exhaling dramatically, he blew the hair around his lips sideways. "Such a loyal friend, indeed," he said with a hint of sarcasm. "Anything to get you out of the battle, I suppose." Wes bristled at the man's tone, but held his tongue. "Well, lead on, then."

Wes led the way back to Jack who had slumped sideways to the ground. He was only partly conscious and looked up hazily as the doctor knelt to examine his wound. After a moment, the doctor glanced up at Wes. "This boy's a Yankee, you know."

Wes smiled wryly at him. "Yeah, I noticed."

"I've got lots of wounded Confederates worse off than this one," he grumbled, starting to get to his feet.

Wes was startled by the man's coldness. "But, he's a friend," Wes blurted before he could think. "We grew up together." The two stared at each other for a moment. Wes, wondering what the doctor's next move would be, said in a small voice, "Please."

The doctor turned back impatiently to Jack. "Well, I suppose a wound's a wound. Peter, fetch me my bag."

The assistant returned carrying a black medical bag. The doctor reached inside and pulled out a bottle. Wes, thinking it was something to help heal the wound, was shocked when the doctor took a long swig from it. Replacing the bottle, he pulled out another, pouring the contents liberally onto a rag which he pressed against Jack's shoulder. The reaction was electric; Jack straightened up and screamed in pain. "Stings a little, no?" said the doctor without emotion.

The shock of the pain seemed to leave Jack senseless, allowing the doctor to probe the wound in his shoulder. Wes leaned in to get a better view, but a scowl from the doctor made him back away. The doctor muttered to himself for a bit, then turned to Wes. "Done."

"Done?" Wes asked, trying to mask his incredulity.

"Well, there's not much to *be* done. Looks like the bullet hit the collar bone at an angle, tore up the shoulder and lodged inside somewhere. I could open him up, but he'll probably be better off if I don't go exploring. Either he'll get better or he'll die." Jack gasped. He had apparently been conscious enough to hear this cold assessment of his condition. Then the doctor was gone without another word to either the patient or his friend.

Wes sat wearily beside Jack, leaning against the front of the building. They stared off together into the falling night, and Jack's mind seemed to clear. He smiled at some thought and Wes looked at him, waiting for him to speak. "I was just thinking," Jack said, "about the time we tossed you into the creek when we were kids. It's like we were both somebody else back then." He paused, struggling to overcome a fresh wave of pain. Then his face relaxed again. "You're the last person I would have expected to come to my rescue."

Wes nodded. "I've hated you for a long time. I thought I still did. I expected it would give me pleasure to shoot you."

"I suppose I deserve that. You and I have had a lot of bad blood." Jack's voice was a whisper. "War changes you, whether you think it will or not." He looked Wes in the eye, sizing him up. Finally, he said, "I'm not going to make it back, Wes."

Wes started to argue with him, but was silenced by Jack's intensity. "No. You know when it's gonna happen. I've had this feeling for a couple of days now. I'm not gonna get back home."

Wes stifled the urge to talk Jack out of his mood. He had heard others go on like this before, and had been surprised to find that they were often right. There must be some kind of warning, some inner voice that never speaks until the final moment is near. Since he couldn't argue with him, Wes listened.

"I need you to do something for me," Jack said. He paused a moment, then searched Wes' face again. "Will you do something for me?" Wes nodded. "I don't know if you'll ever get back to Gettysburg. But you're headed north. Hell, the way things are going, you may just win this damn war." He winced in pain for a moment. "Anyway," he said, gasping, "if you ever do get back, I want you to get a message to Ginnie for me. I wanted to write her a letter, but..." – he motioned toward his useless arm.

Jack was silent for so long that Wes thought that he had fainted again. He leaned over to check him, and saw that his eyes were open. Deciding that he was trying to think of what to say, Wes waited. At length, Jack said, "We were supposed to get married in the fall. On my anniversary leave. But, I guess now...."

"Jack," Wes protested, "you still might make it."

Shaking his head Jack said, "If I do, I'll just be in some prison camp down south. Hell, I'll probably starve to death. I've heard stories about your prison camps. Anyway, I want you to write a letter for me. I haven't treated her real well. I want to straighten things out between us. So she'll know what happened."

Wes got pencil and paper and, for the next ten minutes, wrote while Jack poured out his heart to Ginnie. It was an eerie experience, writing a letter from his former worst enemy to his former best girl. The words could almost have been his own although, he noticed with annoyance, Jack was much more polished at using them than he was.

As he wrote Jack's apologetic words to Ginnie, he felt his own love resurrected, born afresh out of the place that was left blackened by her rejection a year ago. Jack's wound, while ending Jack's hopes for the future, had rekindled his own. He tried to concentrate on his task so that Jack would not notice his rising joy. After Jack had explained about the wound, and the possibility of death or prison camp, he paused, unable to go on.

They sat in silence for a time, watching others hurry past the door. Then Jack looked at Wes. "You know, it's strange. I never held much faith in God. But just before you came up, I was praying that I would find somebody to take a message to Ginnie. I can't believe it's you. But I guess, in a way, you're the perfect one. It's funny, sometimes, how God answers prayers." After a pause he added, "She could never put you out of her mind. Even though I wanted her to."

The sun was setting, and they each were lost in their own thoughts. Wes could see tension in Jack's face, a pain that did not seem to come from his wound. At length, Jack spoke, choosing his words carefully. "Wes, there's more," he said, suddenly on the verge of tears. He opened his fist for the first time and Wes saw a scrap of paper, crumpled and bloody. "You have to know about it....There's going to be a baby. Ginnie's and my baby."

Wes was struck dumb, completely unable to move or think. After an eternity, he whispered in disbelief, "A baby?"

"In the winter, sometime," Jack said, his lip quivering. "She wanted to get married sooner than September, because of the baby. But that's all changed now. I can't get back to make a home for her or to give the baby a name. She's scared, Wes. If I don't get there to marry her, I don't know what she'll do. She'll be ruined. You'll look after her, won't you?"

Wes hesitated again, thunderstruck. He felt torn in two. Ginnie had given herself to someone else, and now she was in desperate trouble. But perhaps he was the one person who could save her. The irony of the request astounded him. He fought off anger, joy, pain; what was left was a vacuum, a place where he felt nothing. He looked at Jack who was caving in to his pain, and said quietly, "Tell her I'll do it. Tell her I love her, and I know about her problem. Tell her I'll take care of her." Wes picked up his pencil again. "Tell her that. In the letter."

When Jack finished his dictation, he succumbed to his exhaustion and pain, fainting into sleep. Wes pocketed the letter and leaned back, closing his eyes and shutting down his mind before his emotions completely tore him apart.

He awoke the next morning still sitting beside Jack. He shook him gently but was unable to rouse him. Leaning closer, he saw that Jack's face was a pasty white, and for a moment he thought he had died in the night. But his chest was still moving, although very slightly, and it was apparent to Wes that Jack had only a short time. Knowing that he could not just leave him, he looked around for help.

A wagon train of wounded soldiers and northern prisoners was moving south on the road in front of them, so Wes had Jack loaded aboard. A doctor looked briefly at him and said to Wes, "He's not going to last long."

Wes merely nodded. He walked alongside the wagon for a few minutes, then stopped and watched the train disappear into the distance. Unconsciously, he put his hand into his pocket to make sure that Jack's letter was really there. Finally, he turned away to search for his company, to begin the northward march toward home, back to Ginnie.

Chapter 18

THE COMING THUNDER

Gettysburg, Pennsylvania
June 26, 1863

Ginnie sat bolt upright in bed, startled awake by a banging on the front door. Even as she pulled herself out of bed she knew what it was. Georgia's baby was coming. She saw her mother hurry past her door, pulling an old robe around her.

When they opened the front door, they found a young girl with disheveled brown hair standing there in the dark. Ginnie recognized her immediately – Mina Williams, the niece of the Haskells who owned the Wagon Hotel. The hotel stood immediately across Baltimore Street from Georgia's home. It was apparent that the girl had been roused out of bed by her mother to bring them a message from Georgia. But Georgia was not due for another two weeks.

Mina said, "Miss McClellan said for you to come right away. She said she's got the pains."

Mary nodded and told the girl to come in while she gathered her things. Hurrying to her room to dress, she began issuing orders at the top of her lungs, giving Ginnie instructions about what to do while Mary was at Georgia's, a third of a mile away, south of town.

Ginnie interrupted. "I'll go with you."

"No, you won't," Mary replied sharply. "I need you to stay here and take care of the house and look after the boys. Anyway, there's sewing to be done."

"I can do it there," Ginnie protested. "I'll bring the boys with me and look after them so you don't have to worry about them."

Her mother rushed past her into the kitchen. "Nonsense!" she said. "That house is too little for all of us. Besides, I don't want the boys there when the baby comes." And with that she grabbed her hat and was out the door, with Mina in tow.

As Ginnie shut the door, she felt the familiar nausea creep over her. Resting her hand on her stomach, she thought of the life that was growing there. It had been a month since she had written to Jack about her pregnancy. With each new day, the anxiety caused by his silence grew deeper. She fretted that he might have gotten the note but had chosen not to respond. Or perhaps he was....She didn't want to think about it.

With sleep out of the question and dawn not far away, Ginnie decided to start her morning chores, the first of which was to get her brother Harry and their boarder, Isaac Brinkerhoff, out of bed. Isaac was six years old, the son of Wilhelm and Gretchen Brinkerhoff. Mrs. Brinkerhoff was a lady's maid and housekeeper for Mrs. David Wills, the wife of a well-known attorney in town. She lived in at the Wills' home and was free only on Wednesday evenings and Sundays. Since Mr. Brinkerhoff worked long hours at the Rupp Tannery, they were unable to keep Isaac at home and were forced to find some place to board him. Mary Wade had offered her services, since it would mean extra income for the family.

Isaac required special care since he had been crippled from a childhood disease and was unable to move his legs. As time went on, a greater portion of his care had been entrusted to Ginnie. Now that Georgia was ready to have her baby, Ginnie found herself charged with the care not only of Isaac but also the youngest of her three brothers, eight-year-old Harry, in addition to her normal chores of cleaning, cooking and assisting with the sewing.

Halfway through the morning, the clatter of hooves sounded outside in the street. The front door opened with a bang, and Ginnie sighed to herself, suddenly remembering that she had told her brother, Jack, to stop by that morning.

John Wade was seventeen and had joined the army only three days earlier, enlisting against his mother's wishes in the 21st Pennsylvania Cavalry Regiment which had been stationed in Gettysburg for the past week. He was small for his age but, because he was a good horseman, they had accepted him and made him a bugler. However, the uniform he had been issued was much too large for him, and Ginnie had told him to bring it home so she could alter it.

"Mama! Gin! Where the hell is everybody?"

Ginnie snapped, "Watch your tongue around the boys."

"Sorry, Gin. Where's Mama?"

"At Georgia's," she told him. "The baby's coming early."

Jack frowned. "God damn! Just when I'm leaving town."

Ginnie started to reprimand him again, then checked herself. Jack was a soldier now, trying to act like a man, and was probably facing real danger. She smiled at him and said quietly, "Take off your uniform if you want me to work on it."

She watched him as he stripped off his jacket. He was skinny and fragile looking, not more than a boy, and she shuddered as she imagined him in the midst of a far away battle, surrounded by flying bullets and dying men. As he handed her the jacket, Ginnie held it for a moment, the fragrant wool suddenly reminding her of Jack. She picked up her thimble and needle and went to work quickly before the tears could overwhelm her.

"Hurry up," he urged her. "My regiment's about to leave. I'll be absent without leave. They'll court martial me and I'll spend the war in jail!"

"Nonsense," Ginnie said, grinning. "You're a bugler. They don't put buglers in jail. Unless you blow the wrong bugle call. Maybe you ought to practice while you're waiting for me."

About 12:30, they heard a commotion on Baltimore Street – shouting voices and the noise of several horses. Jack ran outside to find out what was going on, and was back in a minute. "Ginnie!" he shouted. "The rebs are coming. That was some of the scouts from our regiment. The rebs are coming down the Chambersburg Pike and they'll be here in an hour!" She jumped to her feet and looked at him in horror. "I've got to *go!*" he yelled, grabbing the uniform out of her hands.

"Are you sure the rebels are coming?" she asked in alarm. Each day brought fresh rumors that Confederate armies were approaching from every direction but, so far, no gray uniforms had appeared.

"I'm not going to stay around to find out," Jack shouted. "My regiment's already left and I have to catch up with them." He started for the door, still struggling into his uniform.

"Jack!" she called sharply. He stopped and looked at her, realizing for the first time that she was afraid. He walked over and hugged her. Clutching him desperately and trying not to cry, she told him, "You be careful. Don't get up front where they can shoot at you. I don't want you to get hurt."

He smiled confidently. "Don't worry, Ginnie. I can take care of myself. You just stay indoors when the rebs come and you'll be all right. They're looking for me, not you." Ginnie reflected on that thought, suddenly wondering who would help them if he was wrong. She watched him ride off, nearly numb with worry.

As Jack headed toward Baltimore Street, Ginnie saw him wave to their eleven-year-old brother, Sam, who was standing in front of the James Pierce house on the corner. Sam, the middle of the three Wade boys, lived with the Pierces and helped them with their butcher business. At the last moment, Jack saluted Ginnie as he turned left, galloping north toward town. She waved a restrained goodbye, suddenly aware of how frightened she was.

She spent the next hour shuttering up the house, doing everything she could think of to make it secure, or perhaps to convince any rebels who might chance by that no one was home. Finally, unable to bear the tension any longer, she decided to take the boys to Georgia's house so that everyone could be together if the rebels really did come. She gathered a few things, then picked up Isaac and pushed Harry out the door. As they started toward Baltimore Street, a noise behind her made her turn toward Washington Street at the opposite end of Breckenridge. What she saw made her stop in terror.

175

There, at the far end of her block, marching down the middle of South Washington Street, was a column of Confederate soldiers. The battle flag at the head of the column, its blue "X" filled with stars, left no doubt about their identity. They moved silently, almost ominously, while she stared at them, rooted to the spot in shock.

Wavering in indecision, she turned back toward Baltimore Street hearing loud voices from that direction, and saw several soldiers in gray uniforms walking by. It was true. The feared moment had finally come. They had been invaded! With the road to Georgia's house blocked, there was nothing to do but return home and bolt the door.

A few minutes later, Sam was pounding on the locked door. When Ginnie let him in, he explained breathlessly, "Mr. Pierce told me to take their horse and ride it south down the Baltimore Pike and hide it in the woods somewhere, and wait until the rebs leave. If I don't, they'll steal the horse."

"I can't let you do that," Ginnie protested. "Mama wouldn't let you go if she were here. There are rebel soldiers all over the place." Sam ignored her, rummaging through his things for his Gettysburg Zouave uniform. Ginnie, trying to keep control of herself, shouted, "You're not going!"

Sam, deaf to her protests, jammed some bread in his pockets, clapped his fez on his head, which was as much of his uniform as he could find, and said, "Well, at least they'll know I'm a Zouave." He headed for the door, but Ginnie blocked his way. Dodging her adroitly, he said, "If you slow me down, they'll have a better chance of catching me." And he was gone.

Near panic now, Ginnie started to follow him, but a moment later he appeared from behind the Pierce's house, mounted on their valuable iron gray mare, and clattered onto the road, heading south at a gallop. He leaned on the horse's neck, his red fez planted tightly on his head. Ginnie called to him but he rode on.

Returning to the safety of the house, she watched at the window for a few minutes, engulfed by uncertainty. Was her mother safe? Had the baby come yet? Would Sam make his escape? She moved back to her sewing, but before she had even picked up the needle, she heard more voices in the street. Looking out the front window again, she saw Mrs. Pierce shouting, "You don't want the boy. He's not our boy." A flush of shock washed over Ginnie.

Opening the door, she saw a group of soldiers on Baltimore Street leading a gray mare north. It was the Pierce's horse, and Sam, missing his fez, was sitting on its back looking small and scared. Ginnie ran out onto the porch and heard the soldiers laughing at her brother as they led the horse by its reins. Sam slouched in the saddle, his hands tied to the pommel in front of him.

Mrs. Pierce was shouting at the soldiers from her front door. "That's our horse. That boy doesn't belong to us. He just works here. We told him to hide the horse. Let him go. You don't want the boy." The soldiers looked indifferently at her, ignoring her words.

Ginnie ran down to the corner and, before she thought better of it, found herself in among the soldiers, grabbing the bridle at the horse's mouth. Sam looked down at her in naked terror. His face gave her the courage she needed.

"Stop!" she shouted to the group. Surprised, then amused by her appearance, they started to make rude comments, but she fixed her angry gaze on the soldier who had hold of the reins. Noticing that he was wearing Sam's fez, she felt a sudden fury. "This is my *brother*," she shouted at the man. "The horse doesn't belong to us. He was only doing what he was told to do. Let him go! You can have the horse. But let him go."

They responded with laughter, crowding around to get a closer look at her. In a boiling rage, Ginnie turned to the nearest soldiers and screamed, "Is this the kind of cowards you rebels are? Do you make war on eleven-year-old boys? Does that make you feel big and strong?" The words were coming without conscious thought.

The soldiers looked at each other sheepishly, cowed by her contempt. The man wearing the fez took it off and held it in front of him. He said flatly, "We have orders to bring all horses and riders in. You'll have to come up and talk to the lieutenant." And with that they quieted down, turned their eyes north and kept going.

Ginnie was left standing in the middle of the street, helplessly watching as Sam turned in the saddle to look at her with pleading eyes. "It's OK," she called to him. "I'll get Mama. We'll make them let you go." She turned, and saw Mrs. Pierce still standing in her half-closed doorway, the only remaining target for Ginnie's fear-driven rage.

Walking toward her, she stood in the middle of Breckenridge Street and shouted, "What were you thinking when you told an eleven-year-old boy to hide your horse? Are you crazy?" Searching for words, she finally said in a threatening tone, "If anything happens to Sam, I don't know what I'll do with you!" She whirled and ran back to the house, then dragged the boys hurriedly over to the Pierce's. "Here," she demanded. "The least you can do is watch the boys until I get back. I have to go get Sam."

Without waiting for a response, she ran down Baltimore Street, looking nervously in every yard and around every corner for armed men who might stop her. She saw several groups of rebels but kept her eyes forward and hurried as fast as she could. When she arrived at the McClellan house, she burst in through the door with a half-sob of exhaustion and relief.

Mary looked up from her seat in the parlor. "Ginnie, what's wrong? Where're the boys?"

"Mama, they've taken Sam!"

Mary rose and came into the kitchen, shutting the parlor door behind her. "Who's taken Sam?" she demanded.

177

"The rebels," she said, half in tears. Suddenly, she felt responsible for Sam, wondering if her mother would blame her for this predicament. Then Ginnie saw the little form wrapped in the blanket and cradled gently in Mary's arms. Overwhelmed by a sudden rush of emotion, she took the baby from her mother.

"It's a boy," said Mary while she gathered her things. "Louis Kenneth McClellan." Ginnie stroked the baby's soft face, mesmerized by the tiny life which had made its appearance in the midst of such chaos.

The double house was home to two families, and each one had its own entrance fronting on Baltimore Street. Mary slipped out their front door and ran the few yards to the other front door, the one that led to the opposite side of the house where Catherine McClain lived with her four children. Catherine's husband, a Federal soldier, had been killed in Virginia several weeks earlier and Georgia had helped the grieving widow by watching her children, despite her late pregnancy. Catherine now offered to watch the new baby so that Mary and Ginnie could go into town to find Sam.

"We'll be back as soon as we can," Mary assured her before rushing outside again.

Mary and Ginnie walked rapidly up Baltimore Street toward the Diamond. They saw many gray clad soldiers, marching in groups, standing idly on porches, arguing with citizens. Ginnie watched them warily, feeling threatened by the dozens of eyes that followed them as they walked resolutely up the center of the road.

No one stopped them, however, until they neared the Diamond where a gruff looking man with black whiskers stepped off one of the porches and told them to halt. "Where are you heading?" he asked, eyeing Ginnie.

Mary turned to the man and looked him directly in the eye. "I'm looking for your general."

The man, obviously amused by Mary's forwardness, asked, "And which general would that be, ma'am?"

Mary's eyes blazed. "How should I know? He's *your* general, isn't he?"

"Well, yes, ma'am, I suppose he is."

Another soldier, this one dressed in the uniform of an officer, stepped forward. "Can I be of service, ma'am?" The whiskered man backed off with a deferential look at the officer.

Mary turned toward the young man and repeated her request. The officer asked why she should want to see a general, then listened attentively as Mary explained the situation. Clearing his throat politely he said, "Well, ma'am, I'm General Early's adjutant. Perhaps I could arrange for you to meet him briefly to repeat your story."

Mary nodded, and she and Ginnie followed the officer to Fahnestock's store where they were told to wait outside. A moment later, he returned and led them inside to a group of men sitting around a table. One particularly dirty officer leaned back in his chair, his feet sprawled on the table in front of him. Ginnie stared at him, unable to believe that someone who looked so disreputable could be a general. His uniform was in tatters, his huge beard matted with dirt and mud, his eyes sullen. He glanced up at Mary and Ginnie as though they were intruders. Chewing on the wad in his cheek while he slowly examined them, he spat noisily on the floor at their feet before speaking.

"Well, damn it, woman, speak up. What do you want?"

Mary stiffened at the affront. Ginnie put her hand on her mother's arm, but Mary was already moving toward General Early. "General, I know you're busy, what with invading *my town* and all. But your soldiers have arrested my eleven-year-old son for trying to ride out of town on a horse that wasn't even ours, but belongs to a neighbor. You've got the horse. I would like my son back! You have no right to keep him."

Early smiled sarcastically. "Oh, I don't know. It seems to me I can do just about anything I god-damn please – and there ain't a whole shitload you can do about it." He cleared his throat. "Ma'am."

Ginnie's mouth dropped open, incensed to hear such talk directed at her mother. But Mary glared at the general for a moment while she gathered her thoughts. At length she said, "General, I've heard many stories about how ill-mannered you rebels are. And you, sir, certainly live up to every one of them. You terrorize young boys, and you show no respect for women. You ought to be ashamed of yourself. And you, supposedly a general!"

There was a deathly silence in the room as the officers waited uncertainly for General Early's reaction. He pulled his feet down from the table and leaned forward. Bursting into a great guffaw, he looked around the room as the rest of the men joined in the laughter.

"Men, this here's why I stayed a bachelor all my life." Early muttered something to the young officer, who turned and motioned for Mary to follow him. She did so without another word to the general. Ginnie scurried along behind them.

Outside the store, Ginnie watched as the officer opened a cellar door and disappeared inside. He reappeared a moment later with Sam in tow. Sam broke from his grasp and ran into Mary's arms, burying his face in her shoulder. She pulled him down the road toward home, but paused after a few steps and turned back to the officer.

"Thank you, sir. You have been most kind." The man dipped his hat gallantly to her and smiled. Mary asked, "May I know your name?"

"I'm Major Douglas, ma'am. Henry Kyd Douglas. At your service." And with that he turned and walked back into the shop.

That night Ginnie stayed barricaded indoors with the boys, jumping in alarm at every noise. Mary had returned to Georgia's for the night and the quiet in the house frightened Ginnie. Out the window, she could see the sky glowing red with the reflection of some distant fire. Fear that the rebels might burn the town made sleep a long time in coming.

She was up early the next morning. The stillness outside was frightening, as if everyone had fled the town and left her alone. She made her way to Baltimore Street before the boys woke, relieved that no soldiers were in sight. Seeing Mr. Buehler, the postmaster, talking with Professor Jacobs from the Seminary, Ginnie walked over to them and asked, "Are they gone?"

Mr. Buehler nodded, but his face was a mask of anger. "Yes, they are. But they left a mess behind them. They burned the railroad bridge over the creek, they cut the telegraph lines and they made off with most of the food in town, like the vultures they are. They even stopped the mail."

Ginnie sighed in relief. The news about the rebels leaving was so good that these acts of destruction sounded minor by comparison. The red glow in the night had only been the bridge; and telegraph lines could be repaired.

Being cut off from the outside world, however, did not stop the rumor mills; instead, it caused them to work overtime. Primary, of course, were rumors to the effect that the entire Confederate army was about to return and surround the town. People were saying that the force that had occupied the town was only a small part of the army, sent ahead to scout for supplies, and that the rest of the army would soon be coming through. Ginnie found it hard to imagine more soldiers than those she had already seen. They had been everywhere, in all the buildings, filling the streets, eating all the food. If that had been only a small part of the rebel army, she wondered how the Federals would be able to fight the main army. And where *were* all the Federal soldiers? Had Gettysburg simply been abandoned to the enemy?

During the next days, many of the store owners left town with their goods, fearing that the rebels would return. On her daily trips to her sister's house, Ginnie saw the few remaining carts and horses being piled high with anything of value. In the backyards of many houses she noticed families burying their treasures, the surest way of protecting them from scavengers.

On Sunday, June 28, Ginnie took Isaac to his parents and walked with Harry all the way up to St. James Lutheran Church, a block east of the Diamond. As she sat in the pew, the prayers spilled out of her – for the safety of the town, the baby, her family. For Jack's safety, and for his return to help her.

The prayers relieved her mind a little and after the service her mood was the happiest it had been in days. As she walked through the Diamond on the way home, she saw a cheering crowd gathered. Looking down Baltimore Street she saw one of the most splendid sights she could remember. There coming up the street was a long column of Federal cavalry, horses two abreast, mounted troopers in mud-spattered uniforms, spurs and gear clanking. As they rode into the square in the noonday sun, the crowd pressed around them on both sides of the street, forming a human corridor through which they passed. Ginnie could see from their sweat-streaked faces that they were weary from hours in the saddle. Nevertheless, they smiled at the reception and waved to the crowd.

As though from nowhere, buckets appeared by the side of the road and women raised overflowing tin cups filled with cold water. This boon was greedily accepted by the troopers, many of whom stopped their horses in the middle of the street so that they could satisfy their thirst. Ginnie saw one soldier take off his hat, pour the cup of water over his head, then lean down to return the cup to the young woman who had offered it, only to embrace her with his free arm and kiss her lustily. Such was the mood of the crowd that it applauded this somewhat unseemly show with cheers and laughter.

The feeling of security evaporated, however, the next morning, Monday, the 29th, when the cavalry mounted their horses and rode south out of Gettysburg. Ginnie, standing at the end of Breckenridge Street, felt oppressed by a fresh sense of abandonment as she watched them clatter by.

There was no mail again that day or the next, and the lack of a reply from Jack created a growing anxiety in Ginnie. More than once she found herself frozen in the midst of some chore, her thoughts miles away. Her mind kept drifting back to the postal stoppage. If the mail could not get through, how would Jack be able to? What if he were trying to get back to Gettysburg right then, only to be captured by the rebels? The thought was horrible, Jack in one of those awful prison camps because of trying to get back to her. And with him a prisoner, the wedding might not be able to take place until it was too late. And what would the town think then? Or Mrs. Skelly, or Georgia...or, worst of all, her mother?

After breakfast, she dropped the boys at the Pierce's, saying she needed to go to Georgia's to help her mother. But she turned north when she reached Baltimore Street, walking slowly as though uncertain of her destination. A short time later she found herself standing in front of Jack's house, staring at the door. She was trying to decide whether to knock when the door opened. Mrs. Skelly stood in the doorway, a look of surprise on her face. "Virginia?"

Embarrassed, Ginnie struggled to think of some reason for the visit. Mrs. Skelly looked at her uncertainly. "Can I do something for you?"

Ginnie found herself on the verge of tears. "I just need to talk to someone. I'm so scared."

Mrs. Skelly opened the door and ushered Ginnie into the parlor where they sat facing one another. Even before she opened her mouth, however, Ginnie was unnerved by the meeting. She was certain that guilt was written all over her face. She looked at Jack's mother for a moment, thinking seriously about telling her everything. It would be such a relief to let it out, to stop carrying the burden alone.

But with that thought came the realization that Mrs. Skelly would not believe her, that she had no proof that Jack was the father, that this woman who never had liked her would certainly rush to defend her son against what she saw as a slanderous charge. Ginnie sighed, closing her eyes and feeling exhaustion in every muscle in her body.

Mrs. Skelly asked with concern, "Are you ill, Virginia?"

"No," she said wearily. "My sister just had a baby and my mother has been with her for several days. I have the house and the boys to look after, and I guess I'm just really tired. And I'm so worried about the rebels coming back."

"Yes, isn't it awful what they did to us," said Mrs. Skelly, shaking her head.

Desperate for something to say, Ginnie asked, "Have you heard anything from Jack? I haven't gotten a letter in weeks."

"Yes," she said slowly. "Jack told me that you two were writing. That's very...nice," she added, her tone betraying her disapproval. "He writes me regularly, of course. And tells me everything," she added, as though to warn her. "But I haven't received a letter for about two weeks. I'm sure it's just because the mail has been delayed. There is a war, you know," she said, feigning light-heartedness.

Ginnie glanced at the floor, her nervousness making her almost incoherent. "I just don't want him to get hurt," she mumbled.

"Of course you don't," Mrs. Skelly said soothingly. "We don't want anyone to get hurt. I'm sure we'll hear from him soon and find that everything's all right." After an awkward pause, Mrs. Skelly asked, "Is there something else?"

Ginnie, her nerves near the breaking point, stood and moved toward the door. "No. Thank you. With my mother gone, I just needed to talk to someone. Thank you." She slipped out of the door without looking back.

It was nearing noon as she started dejectedly back toward the house. The visit had been a disaster. Mrs. Skelly was certain to sense that something was wrong. As she walked, deep in thought, two girls from her class in school saw her and ran up excitedly.

"Isn't it wonderful? All the soldiers!" one asked enthusiastically.

Ginnie frowned, "What soldiers?"

"The army's here," they told her. "Our troops have returned. They're up at the Diamond right now. The rebels were coming back into town, but they ran off when they saw our troops. Come up with us to see them."

Ginnie felt a momentary excitement, then remembered that her mother was waiting for her at Georgia's. She shook her head, "You go on without me." She watched as the girls moved off north, giggling as they talked about the possibility of meeting some eligible soldiers.

She spent the afternoon helping her mother with the chores and watching the baby. Outside, carts and horses rushed up and down the street, causing Georgia to complain about the noise. Watching from the window as the troops milled about, Ginnie wished that one of them would turn out to be Jack.

It was well after dark when she walked back to the house on Breckenridge. Not ready to deal with putting the boys to bed and cleaning up around the house, she walked past the house toward Washington Street and stood for a long moment staring west into the night. On one of the far hills, she could see hundreds of camp fires twinkling in the night. Knowing that so many troops were nearby to protect them was a comforting thought.

Hoof beats broke her reverie and she turned to see two troopers reining in their horses. Both appeared unaware of Ginnie's presence in the darkness. One dismounted and moved to the side of the road to look at the fires.

After a moment, the trooper turned and saw Ginnie standing there. He tipped his hat to her with a quiet, "Evenin', miss."

"Am I glad to see you," she exclaimed. "Where are you men from?"

The trooper, looking off to the west, said, "The 8th New York Cavalry, Miss. We're General Buford's troops."

"Are you going to be staying here long?"

The trooper, still looking anxiously toward the west, muttered, "As long as we can – as long as they let us, Miss."

"Who?" Ginnie asked.

"Them." The trooper pointed toward the distant campfires.

"You mean those aren't our soldiers?" Ginnie asked, suddenly sensing the tension in the trooper's voice.

He turned and looked grimly at Ginnie. "No, Miss. That's an entire corps of General Lee's army. Thirteen thousand men."

"But you can hold them, can't you?" Ginnie asked, feeling the fear creep up her spine.

The soldier sighed wearily. "I don't know, Miss. There's only twenty-five hundred of us. But we'll fight to the last. That's all I can tell you."

"Oh, my god," was all that Ginnie could manage before she fled back to the questionable safety of her house.

Chapter 19

THE FIRST DAY

Gettysburg, Pennsylvania
July 1, 1863

Ginnie's eyes snapped open as she struggled to remember the dream. It trickled out of her mind like water, however, and she was unable to grasp more than a few disturbing images. There was fighting, soldiers were shooting at each other. Her baby was there, but somehow it was lost. She remembered feeling terrible anxiety, looking for the baby, looking for Jack...and finding neither.

Sitting up she realized that it was later than she had thought. The sun was well up and she heard the sounds of Isaac and Harry playing quietly in their bedroom. For once, her stomach felt fine with no trace of morning sickness. Then she remembered the nightmare of the troops outside. They were not a dream, and the fight that was coming would be for real.

Dressing quickly, she looked out the window, but there was no one to be seen. The streets were empty and once again Ginnie wondered if the troops had left in the night. This time she would be thankful for their departure; if there were no troops, there would be no fight.

She fed the boys and busied herself doing some of the necessary housework. Harry kept interrupting her with the same request. "Gin, I want to go up to the Diamond with Tom and Dillie to see the horses and the soldiers. Their mothers let them go yesterday."

"You're not going," Ginnie said for the fourth time. "That's final!"

"But Dillie got to lead a horse for one of the soldiers. They said today he could ride him, if he goes back." Ginnie tried to ignore him. Finally Harry said, purposely under his breath, "Well, I'll just sneak out when you're not looking."

"You'll do no such thing," Ginnie said sternly. "If you even try, I'll take you down to stay with Mama."

Half an hour later, some time after nine o'clock, Ginnie heard a distant booming. "Is that thunder?" Isaac asked with a worried look.

Ginnie listened to the rhythmic thuds hoping that Isaac was right. But when higher pitched explosions punctuated the deep booms, she knew immediately that it was artillery. Her worried face confirmed the boys' fear. Harry, his face tense, asked, "Are they going to shoot at our house?"

She went to them, putting her arms around Harry's shoulders and looking into Isaac's frightened eyes. "We're going to be fine," she assured them. "Those guns are shooting way outside of town" – she gestured vaguely off toward the northwest – "and our soldiers will take care of those bad rebels." She hugged them with a little laugh, trying to humor them out of their worry. "If they try to come in here, I'll hit them over the head with my broom handle."

Isaac laughed, but Harry's expression didn't change. "If those cannons shoot our house, it'll fall down and we'll burn up. I've seen pictures of how cannons shoot houses."

"Harry, if the shooting gets any closer, we'll go down to Georgia's, all right? We'll be safe there. And you can see the new baby! Maybe you can even hold him," she added as an inducement.

"I don't wanna hold no baby!" Harry said with a frown.

Trying to decide what to do, Ginnie peered out the front window and saw a group of neighbors standing in the middle of the street, huddled together as though for protection, busily engaged in conversation. Telling the boys she would be back shortly, she slipped across the street to the group.

"They're fighting west of town," James Pierce was repeating for the benefit of newcomers to the group. "They've been fighting since early this morning, and the rebel guns are trained on the northwest corner of town."

"Do you think they'll come down this far?" a woman asked. "I don't want to get caught here if the rebels overrun the place again."

Pierce answered, "There's no chance of that. Our boys'll keep them outside of town. That's what they're here for, to protect the town. I don't think we need to worry."

"Just the same," said the first woman, "I think I'm going to leave. I won't get any sleep tonight, anyway, worrying about whether I'll wake up in the morning surrounded by Confederates again." Then with a perplexed look on her face she asked, "What are they doing here, anyway? Why did they pick on Gettysburg, of all places?"

Pierce shook his head. "I don't know. But I don't think it's wise for you to leave. An empty house is an invitation to looting. Look over there." He pointed to a house at the end of the street vandalized during the earlier rebel occupation. "I don't want that to happen to my house." The group stared bleakly at the broken windows, the still-open front door and the belongings scattered in the yard.

A new series of cannon shots sounded, much closer than before. The group, startled by the sound, looked anxiously to the northwest and then eyed each other uncertainly. As they started for their homes, a horseman came riding hard down Baltimore Street shouting as he passed every house: "The rebels are shelling the town. Get into your cellars or you'll be killed."

The group fled to their houses. Ginnie ran as fast as she could, cringing and waiting for the first shots to fall. She picked Isaac up by one arm, ignoring his cry of pain and herded Harry to the cellar. The next hours were hellish and Ginnie was afraid she would lose her mind. Between the boys weeping and the continuous explosions overhead, the confusion was simply overwhelming.

Finally, about eleven o'clock, she decided that it would be better to go down to Georgia's where they would be farther out of range. Leaving the boys in the cellar, she went upstairs, packed some clothes, gathered a little food together, then stuck her head out the back door for a minute to listen to the sound of the cannons. She thought it was definitely getting louder. As she listened, she heard a new sound for the first time: tiny snaps that sounded like fireworks. Realizing that this was the sound of rifle fire, she hurried to get the boys ready to leave.

She put the two large satchels on the porch and shifted Isaac to her left hip, then locked the front door. She turned to look for Harry as she slipped the key into her pocket. He was nowhere to be seen.

Alarmed, she ran down the steps to the sidewalk calling Harry's name. As she looked to the west up Breckenridge Street, she saw a long column of blue-uniformed men trotting rapidly up South Washington Street. And there, right on the corner, watching them with such enthusiasm that he was literally jumping up and down in time to the beat of their feet, was Harry.

Ginnie ran west to the corner, half to recover Harry and half to get closer to the soldiers, the sight of whom had filled her with relief. A small crowd had gathered along South Washington Street, and they were cheering and clapping as the soldiers ran by at the double-quick. There seemed to be an endless line of them moving north. She heard someone mention, "Eleventh Corps," though she wasn't certain what that meant. Cannon fire could still be heard in the distance, and the whole scene had an unreal air to it. The celebration seemed out of tune with the booming of cannon which might at any moment destroy the houses around them. But, if there was to be salvation for them, these men, moving smartly up the road in spite of their obvious weariness, would be the ones to bring it.

Women offered tin cups of water to the soldiers, who broke ranks and stopped for a moment to drink. Their officers shouted at the soldiers and, in tired and impatient voices, asked the people lining the road not to slow their progress. But the drinks continued to be offered; the soldiers stopped in little clusters to cool their thirst, then marched off with smiles, promising to protect their benefactors from the outrages of the nearby enemy.

Ginnie caught Harry by the shoulder and started to draw him away. But he protested, "Aw, Gin, let me stay and watch. You wouldn't let me see the horse soldiers this morning."

She looked back at the house with the two heavy satchels still sitting on the porch, and realized that her back was already tired from Isaac's weight. Glancing to the left down South Washington Street, she saw an endless line of soldiers flowing toward them. There must be thousands of them, she thought, certainly enough to defeat the rebels on the hills to the west. Realizing that it would be a while before the procession ended, she relented. Admonishing Harry not to stir from the spot, she walked briskly to Georgia's house and deposited Isaac. Returning to collect Harry and the clothing, she rattled the doorknob once again to make certain it was locked. She picked up one of the satchels and helped Harry with the other, and together they set off down Baltimore Street.

Up ahead they noticed another parade, this one going in the opposite direction, heading south. As she caught up with them, she saw that the huge column was made up of rebel prisoners, perhaps a thousand of them, stretching for several blocks. The column was composed of the most wretched, dejected, filthy men she had ever seen. Some were dressed in gray or butternut battledress. But many were simply barefoot and clad in rags, the remnants of their tattered clothing no longer having any appearance of the military to it. The men shuffled along, looking totally exhausted and humiliated. In contrast, the Federal soldiers who escorted them, spaced every few feet on either side of the captives, were neatly dressed as they walked with their rifles at the ready. Civilians lined the street, many jeering at the defeated enemy. As Ginnie walked past them, she could not help staring at their faces, and one young prisoner caught her eye for a second. She was surprised that he looked not like an invading terror but like a lost little boy, almost like her brother.

The farther down Baltimore Street they went, the more Union soldiers they encountered. When they reached her sister's house, Ginnie was surprised to find it surrounded by Federal troops. A great number of them stretched out along the Emmitsburg Road and up the Baltimore Pike toward the cemetery. They seemed to be everywhere. At first she was disturbed by the noise and commotion caused by all the military activity, which totally transformed the atmosphere of this normally quiet corner of Gettysburg. Then, realizing that the safest place to be was at the center of the Union army, she relaxed a bit.

She took Harry into Georgia's tiny house and started to ask her mother what needed to be done, when a knock was heard at the front door. There were two doors in the house, the front door that opened to Baltimore Street from the parlor, and a side door which led to the kitchen. Over the past two months Georgia had begun using the parlor as her bedroom in order to avoid having to negotiate the narrow staircase to the house's second level. Ginnie, therefore, opened the kitchen door to call the visitor around to the side door. A large Union soldier appeared, his hat respectfully in his hand. He looked pleadingly at Ginnie through dark, expressive eyes.

"Excuse me, Miss," he said, "but I just saw you go in the house. Do you have any food you could spare? We're short on rations and some of my men didn't eat all yesterday." Ginnie was uncertain how to respond. Mary appeared beside her in the doorway and sized up the soldier. He added quickly, "I'll be glad to pay you."

"Nonsense," her mother said. "We're glad you're here to protect us. Ginnie, give him some bread."

When she handed him a couple of loaves, the man thanked her and said, "How much do I owe you?"

Mary shook her head, motioning for him to leave. "You do the fighting, and we'll try to feed some of you." When he was gone, Mary said to her daughter, "You'd better mix up some dough. He won't be the last one to come begging."

The soldiers arrived in a steady stream, and the women handed out what food they could spare. Many offered to pay, but Mary said, "I haven't charged the others, so I won't charge you. You just be sure to keep them rebels away from us."

When the food was gone, except what they were saving for their supper, they told the soldiers to come back later after they had had time to bake more bread. Ginnie left the dough to rise and, taking the water pail and a metal ladle, went to the windlass well behind the house and let down the bucket. The day was hot and the dust stirred up by hundreds of soldiers hung in the air, making it seem even hotter and more uncomfortable. She was perspiring heavily as she cranked the bucket back up and filled her pail. Lugging it to the street, she approached a group of cavalrymen standing on the sidewalk in front of the house and asked if they wanted a drink of water. They eagerly lined up around her, offering her their canteens to fill. She ladled the cold water into dozens of canteens and cups, looking into their sweat-streaked faces as they thanked her for her thoughtfulness.

In no time the pail was empty, and she returned to the well for more. She made the trip many times in the next hour and a half, sometimes with a soldier coming along to help crank, but often having to work the windlass by herself. She began to wear a path through the dry grass between the well and the sidewalk. Her arms and back ached from the labor, and her dress was soaked from the waist down. There seemed to be no end of soldiers waiting for the cool water in her bucket, but before long her mother called for her to come help with the baking.

Half an hour later, a little after four o'clock, the level of noise in the streets suddenly increased. Ginnie stepped out the kitchen door to see what was happening. Galloping horses thundered down Baltimore Street, dragging artillery caissons and supply wagons, their drivers whipping the teams in a frenzy of speed and confusion. Mixed in among the wagons were dozens of mounted officers, shouting orders, wheeling, dodging in and out among the teams, and turning to look back toward the north. As Ginnie followed their gaze, she could see hundreds of soldiers running toward them from town.

A wagon went by her, then turned sharply and stopped in front of the hotel. Two men jumped down from the seat and went around to the rear of the wagon, where a dozen men were piled together, writhing in pain. Many of them were drenched in blood. Ginnie could not tear her eyes away from them. As the drivers carried one man toward the hotel, he let out a scream which verged on madness. The sound struck terror into Ginnie's heart; she felt lost in the middle of a hellish nightmare.

She moved unwittingly toward the wagon to look at the other men still inside, but was distracted by another group of soldiers coming toward her on the sidewalk. Two of them were dragging a third between them; his head was bowed and he seemed unable to walk. As they passed her, Ginnie could see that his face was covered with blood which was dripping directly on the sidewalk as they pulled him along, his inert feet smearing the blood in a dark trail behind him.

She lifted her gaze from the first individuals she had noticed, and realized that the whole street was filling with a mass of wounded and fleeing Union soldiers. There seemed to be an endless stream of them, panicked and out of control, some running madly down the street, others hobbling along using their muskets for crutches, some crawling on hands and knees. Soldiers hurried quietly in groups or ran singly through the mob as though pursued by devils. The wounded appeared in increasing numbers, hastily bandaged in bloody rags, displaying every type of injury, carried on stretchers or roughly tossed across the shoulders of other men. Every so often a soldier would simply fall on the ground, sometimes to be helped by his comrades, sometimes to lie there while the torrent of escaping humanity parted to flow around the inert body.

Transfixed, Ginnie's senses were overwhelmed by this endless stream of suffering. Soldiers threw away their guns and ran, others sat on the sidewalk gazing blankly at the road; one man was vomiting between his legs. Everywhere there was blood. A man limped along, his right arm around the neck of a comrade, his left arm only a shattered stump, his head thrown back and his mouth agape in silent agony. When she came to her senses, she found herself gazing blankly across at a soldier who stood urinating into the street without apparent self-consciousness.

She was snapped out of her trance by a soldier who shouted at her as he ran by, "Get out of here, Miss! The rebels are coming." Suddenly jolted to awareness, she gathered herself and ran back into the house, where she collapsed on the kitchen floor and broke into hysterical sobbing. Her mother knelt alongside her, trying to calm her. After a moment, Mary led her into the parlor and had her lie down on a lounge under the north window.

Ten minutes later, about four-thirty, the sound of gunfire was heard in the street north of the house. Mary rushed to the window over Ginnie's bed and Ginnie sat up to see what was going on. They were horrified to discover that the road out front was literally choked with men, thousands of them, so many that they completely filled the street, a struggling torrent of humanity flowing south, running, yelling, shoving each other out of the way, desperate to escape whatever was bearing down on them from the north.

As they looked up the street, the women could see the blue mass thin out, giving way to a relatively open space filled with individual stragglers. Then, to their horror, they could see more men, men in butternut and gray, running down the street toward the retreating mob. The Confederates were hiding behind houses and fences and trees, shooting into the backs of the fleeing Federals. Some of the escaping bluecoats tried to fire back but most ran desperately to escape the gunfire behind them.

Ginnie and her mother looked at each other in mute shock. Their soldiers were giving way to the rebels and it looked as though in a minute their house would be surrounded by the Confederate army. They stared transfixed out the window, praying for the tide of battle to turn, horrified by what they saw but unable to look away.

They saw a Union soldier limping down the street, hobbling as fast as he could with a badly injured leg, his musket serving him as a crutch. They felt his terror as he hurried along, his back exposed to the rebel sharpshooters. A moment later, the women saw a puff of smoke appear from his chest and watched as he pitched forward on his face and lay perfectly still. They both cried out in anguish and turned from the window.

Georgia was whimpering with fright, and the other two women went to the bed and lay down with her, huddling close for comfort and reassurance. But they could not block out the sound of gunfire which went on for another half hour.

Suddenly they heard the smack of a bullet against the side of the house. Georgia cried out in alarm, aware that bullets might come in through the window. Lying on the bed, they were in the direct line of fire from the rebel soldiers up Baltimore Street.

Ginnie jumped up and shouted, "We have to move the bed." Mary came to help her, and together they tried to slide the bed. But with Georgia's weight, it was difficult to move. Since the head of the bed was to the south wall alongside the fireplace, the women grabbed the foot of the bed and swung it into the inside corner of the room, next to the kitchen and away from the window. Then they rearranged Georgia and the baby so that they were lying with their heads to the foot of the bed, nearest the kitchen. Finally, they lay down with her, feeling a little safer, although the gunfire and shouting continued for some time.

A little after five o'clock, the noise outside subsided and there was a relative lull. When Ginnie investigated by cautiously peering out the front window, she saw Union soldiers alongside the house and across the street surrounding the hotel. In great relief, she said to the rest, "It's all right. They stopped them. We're inside the Union lines; the rebels didn't get down this far." There was a noticeable decrease of tension in the room.

Mary went into the kitchen to prepare a little supper for them, even though no one was hungry. They sat together in the growing darkness, talking quietly and praying for night to come so that the fighting would end. Every so often there was a resumption of shooting, and several times they heard the unmistakable sound of someone being shot nearby. In the lulls between shooting, they could hear the moans of the wounded.

A cry near the house made it clear that someone had been hit by musket fire. Ginnie looked out the front window. There on the sidewalk directly in front of the house was a Union soldier, lying on his right side, holding his left leg and frantically trying to drag himself closer to the house for shelter. She muttered sympathetic sounds as he struggled toward her, trying to get away from the exposed position in which some rebel sharpshooter had found him. Just as he was about to reach the front wall of their house, he was struck again in the left shoulder. Ginnie saw his shoulder explode as the bullet hit him, spraying his shirt and the sidewalk with blood. She screamed in shock at the same moment he did, and watched him roll over on his back in the partial protection of the house. Before she thought about it, she was opening the front door to go to his aid. But her mother stopped her. Quietly she said, "You'll have to wait until dark. You know they'll shoot at you if you go out now."

As darkness fell, Ginnie attempted to light one of the gas lamps in the kitchen. To her consternation, there was no gas pressure when she turned the handle. "The gas isn't working," she said, perplexed.

"The rebels have probably turned it off," Mary responded. "We'll have to get along with candles."

Finally, after gathering some bandages, biscuits and what few medicines they had in the house, Mary and Ginnie judged that it was safe to take a chance. The firing had almost completely stopped because of the growing dark. Mary tied a large white scarf to a broom handle and handed it to Ginnie as a possible protection against snipers. Ginnie opened the door, held the white flag out the door for a moment, then slipped out the door and ran in a crouched position to the man lying against the front wall. At first she was afraid he was dead but, as she touched his shoulder with the bandage, he moaned. She bound up his shoulder, then attempted to rip his trouser material to get at his leg wound. The bullet hole in his leg appeared to be clean and she merely bound it to stop the bleeding. He never regained consciousness and did not appear to know she was there.

She rose, holding the white flag over her head, and looked around for other wounded men. She noticed in the vacant lot to the north of the house – the direction from which the rebels were firing – two men lying close together. She walked quickly to them, holding the flag in plain sight, and knelt by the first man. He looked up at her in gratitude and asked, "Do you have any water, Miss?"

Ginnie dropped her supplies in a little pile, and ran to the house. In a moment she was back with a pitcher of water and two cups. She poured water into one of the cups and gave it to the soldier. "Where are you hurt?" she asked.

"My back," he said. "Something hit me in the back. I can't walk." He tried to sit up but grimaced in pain.

As he drank the water she asked, "What's your name?"

"Kahlar," he told her. "Will Kahlar, 94th New York. Is that your house?"

She helped him drink the water, since the effort obviously caused him great pain. "No, my sister lives here. She just had a baby and we're helping her."

He glanced at the house. "That's not a very good place to be. You're right between the lines." He handed back the cup. "You should get back inside, Miss. The rebs are shooting anything that moves."

She took two biscuits out of her bag and gave them to him before moving to the other soldier. "I'll be all right," she assured the first soldier. "I have my flag of truce." She waved her banner and smiled nervously.

The second soldier appeared to be unconscious. She could see a massive wound on his left leg. She checked his breathing and then shook him gently. He opened his eyes, focused on her, and smiled. "Do you want some water?" she asked quietly.

"Yes, please," was his only reply. She held his head as he drank. "More," he said when he had drained it. She poured a second cup, asking as she did, "What's your name?"

Kahlar answered for him. "He's our orderly sergeant, Al Brewer."

"Well, Sergeant Brewer, I'll leave this cup here and come get it later. You can both share it."

She got to her feet and walked along the side of the road in the fading light, checking the soldiers who sat or lay there. Giving out biscuits until they were gone, she applied several more bandages and returned to the house two or three times for water. On her final trip to the well, she stumbled over a soldier on the southeast side of the house, lying up against a fence. Kneeling to examine him, she rolled him onto his back. A cold shock ripped through her body as she saw that he had no face; what remained was only a mass of torn flesh and bone, eerie in the twilight, unrecognizable as a human being. This final fright pushed her past the limit of her endurance. Shivering in terror and exhaustion, she dropped her supplies and ran back into the house. She had done all she could that night.

Lying on her lounge under the window, with the groans of the wounded echoing through the room, she stared into the dark, appalled by the unbelievable events she had seen, trying to relax and sleep but unable to shut from her memory the ghastly images of wounded and dying men.

Each time she closed her eyes, she saw once again the apparition of the faceless man. Her mind pictured Jack lying alongside the mutilated corpse, sometimes becoming the corpse. Eventually, the waking nightmare of the day blended into a series of frightening dreams that continued to haunt Ginnie's troubled sleep.

Chapter 20

THE CONQUERING HERO

Gettysburg, Pennsylvania
July 1-2, 1863

The weeks since Wes' meeting with Skelly had passed in a blur. The army continued its march northward, moving without opposition through quiet towns where eyes peeped from behind windows to watch the invaders pass. Moving past Gettysburg many miles to the west and north, they had eventually turned south, drawn ever closer to Wes' birthplace by some mysterious plan from on high. It seemed that God and the generals had all conspired to return him to Ginnie.

The heat of summer had set in, drying the roads along which they marched. Dust trailed high into the air, covering men and animals with a buff-colored film, working its way into noses, throats and eyes. But this march, a repetition of a hundred weary movements in past years, did not feel nearly as tiring to Wes. All around him, men talked of the strangeness of this enemy place, of how lush it was, untouched by the ravages of war. They were amazed by the amount of food stored in the barns they passed. Wes, however, looked out upon the familiarity of everything he saw, and it calmed his soul.

A few weeks back, his life had seemed empty and hopeless; now, everything he had once prayed for seemed to be happening. There was little chance that the North would be able to stop them now. With General Lee leading them, they had won all of the significant battles. Their confidence was high, food and water were plentiful, and they effectively controlled much of south-central Pennsylvania. Who knew how much farther they might go? Newspapers were calling for a cessation of hostilities, and many thought the war would soon end with a negotiated settlement. That would mean the rebels had won. They didn't want to conquer northern territory; they just wanted to be left alone in their new southern country.

But most of all, in Wes' breast pocket was a secret that outweighed all the victories of war. Jack's letter was certain to bring Ginnie back to him.

As the march dragged on, there was word of a battle in progress, but no one seemed to know where it was taking place. They had already marched twenty miles since dawn, and Gettysburg was still several miles ahead. As he strained to see familiar landmarks, he noticed a great pall of dust and smoke floating over the hills in the direction of home. This could mean only one thing: the battle was there. A cold fear gripped him. His sisters were there...and Ginnie was there. They knew little about the mindless savagery of war. What was happening to them? Perhaps, he thought, they had fled the town.

They arrived southwest of Gettysburg after the sun had set, and were ordered to bivouac within sight of the rocky hill that Wes knew well. He studied it in the dark, unable to believe how close he was to his childhood haunts. They had heard the sounds of fighting, smelled the acrid scent of gunpowder. Now, as they made camp, the guns were quiet. But the men were restless, voicing their concerns in the darkness around Wes.

"Why are we tenting here? We should have pushed on up that hill before them Yankees can dig in."

"Yeah. Old Jack wouldn't have let us lay about in front of them bluecoats."

"That hill's going to give us a heap of trouble. What's the name of this place, anyway?"

"Gettysburg." Wes spoke without thinking. They turned to him in the darkness.

"Who's that? Culp? That's right, boy, these are your stomping grounds, ain't they. Where abouts did you grow up?"

Wes, staring at the dark hill, did not turn to face them. "Here," he said. "This is my family's land. That there is called Culp's Hill." His voice was low, but it carried in the warm night air. They quieted thoughtfully, understanding the implications of Wes' words.

"You been up that hill before? What's it like?" someone asked, after a time.

Wes looked up the hill, sobered by his recollections. "Oh, it's just a hill," he said, finally. "Lots of rocks on it. Have to cross a creek to get to the top." There was more he could have said, but he decided against it.

He wondered to himself: what were the odds against something like this happening? He had planned to stay in the South, but the tides of war had washed him up on these shores once again. A year ago, when he had tried to get here by himself, he had been stopped. Now, it was as if the colossal events of this war had been designed for one purpose: to allow him to fulfill his personal destiny.

When Skelly had said to him, "If you ever get to Gettysburg, give Ginnie a message for me," he had enjoyed playing with the idea of returning in triumph; but he realized that that was a fantasy. Yet, here he was, home again, not as a prisoner, but as a conqueror.

Ginnie was probably no more than a few hundred yards from him at this moment. He wondered how he could get to see her before the battle ended. He was close, but that final distance seemed farther than all the other miles combined. Frustrated, he bedded down well after midnight.

The thunder woke him long before the sun rose. He drowsed on the damp ground a moment, his first waking thought the same as his final thought the night before – how could he get to see Ginnie? He dreamed of her face, excited by what he had to tell her. The explosion of a shell nearby interrupted his reveries and shook him instantly awake.

The early morning was clear and warm, belying the thunder from the top of the hill to his front. The Federals had begun their bombardment early. Wes watched for a moment as the big guns spit their fire into the darkness. He heard the rumbling roll lazily down the hill, heard the high pitched wail of the projectiles which followed, saw the explosions which turned night into day for an instant. One of the shells impacted only a hundred feet away, causing Wes to duck reflexively, shielding himself against the hot metal rain that riddled the area.

The company was formed up and moved out to a point behind a slight ridge. Without having to be told, the men lay down, heads forward, and listened to the rhythmic explosions. Wes wasn't afraid in the usual sense; it was merely an aggravation to have to face such danger when there were so many things he wanted to do. Let him see Ginnie, give him time to get this most important task accomplished, and then he would be ready to face anything.

It had been a long time since he had really feared death. The anticipation of battle was different than the fear of death. When he returned from prison, he had had nothing to live for and had approached the dangers of the battlefield indifferently. Now, however, with everything to live for, the thought of death here, at this moment, frightened him in a way it never had before.

After several minutes, the captain formed up the men and marched them to the southeast, away from the cannons. Wes was relieved, but felt the urge to move as fast as possible, fearing that at any moment a shell might explode overhead.

They reached the Hanover Road and marched eastward toward the Deardorf house. Wes had known one of the Deardorf boys in school and had worked on their farm a few times to earn extra cash. Before they reached the house, however, they were ordered off the road into position along a ridge that ran north and south across the road. He looked down on the fields below. In the first rays of sunlight, he could see a few houses dotting the landscape, like islands set down in a sea of wheat. Every place carried a memory. He remembered hiding in the woods with Will down to the left and throwing rotten apples at Storrick's mule. He recalled how the old farmer had stormed

197

up the hill after them, a stick in hand, his face red from the exertion. They had run away, easily eluding their pursuer, peppering him with a volley of youthful laughter.

As he looked down past the houses, there in the distance he saw a troop of cavalry, their blue coats just visible in the feeble morning light. The men around Wes questioned the sergeant as to why they had been brought here. They were told that they formed the extreme right flank of the Confederate line. As such, they were responsible for any Federal attempt to outmaneuver them. Such a movement could seriously jeopardize the entire Confederate position. The opening cannon fire had coincided with a Federal move to the east, and General Johnson had ordered that a regiment be sent to investigate. Since the 2nd was closest, Wes and the others had been pulled out of the frying pan and thrown into the fire.

Colonel Nadenbousch, Wes' regimental commander, stormed by on horseback, field glasses out, surveying the Federals who were riding west down the Hanover Road toward them. He could see that they were sending skirmishers forward, so he called for his own skirmishers. One of his aides rode over to Wes' company commander. As the two of them conferred, Wes held his breath; he knew what was coming.

He was to go forward with the rest of the company as skirmishers for the entire regiment, to fight in the very front lines. This was done to blunt the enemy attack by harassing them and weeding out any possible ambushes. In theory, the skirmishers were then to give ground, falling back to the main line where the battle would be joined. In both cases, the skirmishers were vulnerable, the first targets the enemy would see.

Wes heard the sergeant yell, "Form skirmish!" This was echoed down the line and the men stood, spreading out several paces from each other. "Forward, march!" echoed across the ridge. Wes felt the fear settle in his knees, the thick, heavy knowledge that the enemy was in sight, and that he saw you. He also knew that the eyes of the entire regiment were watching them move down the hill. Wes marched with his gun in front of him, waist level, the bayonet glinting in the morning sun.

It was difficult to see the Federal skirmishers because of the sun. But as the troops moved forward, he began to feel the firmness return to his step. As he waded into the foot-high wheat, he could make out the horsemen, now dismounted, moving forward to the right of a clump of trees in Storrick's yard. A high-pitched whizzing sound over his head made him instinctively flinch. The line stopped, without a command, at a shallow indentation in the ground. Wes saw several of the others lie down and followed suit. Raising himself to look over the wheat, he fired his first shot, aiming with great care. He could see the Federals strung out along a line a hundred yards away. The pop-pop of the Federal carbines was higher-pitched than the low concussions of the Confederate rifles, and the morning air was filled with a continuous exchange of fire.

It had taken Wes time to get used to his new rifled musket. But like his old smoothbore, he had shortened its stock and carved his name in it, and by now was something of an expert marksman. He lay on his back to reload, pulling the ramrod up past his head and leaning it against his shoulder. He reached down into his waist pack, pulled a charge from it, then leaned off to the side to tear the paper away with his teeth. Carefully tilting the rifle up as far as his arms would allow, he poured the powder down the barrel. A sudden breeze blew some into his eye, temporarily blinding him with pain. After trying to clear his eye with filthy hands, he pushed the ball into the mouth of the barrel, holding it tight with his left thumb. With his right hand, he reached up, took the ramrod leaning against his shoulder and shoved the bullet home. Then, as he had a thousand times before, he rubbed the carved letters of his name for good luck and looked toward the enemy to pick a target. He squeezed his trigger and felt the familiar concussion against his shoulder.

This maneuver was repeated over and over with mindless precision: loading, aiming, firing, reloading. It was difficult to tell whether he was actually hitting anything. But he didn't really care, and it seemed that the men across the way were equally unconcerned. Both sides seemed content to hold each other at bay with only cursory attempts to gain ground. Occasionally, one of the Confederates would run forward a few paces and dramatically throw himself down behind a larger boulder or into a deeper gully which offered a little more protection. It looked heroic but Wes knew that in most cases it was motivated only by a desire for self-preservation.

Wes had a veteran's knowledge of what created heroes in war. It usually had nothing to do with cowardice or courage; most often it involved sheer luck. To this point, Wes reflected, he had been a little shy on luck, always too late or in the wrong place. A common foot soldier's primary goal was to fight and to stay alive. But now, in this place, perhaps his luck would begin to change.

The sun began its descent into late afternoon. He had lain in the field most of the day and his waist pack was almost empty for the second time. A brave ammunition boy scurrying along the line had filled it once. Somehow, the boy had managed to avoid the bullets that whizzed past him, his movement among the men making him a prime target. But Wes, searching for him now, could not see him anywhere and wondered briefly whether he had been killed.

Suddenly, he heard a loud cheer somewhere to the rear, the high-pitched wail of Confederates on the move, and he knew that the order had been given to advance. He was up on his knees before the sergeant gave the command.

The skirmishers moved forward as one, hunched low and sweeping through the wheat toward the slight rise which the Federal troopers occupied.

Wes' heart pounded with excitement, his fear vanishing as adrenaline surged into his blood. Bullets whistled past him, but as they closed the space between the lines, leading the way for the rest of the brigade, he saw the troopers begin to waver. Wes ran, still holding his rifle at waist height, bayonet forward. The Federal troopers watched them come, the sun from the west now in their eyes.

One enemy soldier, directly in front of Wes, looked at him, then turned his head from side to side as if trying to see what his comrades were doing. They both noticed that the Yankee line was beginning to collapse. Finally, as the distance closed to several hundred feet, the man in front of Wes aimed and fired directly at him, then turned and ran. Wes never missed a step, never heard the bullet pass, which told him that it had missed by a wide margin. The Confederate skirmishers paused at the top of the rise that had until a moment ago been held by the Federals. They turned to the main body of troops, storming up behind them, and shouted their triumph. Wes waved them forward, then took off down the hill after the retreating bluecoats.

It was a wondrous feeling, exhilarating. He was on the leading edge of this victory and the glory lust was in his blood. The main line of Federal troops waited at the crest of the next rise, off the Hanover Road toward the Storrick farm. Wes and the rest of the skirmishers sprinted toward the troops with a blood-chilling yell, caught up in the fury of battle.

A bugle call sounded ahead of him. Wes recognized it as a call for retreat and ran all the faster. The enemy line began to recoil away from the assault in confusion. Up ahead, Wes saw a man on horseback, his epaulettes marking him as an officer. He was looking the other way, his pistol raised over his head, trying to control his men as they pulled back. Thus, he was momentarily unaware that the leading Confederate skirmishers were bearing down on him.

Wes never broke stride. Holding his empty rifle by the barrel, he swung it with all his strength, using his momentum to add power to the blow, and struck the horse solidly in the chest. The mare, rearing, caught the officer off guard. The man slid out of the saddle, his hands clawing at the air as he fell. The horse bolted and the officer landed squarely on his back, the pistol bouncing out of his grasp. Wes grabbed it from the ground just as another Federal soldier rushed forward to cover the fallen officer. His rifle was pointed directly at Wes, the bayonet twenty feet away. Wes fell to one knee and fired instinctively, hitting the man in the shoulder. Spinning from the impact, he fell sideways with a scream.

The unhorsed officer was struggling to his feet, but Wes immediately rammed the tip of his bayonet against the man's chest, shoving him back to the ground and holding him there. Looking around for support, Wes realized that the three of them were alone. The rest of the Federals had retreated, and the main body of Confederates was still several hundred feet away, marching forward at a deliberate pace. Wes stood waiting, his bayonet point firmly pressed against the chest of the officer, whom he now saw to be a captain. The trooper whom he had shot lay on his back, and Wes could see that he was too badly injured to cause a problem.

The Confederates finally arrived, running past him in pursuit of the main body of northern troops. An officer riding past stopped to gaze down at Wes and the captured officer.

"Good work, soldier. Take them back to General Walker. He's up on the hill."

The officer returned Wes' salute and spurred off after the troops. A tingle of pride worked its way up Wes' spine. Trying to sound gruff, he ordered, "On your feet." He watched the officer struggle up from the ground and pause to brush off his soiled uniform. The wounded man had his eyes open now, and Wes walked over to kick the man's rifle away. The officer turned to the wounded man and, ignoring Wes, knelt beside him.

"Sergeant Dow, can you walk?"

The sergeant tried to rise, grimacing in pain. "With a little help, I believe I can, sir."

The captain assisted the sergeant to his feet, holding him up by his good arm. Without pausing to see if Wes was ready, they began to stumble toward the Confederate rear, a ridge now vacant save for a few officers peering through field glasses.

Wes followed behind the men, his bayonet at the ready, the pistol tucked into his pants. The fading light cast a golden hue on the wheat, and a gentle breeze blew over Wes' face. Never had he felt prouder than at this moment. For once, he had been in exactly the right place at the right moment.

Wes' charges stumbled to a stop before the officers lining the ridge, watching the action below. Indicating General Walker, the brigade commander, sitting on a fence rail eating an apple, Wes nudged the men in his direction. He escorted them proudly to the general who looked up with a slight smile.

The Federal captain stepped forward, after judging that the sergeant could stand alone, and saluted. "Captain Lownsbury, 10th New York Cavalry. Sir."

General Walker returned the salute, his pocket knife still in his hand. "At ease, Captain." Wes stood back as the general quizzed the prisoner about the forces in the field below, trying to discover whether there were reserves beyond sight.

Ben walked up to Wes and nudged him. "Looks like you had a good day, soldier," he said quietly, so as not to disturb the General's conversation. Wes beamed at his friend, nodding. "You'd better knock that grin off your face," Ben added, "or somebody's going to think you enjoy capturing Yankees."

In an instant, Wes' mood changed. He whispered urgently, "Ben, I have to get a pass. I have to make sure she's all right."

Ben looked at Wes for a moment, considering the request. Then he broke into the familiar smile which Wes knew so well. "You think you've earned it, eh? Well, see what I can do."

Wes closed his mouth, trying to look serious but the grin kept creeping back. The General was talking and Wes tried to concentrate on what he was saying to the prisoners. "Well, I think this battle is well in hand. If we're victorious here, I believe it'll just about end the war. Which means that you shouldn't be a prisoner overly long. But, until we can properly dispose of you, you'll be placed in a holding area to the rear. Pendleton!"

Ben stepped to the general's side and saluted. "Sir?"

Walker craned his neck to look at him. "See that these men are taken to the stockade, and make sure that the sergeant gets some medical attention." The general, paring another apple, used the knife to indicate Sergeant Dow.

Ben said loudly, "Yes, sir." Then he leaned toward the general, speaking quietly. Walker listened intently, then looked at Wes. He stared fiercely for a moment until Wes' neck began to prickle. Then he said something to Ben, who beckoned for Wes to approach. Wes walked up awkwardly, both frightened and in awe at being in the presence of a general.

"General Walker, this is Private Culp," Ben said quietly

"At ease, Private." Wes relaxed slightly, allowing his eyes to brush across the large man's collar with its silver star.

"Pendleton here tells me this is your town." Wes was momentarily confused, wondering if the general disapproved. "He also tells me that you're a damned good soldier," Walker continued. "I must say, it's a pleasure to have a Pennsylvania man fighting in the Stonewall Brigade."

Wes was so surprised by this unexpected remark that he looked the general in the eye and was rewarded with a broad smile.

"Take these men you captured back to the stockade near town. And in return for your good effort today, you're granted an eight-hour pass to see that your people are safe." The general's expression sobered as he added, "As long as you promise to get back here on time. We'll need every man we have tomorrow." He scribbled something on a scrap of paper and handed it to Ben.

Walker saluted as a sign that Wes was dismissed. Wes stood there for a moment, astonished that the general had saluted him first and, eventually, had the presence of mind to return the salute. But the general had already gone back to the business of peeling his apple. Wes turned smartly and marched off to where Ben stood.

"Well, get out of here," Ben said. "Time's a-wasting." He handed Wes the pass, then pushed him and his prisoners off in the direction of Gettysburg.

Chapter 21

TORMENT

Gettysburg, Pennsylvania
July 2, 1863

The hours before dawn seemed to drag by so slowly that time almost stopped. Ginnie desperately groped for sleep, but her mind was so laced with the stimulant of fear that she was unable to relax. She shuddered, listening to the noises that spewed from the darkness. Moans, curses, screams of pain and pathetic cries for help were blown into her room by the hot July breeze, adding to her torment. She could hear her mother tossing in her bed. The baby lay quietly next to Georgia, innocent of the chaos surrounding him.

She must finally have dozed because she became aware that her mother was in the kitchen, working by the light of a single candle. With a sigh, she rose quietly so as not to wake Georgia or the children. She joined her mother and, without a word, began to knead the dough that she was preparing. They worked until the light from the window finally overwhelmed the candlelight.

But with the light of the new day came the sounds of gunfire from all sides of the house once again. As Ginnie stopped kneading to listen to the shots, she could feel the terror returning. She turned back to her work and was surprised to see her mother, her face buried in her hands, weeping softly.

"Mama!" She moved to her, putting a hand on her back to comfort her. Seeing her mother like this was almost more frightening than the violence all around them. Mary Wade had always been the pillar of strength upon which they all relied, never crying or showing any sign of weakness. Ginnie could do nothing but hold her and feel the dread that shook her body. Finally, Mary straightened, wiped her eyes with the back of a flour-covered hand and returned to her work without looking at her daughter. Knowing better than to press her mother, Ginnie also resumed her work, her waning sense of security even further shaken.

As the morning progressed, the gunfire continued. There seemed to be no pattern to the shooting; sometimes it was intense, then it would stop for fifteen minutes or more. Each renewed barrage made Ginnie cringe, but with the sunrise her fear decreased and they worked faster, the warm loaves piling up on the kitchen table.

Even before the sun was fully up, there were renewed knocks on the door by soldiers looking for food. Since both of the doors to the house were in view of Confederate guns, it could be a dangerous mission to stand there waiting for bread. Many men made it with no problem, but often they had to dodge bullets as they dashed off with their prize. Ginnie and Mary stood well clear of the door each time it was opened, closing it quickly when the visitors left. Ginnie heard one man receive a gunshot wound as he tried to get around the back of the house with two loaves of bread. She glanced quickly out the window to see him crawling painfully for cover on his knees and elbows, holding the loaves carefully in his hands so as not to soil them.

As the heat increased in the early morning, the cries of the wounded near the house could be heard: "Water. *Water!*" Georgia lay with her baby in the next room, her face to the corner, listening to the pleas from outside. "Why can't they be quiet?" she exclaimed finally, more frustrated than angry.

Ginnie felt the same way. She wished it would all stop. The agonized pleas were making her skin crawl. Finally, she jumped up, grabbed a bucket and a small cup, and said, "I can't stand it anymore. I have to go out."

Mary looked up from where she sat, her eyes reflecting her concern. But she nodded silently. Ginnie held her white flag out the open door and waited for a moment. With a final glance at her mother, she took a breath and stepped into the light. Standing there for a second, she could imagine the rebel rifles across the way trained on her, and she waited for the first shot to come. But there was only quiet, so she stepped around toward the well on the opposite side of the house.

Cranking up the bucket for the first time that morning, she glanced around the area, stunned that one day could so totally transform the place. Everywhere there was wreckage. Carts had cut dark brown gashes into the green grass. Men lay in every possible spot where there was protection from rebel guns, some wounded, others just resting, still others firing from time to time. Countless small breakfast fires burned all the way out the Baltimore Pike, sending columns of black smoke aloft like a forest of spectral trees.

The eyes of nearby soldiers followed her as she went about her work, pouring water from the well's bucket into her pail. The faces that watched her were completely devoid of emotion: no fear, no pain, no happiness, no apparent feeling at all. It seemed to Ginnie that she had been suddenly transported to some alien place where life had taken on a violent and inhuman aspect, and she realized how alone and vulnerable she felt.

She went to the nearest wounded man, knelt cautiously beside him and dipped her cup into the water. He took the cup gratefully and held it to his lips, while his eyes remained locked on hers. Finally, he lowered the cup and she saw that he was smiling. "Thank you," he whispered. She nodded and moved on to the next soldier. The bucket was repeatedly emptied as Ginnie knelt by dozens of wounded men, spending a few moments with each one, talking and trying to bring relief.

As she walked back to the well the fifth time, she noted that everyone else was either lying or sitting, trying to be as inconspicuous as possible. She, on the other hand, was the only one standing and moving about. It filled her with a constant fear, and yet, during this period of time, the firing had ceased. Men on both sides seemed to be watching in fascination as Ginnie went about her work. Soon, Federal troops at some distance were shouting for her to bring them water, also. She could even hear a few calls from equally tired and thirsty men on the rebel side of the line.

After emptying the pail for the fifth time, Ginnie returned to the well again, but stopped on the far side of the house to see if Catherine had fled with her family. She called in through the side door, "Catherine, are you all right?"

A moment later, a voice came through the slanted cellarway door. "We're down here."

Ginnie opened the door and peered into the dark cellar. Catherine came to the steps, squinting in the light. "Are you all right?" Ginnie asked again.

The woman was white and shaken. She held the baby in her arms, and the other children crowded around her for protection. "We're pretty scared. I bring them down here when there isn't something we have to do in the house. I'm thinking about taking the children up the hill to the Federal lines until this is all over."

Ginnie said, "That might be a good idea. But you're pretty safe on this side of the house, I think."

"Yes," Catherine said, concern in her voice, "but aren't you in danger on your side? Can't they shoot right into the house?"

Ginnie smiled. "Well, we're pretty safe. A lot of bullets have hit the house, but the brick is strong. We're all right."

"Do you want to come down here with us?" Catherine asked.

"No. Thanks anyway," Ginnie said. "We can't move my sister yet. If it doesn't get any worse than this, we'll be all right." As she started to leave, Ginnie asked, "Do you need anything?"

"No, thank you." Catherine smiled weakly and started to close the cellarway door, then opened it again and asked, "How's the baby doing?"

Ginnie smiled. "He's fine. Big and strong. He thinks all this noise is normal. Sleeps right through it." She waved goodbye, filled her pail once more and dragged it to the men lying in her yard. Finally, she returned to the house to do some more baking.

About ten o'clock in the morning, they were startled by a loud knock and a woman's voice at the front door. Ginnie cautiously opened the door. She was surprised to see Julia Culp, and even more shocked to see standing behind her a Confederate officer. He had in his hand a staff from which fluttered a white flag.

Julia said, "Ginnie, I don't have time to explain but I wish you'd come with me right away. You'll be all right. They've arranged a temporary truce so that we can tend to our wounded."

Ginnie didn't know what to say. She looked at her mother, who had come to see who it was. Mary scowled and shook her head slightly. Julia saw the gesture and took a step forward. "Mrs. Wade, they're taking over all the vacant houses in town for hospitals, and yours may be one of them." Ginnie and her mother glanced at each other in alarm. "If they do, one of you ought to be there," Julia went on, "to protect your belongings, but also to help our wounded boys. The rebels have told us we could care for them, because they're too busy looking after their own men. If we don't, some of them will die." The officer behind her said something impatiently, trying to hurry them up. "I helped all day yesterday," Julia added urgently. "I was quite safe. But we have to hurry!"

Mary sighed, shook her head again, and said, "Very well, maybe you ought to go." She looked at Ginnie, her eyes pleading. "Be careful."

Ginnie gathered a bundle of rags and quickly kissed her mother. "I'll be fine." She rushed out to join Julia, who stood waiting next to the rebel officer. The three of them walked briskly up Baltimore Street, the little white flag on the officer's staff fluttering as they moved.

Ginnie was stunned by the ravages that the town had suffered in the last twenty-four hours. The first thing she noticed as they walked toward the Confederate-held area of town was the smell. For some reason, she hadn't noticed it as much down by Georgia's house. It was as if the whole town had turned into a sewer. The air was filled with the odor of badly tended outhouses and the sickly sweet smell of rotten meat. But it was the strength of the smell that suddenly nauseated her; the overpowering weight of the stench was much greater than anything she had ever experienced. At first she thought she was going to be violently ill, but she covered her mouth and nose with a handkerchief and kept going.

As they walked up Baltimore Street, she began to see some of the sources of the stench. In front of Harvey Sweney's house, a block north of her sister's home, a dead horse lay on its side in the middle of Baltimore Street, its upper rear leg propped grotesquely in the air by the bulk of its belly. Its eyes were open and its tongue, draping out of its jaws, licked the dirt. It gave off a rotten air of decaying flesh. Ginnie made a disgusted face and looked away.

Inside a fence farther up the street lay two dead Federal soldiers, already turning black in the heat. One was still in uniform except for his shoes, while the other lay stripped to his underwear with his infantry kepi lying on his stomach. In his dead hand he held a small American flag, placed there as a joke, no doubt, by some Confederate soldier. She heard the soldiers near the house laugh as they watched her look at the bodies, then turn quickly away. The officer escorting them glared at the men.

On both sides of the street she could see Confederate soldiers, hiding on porches or behind houses, trying to get out of the line of fire of Union snipers to the south. The troops eyed the women as they passed but, seeing the officer, said nothing. Ginnie felt uncomfortable under their gaze, and tried to keep her eyes averted. But she couldn't help seeing several men with their trousers down, urinating against the buildings as they watched her pass. Disgusted and embarrassed, she wondered why they didn't use the outhouses behind the homes along the street. Then it occurred to her that, while the entire town had outhouses for only 2,500 people, there must have been that many soldiers along Baltimore Street alone. No wonder the place stank; the whole town was being turned into one gigantic cesspool.

As they approached Breckenridge Street, Ginnie was surprised to see a barricade across Baltimore Street. Composed of large rocks, sections of fence, logs and anything else the rebels could find, it was providing a haven for a number of sharpshooters who were lying behind it.

Julia said, "Could we stop at your house and get some old sheets and clothing to use for dressings? We're desperate for material to dress wounds with." Ginnie glanced at Julia uncertainly, then fished in her pocket for the house key. In a minute, they were inside the empty house which, to Ginnie's relief, was undamaged. Rummaging through closets and chests in the bedrooms, they came up with a large armload of material.

They continued two blocks north to the new Adams County Courthouse which had been taken over as a hospital. As they walked up on the front porch, Ginnie noticed what seemed to be a crude box, about the size and shape of a coffin, underneath an open front window. Fearing that it contained a dead body, she tried unsuccessfully not to look at it. But out of the corner of her eye, the contents of the box suddenly registered on her mind, and she covered her mouth in horror. Julia put an arm around her, and led her quickly into the courthouse lobby. She said quietly, "You'll be all right. You get used to it." The box contained half a dozen amputated arms and legs, tossed out the window into the container following surgery.

Over a hundred wounded men were already lying in the rooms and hallways of the building. The floors had been covered with straw for the comfort of the sufferers and also to absorb the blood and excrement. The smell was revolting and Ginnie, already nauseated, feared once again that she would be sick.

Julia said quickly, "You get used to this, too. Breathe through your mouth. Come along. They need you in here." She led the way to a back room. Ginnie followed, suddenly sorry that she had agreed to come. While the Confederate soldiers in the rest of the building were receiving some medical attention, the Union casualties had been thrown together in a large meeting room where, aside from their guards, they were receiving no attention at all. "The rebels said they can't spare doctors to help our men," Julia explained, "but that we could care for them." She looked around, pointing out the condition of the suffering soldiers to Ginnie in a whisper. "Unless we do something, some of these men are going to die."

Ginnie, sickened, dizzy with shock, looked at the hellish chaos and shuddered with revulsion. The room was filled with the prone bodies of suffering soldiers, some propped up against the wall smoking, others lying flat on the bare floor, moaning in pain. Their clothing was filthy and matted with blood, with pieces torn off to expose their wounds. Some of the men were entirely naked, covered only with newspapers. The place was alive with flies and stank of vomit and excrement. In the narrow pathways between the wounded, several volunteers moved among them, cleaning up the mess, spreading new straw, caring for those most in need of attention.

Julia spoke to one of the Confederate guards. "This is Ginnie Wade. She's going to help with these soldiers." Without waiting for a response, she turned to Ginnie and said, "Here, start anywhere with these boys. I'm going to try to find Dr. Horner and tell him that there are some new Union soldiers here since yesterday."

As she started to leave, Ginnie looked after her in bewilderment. "But what am I supposed to do?" she asked anxiously.

"Do what you have to," Julia called over her shoulder. "They'll tell you what they need." As she left the room she said, "I'll be back as soon as I can."

Ginnie turned and looked at the men, jammed together on the floor. Taking a deep breath, she forced a smile and walked to the man nearest her who was holding onto a bloody wound in his leg. She said simply, "What can I do to help you?"

For the next half hour, she ran errands, brought buckets of water, bound up wounds, hunted for food, and spoke comforting words to the suffering men who were captives in her town. She was surprised at how quickly she got used to the sight of blood and how adept she became at dealing with various ugly wounds. She discovered that if she looked at the man's face before she looked at his wound, she could concentrate on his feelings instead of her own. She learned which ones needed only water and reassurance, and which needed constant attention to stop the bleeding or to calm them so they wouldn't further injure themselves.

Going back through the courthouse to get more water, she happened to notice a strip from one of her gowns adorning the arm of a rebel soldier. At first she was infuriated – she had expected to use her things for the Federal soldiers. But then, realizing that it was too late to do anything about it, she said to the soldier as she passed him, "That gown looked a lot better on me that it does on you!" The sarcastic tone in her voice made her feel much better. The soldier, baffled, looked at her in silence.

Realizing that a guard in the back room had scooped up the things she had brought and given them to the rebel doctors, Ginnie looked around in an effort to find the rest of her belongings. She saw a wounded Confederate ripping up a blanket which, only that morning, had been in her hope chest.

"Give me that!" she shouted, marching up to him.

He looked at her in surprise. "Who are you?" he inquired casually.

"This is my blanket," she said angrily.

The soldier smiled. "Not any longer, it ain't, Miss. This here is 'captured goods'."

Ginnie stamped her foot in frustration. The soldier looked up and commented mildly, "If you got a problem, Miss, you'll have to see my lieutenant." He laughed to himself. "But then, of course, you'd have a bigger problem, so I wouldn't advise it. Miss!" he concluded, with forced politeness.

In the early afternoon, Julia returned. "I left several messages for Dr. Horner," Julia told her, "but he's so busy I don't know when he'll get here." They had done everything they could for the moment and, feeling exhausted, sat down by the door for a moment to relax with a cup of cold tea.

After a while Ginnie asked, "Have you heard from Will?"

Julia shook her head. "No. The mail's so slow. I worry about him." She trailed off into silence, her face masked by the vacant look that Ginnie was beginning to find familiar.

Ginnie shifted in her seat. "What about Wes?" Julia's look darkened further and she shook her head. "Is he still in prison, do you think?"

"I don't know," Julia confessed. "I think if he were, we'd have heard from him. Sometimes they exchange prisoners. He said in one of his letters that he might be exchanged. But I haven't heard anything more." She shook her head. "It sounds funny to say, but I hope he's still in prison. At least, that way he's safe."

They sat in silence for a while, weary, absorbed in their own thoughts. "Wes was never a happy boy," Julia said suddenly. "He had impossible dreams, but nothing ever seemed to work out for him. He thought everybody looked down on him because he was small and poor. He was my big brother, but I always felt like I had to take care of him. He was always getting hurt."

Ginnie nodded slowly. "And I'm one of the people who hurt him."

"That's not what I meant," Julia said earnestly. "You had to do what you did. I always thought we'd be sisters some day. But the war changed...everything. It's so hard, having him on the wrong side. Hard for the family, hard for him, hard for everyone."

The two women were kept busy by the arrival of more Union wounded, who were carried unceremoniously into the room and dumped on the floor. By 3:30, when Dr. Horner finally showed up, Ginnie began to feel faint from hunger, exhaustion, the effects of her hidden pregnancy, and the eighty-degree heat. When Julia suggested it was time for her to go home, Ginnie agreed readily.

As she walked through the main rooms, filled with Confederate wounded, a young officer stopped her. "Where are you going?" he demanded.

"Home," she answered, somewhat taken aback by his question.

"Would you come upstairs with me for a moment," he asked, his voice somewhat more subdued.

"Why should I?" she retorted, unwilling to be cowed by this boy in a man's uniform.

"Because there are some more of your officers up there. I'd like you to look at them before you leave. Please."

"More? Why didn't you tell us about them before?" But before she finished the question, the lieutenant was halfway up the stairs. She followed him, filled with apprehension. Part way up, she stopped, debating whether to call Julia or not. Deciding that she could talk to her after seeing what was upstairs, she continued.

He led her into a small room where three men were lying on their backs, side by side on the floor. All three wore the uniform of Federal officers. Horrified by the realization that they had been completely neglected all this time, Ginnie rushed in and knelt by the nearest one. When she spoke to him, she noticed his slack jaw and dull, half-open eyes. She was struck by a cold chill. Looking at the other two, she realized that all three men were dead.

Jumping to her feet, she confronted the young lieutenant who was standing in the doorway, a leering smile on his face. "They're all dead," she said, an accusing tone in her voice.

"Do tell? Well, that don't say much for your nursing skills. Does it?" The leer deepened, his eyes glittering with passion.

Suddenly aware of what was happening, Ginnie started for the door. The man did not move. "Get out of my way!" she commanded. He grinned at her with the expression of a predator playing with its prey. She felt a hot flush of fear. "What do you want?" she asked, her voice quavering.

Stroking his scanty mustache he said, "Well, everything in this courthouse is a prize of war. So, I guess that includes you."

Truly frightened now, she started to push past him but he stopped her. She tried to scream but he grabbed her around the waist with one hand and clamped the other firmly over her mouth. As she struggled, he shifted his left arm around her neck, locking her to him and covering her mouth, while with his right hand he started pawing the front of her dress. Half terrified, half enraged, she wrenched her left hand free and clawed his face as hard as she could, plunging her thumb nail into his eye. He let out a roar, broke his grip and she escaped, screaming for help as she ran down the stairs.

A doctor stopped her and tried to calm her down. Julia came running from the back room and embraced her as she sobbed. When she explained what had happened, the doctor detailed a soldier to accompany her home, again under a white truce flag. Without saying goodbye to Julia, she ran out the front door so quickly that the soldier had to jog to keep up with her. As they hurried down Baltimore Street, they heard a distant explosion, then a second, and immediately realized that a new cannonade had begun. Panicked, oblivious of the snipers around her, thinking only of the need to get back to the safety of Georgia's home, Ginnie ran blindly down the final block without even looking back to see what had become of her escort.

Forcing herself to remain calm, she entered Georgia's house and gave only a mumbled description of the day's horrors. She said nothing of the incident with the officer. Suddenly, they heard the scream of a shell followed immediately by an enormous crash that shook the whole house as though they had been struck by an earthquake. The impact was followed by the sound of falling bricks and splintering wood as debris showered down upon the upper floors, filling the stairwell with a cloud of plaster dust. Ginnie fainted onto the kitchen floor.

Her mother ran to her side, afraid that she had been struck by some of the debris. Gradually, Ginnie came around, revived by a drink of water. She sat up, dazed, trying to make sense of all the noise around her. Mary was saying something to Georgia about going to the basement, but Georgia and the boys were busy screaming. Mary went toward the kitchen door, but a particularly loud series of explosions nearby sent her running back into the parlor, dragging Ginnie behind her. Resuming their prone positions once again, below the level of the windows, they huddled together, weeping in terror and praying for deliverance.

As the light faded, the rifle fire let up and people could be seen walking about on the streets again. Ginnie said to her mother, "I think the worst is over. The shooting seems to have stopped."

At that moment, somewhere nearby to the east, the guns began again, closer than ever before. It sounded as though the fighting was almost behind them, up on the east side of Cemetery Hill. The sound was deafening, its nearness raising the women's fears to a new level, as the house actually shook from the concussions. There was nothing to do but stay down.

Around ten o'clock, quiet finally returned. They lay still for more than an hour, listening, too afraid to move. Eventually, Mary went into the kitchen. "Where are you going?" Ginnie asked.

"We need to make more dough for tomorrow." Ginnie stood and followed her, feeling the weariness in every muscle. She fought off a wave of dizziness and managed to gather the strength to help her mother. Together, they started a new batch of yeast which they mixed into sponge and left to rise until morning.

It was well after midnight before they finished their work and lay down again on their beds. Despite her weariness, Ginnie had a hard time falling asleep. She continued to tremble as the horrors of the day replayed themselves in her mind.

Chapter 22

REUNION

Gettysburg, Pennsylvania
July 2, 1863

There was an unnatural stillness in the town. Everywhere Wes looked there were soldiers quietly settling in for the night. He had dropped his prisoners at the makeshift pen on the edge of town and was now in search of his sister Annie's house. He had never been to the Myers' home; Annie had not been married until 1861, just before her husband, Jefferson Myers, went off to war. But Julia had told Wes where the home was, on West Middle Street, directly across from Jack Skelly's family. It seemed safer to see Annie and Julia first. Ginnie would come later.

When he reached Annie's house, he was disappointed to see no light inside and wondered whether his sisters had fled the fighting. He knocked quietly, trying to remain inconspicuous. There was no response. He knocked again, louder this time. Finally, he heard movement inside. A tiny, frightened voice called, "Who is it?" The door opened a crack and a faint light spilled out onto the street, illuminating Wes' face.

He recognized Julia, and smiled in relief. She stared at him, uncomprehending for a moment. Then, in a flash, recognition spread across her face and she broke into a bright smile. Swinging the door wide she exclaimed, "Wes! I can't believe it's you." Wes stepped through the doorway as his sister called back into the house, "Annie, it's Wes." Then Annie was there, too, and it was as though all the loneliness and horror of the past year had been erased in a moment.

They each hugged him, and then Julia hugged him a second time, staring into his face as though to convince herself that it was really him, and that he was well. They seemed awed by his presence, excited but stunned, not quite certain how to act.

"I thought it was the rebels..." Annie began, then stopped herself, embarrassed.

Julia, in an effort to cover the blunder, said, "No, she means we've been afraid that some dirty rebel would break in and...." That also sounded wrong, and she fell silent in confusion.

213

Wes, amused by their discomfort, looked apologetically down at his filthy uniform. "Well," he said, in his best southern drawl, "I'm afraid that this dirty rebel *has* broken into your house." That relieved the tension and, amid appreciative laughter, they moved into the parlor and sat down.

"How did you get here?" Annie asked. "Did you run away?"

"No," he said, chuckling. "Believe it or not, my regiment came here with the rest of the army. I got a pass just so I could visit you. A general gave it to me. Personally. He gave it to me because I fought so well today. I captured a Yankee officer and his sergeant, single-handed." Annie's face dropped slightly, her brow furrowed. Wes noticed this and stopped talking. There was an awkward pause as they each tried to find some neutral subject about which to talk.

Julia laughed and said, "Well, we were worried when the rebels captured the town, but I guess it wasn't all bad. It meant you were able to get here."

Annie stood suddenly. "But look at you," she said. "You must be starving."

He nodded, pulling his hat off and slumping on a couch. "I'm exhausted, and I can't even remember when I had anything to eat." Annie ran to the kitchen for tea while Julia continued pummeling Wes with questions, not allowing time for him to answer. He sat listening to her, a contented smile on his face.

Annie called from the kitchen, "Don't say anything important," then returned shortly, bringing him a steaming cup of tea and the promise of food. She settled herself across from him, folded her hands in her lap, and prepared to listen. Wes sipped his tea, basking in a sense of family warmth that he had missed for so long.

He answered their endless stream of questions. When did he get out of the prison camp? How was his health? What were the rebels like? What would they do to the civilians? Who was winning the battle? When would they be gone? And so on until he grew drowsy from the warmth of the house and his own weariness.

"Let's go in the kitchen and get you some food," Annie said after a while.

He ate greedily, realizing how much he missed the comfort and routine of a regular home. The smells of the kitchen triggered powerful memories which transported him to his childhood home. He could hear his mother rattling around in the kitchen, humming, while his father worked in the attached shed, yelling about something. He saw the big Sunday afternoon gathering around the table as though it were yesterday, complete with aunts, cousins and guests. His sisters ran through his reverie in their childish forms, innocent and fresh, back before.... The mood was broken as Annie pushed another plate of food in front of him.

The first thrill of seeing each other was passing. Painful questions began to invade the pleasantries. No matter how they tried to avoid it, he was the enemy, and they were taking chances by having him there. The neighbors might see and spread the word. Julia would always give him unquestioned acceptance, but Annie could never quite forgive what Wes had done. Now, with her husband and Wes on opposite sides in the war, she was even less sympathetic. He began to fear that she would make the situation awkward.

To divert the direction of their talk, he cleared his throat and asked the question that had been foremost in his mind since he arrived. "Is Ginnie still in town?" The women glanced at each other.

Julia nodded, her words almost a whisper. "Yes, she's here. But you can't be thinking about seeing her again, can you?" The question was accompanied by a pleading look. "She's getting married, Wes. To Jack Skelly. You know that."

Shaking his head he said, "Skelly's probably dead." The girls reacted in honest horror. "I saw him a few days back," he continued, "when our company passed through Winchester. We captured most of his brigade. He had a bad wound and they left him behind. I found him and took him to a hospital. But I don't think he's coming home. If he lives, he'll be a prisoner." He shook his head again. "But the doc said it didn't look good."

Annie stood, moving to the mantle, her face turned away. Wes could see her shoulders shaking slightly and his heart went out to her. She turned from the fire, her eyes brimming with tears. "Wes, do you know if Will was there when you captured Jack and the others?"

"He wasn't captured," Wes said emphatically, pleased that he could give her this assurance. "I checked with Jack and some of the other Yankees there. They all said that he got away. He could be here for all I know."

Annie shook her head vehemently. Will was the oldest, and he and Annie had always shared a particular fondness for each other. "No. If he was here, he would have let us know. Why hasn't he come home? He could be lying dead in some field for all we know."

Wes nodded sympathetically, but he was impatient with her ignorance of the army. "There's no way he could get here right now," he explained carefully, trying to measure his words. "He'd have to pass through half the Confederate army. If he tried it, he'd get himself captured and end up in one of those prison camps. And, trust me, he'd be better off dead." Wes tried to hide his revulsion as a swarm of memories welled up in his mind.

"That's a terrible thing to say," Annie snapped indignantly. "No," she insisted, "he'd find a way to get here."

"Annie," Wes said, his exasperation returning in spite of himself, "Will could be here in town right now. There are thousands of Federals here. But he just can't get *here*, to the house. He'll be able to come when the battle's over." He should have let it go at that, he knew, but he added, "Unless we win."

215

They looked at him in dismay. "Oh, do you suppose you will?" Julia asked, obviously unhappy at the possibility.

Her reaction made Wes feel defensive. "What do you want me to say?" he asked hotly. "That I hope we lose?" He scowled at them for a second, at an impasse. He knew that if he said anything else, he would only make things worse. Finally, backing down, he said with a sigh, "Only God knows what's gonna happen."

He reached a hand out to Julia, touching her gently. "I'm sorry Jules. About all this. I never thought...." He trailed off unsure of what he wanted to say. Finally, he said simply, "I've missed you." They looked at each other in a silence more eloquent than words. A tear formed in the corner of Julia's eye and slowly trickled down her cheek. Wes watched it with a kind of sad resignation.

Trying to change the subject he said, "Ben asks after you every time I see him. In fact, he's the reason I got to come here tonight. He's working on General Walker's staff now."

Julia smiled faintly, wiping the tear away. Her cheeks flushed a bit at the thought of Ben, remembering how it felt to dance with him so long ago. "Ben's here? In town?" she asked, incredulous. Wes nodded, but he saw her eyes cloud over again. "Are you sure Will was there, in the battle with you?" she asked hesitantly.

He sighed and said carefully, "I think I saw him."

Annie turned around abruptly. "You saw him?" She almost shouted the question.

"I said I *think* I saw him. Things get pretty confused during a battle."

Julia caught her breath and looked at him obliquely. "You could have killed each other." It was a statement, not an accusation. She was confirming a terrible truth that had been haunting her.

"Julia, people are killing each other all the time. There are people dying right now, here in town. And there's nothing you or I can do to change that. I can't stop this war." He shook his head slowly, adding, "I only wish I could."

Her eyes filled again, glittering with pain as she thought of the awful things that were happening all around them. She had one final question, and she had to ask it or it would continue to haunt her. Haltingly, she spoke the words. "If you knew it was him....if he was standing there, right there in front of you, and you knew it was him, would you have pulled the trigger?"

Wes thought again of that moment in Winchester, that terrible instant when he realized that it was his own brother in his gun sight. He was thankful now that he had not pulled the trigger that day, thankful not for himself, not even for Will, but for Julia. He could not have survived her grief. He could never confess to her what nearly had happened, so he said in a soothing tone, "What a question! No, of course not, Jule. He's my brother."

These last thoughts had a numbing effect on the conversation. After an uncomfortable silence, Wes returned to an earlier question. "You say Ginnie's still in town?"

"Yes," Julia said, then asked with deep concern, "Do you really think Jack might die?"

Wes thought about the question. He had known Jack all his life, but the fact that he was probably dying someplace right now produced no emotion in him. Jack had been two months away from marrying Ginnie, and now Jack was dying and Wes was here, alive.

"That's what the doctor said," he told her flatly. Then, pressing her, he asked, "Where is she? At her place?"

"I was with her today," Julia said quietly. "We were working together at the Courthouse. They're using it as a hospital, and we were tending some of the Union soldiers." She paused, but Wes urged her on.

"You saw her today?" he asked excitedly. "How is she?"

"Fine. She's staying with her sister down by the Inn. Georgia just had a baby and the family moved in with her for a while, to help. And to be safer."

The news relieved Wes' mind: the thought of Ginnie caught in the middle of the battle had been worrying him. "I'm glad," he said. "It's hard to believe that the war's come to my hometown. After all the places where I've fought, I never thought I'd end up in Gettysburg. These past days, I've been worried about you all. And...Ginnie."

Annie came over to pile more food on his plate and Wes continued gobbling his first hot meal in weeks, wondering if he would ever feel full again. Julia asked, "Are you going to try to see her?"

Wes paused between bites. "Yes, tonight, after I leave here. I have a message from Jack that I promised I'd deliver."

Annie and Julia exchanged a glance: this added a whole new element to the story. They looked back to Wes, who continued eating, ignoring their curiosity. Finally, Julia could stand it no longer and leaned forward conspiratorially. "Oh, do tell, please."

"I can't. It's a private message. You'll find out soon enough what it's all about." Smiling, he added, "Everybody'll find out."

"You mean," Julia pressed, suddenly very serious, "about Jack...maybe dying?"

"That. And...other things," he said, wishing that he had kept his mouth shut.

Peevishly, Julia muttered, "Oh, I wish you'd tell."

"But how will you get there tonight?" Annie put in, sounding worried. "That part of town is in Federal hands."

"The General told me we have the whole town. I can go anywhere I please. But I have to go soon. I've got to be back before morning roll call or

217

they'll list me as a deserter. Her house is only a couple of blocks from here."

"No," Julia broke in. "Don't you remember. She's at her sister's place across from the Wagon Hotel."

That reminder jolted Wes for a moment, and he whispered, "Damn! You mean she doesn't go home at night?"

"No, she's living there for a while. Oh, Wes," Julia beseeched him, "you'll be careful, won't you? I don't want you to get captured again."

Wes pushed his empty plate away and stood, reaching for his hat. "Of course I will. I wasn't fond of being a guest of the Yankees. But I have to find her tonight. We might move out tomorrow and this may be the only chance I get."

"Do you really think the battle might end tomorrow?" Annie asked hopefully.

"I don't know," he admitted. "It has to be over soon. We can't go on like this much longer." He wanted to say that the Yankees were about to collapse, but decided against it.

"Please don't go so soon," Julia whispered. Her sad eyes pulled at his heart, but he took a deep breath and moved toward the door.

"I have to. I'll come back if I can."

Annie hugged him, "Please do. And be careful in town. There are some people here who wouldn't mind seeing you dead."

Julia wrapped her arms tightly around his neck and squeezed until he could barely breath. He pulled away finally and saw that her eyes were filled with tears again, tears of love for him. That sight touched him more deeply than anything else had the whole evening. Feeling his own eyes begin to moisten, he kissed her cheek gently and smiled. "I'll come back, Jule. I promise. Tomorrow, after the battle." She smiled weakly and Wes went out the door quickly before she could see his trembling lip.

Looking back, he could see Julia's form in the lighted crack of the door. Then the door closed and the light was extinguished, leaving him alone in the darkness. He moved again through the town, down Baltimore Street and toward Ginnie. A guard stopped him, telling him that he could go no further that night since the Federal line ran between them and the house where Ginnie was staying.

He stood for a long time, his fists clenched, looking down the street at the house in which she was probably asleep by now, unaware of his presence. He had waited so long to see her and at this moment he was so close to his goal. Why would God mock him by throwing this agonizing frustration in his path? He patted the note in his pocket again, reassuring himself that he had finally gained a weapon with which to win his long battle for Ginnie. He turned and started to walk back to camp.

The guard laughed, his cackle stinging Wes. "She'll still be there tomorrow. Unless the Yankees get to her first." Wes almost responded angrily, then stopped himself. Like it or not, the old man was right. He was just going to have to wait one more day.

*   *   *   *   *   *   *   *

Gettysburg, July 3, 1863

Several hours later, as the mantel clock struck 4:00 a.m., Ginnie was awakened by another nightmare. She lay in bed, trembling, listening nervously for the threatening sounds of battle to resume. She had slept fitfully. The heat had been suffocating all night, intensified by their fear of opening the windows; the hideous moans of suffering men, hiding in sheltered places around the house, had echoed constantly through the house; Georgia's baby had been fussy because of the heat, and Ginnie had been up several times to quiet him. Each time it had taken longer to fall back to sleep. The horror of the past two days infected her dreams, producing nightmares which made sleeping almost as frightening as wakefulness.

Finally, she gave up and got out of bed. She checked the boys, sheltered on their trundle between the big bed and the back wall, then peered over her mother's prone form at the baby, snuggled against Georgia. Her mother whispered in the darkness, "What's wrong?"

"Nothing," she said, leaning toward her. "We need more wood for the fire. I'm going to get it before it gets light. It'll be safer in the dark." Mary started to sit up, but Ginnie gently held her by the shoulder. "You stay there. I'll get Sam to help me." Then she added, "I'll be careful."

Already dressed, she fished the chamber pot from beneath the bed, afraid to use the outhouse in the backyard: last night, she had found a Federal sharpshooter sleeping in it. She carried the pot into the kitchen for privacy, replaced the cover and slid it back under the bed. She had pulled on her shoes and started to move toward Sam's bed when she paused for a moment. Turning around, she returned to her own bed and dropped to her knees. Looking out the window toward town, toward where the rebels were hiding, she folded her hands and lifted her eyes to the stars. "Oh, Father in heaven," she pleaded silently, "please be with us today. Protect the baby and all of us, and keep us safe from harm. Help this terrible time to be over. Soon."

She shook Sam gently, and with a sleepy moan he got out of bed and followed her. Opening the kitchen door, she peered out cautiously. She was startled by how quiet it was: no voices for the moment, no movement. Aware that she was facing the enemy, hidden behind dozens of windows up Baltimore Street, she wondered if they could see her. To her right, she thought she could see the first streaks of light touching the horizon. She whispered to

219

Sam, "Come on! And be quiet," and stepped out into the yard. They went on tiptoe, fearful that any sound might attract the attention of those hidden marksmen.

As she reached the woodpile, the sudden blast of a nearby cannon made her scream in terror. She grabbed for Sam and pressed him against the brick wall of the house. A second distant explosion shook the air almost immediately, and Ginnie realized that a cannonade had started over to the east, toward Culp's Hill. Steeling herself and trying to calm Sam, she reasoned that the noise of the bombardment might distract the soldiers nearby and mask the sound of their work. Stumbling in their haste, they each carried an armload of wood to the kitchen where their mother now stood anxiously holding the door for them.

Ginnie told Sam to take the bucket around to the well on the other side of the house to get the morning's water supply. She could hear the windlass squeaking in the dark as twice more she filled her arms with wood. As she started back with the last load, Sam struggled past her, staggering under the weight of the bucket.

Suddenly a voice from the dark said, "Miss!" The appearance of a man by the kitchen door startled her so violently that she dropped her armload with a cry of fright. The wood clattered noisily onto the walk.

"What?" she choked, barely able to speak. Her mind raced: Was he federal or rebel? "Who are you?"

"I'm with Doubleday." Ginnie relaxed a bit; he was a Federal soldier. He said, "I was here yesterday and you gave me some bread." Though he was trying to speak quietly, the cannons booming off to the east made that impossible. He raised his voice just as the cannons paused for a moment so that he was shouting in the sudden quiet. "Do you have any more?"

"You have to get away from here," she said urgently. "It's not safe. I don't have any bread now. I'm going to bake some, and some biscuits as soon as I can. Come back in a couple of hours and I'll give you some." She stared at his silhouette in the dark, and suddenly he was gone. She hurried into the kitchen after Sam, who dropped his heavy bucket under the kitchen table and went back to bed.

The baby was crying again, and Mary went to get him. Ginnie closed the parlor door, so as not to disturb Georgia and the baby, though that was unlikely: the cannonade off to the east, around Culp's Hill, continued for about an hour, jarring the house with its heavy concussions. She lit a single candle in the kitchen, and for the next hour prepared more bread dough, using the sponge they had mixed the night before. By 6:00 the cannons had finally grown silent; it was half-light outside and, since she wouldn't be getting the boys up for breakfast for another hour, she decided to lie down again while the dough rose.

She had just returned to the kitchen at about 7:00, closing the door between the rooms again, when the sound of musket fire erupted toward town. As she turned involuntarily to look north toward the sound, an explosion followed by shattering glass blasted through the parlor, instantly accompanied by frightened screams. She tore open the door, terrified by what she might find. Her mother was on her hands and knees on the bed, straddling Georgia and the baby. Isaac's enormous eyes peered over the edge of the bed, looking at the broken north window in disbelief.

"Harry! Where's Harry?" Ginnie screamed. Her mother looked around in a panic until a tiny voice from under the bed said tearfully, "I'm here." Ginnie dropped to her knees, searching under the bed where the shivering eight-year-old was huddled in a ball, his eyes clamped tightly shut. "Good, stay there!" she ordered him, her voice loud with anxiety. At that moment, the sound of gunfire increased, and they could hear the repeated smack of bullets against the bricks on the north side of the house.

"Get off the bed!" Ginnie yelled at all of them as she crouched on the floor. Her mother crawled awkwardly off the side of the bed toward Ginnie, while Georgia rolled off the other side onto the trundle, practically crushing Isaac as she landed. "The baby, get the baby!" Ginnie shouted, but Georgia was already reaching for him, pulling him down behind the fragile fortress of the bed's mattress and frame. Ginnie moved to make room for her mother on the floor, and suddenly cried out in pain. She realized only then that the floor was littered with glass. Her forearm was cut in two places, and blood was running down the sleeve of her dress.

Her mother saw what had happened, and pointed in shock at the lounge under the north window. "Look at your bed, Ginnie! It's covered with glass. If you had been in it..." but she was unable to finish. The firing, which had continued during all of this, suddenly increased in volume, and a moment later another loud crash filled the room, making them all duck in terror.

Mary lifted her head to check whether anyone was hurt and then said, in an awed whisper, "Gracious God, look at that!" When Ginnie and Georgia followed her gaze, they saw a spent minie ball lying on the pillow at the foot of the bed where only moments ago the baby had lain by Georgia's head. They stared at it for a moment, as if in a trance, and then Mary reached up and touched it. "It's still warm," she said in wonder. Then her eye caught Georgia's across the mattress, and she burst into tears.

Ginnie tried to soothe her. "Mother, God spared both Georgia and me this morning. We're in his hands. Don't worry. We're going to get through this." When the firing quieted down, the two women cleaned up the broken glass, hung a blanket over the shattered window, and tried to make the room as comfortable as possible.

By 7:30 it was full daylight. The rifle fire had diminished enough that

Mary felt she could safely move her little family into the kitchen. There, behind the strong side door, away from the windows, they felt more secure. Georgia joined them in the kitchen for the first time. They gathered around the table and ate a meager breakfast of bread, butter, applesauce and coffee. Harry was still shaking, his eyes filled with a bright liquid terror. "Are they gonna shoot us again?" he asked repeatedly, brushing off their assurances to the contrary. "Can't we go somewhere, so they can't shoot us anymore?"

The same question had tortured both Ginnie and her mother, although neither had put it into words. Georgia was having trouble walking; they couldn't carry her, and anyway, where would they take her? It wasn't safe to go outside; the rebels were shooting at anything that moved. They would be safer in the basement, but the only entrance was outside, and getting there would expose them to sharpshooters. There was another basement on the opposite side of the house, but there was no way to get to it from inside. It was probably no safer upstairs, and in any event they wanted to be near the doors in case the house caught fire. They knew all this without discussion; putting it into words would merely acknowledge their helplessness.

So Ginnie simply said, "No, Harry, we're as safe here as we would be any place." He was not convinced. Neither was she, but at the moment she couldn't think what else to do.

When they were finished with breakfast, Mary ordered them all back on their beds in the parlor for safety.

"Read us something, Gin," Georgia suggested weakly.

Ginnie pulled her Bible from under the bed. Lying on her back, consciously staying away from the blanket-draped window over her bed, she opened the Bible to the place where she had stopped reading the day before.

"Psalm 27," she read aloud. *"When the wicked, even mine enemies and my foes, came upon me to eat up my flesh, they stumbled and fell. Though a host should encamp against me...."*

She raised her head to look at Mary and Georgia on the bed, an amazed smile on her face.

"Though a host should encamp against me, My heart shall not fear: Though war should rise against me, In this will I be confident.

"Now shall mine head be lifted up above mine enemies round about me....Deliver me not over unto the will of mine enemies. I had fainted, unless I had believed to see the goodness of the Lord in the land of the living. Wait on the Lord: Be of good courage, and he shall strengthen thine heart: Wait, I say, on the Lord."

"Amen," Mary whispered quietly. Ginnie smiled, suddenly feeling safe, confident that God was watching over them. They huddled together for a while, listening to the chaos around them, a quiet island in the midst of a human storm.

Chapter 23

THE WILL OF MINE ENEMIES

Gettysburg, Pennsylvania
Friday, July 3, 1863

Ginnie, her mother, Georgia and the boys all lay silently on their beds in the converted parlor, waiting for the firing to begin again. After a while, Mary said wearily, "Well, we'd best be getting the baking done. Those soldiers will be coming soon."

Going into the kitchen with her mother, Ginnie stood again at her mixing tray and began blending ingredients for biscuits. Working up a large lump of dough, she kneaded it on the tray, wondering if there was some way they could increase the number of biscuits they could bake at one time.

Mary, who was starting the fire in the bake oven, came back past Ginnie to get more wood. The door to the parlor stood open, so that it formed a barrier behind Ginnie as she stood at the dough tray. Her mother started to close the door so that those still sleeping in the parlor would not be disturbed by the commotion in the kitchen.

"Leave it open, please," called Georgia. "I like the smell of the dough."

Ginnie looked at her mother. "It's all right. Leave it open. I feel safer here behind it."

*   *   *   *   *   *   *   *

At that moment, in the home of Harvey D. Sweney, 350 yards north up Baltimore Street, a Louisiana sharpshooter began his day's work. He was tired from the constant fighting on Thursday. He had climbed countless flights of stairs to check the views from the second floors or garrets of many buildings. Firing five or six dozen rounds, he had personally picked off three Yankee soldiers that he knew of, and had drawn the angry return fire of several squads of Union riflemen. Two windows had exploded in his face but, aside from cuts and bruises, he was uninjured. He took pride in his marksmanship. Back home in Louisiana, he bragged that he could pick off a squirrel with a single shot at 100 yards. But shooting Yankees on their own land was the supreme pleasure of his life. He didn't know about politics; all he knew was that he

225

was tired of being pushed around by the northern politicians. He was up here to do a little pushing back.

He had found this single garret window in the south side of the Sweney house last night about twilight. It was quiet and dry in the garret and, since the window was too small for more than one rifleman, he was alone. There was scattered firing from windows all around him, from the Rupp Tannery with its tall smokestacks to his right, and from some buildings to his left across the street. He had squeezed off a few shots for the pleasure of harassing the enemy, but it was soon dark, so he had eaten a bite and gone to sleep.

He slept late into the morning, something unusual for him. It was after 8:00 when he woke, alerted by the resumption of musket fire. He started to go look for an outhouse, then decided simply to urinate in the corner of the garret. Before he loaded his weapon, he paused to chew a bit of hardtack for breakfast. Finally, looking out the window for a target at about 8:30, he spotted a blue-coated figure hurrying across Baltimore Street halfway up the north slope of Cemetery Hill, crouched as though his posture would make him invisible to the enemy. The man in the garret aimed and squeezed off a shot. His quarry never slowed or hurried his pace, did not even seem to notice the shot. Odd. At this range, it should have been a certain hit. The marksman looked up at the tree branches. They were visibly moving. Wind. That was the problem. He would have to correct for windage.

There was a simple way to do that: fire at a stationary object, calculate how far off the mark the shot registered, then adjust in the opposite direction to allow for the effect of wind. He looked for a target. Up the hill to the south, a little over 300 yards away, was a house with a door which faced north. The door had a clearly visible knob on the left side just the right size and at the right range to help him make his calculation. He aimed at it and fired. A puff of smoke and splinters appeared about two feet to the right of the doorknob and a few inches lower. That was the correction he would need to make. Satisfied, he went on about his sharpshooting.

The lead slug, missing the doorknob by two feet, had blasted through not only the outside door on the north side of the McClellan house, but also had gone through the inner parlor door, the door which stood open so that Georgia could smell the bread dough, the door which gave Ginnie an added sense of safety. Slowed by its progress through both wooden panels, it needed to travel only two more feet to strike Ginnie precisely in the spot below her left shoulder blade which would allow it to penetrate her heart. It had barely enough momentum left to exit her body, after which it was spent, ending up wedged between her corset and her left breast. Virginia Wade, twenty years of age, was dead before her body crumpled to the floor.

Mary, reaching for more wood in the corner of the kitchen, was startled by the splintering crash of the bullet tearing through the two doors. She straightened up in time to see Ginnie slump over the mixing tray, then slide backwards onto the floor, pulling the tray with her. With a choked cry, Mary knelt alongside the body, shouting, "Virginia! Virginia!" as she lifted her daughter's head and peered into her lifeless eyes.

*   *   *   *   *   *   *   *

Wes' company, huddled together at the base of Culp's Hill, heard dawn break as it had the day before, with thunder. The explosions were much closer, however, and from where Wes lay he could see the muzzle blasts from the hilltop. The shots fell with great accuracy across the regiment's front. Suddenly, musket fire erupted from a breastwork only thirty yards away. Wes and the others were shocked by how close it was. When they had arrived in the pitch darkness some hours ago, those breastworks had been invisible. Now, as the sky began to lighten, Wes could see clearly that the Federals had built a strong wooden wall atop their trenches, and were pouring a devastating fire from behind the safety of their log fortress.

Colonel Nadenbousch rode by yelling orders, obviously unhappy with their situation. He told them to fall back and shift to the left. They took up a new position to the right of the little creek that ran down the hill. Wes knew the place well. The water hole that he had played in as a boy was across the creek and over the next rise. Above them, more Yankees crouched behind another set of breastworks. They began to fire as Wes' group moved into place.

Wes looked to the rear, wondering what they were going to be asked to do. There he saw their colonel conferring with General Walker. Ben sat on his horse nearby, waiting for orders. All at once, the colonel turned to Ben and spoke a few words. Ben saluted and spurred his horse toward the 2nd.

Dismounting, he ran over to where Wes and his company were posted. He spoke to the captain, and a moment later they both turned and looked at Wes, motioning for him to join them. Wes jogged the few steps and knelt beside Ben, filled with both curiosity and apprehension.

Ben explained, "The general wants me to scout the area over the creek to see if it's possible to attack that breastwork from the flank. He asked me if you'd help since you know the area."

"Of course. Are we going now?'

"Soon. Drop your pack and just take your rifle. We can move faster that way."

A little after 8:00 in the morning, the two of them moved off to the left. They stayed in the trees until they came to the creek. Jumping into the water, they splashed across quickly, worried about becoming targets. Ben made it in several strides, but the water came up to Wes' thighs. The current was swift and he had trouble keeping his footing. The icy cold had already numbed his legs and, by the time he pushed up the far bank, Ben was off again, running into the cover of the woods.

As he watched Ben run ahead of him, Wes had a flash of memory from his childhood. He was chasing Will up this same hill. His short legs had always made it impossible for him to catch his taller brother. They had splashed through this creek, laughing and yelling. Then, lying on the rocks ahead, near the trees which Julie and he had called their "houses," they had dried themselves in the sun, enjoying a fraternal bond which, sadly, had faded over the intervening years.

Ben now lay among those same rocks, peering around the edge of one of the larger boulders to study the Federal line. Wes crawled in beside him and turned onto his back. Looking up, his eyes found "his" tree, twenty-five yards or so to his right. As he examined it, a cold shudder ran through him. The tree had been blasted by artillery and rifle fire until it was missing a good part of its foliage. Light patches in the trunk, among the darker toeholds which he had gouged so many years ago, showed where bark had been shot away to reveal raw wood. Several branches were missing, and their absence revealed something which he had almost forgotten about, a crooked twist in the trunk halfway up which made the tree look as though it had suffered an injury long ago.

Ben looked down at Wes. "What're you doing? We're supposed to be checking on the Federals and you look like you're taking a nap."

"See that tree over there?" Wes asked absently.

"What tree?" Ben asked without looking, still nervously searching for enemy activity.

"That crooked tree over there, that's been all shot up. I used to sit in that tree when I was a kid. And talk to my sister." All of a sudden, his throat choked up and he had an irrational desire to weep. Dizzy with emotion, he realized that part of what he was feeling was fear. He wished he had not seen what the battle had done to his tree.

Ben kicked him in the shoulder. "What the hell's the matter with you? We've got Federals all over the place, and you're going on about trees."

Wes took a final glance at the tree, then flipped over onto his stomach alongside Ben. In that instant, his mood changed completely. "I just realized that I've come home," he said. "I had to join the rebel army to get back where I belong. This land is mine." He scooped up a handful of earth with his fingers. "I didn't have to go south to look for a plantation. It's right here. When we win, this will all be mine. Mine and Ginnie's." He punched Ben on the arm, satisfaction blazing from his eyes.

Shaking his head, Ben cautioned him, "Well, then, you'd better watch yourself. We have to win this thing first." He looked at him sternly. "Let's concentrate on what we came to do." But even Ben's sharp words could not dampen Wes' euphoria. It was all here before him: the land, the future, Ginnie, and the opportunity to make all of them his.

Ben pointed to a large boulder farther off to the left. "Go over there where you'll be closer to their flank. I'll go up around here" – he pointed to the right – "to that boulder, so I'll be on their front. Let's shoot from those two directions at the same time and see if we can make them reveal how many troops they have and where they're posted."

Wes scurried to the left, dodging from tree to tree, finally hiding himself behind a large rock facing the enemy flank. From there, he could see Ben's boulder with his rifle sticking up above it. The rifle lowered and fired into the front of the Federal trench. Wes saw two enemy soldiers turn behind the log breastwork to return the fire. From Wes' position, he could support Ben, covering him from the Federal fire. If Ben could entice them to show themselves, Wes could fire at them while their attention was focused elsewhere.

Swiftly loading his gun, he waited until Ben fired again. For the second time, he saw two Federals turn from their flank position to fire toward Ben's boulder. They were behind their log fortification, but Wes could see their movement through the firing slit. He aimed, fired, and heard a shout. He reloaded and looked toward Ben, waiting for his next shot. But in his excitement, he peered over the boulder instead of around it.

The bullet struck him in the forehead. Ben saw Wes topple over backwards, his arms outstretched, his rifle still clenched firmly in his fist. The bullet seemed to lift him off the ground and push him backwards. Ben watched in horror as Wes' outstretched body fell to earth again, sliding backwards downhill into a small gully. He landed on top of his rifle among the jagged rocks at the base of a dry wash and never moved.

Ben screamed, "Wes!" He wanted to run to him, but he was trapped where he stood. The Union soldiers, aware of his position, fired continuously and the bullets struck around the boulder every time he tried to move. He hid behind the rock, firing repeatedly, until his ammunition case was empty. Then he sat watching the place where Wes lay, hoping for some sign of life. It was half an hour until the regiment, deciding that the two of them had been killed, made its assault. There was desperate fighting for twenty minutes, during which the 2nd Virginia suffered a terrible number of casualties. While the Federals were distracted by the fighting, Ben was able to work himself around to where Wes lay.

He felt for his pulse, but Wes' face was gray and there was no life in his eyes. Ben choked out his name, amazed once again at how quickly a life could be snuffed out. As he stared at the dead eyes of his friend, he was overcome with rage. It was his fault; he had asked Wes to come with him. He had gotten his own best friend killed. He stared at Wes' body in disbelief.

Finally, he dragged him over to the group of trees that Wes had pointed out to him and laid him carefully alongside them. When he moved the body, Ben discovered that Wes had fallen on his rifle, breaking off the stock. He returned, picked up the stock with the letters "W. CULP" carved into it, and tossed it alongside the body to help identify Wes. As he looked down at his friend, his eyes filled with tears and he whispered, "Goodbye, Wes. Old friend." Then he was off, running to catch his comrades as they retreated back down the hill.

In the sudden silence, a bee buzzed on a flower, unaware of anything but the work it had to do. A breeze whispered through the shattered branches of the familiar tree overhead, opening and closing them rhythmically. Wes lay under the tree, back on his own land, his vacant eyes looking up through the lacy foliage into the blue July sky.

*   *   *   *   *   *   *   *

From the parlor Georgia called, "What's happened? What's wrong, Mama?" Mary, feeling as though she were paralyzed, barely able to breathe, started to rock as she cradled her daughter's head and shoulders in her lap. "Oh, God!" she repeated over and over. "Oh, God! Oh, God!" With her right hand, she reached behind Ginnie's body in an irrational effort to stand her on her feet, but immediately felt the blood oozing from her punctured heart and lung. Hysterically, she snatched her hand away, looking in horror as the blood dripped from it onto Ginnie's gray cheek. Mary no longer doubted the truth.

Georgia shouted again, her voice rising in fear. "Mother, what's happened?" Gently placing Ginnie's head back on the floor, Mary stood up and went into the parlor. When Georgia saw her face and the blood smearing her dress, she instantly knew the truth but could not comprehend it. "What?" was all she could say.

Mary stood in the door, faint and white with shock. "Georgia, your sister is dead," she said simply. "A bullet hit her in the back."

Georgia's horrified screams were joined by a frightened wailing, first from the two boys and then the baby. Mary stood immobile in the doorway, too stunned to think or even to feel.

The moment of paralysis was broken by a pounding on the side door, the one through which the fatal bullet had just passed. Two large men in blue uniforms burst into the kitchen. Mary turned to face them, too bewildered to be surprised by their appearance or to wonder what they wanted.

"What is it, Ma'am?" one of the soldiers, a sergeant, shouted. "What's wrong." Then they saw Ginnie's body on the floor. The men knelt alongside her, feeling for a pulse. After a moment, they looked up at Mary, their faces confirming what she already knew.

"She's dead, isn't she?" Mary said, regaining some of her usual poise.

"I'm afraid so, Ma'am," said the sergeant. He glanced at the door, noting the bullet hole. "Must have been a stray bullet." Then, standing up, he quickly took charge. "We have to get you out of here." He spied the two boys, peering in through the parlor doorway at them. "You and the children shouldn't be here. This house is between the lines, and it's dangerous," he said, stating the obvious.

"We wanted to go to the basement yesterday," Mary told them, "but we were afraid we'd get shot when we tried. And my other daughter," she said, indicating the parlor, "has a new baby, and we couldn't move her."

"That's all right," said the sergeant. "We'll help you."

He ran up the stairs to see what was on the second floor, then descended quickly and ordered, "Gather the children, and follow me up there."

"No!" said Mary firmly. "Georgia can't climb stairs and I'm not going to leave Ginnie here on the floor!"

The sergeant put his arm around her shoulder. "We have to get you out of here," he said firmly. "We're gonna take you and your girls over to the other side of the house."

By this time, Georgia was standing in the doorway holding the baby. The parlor door screened Ginnie's body from her sight. "Where's Ginnie?" she asked, her tear-streaked face haggard with shock. Mary closed the door so that Georgia could see Ginnie's body, lying with her head toward the north door. Her feet were partly under the kitchen table, the dough tray was alongside her on the floor, and the whole scene was covered with spilled flour and baking ingredients, slowly turning red where blood seeped out from under her body.

Georgia began a high keening wail. Her mother went into the parlor and rummaged through the chest, returning with two quilts. One she threw over Georgia's shoulders to hide her nightgown from the soldiers, the other she held up for her daughter to see. "We have to cover Ginnie with something," she said quietly. "Shall we use this?"

Georgia recognized one of her own quilts, one she had pieced together as a child. She nodded without saying a word, staring at her sister's body on the floor. Mary spread the quilt over Ginnie, carefully arranging it so that it covered all but her feet. When she stood up, she broke into tears. "I can't leave her here."

"We won't leave her," the sergeant said impatiently. "But we have to get you out first. We'll come back for her." He pushed Harry toward the stairs and indicated for Isaac to follow him.

When Mary explained, "He can't walk," the sergeant scooped him up and beckoned to Mary to precede him up the stairs. Halfway up, Mary suddenly realized what they were doing. "I don't want to go up here!" she shouted. "It's not safe up here!"

"We're not going to stay up here, Ma'am," responded the soldier. "This is the way to safety." As Mary reached the top of the stairs, she saw what the soldier already knew. Straight ahead, on the left side of the front bedroom, where an impenetrable brick wall had always separated the two halves of the house, was a ragged hole made by the shell which had torn through the upper floor yesterday. Mary understood: the thing which had almost killed them a day earlier was now providing the route for their escape.

The private was enlarging the opening by tearing away lath and plaster and kicking at the bricks which framed the hole. When he was done, he took the baby from Georgia, watched as she gingerly squeezed through the opening, then handed the baby back to her. When the others had passed through, the sergeant started after them.

"No!" Mary shouted again. "You said you'd bring Ginnie. I'm not going any farther without Ginnie!" The two soldiers returned to the kitchen where they laid the quilt on the floor, lifted the limp body onto it, and covered it carefully. The sergeant then lifted her over his shoulder and struggled back up the stairs. Once on the other side, they led the family down the opposite stairs into the empty south side of the house, then out the door and down into the cellar, which had been abandoned by the McClain family the day before. There they collapsed on the floor in exhaustion.

The sergeant placed the body on a table in the corner and then, seeing that Georgia had no place to sit, returned to the house and brought down a split-bottomed rocking chair. Ordering the private to stay with the family for a while, the sergeant left.

Mary, upset by Ginnie's disheveled condition, began to undress her. As she did so, she felt something in the pocket of Ginnie's apron. Pulling out the contents, she discovered, in addition to the key to their house and a small purse, a photograph of Jack Skelly in uniform. She stared at the photo for a minute, her eyes filling with tears. Then, without showing it to anyone, she slipped it back into Ginnie's apron pocket. As she removed Ginnie's dress, the lead minie ball fell onto the table with a clatter. She checked the wound and discovered that the bullet had gone entirely through her body. She tried to clean up the blood and remove some of the flour and dough which still stuck to Ginnie's hands but, without water, she could do little more than wipe the body with Ginnie's stained garments. She replaced the dress, tried to arrange her hair, covered her once again with the quilt, and sat down on a bench next to Georgia, who was trying to nurse the fussy baby.

Mary felt the pain constricting her throat, but the tears would not come. Georgia sat rocking the baby in her arms, a dazed look on her face. The sergeant returned some time later, standing uneasily on the cellar stairs. He cleared his throat and asked, "Ma'am, I know this is a bad time and all, but I saw the food in your kitchen. My men are hungry. Most of them haven't eaten much at all in the past couple of days. Do you think I could go and get some of it for them?"

Mary, emotionally exhausted, turned to the sergeant and saw the empathy in his eyes. Slowly, she stood up, glancing back at Ginnie's quiet form. There was nothing she could do for her daughter now. "I'll finish the bread," she said quietly.

The sergeant began to object, but Mary raised her hand to quiet him. She went with him back up the staircase, through the shell-hole and crossed into Georgia's empty house. As she turned left from the staircase into the kitchen, her eyes moved to the floor behind the parlor door. There she saw the ghastly stain from Ginnie's blood, darkening even now as it soaked into the wood. With a stifled cry, she moved to the table and began to work. The soldier wiped up the bloodstain as well as he could, then stayed to help. Using the dough which Ginnie had prepared the day before, Mary baked another fifteen loaves of bread which the soldier distributed to members of his company. The last loaves were gone before noon, and Mary returned to her family in the basement.

The five of them – Mary, Georgia, the baby and the two boys – settled into an uncomfortable vigil which lasted almost thirty hours. It wasn't until past noon the following day, Saturday, that they were finally convinced that the battle was over and it was safe to come out into the open once again.

*   *   *   *   *   *   *   *

Julia and Annie hurried back to Annie's home on West Middle Street after dark on Friday night, worried that they might have missed Wes. He had promised he would visit them again before he left with the army, but they reasoned that he would not be free to come until nighttime, after the fighting stopped.

They had spent most of the afternoon in the basement of their cousin, Mrs. William Stallsmith, on York Street. There, on the east side of the Diamond, they were farther away from the terrible bombardment which took place that afternoon somewhere off to the southwest. Annie's home was in the most exposed portion of town, and she feared that stray shells might hit it. But for several hours now it had been quiet, and they felt justified in returning.

Unwilling to go to bed, they sat in the parlor impatiently waiting for Wes to arrive. Around 11:00 there was a knock at the door. Julia jumped up, with Annie a step behind her. As they peered through the curtain on the door, they saw a Confederate uniform. Wes. He had been able to return.

Julia hurriedly opened the door, then stepped back in surprise. It was not their brother. A stranger in the uniform of a rebel officer stood before them, removing his hat respectfully. Annie's surprise turned to fear. She was even more startled when Julia suddenly said, "Why, Mr. Pendleton, of all people! How nice it is to see you again." She offered him her hand, which Pendleton grasped, bowing slightly.

"Good evening, Miss Julia," he said. A smile crossed his face when he realized that she remembered him. "It's a pleasure to see you, too."

Julia turned to her sister and said, "Annie, this is Mr. Pendleton. Mr. Pendleton is in Wes' company, and I met him when I was in Shepherdstown. Mr. Pendleton, this is my sister, Mrs. Barbara Ann Myers."

Pendleton bowed politely to Annie, murmuring, "Mrs. Myers." Julia turned back to him, her face flushing at the thought that he had come to the house. She wondered why. Could it possibly be that he wanted to see her? She smiled to herself.

"Won't you please come in, Mr. Pendleton?" Annie said tensely, torn between her desire to be polite to a friend of Julia's and her distaste at the thought of entertaining a rebel officer. As he stepped into the front room, his discomfort betrayed him; the smile slipped from his white face and his lip began to quiver.

Julia suddenly knew the truth: he had not come just to see her. Trying to hold back the conscious thought, she started to chatter. "Oh, dear, I wish Wes were here to see you. He was here last night. We were so glad to see him. I hadn't seen him for ever so long, you know, with the way things are. Why, we can't even get mail back and forth. He said he would come back this evening and we hurried home to see him and...."

Annie broke in. "Something has happened, hasn't it, Mr. Pendleton? That's why you're here."

Ben looked down at the hat in his hands, nervously running his fingers around its brim. "I'm afraid so," he said softly. Julia, unable to hold back the realization any longer, burst into tears and turned to embrace Annie.

Trying to stave off the inevitable as long as possible, Annie asked, "Is he badly hurt?"

Pendleton shook his head. "I'm so sorry, Mrs. Myers. I'm afraid he was killed." Julia stifled a scream as Annie's face crumpled. The women held on to each other, sobbing. He continued, "I can't tell you how I hate to bring you this kind of news. But I wanted to do it myself. I thought a lot of Wes. He was my best friend. I'll miss him a lot." He stood, shifting from one foot to another, uncertain what to do next.

Annie, regaining her composure, said, "Mr. Pendleton, please come in and sit down." As they walked into the parlor she said, "I know this was a difficult thing for you to do. You've had a hard day, and I know Wes was a friend of yours. We want you to tell us everything you know. When did he die?"

"This morning, Ma'am," he began. "Mainly, I wanted to tell you where to find your brother. I knew that you would want to bring him back home, so I took special care to put him where you could find him."

Julia looked at him, her eyes red and puffy. "How did he die, Mr. Pendleton? I hope you can tell me he didn't suffer."

Ben looked at her uneasily. He tried to speak several times, but found himself lacking the words. Eventually, he shook his head. "No, Miss Julia, I don't think he suffered." Suddenly, he was afraid he too was going to cry. "It's my fault. If I hadn't taken him with me, he would be alive now."

Julia tried to comfort him. "Surely not, Mr. Pendleton. Surely, it was something you couldn't have helped."

He struggled to regain his composure. "We were attacking on this hill out here, southeast of town, you know, and...."

Julia looked at her sister. "My God, Annie, I hope he wasn't killed on Cousin Henry's property. That would be just too awful." She started to cry again. Pendleton looked in despair at Annie, who nodded for him to continue.

"Well, they sent me up to scout, and I took Wes because he knew the area. He was firing from behind a big rock when...they got him." He paused to clear his throat, his lip quivering. "Those of us in Company B were real close, because we'd been together since before our unit was taken in at Harper's Ferry, you know?" After a moment, he added, "It appeared he was killed with one shot. I think he died right away. You know, no pain or nothing."

He stopped, as though his recital had exhausted his courage. Not knowing whether he was helping or making things worse, he sat in silence, looking miserable. After a moment, Annie asked, "Did you say you buried him yourself?"

"Yes, Ma'am. Well, no, not exactly. After the fight was over, there was a sort of truce to let us recover our dead and wounded. Wes was the only member of Company B who was killed. So, some of the men from Company B went to the clump of trees where I put him and dug a grave. I wanted to tell you where to find him. There's two big boulders part way up the hill. Off to the left are two trees real close together. One of the trees is shell-struck. Half its bark is missing, and it has a funny twist in the trunk, like somebody bent it to the left, and then part way up bent it back up straight again, y'know? You can't miss it. He's buried alongside that tree, on the side toward the boulder." They sat looking bleakly at each other. "You'll need to get some men to go look for him, Ma'am," he added. "That's no place for ladies right now. There's lots of bodies still not buried out there."

Julia straightened and said with conviction, "That doesn't matter. I'm going to go look for him."

Annie reached over and stroked her hair. "Oh, Julia, you can't do that alone. We'll ask Cousin Henry to help us. After all, it's his property. He knows it better than anyone."

"Annie!" Julia shouted. "Cousin Henry hates Wes. He thinks he's a traitor. He says he should be shot if he comes home."

Annie tried to calm her. "Hush, Julie. Wes is gone now. He's paid for whatever sins he committed. They can't hold any hard feelings now. It's too late for all that."

There was another long silence. Finally, Ben said, "I wish I could help you, but I have to get back to my unit. I think we may be pulling out tonight."

Annie brightened. "You're pulling out? Does that mean the battle might be over?"

"Maybe," he said nodding, his face a picture of frustration. "I think we're plumb wore out. I don't think we can make another assault. I can't say for sure. If you wait 'til tomorrow to go look, I think the hill will be clear. Anyway, tonight it'd be way too dangerous. There's lots of nervous men out there. They shoot at anything that moves and find out later who it was." He rose, picked up his hat, and bowed awkwardly. "I'll take my leave now, ladies. If you'll excuse me."

Julia got up quickly and went to him. Grasping his hand, she looked into his face, her cheeks stained with fresh tears. "You have done us a great service, Mr. Pendleton. We can't thank you enough for taking care of him, and for letting us know where to find him. He treasured your friendship."

Annie added her thanks. "We know you didn't have to do this, and that it was dangerous for you to come here. We will always be grateful." He shook hands with each of them and, with a final long look at Julia, turned and left.

Julia stood in the open doorway as Ben's dark form blended into the night. Listening to his footsteps fade away, she strained to hear some final sound in the deepening silence. Then, raising her eyes, she saw, directly overhead, a single star burning in the black night sky.

Chapter 24

BURIED DREAMS

Gettysburg, Pennsylvania
July 4, 1863

With the entryway doors closed and a single candle for light, the cellar on the McClain side of the house was damp and gloomy. Mary Wade and her little family huddled together for comfort all night, trying to sleep, still in a state of shock. But for Mary, sleep was out of the question. In the hours after midnight, she was constantly drawn to the far end of the basement where the body of her younger daughter lay on a table, covered with a stained quilt.

She had seen the slight curve in her daughter's abdomen and guessed at its meaning. Her astonishment was tempered by the sorrow of a second loss, one which she would never completely understand. In the pocket of Ginnie's apron Mary had discovered the picture of Jack, looking proud in his uniform. Mary wondered if he would return for Ginnie some day soon, expecting to find a wife and a child, but finding instead a grave.

She lifted the cover a dozen times to gaze at Ginnie's face, as though she needed to convince herself that this thing had really happened. Stroking the rumpled hair, she muttered quiet words which the others in the room were unable to hear. As Saturday morning dawned, she fell asleep for a time, sitting by the table holding Ginnie's cold hand.

*   *   *   *   *   *   *   *

For Julia, the long night seemed as if it would never end, the dull ache in her throat threatening to suffocate her. It had begun to rain late in the evening, and the downpour had not stopped all night, nor had her tears. She was standing at the window, her forehead against the glass, watching the scurrying drops chase each other down the panes. Looking up, she saw that the star was no longer visible. It felt as if the whole world was drowning in sorrow.

The rain slowed as the sky turned a lighter shade of gray. Feeling a hand on her shoulder, she turned to see Annie already dressed. Julia stared at her sister, searching in her eyes for a pain to match her own. But Annie's eyes, warm and bright, showed no sign of the weary ache that Julia felt. Resentment flared deep within her as it suddenly became clear that Annie was not mourning Wes. Perhaps she might even be glad that he was gone. No longer would his existence divide the family. Julia closed her eyes to prevent the tears that threatened again.

She dressed, and together the two sisters hurried east through the drizzle toward their cousin's farm. The world of Gettysburg had suddenly become alien to Julia as she peered from beneath her scarf. Fences and tree branches lay strewn about as if some great wind had blasted the town. The grass alongside the road was deeply rutted, torn by the wheels of carts and cannon. The ruts, filled now with water, turned the ground into a quagmire that sucked at the girls' feet. Silent blue and gray heaps covered the fields beyond, laid out in drab and muddy rows. After days of working in the hospital, Julia thought she was immune to death. But here the smell of broken bodies and broken earth tore at her nostrils. Through the mist, two soldiers in the distance struggled with a corpse, flinging it carelessly into line with the others. They paused to watch the girls pass, their eyes as hollow and lifeless as the dead men they carried.

Annie grasped Julia's shoulder, steadying her as they moved past a dead horse, its eyes staring unblinking into the rain. An odd silence had settled on the town as if the thousands of men who had caused this vast horror had suddenly stepped back from their deed in remorse. The only movement Julia could see was the two soldiers returning to their chore. For a ghastly moment she wondered if everyone had finally been killed and only these two were left to bury the dead.

Annie knocked at the door of the Culp farmhouse and called softly. Their cousin Henry swung the door back, a stern look on his face. He brightened when he saw the girls, hurrying them inside where his wife helped them dry out and wrapped them up in blankets.

Since their father's passing, Henry had looked after them like a second father. He was a good and kind man, but Julia knew that he harbored a deep hatred for Wes. He despised the thought of what he had done, fighting for the rebellion, and he took it as a personal affront to the family. Julia, studying her cousin's face, trembled as she thought of relating the news. She feared that in his anger he would refuse to help her find Wes' body because, in this house, Wes was the enemy. But she still loved him, and it therefore fell to her to say some sort of farewell.

"What is it?" Henry asked with a worried smile, grasping Julia's hands to warm them.

Annie leaned toward him and said softly, "It's Wesley."

He looked at Annie for a moment, his expression darkening. "He was here?"

238

"He was killed yesterday," Annie told him. Henry's wife gasped and Julia felt his hands tighten around hers. She waited for him to say good riddance, to tell her that Wes was better off, that it served him right for what he had done. But there was only a pained silence.

After a moment, Henry shook his head sadly. "That poor boy."

"Where was he killed?" Mrs. Culp asked quietly.

"Right here on your land," Annie answered. "Up on the hill." She went on to explain about their visitor the night before and what they knew of Wes' burial. There seemed to be no emotion in Annie's voice as she talked. Julia fixed her eyes on Henry, drawing strength from him, gathering courage to ask for his help.

When Annie was done, Henry turned to Julia. "You want to…you want to go find him?"

She nodded, relieved at not having to ask. Henry sighed, dropping his head for a moment as he considered the situation. When he spoke, his voice was deep and firm. "You know how I feel about Wes fighting with the rebels. And you know what your father thought. There ain't nothing that's going to change that." He paused and Julia saw that there was pain in his eyes. "But I suppose none of that really matters a lot now, does it? Wes paid the price for what he did, and someday I'll have to pay for my own sins. Right now, that boy isn't a rebel or a traitor. He's just a boy. And I suppose he's still our boy. He's part of our family." He caressed Julia's cheek in an effort to wipe off several drops of rain. "I'll get my shovel and a tarpaulin. Let's go find him."

There was nothing to say. They rose, and Julia wrapped her arms around him in silent gratitude.

*   *   *   *   *   *   *   *

The sergeant opened the cellar doors. As the women peered up at him, squinting in the morning light, he said, "I thought you'd want to know, we beat 'em good yesterday. I think the fighting's over." He looked around the gloomy cellar with concern and asked if there was anything they needed.

Mary stood, brushed her skirt off, and said softly, "My daughter will need to be buried today. Do you think you can find a coffin for us? The army ought to have…." Her voice trailed off. The sergeant hesitated but, seeing the misery in Mary's eyes, he nodded and backed up the steps.

Mary followed him, desperate for some fresh air. Going into the house, she began straightening up the kitchen which they had so frantically vacated. She put the dishes in their proper places while carefully avoiding the dark stain on the floor. In the yard, she found the bucket that Ginnie had used to fetch water for the soldiers and took it to the well. Returning to the kitchen, she found an old brush and set to work, painfully scrubbing away the blood.

239

Several hours later, the sound of a cart brought Mary back outside. She was relieved to see that the sergeant had been able to find a coffin. "I hope you don't mind, ma'am," he explained apologetically. "This was meant for a rebel officer. But he won't be needing it."

While the downpour continued, cleansing the earth of the ravages of the past several days, the women got ready for the burial. Around five o'clock, when the rain finally let up, the soldiers set the pine coffin on the brick pavement outside the south cellar. Several of the men, caked with mud from digging the grave near a bed of flowers in the rear yard, stood mutely by, leaning sympathetically on their spades. As the family gathered around the coffin, the sergeant disappeared into the cellar. He reappeared a moment later with the quilt-covered form in his arms, and placed Ginnie gently in the coffin.

Suddenly, Mary dropped to her knees with a sob and pulled back the quilt from Ginnie's face. The features were so familiar, the hair with its braid over the crown of her head looking the same as always. But her eyes and her mouth were partly open, and the bluish tint to her skin was nothing like the Ginnie they had known a day earlier. Mary stroked her cold cheek, rocking slowly back and forth and moaning with an inner agony.

Opening the quilt farther, she held up Ginnie's left hand. "Look," she said. "She still has the dough on her hands." She dusted some lingering traces of flour off the front of Ginnie's dress. "I wish I had had time to clean her up better," she moaned. The soldiers looked on, strangely moved by this tiny island of tragedy in so vast a sea of misery.

When she finally stood up, one of the soldiers nailed the lid tight. Others lifted the coffin and carried it to the garden. The family followed in a straggling procession, gathering around the grave which had several inches of water in the bottom. They watched as the soldiers forced ropes under the coffin, struggling to lower it into the muddy hole where it settled into the water. Mary winced as the soldiers began to shovel scoops of dirt into the hole. The clods made hollow sounds as they hit the top of the coffin, like drumbeats for the dead, sending chills up Mary's back.

Mary suggested to the sergeant that someone should say some appropriate words, but he merely nodded. Mutely, she stared into the muddy hole, realizing that Ginnie was the one who knew the Bible. "Well," she sighed after a long moment, "I guess God will have to say his own prayers for her. She was ready to meet him if anyone ever was."

*　　*　　*　　*　　*　　*　　*　　*

Henry led the girls up the hill in the midst of a steady rainfall, carefully helping them over each obstacle. In time, they found themselves near the boulders that Ben had described. They spread out to search the area, but it was not long before Henry called the girls to two large trees near the top of a ridge. He held a piece of wood solemnly out to Julia. She saw that it was the splintered stock of a rifle. Turning it over, she stifled a cry as she saw, carefully carved into the old wood, the letters, "W. CULP." She traced the letters with her fingertip, then looked sorrowfully up into the tree overhead.

She had not recognized the place before because the damage caused by the battle had effectively disguised it. But now she examined the surrounding area to make certain. Their two trees were blasted, shattered by thousands of bullets until they were nearly unrecognizable. But the limbs of the farther tree were low and inviting and the twist in the trunk of the tree in front of her was unmistakable. It seemed like a million years ago on a different planet, but when she looked up she could still see Wes sitting among the leaves, his legs dangling over one of the branches.

"He's here," she said simply.

Henry carefully dug at the base of the tree, removing the soft earth from a mound they discovered under some loose branches. He stopped when the blade of the shovel touched something solid. Kneeling, he brushed away the dirt with his hands to reveal an area of gray cloth. Annie knelt and helped her cousin as they carefully cleared away the earth from around the body. Julia felt the dread build inside her, knowing what they would find but secretly hoping that the face they were about to see would be that of a stranger.

With an enormous effort, Henry pulled the body loose from the earth and laid it on the ground alongside the shallow grave. Annie sobbed as Julia knelt and began to clear Wes' face of the dark soil which clung to it. The rain, falling through the trees, helped to wash his features, revealing his blue lips and giving Julia the odd sensation that he was crying. She looked at the black hole in his forehead and was overcome by weeping. Noticing that Annie was also lost in misery, Julia chastised herself for thinking that her sister was indifferent to Wes' death. She hugged Annie tightly and the two held each other for a long moment.

"What should we do now?" Henry asked quietly. Julia looked at him in surprise. She had not considered what she wanted to do once they had found Wes' body.

"Shouldn't we bury him proper, in the cemetery?" she asked.

Henry shook his head firmly. "The town wouldn't stand for it. And I'm not sure that I would either."

Julia nodded. Her eyes traced the weathered toeholds as they moved upward on the battered tree trunk. Quietly, she told them, "This is where he belongs."

Henry set to work digging the hole deeper. The soft ground moved easily but it took a great deal of effort to get through the roots of the big elm tree.

Henry then pulled the tarpaulin open and laid it in the grave. Carefully, they lifted Wes' body onto the wet tarpaulin and wrapped it tightly around him. Julia and Annie each threw clods of dirt into the grave, speaking words of love and blessing to their brother. Finally, the grave was filled in and covered with leaves and branches to disguise it.

Silently, they started back down the hill. Part way to the creek, Henry stopped. "I want you to promise me something," he said, looking intently at the women. "I don't want you to tell anyone that he's here." Julia glanced at Annie, her sad expression indicating that she understood what Henry was saying. "I don't want anyone to know that we even found him. As far as the town knows, he never got back to Gettysburg. He went south…and that was the end of that." He paused, waiting for their response. Annie nodded and looked at her sister.

"So, it'll be our secret?" Henry asked pointedly, staring at Julia. She glanced back at the tree once more in a final farewell. Then, sighing, she nodded her agreement and they set off down the hill toward home, leaving the grave behind.

The wind blew through the torn and broken branches of the old elm. Wesley Culp had come home to stay.

Epilogue

A NEW BIRTH

Gettysburg, Pennsylvania
Thursday, November 19, 1863

Julia climbed the hill again as she had many times in the past months. The dead leaves underfoot crackled in the fall air. In a formal black dress, she suddenly felt foolish. She had meant to go to the ceremony at the cemetery today to hear Mr. Everett and the President speak, but somehow she found herself here instead. The faint music of a brass band floated on the air from below in sad celebration.

She paused at the foot of Wes' tree, looking again at the pile of dirt, leaves and branches that served as the only marker of her brother's grave. She could not forget the sight of his face, caked with the dark muddy earth. That awful final picture had blotted out the living Wesley, and left her unable any longer to remember his voice or his smile, or the way he talked about his dreams.

It had been over four months since those three dreadful days in July, but the true horror had begun only when the armies left. No corner of the town had been left untouched by the slaughter. As the people cleared their yards, they did so in a daze, trying vainly to escape the demons that haunted the place. But the nightmare would not stay buried. Each rainstorm uncovered the newly dead, buried hastily in shallow graves.

The worst legacy of the battle, however, was the wounded. For months, they had been everywhere. When the battle ended and the armies left, thousands of wounded soldiers, both federal and rebel, had remained in town. Many could not be moved and had to be put up in temporary field hospitals. These had been established wherever there was water and some kind of shelter. As a result, practically every building in the area had been commandeered for use as a hospital: churches, barns, stores, private homes. For weeks afterward, anywhere Julia walked in town, she could hear the cries of men in agony. For Gettysburg during that dreadful period, the armies might have gone elsewhere, but the battle had not been over. As a result, she spent a lot of time in the quiet of the hills, away from the reminders of the battle, alone with her own private memories.

But today, four months later, the entire nation had focused its eyes here.

243

The scattered bodies of those who had died fighting for the Union were finally being moved to the cemetery where the country's greatest men were gathering to try to make sense of their deaths. They would give mighty speeches about the heroics of the Federals in preserving the Union. They would weep over the deaths of the blue-coated victors. But who would weep over the one boy in gray buried in secret at the top of Culp's Hill? No one but Julia.

*   *   *   *   *   *   *   *

Georgia Wade McClellan sat in the back row on the wooden speakers' platform feeling very much out of place. As she watched the assembling dignitaries, she wished again that she had followed her first instinct and stayed home. But a personal invitation from the President of the United States is difficult to refuse. Her mother had received a letter from Mr. Lincoln, full of sympathy about the death of her daughter. They had been touched by the fact that the President, with all of his responsibilities and worries, should take time to comfort them.

Then, yesterday, an aide to Lincoln had come to the house, inviting Mary Wade to join the President on the speaker's platform when he came to Gettysburg to dedicate the new national cemetery. Her presence would honor her daughter, "Jennie Wade, the heroine of Gettysburg," as she had come to be known in song and poem. Mary refused because of poor health and a natural reticence about attracting attention to herself. But she told the aide that Georgia would represent the family in her place. Georgia tried to protest, but her mother insisted.

Frankly, the Wades were astonished at how the country had lionized Ginnie in the few months since her death. She was being portrayed as a martyr who, while baking bread for hungry federal soldiers and risking her safety to bring comfort to the wounded, had been killed by a rebel bullet, the only civilian to die during the recent, famous battle in their town.

The dignitaries were greeting each other and Georgia looked at them self-consciously. The aide to President Lincoln, who served as her escort, leaned over to whisper the identities of the powerful and famous men who were noisily settling themselves into their seats: various congressmen, several generals including Doubleday and Gibbon, and six governors from the eighteen participating states.

Georgia, awed by the importance of this assemblage, felt increasingly uncomfortable. Her only claim to fame was that her sister had been killed, which was certainly no credit to herself. She wished her mother had accepted the invitation, but Mary Wade was now at home tending to the baby so that Georgia could honor the President's request. Mr. Lincoln had heard of

Georgia's service as a nurse in the days following the battle, and was just as happy to have Georgia accept his invitation, since he wanted to honor all those who had served in similar capacities.

Georgia was still trying to understand why Ginnie's death should be any different than the thousands of other deaths which had resulted from the battle. There was no doubt that her sister had been a good person, but Georgia was amazed at how their personal tragedy had affected people all over the country. She missed Ginnie deeply, and the family was still in mourning. But she resented having to share their grief with those who had never known her.

A commotion off to the left side of the cemetery caught her attention, and Georgia saw a group of people marching toward the speaker's stand amid cheers and applause. There, mounting the steps to the platform, was President Abraham Lincoln. Everyone on the platform rose in respect and, in spite of herself, Georgia was overcome by a sense of awe. She had never seen Lincoln before and suddenly realized that his photographs did not begin to capture the essence of the man.

He was much taller than she had imagined, his head clearly visible above those around him, with his high silk hat adding yet another foot to his height. She saw that he wore a black band wrapped around his hat, indicating that he was still in mourning for his son Willie who had died almost two years earlier. That single feature instantly humanized him for Georgia and linked them in a common bond of sorrow.

Georgia noticed his enormous hands, made to appear even larger by white gloves which stood out in sharp contrast to his otherwise entirely black attire. Somehow his awkward frame and bony features did not seem comfortable in the formal hat and gloves. But as the President walked along the front row of people on the platform preparing to greet those he knew, he removed his high silk hat and white gloves. And by that action, he was transformed. He seemed to recover his true personality, and suddenly the platform was enveloped by the power of his presence. His lined face softened into a warm smile, his intelligent eyes looked openly into the face of each person he greeted, and everyone strained to hear the quiet tones of his voice as he made some personal comment to each person within reach of his long arms.

He raised his face and gave a gesture of greeting to those sitting farther back on the platform. For a moment his eyes rested on Georgia. He did not say anything but he nodded his head slightly in acknowledgment, and for a protracted instant Georgia felt something of their shared suffering flowing between them. Then he turned and took his seat.

The Honorable Edward Everett, whom the crowd had come to hear, was late as usual. Even Georgia, who knew nothing of what was going on, realized that the quiet assemblage was waiting with a combination of impatience and excitement for the arrival of this famous man. Scarcely more than three years ago, most people had never heard of Abraham Lincoln. But Everett had been famous for forty years. A member of both the U.S. House and Senate, Minister to England, President of Harvard University, Governor of Massachusetts, Secretary of State, Vice-Presidential candidate, he had had a much more distinguished career than the low-born President. He was one of the most brilliant and popular speakers of the day. As Georgia looked at the back of Lincoln's head, she wondered how he felt, knowing that he was far less popular than Everett who had been called upon to deliver the most important speech of his career.

Georgia glanced around at what she could see of the new national cemetery. The platform had been set at the top of the rise between Greenwood Cemetery on the right and the site where the burials were taking place. Down below toward the left, behind the crowd as it stood facing the platform, Georgia could see the workers digging new graves and making burials in those already opened. Only about a third of the burials had been completed and Georgia, viewing the long curving rows of graves, realized for the first time the appalling number of deaths that had taken place in her town. And these were only the northern dead.

At the stroke of noon, Georgia saw the large crowd suddenly separate as if by some mystical force. An impression of Moses, parting the waters, passed through her mind as the sea of people opened to the right and the left in front of her, and there, striding between those walls of humanity on dry ground, as it were, came Edward Everett and his retinue. The group walked to the front where they established themselves while Everett mounted the platform with impressive dignity. He walked straight to the President who rose to accept his greeting. Waving first to the dignitaries and then to the crowd, he sat in the central seat of the front row.

The ceremonies began with a prayer by the chaplain of the House of Representatives, Rev. T. H. Stockton, D.D., who spoke to the Lord on behalf of the multitude for about ten minutes. Georgia shuddered to herself; if this was any indication, they were in for a long afternoon. The Marine Band played some loud music which the people obviously enjoyed more than the preceding prayer. And then Edward Everett was introduced. He rose to thunderous and lengthy applause after which he turned and bowed in courtly fashion to Lincoln, saying a respectful, "Mr. President." Mr. Lincoln nodded in return, responding, "Mr. Everett."

Everett always made a striking impression. Just short of seventy years of age, fifteen years older than Lincoln, he was tall and straight, and his strong features were capped with abundant white hair. His appearance was in direct contrast to that of the President. Clean-shaven, handsome for a man of his age, he seemed to Lincoln's detractors to be everything the President was not. He looked like a statesman, he had an air of sophistication about him which instantly earned the respect of others, and he radiated energy and intelligence.

He moved to a little table which stood at the front of the platform and ostentatiously placed a thick manuscript on it, obviously the text of his speech. Just as obviously, he made it clear that he did not plan to read from his notes but to rely on his memory. Georgia's heart sank when she realized the length of Everett's planned speech.

> *"We have assembled..."* he began in a booming voice, *"to pay the last tribute of respect to the brave men who, in the hard fought battles of the first, second and third days of July last, laid down their lives for the country, on these hillsides and the plains before us, and whose remains have been gathered into the cemetery which we consecrate this day."*

After an hour or so, when Everett had completed a detailed review of the Gettysburg battle, Georgia's hopes rose that the end might be in sight. But the speaker had merely presented the background for his true topic, and he went on for another hour detailing the crimes of the Confederacy and specifying just how the federal government should deal with the southern "rebellion." Georgia, chiding herself for not stopping at the outhouse before she left home and chilled by the November breeze, began looking over her shoulder to see if there were some avenue of escape. But the crowd had even crushed in behind the platform cutting off any hope of a quiet retreat. Regretting that she had agreed to this interminable experience and numbed by the endless torrent of words, she sank down inside herself, determined to endure it to the end. To honor Ginnie.

> *"...wheresoever throughout the civilized world the accounts of this great warfare are read, and down to the latest period of recorded time, in the glorious annals of our common country, there will be no brighter page than that which relates The Battles of Gettysburg."*

And he was finished. Georgia had stopped listening and was almost surprised when he concluded and bowed to the audience. The seated dignitaries rose to join the standing crowd in tumultuous applause. Everett stood for a minute, basking in their appreciation, while Georgia thanked heaven for the chance to stretch her cramped muscles and force herself awake again.

The Baltimore Glee Club rose and sang a hymn composed especially for this historic occasion, and then Lincoln was introduced. Georgia noted that, in contrast to Everett's thick manuscript, the President had only two small pieces of paper in his hand. He wore steel-rimmed glasses which he had pulled down to the tip of his nose. Standing before the expectant crowd, he paused for a moment, surveying the sea of faces. Then he began.

> *"Fourscore and seven years ago our fathers brought forth on this continent a new nation, conceived in liberty, and dedicated to the proposition that all men are created equal."*

He was interrupted by applause. Georgia was surprised by the sound of his voice. He was such a tall man that his high, almost shrill voice came as a shock, and his Kentucky accent was something she had not expected. It took a moment for her to adjust to this new voice, after having listened for two hours to the cultured New England inflections of Edward Everett.

> *"Now we are engaged in a great civil war, testing whether that nation, or any nation so conceived and so dedicated, can long endure. We are met on a great battlefield of that war. We have come to dedicate a portion of that field as the final resting place for those who here gave their lives that that nation might live."*

His voice carried clearly on the crisp fall air. But more than that, a powerful emotion filled his simple words. He was speaking straight to the hearts of the people gathered in front of him. Georgia felt herself drawn in and leaned forward on her chair.

> *"It is altogether fitting and proper that we should do this. But, in a larger sense, we cannot dedicate, we cannot consecrate, we cannot hallow this ground. The brave men, living and dead, who struggled here, have consecrated it far above our poor power to add or detract."*

The crowd interrupted him a second time with quiet applause. Georgia thought of her backyard, and the word "consecrated" caught in her mind. No clergyman had been there to speak the word when they buried Ginnie. But the consecrated ground of which Lincoln was speaking was not limited to this cemetery.

> *"The world will little note, nor long remember, what we say here, but it can never forget what they did here. It is for us, the living, rather, to be dedicated here to the unfinished work which they who fought here have thus far so nobly advanced."*

Applause. As though the voice of Georgia's soul was speaking to her, the words struck home. Why had she been allowed to live while Ginnie was taken? Why had she had the opportunity to experience marriage and motherhood while these joys were denied to Ginnie? Her mother had told Georgia of the discovery she had made in the dark cellar, a discovery that compounded the tragedy. The sudden ending of her life had robbed Ginnie of so many things that she had anticipated. Yet she, Georgia, had all of that yet to look forward to. "The living. The unfinished work." The words swam in her mind and filled her with a whole new dimension of awareness.

"It is rather for us to be here dedicated to the great task remaining before us – that from these honored dead we take increased devotion to that cause for which they gave the last full measure of devotion – that we here highly resolve that these dead shall not have died in vain.

Louder applause. Georgia was applauding along with them, unaware of the tears streaming down her face. "The last full measure of devotion." That was it, the perfect eulogy for Ginnie: her bursting desire to be of help, her devotion to those frightened, hungry, hurting men who filled their town, her almost reckless disregard for her own safety, the passion with which she threw herself into her tasks, no matter how mean or degrading. She had been in Georgia's house helping with the baby, spending sleepless hours washing and baking and caring for little Kenny. Ginnie's last full measure of devotion to her family had cost her her life.

"That this nation, under God, shall have a new birth of freedom, and that government of the people, by the people, for the people, shall not perish from the earth."

And suddenly he was finished. He had begun only three minutes earlier and was already sitting down. Those on the platform jumped to their feet to join in the sustained ovation. But this was different. When they clapped after Everett's speech, they were applauding a performance. Now they were telling Lincoln that his simple words had touched them in a much deeper way.

As she rose and looked out on the thousands of others joined in applause, Georgia suddenly knew that her own tragedy was only a small drop in the enormous ocean of the war. She was not the only one who was suffering. But what was she going to do with that suffering? She could live in the past, tied to her painful memories, nursing her anger at those who had loosed this misery on the country. Or she could work to bring meaning to the lives of those who were no longer here.

Ginnie's death had been an accident, but some great common need had transformed it into a symbol. At first, Georgia had resented the poems and the songs, the effort to make her sister into a heroine, into something that she was not and had no desire to be. If Ginnie had stayed in her own house, the soldiers she helped would have worn gray uniforms. It was pure chance that little Kenny had been born just then, placing Ginnie among federal troops when the bullet found her.

It was strange, she thought, how chance makes heroes – and sometimes villains – out of the most unlikely people. In the developing myth, even her name had been changed, to "Jennie." The name was just as wrong as the romantic legend they were creating around her. Yet, when Georgia tried to picture herself in Ginnie's situation, she wondered if she could have shown a similar kind of courage. God had chosen Ginnie for some reason, and Ginnie had lived up to the challenge. People knew that, and that was what they were remembering. It was Ginnie's role to die. Georgia's role was to go on living.

She hardly noticed the final dirge by the choir and the flowery benediction by yet another clergyman. As the crowd began to disperse, she bid her escort goodbye, then walked down the steps of the speakers' platform and away from the long concentric rows of fresh graves. This place had become a national memorial to the sacrifice of thousands of ordinary people who had given their lives that others might live.

Georgia stepped out onto the Emmitsburg Road just as the cemetery workers behind her lowered another crumbling body into a fresh grave. But she did not notice. Her eyes were set on the little house at the end of the street. She strode quickly, with a new sense of urgency, toward home, toward her husband and her new baby.

The End

Authors' Afterword

The story you have just read is based on actual historical records. We have, to the best of our ability, culled all the relevant facts from the most reliable sources and used them in our narrative. But, as in all historical fiction, imagination has been used to link those facts together to create a story which is both entertaining and informative. We hope you feel that history and invention have blended seamlessly in our novel.

Wesley Culp left his home in Gettysburg to work for Mr. Hoffman in Shepherdstown, Virginia (now West Virginia) in 1856. A member of the Hamtramck Guards, he joined the Confederate forces when war broke out and fought in the battle of Manassas with the Stonewall Brigade. He was later captured by Union forces and subsequently exchanged. Eventually, he was killed in Gettysburg on his family's property, an irony which in pure fiction might seem a bit far-fetched. Wes and Ginnie were probably killed about the same time, 8:30 a.m. on Friday, July 3, 1863. The official record states that Culp's body was never found. The conclusion reached in this book is one of several alternate stories which still circulate to this day.

Virginia (Ginnie) Wade was the only civilian to be killed during the Battle of Gettysburg. She died under the circumstances described in the book. Neither the gunman's identity nor his position when he fired the shot have ever been definitely established. Although she has been known to history as "Jennie" Wade, her name was Mary Virginia. It appears that her family and friends called her "Gin" or "Ginnie." The misnomer "Jennie" seems to have been a newspaper error in one of the earliest published accounts. There is no documentation which would indicate that Ginnie was pregnant. However, some who have researched the story and are familiar with its details feel that there is a possibility that she was. For the purposes of our narrative, this possibility serves the plot well. We have tried to treat this part of the story sympathetically, so that it would elevate and not demean her reputation.

Johnston H. (Jack) Skelly was probably engaged to Ginnie. He was wounded in the Union ranks in Winchester, Virginia on June 15, 1863, and died on July 12, 1863. He is buried in Evergreen Cemetery in Gettysburg not far from Ginnie's monument. Before Skelly died, Culp, who had known him when they were boys in Gettysburg, happened upon him in Winchester and, at his request, promised to carry a message to Ginnie. He failed in his attempt to reach her the night before they both were killed, although he did get to see his two sisters. There is no record of what the message to Ginnie contained.

Julia Culp was the younger sister of Wesley, and had a close bond to him even after he became a Confederate soldier. Julia and Ginnie were the same age and were undoubtedly acquaintances in their youth. Julia visited Wes in Virginia before the war, and worked in the courthouse-turned-hospital on July 1. She was later married to John C. Welliver, but died only five years after the Gettysburg battle, in August 1868.

Mary Ann Filby Wade, Ginnie's mother, later received a financial grant from the government as recompense for the financial hardship caused by the death of Ginnie. Born in 1820, she continued to live in her Breckenridge street home until her death in 1892. She is buried in Evergreen Cemetery, as was her husband, James, who died in 1872. He spent his last years in the Adams County Alms House.

Georgia Wade McClellan, Ginnie's older sister, began serving as a nurse to wounded soldiers in the Adams County Courthouse and elsewhere by the end of July 1863. She was invited by President Lincoln to sit on the platform when he delivered his Gettysburg Address in November 1863. Georgia and Louis had five children, the second of whom was named Virginia Wade McClellan. They lived for many years in Iowa, and Georgia could often be found in Gettysburg when significant anniversary events of the battle were celebrated. She lived until 1927.

Louis Kenneth McClellan was born to Georgia, Ginnie's sister, on June 26, 1863. The birth took place in the McClellan residence an hour before the Confederates entered the town. Ginnie was helping out in her sister's home on July 3 when she was killed. Louis, "the youngest veteran of the Battle of Gettysburg," died on Lincoln's birthday in 1941.

The house in Gettysburg in which Ginnie was killed has been converted into a museum called the **Jennie Wade House**.

David J. Sloat – sloat111@gmail.com
John W. Sloat – sloat437@gmail.com

The Cast of Characters in
THE CALM AND THE STRIFE

The Wade Family
James Wade, a tailor: 1814 to 1872
Mary Ann Filby Wade: 1820 to 1892
Georgiana "Georgia" Wade McClellan: 7-4-1841 to 9-5-1927
    Married on 4-25-1862 to:
    John Louis McClellan, carpenter: 4-7-1837 to 3-4-1913
    Co. E, 165th Pennsylvania Infantry
    Their son: Louis Kenneth McClellan: 6-26-1863 to 1941
Mary Virginia "Ginnie" Wade: 5-21-1843 to 7-3-1863
John "Jack" James Wade: b. 3-13-1846
    Company B, 21st Pennsylvania Cavalry
Samuel Swan Wade: b. 8-6-1851
Henry "Harry" Marion Wade: b. 2-4-1855.
Isaac Brinkerhoff, boarder, six years old
    Son of Wilhelm and Gretchen Brinkerhoff.

The Culp Family
Esaias Jesse Culp, tailor: 6-12-1808 to 6-7-1861
Margaret Ann Sutherland Culp: 10-5-1807 to 11-7-1856
William Edward Culp: 8-8-1831 to 10-12-1882
    Co. F, 87th Pennsylvania Volunteer Infantry
    Married to Salome Sheads: 7-30-1825 to 2-15-1912
    Their son: Wilbertus "Bertie": born 1853
Barbara Anne "Annie" Elizabeth Culp Myers: 1834 to 1890
    Married to Jefferson Myers: 1839 to 1883
John Wesley Culp: 1839 to 7-3-1863
    Co. B, 2nd Virginia Infantry Regiment,
    part of the "Stonewall Brigade"
Julia M. Culp: 1-5-1843 to 8-5-1868
    Married to John C. Welliver on 3-5-1868
Henry Culp, a cousin: b. 1809

The Skelly Family
Johnston "Jack" Hastings Skelly, Jr.: 8-4-1841 to 7-12-1863
    Co. F, 87th Pennsylvania Volunteer Infantry

Other Books by John W. Sloat

Lord, Make Us One, 1986
The Other Half, 2001
Memories of My Misadventures, 2008
A Handbook For Heretics, second edition, 2009
Moving Beyond the Christian Myth, 2011
Life Surprises, 2012

CPSIA information can be obtained at www.ICGtesting.com
Printed in the USA
BVOW080037121212

307881BV00006B/11/P